THE MUSIC OF WHAT HAPPENS

THE MUSIC
OF WHAT HAPPENS

ANNIE COYLE MARTIN

Annie Coyle Martin.

McGilligan Books

Canadian Cataloguing in Publication Data

Martin, Annie Coyle
The music of what happens

ISBN 1-894692-02-0

I. Title.

PS8576.A765627M87 2001   C813'.6   C2001-902417-7
PR9199.4.M37M87 2001

Editing & Copy Editing: Noreen Shanahan
Cover Design & Layout: Heather Guylar
Author photo: Wendy Rombough
Front cover photograph: Thanks to the family of Mercedes Shanahan Mahon.

McGilligan Books gratefully
acknowledges the support of the Canada Council for the Arts and the
Ontario Book Publishing Tax Credit for our
publishing program.

THE CANADA COUNCIL | LE CONSEIL DES ARTS
FOR THE ARTS | DU CANADA
SINCE 1957 | DEPUIS 1957

For the Martins and the Coyles, and for all the Monaghans.

THE FINEST MUSIC

Once, as they rested on a chase, a debate arose among the Fianna-Finn as to what was the finest music in the world.

"Tell us that," said Fionn, turning to Oisin.

"The cuckoo calling from the tree that is the highest in the hedge," cried his merry son.

"A good sound," said Fionn, "And you, Oscar," he asked, "what is to your mind the finest of music?"

"The top of music is the ring of a spear on a shield," cried the stout lad.

"It is a good sound," said Fionn.

And the other champions told their delight: the belling of a stag across water, the baying of a tuneful pack heard in the distance, the song of a lark, the laughter of a gleeful girl, or the whisper of a moved one.

"They are good sounds all," said Fionn.

"Tell us, chief," one ventured, "what do you think?"

"The music of what happens," said the great Fionn, "that is the finest music in the world."

James Stephens, *Irish Fairy Stories*

Contents

Harvest

11

Without Land

39

Two Months in Spring

72

Special Intentions

114

Walking After Curfew

171

At Sea

204

How's Your Father?

246

Fixing the Roof

308

HARVEST

IT WAS NOON, the dinner hour in Ireland, the last Thursday of August. Peadar strode down along the edge of the hay field, his watchful farmer's eye noting saucers of pale green growth where the hay cocks had stood. He was headed for the long, whitewashed cottage on the rise across the lane that ran through the hollow and marked the divide between his land and his sister's thirty acres. It curved gently to the right, past the old farmhouse where he'd been raised, and his sister still lived, past Tom Plunkett's place, before it joined the main road to the tiny village of Slanabaille.

Peadar was a tall, lanky man with white skin burnt red by wind and sun. He wore his cloth cap peak to the back to protect his neck and keep his hedge of black hair in place. Though he usually walked as if short of time, now he paused to gaze across at the house he had built, a large kitchen with a bedroom at either end, the big east one behind the hearth for himself and Angela, the west one for their two daughters. In the wide yard the poultry run lay at one end, the stable, pig sty and byre at the other. The tidy little dairy faced the house.

Coming into the lane through a gap in the hedge he saw his sister on her way up from her house and waited. Emer was three years older than Peadar and two years back from America. She was tall, too, with a high forehead and white skin that never seemed to freckle in the sun. Her jet black hair swept back from a widow's peak, and gathered in a knot on her nape. She was a stylish woman for this isolated place, beautiful even, with wide, grey, thoughtful eyes.

Still, none of the few young single men about the village came to court Emer, though she owned a farm. When Meana, Emer and Peadar's mother, had died two years earlier, Emer returned from New York to help her father on their farm. He followed their mother to the grave a year later and Emer was alone. The wonder was that she did not return to New York, but stayed on, a lone woman raising hens and ducks, tilling her garden of potatoes, turnips and cabbages, and letting out her land to her brother.

Peadar would suggest that she go to the dances held at the crossroads on summer nights, or to the winter ceilidhs, but Emer preferred her own company. Villagers said she was proud and full of her own importance. Others whispered she was that strange thing, a woman who loved women.

"A whistling woman and a crowing hen," they said derisively, "should be left at the four crossroads." And winked knowingly at each other.

"How's Angela?" Emer asked as they crossed the lane to Peadar's house.

"Tired of waiting," said Peadar, "and she looks tired, those black rings under her eyes are a worry."

"That's nothing strange," his sister replied, "all the O'Neills had their eyes put in with a sooty finger. You know Peadar, I lost a hen last night, it must have been a fox. It left nothing but a few feathers and a few drops of blood."

"I'll go after him on Saturday," her brother promised, "my gun is still at your place."

"Thanks, Peadar. You needn't worry about Angela. You know how she takes everything as it comes. She'll be all right."

As they came up to the house Una came out carrying little Nan. Una was a fair-haired girl of ten, very thin and tall for her age, yet sturdy. Her light blue eyes traveled over her aunt's clothes, a skirt of black Birmingham cloth that reached to the top of her black boots, and blue blouse, brooch at the neck. When Una grew up she would go to America and have pretty clothes and never come back to Ireland. She would take Nan with her and they would live in New York in a big house where water ran from a tap in a big kitchen and there would be no carrying pails from the pump.

"Is your Mammy well?" Peadar asked, taking up little Nan

and kissing her. Nan was three, a fat baby with her father's black hair and her mother's green eyes.

"She's frying bacon for dinner," said Una.

The sharp aroma of frying pork and potatoes drifted out onto the porch. Peadar set Nan on the porch step and went to the rain barrel at the side of the house. A tin porringer hung on a nail. He dipped it, poured water on his hands and shook them vigorously. The water curdled in the dust at his feet. Angela came out on the porch and sat awkwardly on one of the stools at the side of the open door. She was a small, round woman with masses of dark red curly hair. Her green eyes were sunk in black shadow, her bare feet swollen and dusty.

"It's ready," she said, "I'm waiting on the kettle." The substance of her being was subsumed into her huge belly.

"Angela, before I have the oats in, you will have it all behind you."

"Please God, Peadar," she said, "please God." Una listened to her parents' conversation and glanced furtively at her mother's figure.

"And how are you, Angela?" Emer asked.

"I'm well. I walked to the river today, a walk is good for me, the nurse always says."

"That was a terrible long walk, you could have slipped on the bank," Peadar told her.

"No fear of that, no worry, Una would have pulled me out, wouldn't you," she looked fondly at Una.

"It was little Nan who wanted to go," Una said shyly.

"Yes," said her mother, "She always wants to go to the river and see the fish jump, don't you Nan?" She lifted the little girl in her arms.

"The kettle," Angela said, rising quickly, then her face contorted in pain and she grabbed the door jamb.

"Take the child!" she gasped and sat down again. A flood of rushing amber fluid soaked her skirts and drenched her bare feet. "It's my water breaking," she said helplessly.

"You're alright," Emer told her, "you're alright. Peadar, you go for Maggie." He turned and ran for the paddock.

Emer brought a blanket. Angela stepped out of her wet clothes and wrapped it round herself.

"I'm fine now, Una take Nan for a walk." Una was staring at her wide-eyed and frightened. "I'm fine now, it's nothing, its nothing at all, I'm fine," Angela insisted.

Una obediently took the toddler's hand and they went round the side of the house, by the brambly path past the vegetable garden, the clothesline and the outhouse, to the river. Nan ran ahead and Una ran after her, trying not to think of her mother. She knew the baby would be born dead, so she had made up her mind not to think about what it might be like. Una vaguely remembered two dead babies before Nan, when they had lived with her grandparents. No one told her about it, but she had heard the adults talking and remembered her mother being sick. Una adored Nan. One winter morning, when she was seven, Una got up and found Nan in the cradle at the big kitchen fire and Maggie, the nurse, fussing around her mother. They lived with her grandparents then, in the old house down the lane where Aunt Emer lived now.

Her grandmother let Una hold the baby because Angela had stayed in bed for a week. Now when she was in bed at night she often heard her parents talking at the kitchen fire. They talked about the expected baby as if it would be a boy, born ready to drive the pony and work in the fields. Una was jealous. She knew how to do most of the work but she was still clumsy. Her mother always milked the cows. Una helped, but her mother always said, "Don't bother to learn to milk. I don't want you stuck on a farm." What Una dearly longed to do was drive the pony and trap, but her father said she was too young, maybe when she was twelve. By then Nan would be five and would not need to be watched so carefully, though at five she still would not be able to go to the river by herself.

Una splashed with Nan in the shallows, her skirts held high. The river was wide here, dammed up to make a drinking hole for cattle. The willows along the bank dipped their pale leaves sinuously in the water, and the breeze bent the dark, brown-tipped rushes. The willows had a yellow tinge. Una was thinking of the September when they'd moved to their new house. Uncle Joseph, her mother's brother, had come to help. Joseph was a teacher in

Dublin. Grandmother Maura was very proud of Uncle Joseph. She said what a great thing it was to get wages every month, rain or shine. Her mother always agreed, "There's nothing like steady money coming every month." Uncle Joseph could speak Irish, which Una thought a frivolous thing, learning something not essential or required. The cart was so crowded with furniture Uncle Joseph sat astride the shaft to drive the horse, his feet hanging down beside the horse's hind legs. Una's mother told her he had brought the big iron bed and oak chest to her grandparents' house the day before her parents' wedding.

Uncle Joseph asked Una about school and when she read for him from her school book he said she was a great reader. The new house smelled of new wood and fresh whitewash, a smell that always reminded Una of Uncle Joseph and the weekend when he slept on the floor before the kitchen fire on a bag of chaff and straw. Nan was a baby, asleep in her cot in her parents' room. Una remembered waking up crying in the strange house. Uncle Joseph came and carried her to the kitchen. "Did you have a nightmare Una? How would you like to keep your uncle company in this new house?"

As she lay on the straw with his arms around her, he told a long, long, rambling story about three children who were turned into swans. Una fell asleep as the swan children flew away, before the story finished, and never knew how it ended. If only he would come and she could ask him. But maybe she was too big for stories now, maybe everyone would laugh at her wanting to hear stories. Her mother would be very busy. She understood very well that her mother was about to have a baby, that was why she had been sent to the river. She cringed, recalling her mother's helpless face when her water broke.

What if her mother died? Women sometimes died having babies. She thought about when her grandfather died. The priest wore black vestments to say mass; the looking-glass and pictures in her grandparent's big kitchen were covered in black, except the picture of the Sacred Heart of Jesus that frightened her. The Savior's cloak was pulled aside and His heart had fire around it. He pointed at the heart with a hand bearing a red hole where the nail had pierced it. The wound dripped blood. A small red lamp burned on a little shelf in front of the picture. Aunt Emer had moved the picture into the bedroom. Now, when they went down to visit her for tea, Una didn't see it. She thought about the drip drip drip of the wetted trees as they stood in the rain to bury her grandfather. The shovels of clay were heavy and wet and made a horrible sickening thud when they landed on the coffin. It was soon covered with clay and Una could almost make herself forget he was in the coffin. Aunt Emer wept and Peadar's face had a stern look. They talked together about her Uncle Paddy in America. Una had never seen Uncle Paddy. He'd gone to America before she was born. He had sent home money for her father to pay the bank for their land. Uncle Paddy lived in New York, but he wrote to Aunt Emer to say that in the spring he was moving to Montana. Una liked that word, Montana. You spelled it as you said it, Montana. Una was the best reader in the fifth book at school.

Swallows skimmed across the water and Una remembered Uncle Joseph saying birds were at home in every element: sky, earth and water. That's why there were so many varieties of birds.

"They can make a living anywhere Una, those birds."

Nan was chasing a frog in the long reeds at the edge of the water. Una watched her in case she went beyond her depth. They waded out further, the river almost to their knees, stood on stones and looked down into the sunlit water. Tiny minnows fanned through the shallows, the slippery, soft, little creatures slid against their palms. But in the water out in the middle of the stream, no big fish jumped, plopping up and disappearing to leave a round recess on the surface. That was what Nan wanted to see.

"It's too hot Nan, for the big fish," said Una, "I'll have to bring you back in the evening when it's cooler."

"Promise Una," Nan insisted.

"Oh, I promise," Una told her.

IN HER BEDROOM, Angela closed the curtains. Standing on the rag rug beside her bed, she poured water from a jug painted with blue flowers into a basin and began to wash her body. Emer turned back the bedspread and blankets, placed an oil sheet and a thick pad of cotton and old folded sheets on the bed.

"Emer, I hope Maggie's at home, the pains are quicker now, every ten minutes or so."

"Don't worry! Even if she's not at home, you know Peadar'll find her."

Angela clung to the bedpost through each contraction, holding it tight till the spasms passed. Then she went on helping Emer lay out scissors, thread and towels on the table beside the bed and ready the infant cradle in the corner of the room. "Everything is ready now, Emer, I wish the nurse was here."

"She'll be here soon, Angela. By evening you'll have it over and you'll have your baby."

Back at the river, Una let Nan splash about in the shallows, then they hunted again for frogs in the dark shining rushes and in the long grass at the edge of the water. They walked along the bank till it curved south and tumbled over the little waterfall before flowing down to the village. Una was thinking about her mother all the time.

Returning, Nan was tired. "Carry me, Una." She stood in front of her sister and raised her little arms up.

"You're a big lump to be carrying," Una complained, "and I have to get home. Mammy's sick." But she picked her up and carried her along the dusty path between the brambles and woodbine. Nan clung to her neck. "Don't choke me, Nan," Una said.

When they came round the side of the house, Peadar was taking the pony from between the shafts of the trap.

"How is Mammy?" Una asked.

"Fine, the nurse is there now," her father answered, taking the bridle off the pony and slapping his rump with the reins. The pony trotted off to the open gate of the paddock.

"Peadar, go for Angela's mother," Emer was standing on the porch, "and take Nan with you, if you can."

Peadar scooped the child up under his arm and ran after the pony. Nan crowed with joy at the prospect of a ride in the trap with her father. Another time Una would have gone with them but she understood her aunt would need her to help today.

"Una, you see to the hens and pigs like a good girl," Emer said now, and turned back to the kitchen.

Una took the lid off the pail of kitchen slops, carried it to the dairy, added skimmed milk to the mess and hefted it across to the pig pen. She tipped the bucket up over the side of the pen into the trough. The pigs squealed fiercely and gulped the slop, standing with their trotters in the feed, climbing on each other's backs and changing places to get a larger share. Flies buzzed around the pigs' heads. The pig pen stank.

Una went to the oat box and filled the hen feed basin. The hens were crowded together squawking for food at the chicken wire fence. The rooster strutted at the back of the flock. Una instinctively feared the rooster. He would fly at you and peck your eyes out if he felt like it. She opened the gate and ran to the far side of the run. The hens flocked after her. She flung the chicken feed in a wide arc. The hens changed direction and raced after the oats, fluttering and squawking. Una latched the gate and went to hang the basin on the nail above the feed box. She heard her mother scream, high, sharp, rising and then fading, like the cry of a stuck pig. Una raced to the house and stopped at the door.

All was silent. After a minute she heard Emer's calm steady voice, "You're fine Angela, you're fine."

Una crept behind the hearth to the bedroom door and stood in the shadow, her eyes wide in wonder and terror.

Angela lay on her back, knees bent and spread wide. Una watched. The swollen lips framed in red dripping pubic hair widened, her mother screamed again, and a wet shiny black ball appeared between them.

"Push, Angela, push," Maggie urged as the ball slipped back and the lips closed, a drip of red blood flowing from them.

Her mother's head fell back on the pillow. Una stood, stiffened in fear and shock. She wanted to run but couldn't. Something kept her rooted to the floor.

Emer held a glass to the labouring woman's mouth, Angela raised her head and drank. Red hair was plastered to her head with sweat. She looked up at Emer, her green eyes blazing with energy.

"Now we're getting somewhere," the nurse encouraged. "Angela, next time push harder, don't waste the pain."

Una sunk back into the shadows. Her mother's head arched back on the pillow, blue veins bulging in her neck. The two women gripped her hands and Emer put a wooden spoon between her teeth.

"Take a deep breath, now, push, push," the nurse persisted.

Angela gave a long, guttural grunt, the wet red and black ball protruded between the parted lips and Una realized the baby's head was covered with blood and black hair. Her knees felt weak and she trembled with relief as the head disappeared again, pushing a stream of blood and water in its wake. Una wished the head would never appear again and her mother would never cry out. She prayed silently with all her heart for this horror to end. She noticed a rope looped through the bars of the bed and the sight froze Una's blood. Her heart pounded in fear. What was that for? Why did they need a big rope? The nurse took Angela's hands and placed them on the rope, while Emer wiped her sweating face. The nurse put both hands on Angela's belly, Angela gripped the rope and lifted her head.

"It's coming," she said firmly and gripped the rope.

Emer put the spoon in her mouth. Her belly seemed to rise and contract and Una saw the baby's head push out as her mother screamed and screamed, as if her body was splitting in two.

Una crouched down in panic. She felt her own pelvis contract painfully, again and again, in terror. She covered her eyes. When she opened them her mother was resting, panting hard. The baby's slimy head was between her legs.

Was the baby stuck there? Where was the rest of it? How would they get it out?

The nurse put her hand in at the side of the baby's neck easing first one shoulder and then the other. Her mother groaned softly, then, with a long moan, pushed the child out into the world.

"A fine lad," the nurse said, as she turned the baby over and wiped his face. She held him up by his feet and neck.

Una looked in wonder. What had happened? That pale and

bloody lump of dough was a human like herself. She heard his first cry, sudden, strong and lonely.

Angela lowered her trembling legs and lifted her head to look. "A boy, a big boy. Oh, I'm so glad to see that lovely big boy, thank God, a boy." She then turned her head to Emer who wiped her sweating face.

The nurse laid the crying baby on his mother's belly. Una stared at the thick, bloody, blue and red cord that led from the baby's belly to his mother. She saw the nurse loop one tight string at the child's belly and another an inch away and flinched as she saw her cut the cord with the scissors. Angela seemed to have fallen asleep.

Emer took the wet slithery child and carefully wrapped him in a towel. "Aren't you the fine lad now." She laid him in the cradle.

"We're not done yet," the nurse said sharply, "wake up, Angela." She began to rub the woman's belly hard. "Come on, Angela, push. Push out that afterbirth."

Her mother wearily opened her eyes and Una noticed a thick stream of blood trickling between her legs. Una clutched the door jamb and closed her eyes.

"Take a deep breath there. Come on Angela, push hard, just one hard shove and we'll be done," ordered the nurse, her voice loud and insistent.

Una opened her eyes again, terrified by Maggie's bossy voice. What was wrong now?

Angela pulled up her weary legs, filled her lungs and expelled a mass of clotted blood.

"Try again!" admonished the nurse. "Please try."

Three times Angela leaned on her tired heels and pushed and then lay back. The nurse took the bloody cord and pulled hard on it and Una squeezed her eyes shut, unable to watch, but then couldn't help herself. .

"One more try, now," the nurse pleaded while Emer wiped the Angela's face. "Try Angela, just once more."

Angela bent her knees and a flat bloody mass, gelatinous, like frogs spawn, slopped out of her and lay in a crimson mess of clots, reddening the white sheet between her legs.

"That's more like it, that's the way, now we're done!" Maggie was triumphant, and she picked it up and turned the red slippery mess over in her hands. A rich, fetid, animal stench of blood filled the room. Una's innards heaved in disgust. She turned aside, her palm tight over her mouth and tiptoed away through the kitchen. She sat on the porch steps and leaned against the door. How terrifying it had been, so much blood, such helplessness. She had seen animals give birth but this had been different. She had never seen so much blood, could not have imagined so much. But it was finished. It was over, her mother's labour was over. The afterbirth had come and everything would be alright. Behind her closed eyes she imagined Angela getting out of that stained bed, her labour past, wrapping her shawl about her, sitting in the chair calling "Una." Any minute now her mother would call out to her, "Una, Una, come here," any second now, she told herself, she would hear her mother call. Sounds from the bedroom drifted through her mind as through a sieve, she did not see what was happening there.

Angela had begun to bleed, the bright steady stream pooled on the snowy sheets, a rosy stain spread wider and wider.

Maggie dropped the afterbirth. "That's not all of it, there's more." She began to massage Angela's belly roughly with one bloody hand, the other felt for her pulse. Stringy clots of dark blood rushed from the woman, her breath came fast and shallow. Maggie rubbed hard on her abdomen, her rough face grim and worried. Blood spouted, she stopped the rubbing and looked across at Emer. Her expression signaled alarm, then panic. Emer held Angela's hand and gently stroked her face and said softly. "You have a fine baby boy dear, a lovely little boy."

Angela's huge green eyes stared heedlessly into space. Her pupils widened unnaturally. She was beyond hearing. Silently, Emer began to weep. Maggie, defeated, looked down hopelessly at the woman. She was sinking fast, her lifespan running out in a hemorrhage they were powerless to stop. After a little while Angela turned her face to the wall. She was like a candle burning down. Her breath came quieter and slower. Her eyes clouded over and turned up under her lids. Her breathing faded away.

"She's gone, she's gone." Maggie gasped. She sat down, her hand groping behind her for the chair. She heaved a deep sigh and her face set hard. "Nothing to be done," she said and rising, took the bloody sheet, and wiped her hands on it and spread it over the woman. Then she sat again, exhausted.

Appalled, Emer walked away, out through the kitchen and collapsed beside Una on the step and took the trembling girl in her arms.

"Is it over, is Mammy alright now?"

"Una dear your mother is gone. We've lost her."

"What, what are you saying?" Una tried to rise to go to her mother.

Emer held her fast, "Don't go in there Una, stay here. You can't go there."

An ancient dread that lurked in Una rose to the surface and she resisted it, fought back against the realization of catastrophe. "I thought she was alright, it was over, I thought she was better!" She felt a terrifying chill through to her heart. Was mother really dead?

"Oh, Una, I am so sorry."

"What happened, what went wrong?"

"It was too much for her Una, just too much, that's all."

"What about Maggie? She's supposed to help her."

"There's nothing we could do dear, nothing."

Una began to whimper, a horribly disjointed, rasping, sound.

"Una, Una don't cry, don't cry like that." Emer held her very close.

Una wept uncontrollably, shudders shaking her thin frame. How could her mother be dead? They were supposed to be making tea soon, and that baby, why was he wailing? He ought not to be alive, why was he bawling?

She watched a young neighbor lad run up to them. "My mother saw Maggie passing and said to see if you're needing help." He looked at them round-eyed.

"It's too…late," Emer said brokenly, "too late, but please go for the priest, Stephen."

Una watched him race away. In amazement, she saw the wind turning the light green leaves of the beech tree inside out. The cat was washing her face on the steps of the dairy. Swallows swooped from the eaves, slicing the air like a sword. Over in the chicken run, the hens pecked at worms in the ground. How could the world be going about its business?

Then the sound of the pony and trap was heard. Emer went, face twisted with grief, to tell her brother he was a widower, and Angela's mother that her only daughter was dead. He jumped down from the trap ashen-faced and ran into the house. Una followed Emer, her heart shattered with pity for her father, shocked by his drawn face. She took Nan from her grandmother and held her close in her arms. Her tears rained down on Nan's curly head.

"Come and see the hens, Nan," she whispered.

Emer put her arm around Angela's mother and led her into the house.

PEADAR KNELT for a long time and held his wife's still-warm, lifeless hands. She lay white as milk in the bloody sheets. The grandmother rocked back and forth in a chair, moaning. At intervals her voice rose in a long, keening exhalation. Emer tried to comfort her.

"Don't cry Maura, you have a beautiful grandson, look at him," Maura stretched her hand out timorously and rocked the cradle gently.

Peadar got up from the death bed and Emer put her arms around him, "I am so, so sorry."

He broke away and went to the kitchen, reached up to the clock above the mantelpiece and removed the pendulum. It was four o'clock. Then he walked, stiff-legged, out of the house and stood leaning on the paddock gate. The pony nibbled grass at the edge of the yard, the bit clanging awkwardly against the ground, the trap door hanging open. After a long time Peadar became aware of the pony and released him from the trap. Cassie Plunkett, Stephen's mother, came racing up the lane, her broad, open face shocked and solemn.

EMER, MAGGIE, and Cassie, as if moved by some unseen instinct, took up the work of the day. They went wordlessly about the tasks, stiff shadows moving in the darkening house. They carried the cradle to the kitchen and placed it beside the hearth. Cassie cleared away the frying pan, the dried bacon and the potatoes, the last meal Angela had cooked. Una came in from the henhouse. She held Nan by the hand. "Nan's hungry," she said and began to weep. Cassie sat Nan at the table with a porringer of milk and bread and jam.

"Aren't you hungry, Una?"

Una tearfully shook her head. Emer was readying a bottle for the baby.

"Can you help me, Una?" She gave the infant to Una and showed her how to feed him a mixture of water and sugar from the curved glass bottle with the rubber nipple. The baby kept crying and was slow to grasp the nipple.

"Rub the nipple against his cheek," Emer instructed. Una shivered, despite the blazing turf fire; she kept trying, as much to ease the baby's thin crying as out of any wish she had for the infant. Her mother was dead. What was the use? It was better if the baby died too. His eyes were swollen shut. The nipple just lay in his mouth. Nan climbed down from her chair and came to look.

"Why are you crying, Una?" she asked.

"I'm not crying Nan, this is the new baby."

Nan stared at her little brother and reached out a hand to touch him.

"Would you like to hold the bottle?" Una asked her, trying to keep Nan's attention on the baby, terrified she would ask where her mother was. Nan held the bottle on a slant. "Nan, you have to hold the end up so he gets a drink." The baby had a funny shaped head and a fat puffy face.

Behind the closed door of the death room the women washed the corpse and spread clean sheets on the bed. There was no shroud, so they dressed Angela in her yellowed wedding dress, which they found on the top shelf of the press. Emer closed Angela's eyes and combed her masses of red hair, arranging it around her face. They lit two big candles beside the bed and twisted her rosary of green Connemara stone in her bloodless fingers. They put a penny on each of her dark eyelids. Maura sat watching them, her face a weary screen.

The clop of the horse's hooves sent Emer rushing out to the

yard. Nan stared at the priest as he marched into the kitchen after Emer, stared at the black tube that hung from his neck. It held the anointing oils.

"Una, dear, leave the baby for a few minutes and take Nan outside," Emer said, gently ushering them out the door.

They went round the side of the house.

"Go to the river?" Nan asked hopefully.

"No Nan, we were there already. Let's see if we can see snails on the cabbage."

Una wanted to stay near the house. Through the open window of her mother's room she could hear the priest talk to Emer and begin the ceremony of Extreme Unction.

Through this holy unction
And through His most loving mercy,
May the Lord pardon thee
Whatever sins thou has committed by seeing."

Una began to cry again, and rebelliously pulled Nan along toward the back of the garden. One of the cats was sitting in the long grass and Nan plopped herself down beside him. Una walked on and stood staring down toward the river. Surely her mother had never committed a sin. Una flung herself on the grass her fists clenched in resentful fury. What was this? Her mother was dead and Una wanted the world to stop, she wanted an earthquake, the ground to split. Great spaces should open on the hills beyond the river, the river ought to rear up and spout over the fields. She wanted noise, thunder to roll, rain to lash and strip the willow and the ash trees bare at the river; her mother was gone, what was this little ceremony in the farmhouse? What did the priest care? Her breath came in gasps and she wept, hopeless with rage. She felt Nan touch her arm and sat up.

"What's wrong, Una?" At the sight of the toddler's alarmed little face Una gathered her wits.

"Nothing dear, I'm alright, let's see if there are any spider webs." Una watched herself taking Nan's hand and leading her away, observed herself playing the big sister, as if another person, a different Una, walked with her little sister back toward the house.

"Nan, look at this, silver lines the snail makes, see the holes there where they have eaten the leaf for their dinner." She crouched and pointed out the bright trails, turning the cabbage leaves over. "Look how these have grown and we set them only about three weeks ago." As she spoke she was discovering how she might survive, keep herself safe, keep from collapsing in tears. She heard the priest leave, and this new Una said, "Let's go see the new baby, Nan."

Word of the catastrophe spread in the unerring way bad news passes in the country, and soon the women came, one by one, to stand beside the bed, dip their fingers in the bowl of holy water, sprinkle the bed and make the Sign of the Cross. Then they knelt and prayed for a few minutes and spoke gently to Angela's mother, before they sat with the widower in the kitchen.

"I'm sorry," they whispered as they took his hand, "sorry for your trouble." Their shawled figures bent in sympathy, their homely country faces sad and anxious, hands joined as if in prayer, movements slow and mournful. They wore long, dark red, homespun skirts, and black or dark green shawls. Peadar sat stunned, hardly aware of his surroundings, scarcely responding to them. Many brought round cakes of soda bread, sides of cold pork, hard-boiled eggs, pots of jelly, and left them on the leaf of the dresser.

Outside the light was fading fast. The air cooled and the colours died in the west. The two lamps on the chimney shelf were lit and the kitchen grew very hot. The door was left open to the yard.

Emer took the baby from Una and put him in his cradle. Una sat watching him, trying to hold back her tears, feeling the eyes of the women resting on her in pity. She decided she didn't want their sympathy, what did they know about her or her loss? What was it to them? They were talking together about her mother, whispering. Why weren't they leaving? There was no need for them. How could they know how bereft she was, there was no one who did, no one in the world knew the havoc that had been wrought. She wasn't going to cry, she wasn't going to be seen weeping. No one would have the satisfaction of seeing her helpless with grief. She would be that other Una, the Una who was never moved or broken-hearted.

Nan wandered from one woman to another in the kitchen, showing each her doll and then sat under the table and dressed and undressed the doll, talking to it in her baby voice. A few men from the village arrived to sit with Peadar.

Just after dark Emer led the grandmother out of the death room and sat her beside the fire. She gave her a glass of whiskey. Maura sipped the liquor, all the while her foot moved up and down rocking her infant grandson's cradle, her rosary beads slipped through her fingers.

In the flickering candle light the dead woman seemed no bigger than a child. Emer removed the coppers from her eyes and left the door slightly ajar so Angela would not be alone. Then she whispered to Una that they should see to the milking. They slipped out of the crowded kitchen and went to milk the cows. Una sat on her mother's milking stool. She grasped the cows teats, squeezed and released them. The milk pinged in the pail and then, as the pail filled, the sound softened to a steady, frothy splash. Angela always sang when she milked and despite her efforts to control them, Una's thoughts darted back again and again to the small motionless body laid between two candles. Her nose filled with the rich, fecund odour of new milk and the dry smell of hay. For a second she thought she might faint, but the feeling passed. Indeed, she and Emer were glad to be away from the talk of the crowd in the kitchen. The rhythm of squeezing and release of the cows' teats was familiar and soothing. The cows munched hay from their cribs and the lanterns threw grotesque shapes on the byre walls. The two grey cats sat watching, patiently waiting in expectation of a saucer of milk. They occasionally mewed piteously, as if they had not eaten for days. Una's eyes ached with unshed tears. She felt the new, brave Una slip away from her. "Mammy never wanted me to be milking, Aunt Emer," she sobbed.

"No harm in milking Una, if the cow's your own."

Una's fingers were neither nimble nor practiced enough to finish milking the cow, her hands seemed not to obey her will. Emer took her place, when she had finished her own task.

"I heard the priest talking, he said it was God's will."

"Don't mind him Una! God willed no such thing."

"Then why is Mammy dead?"

"Because we have no doctor here."

Emer stood up, finished with the milking, and wrapped her arm round Una.

"You listen to me, Una, God is like the rain or the air or warm milk. He is there all the time for us."

"Why didn't He stop Mammy dying?"

"Because He opposes nothing. He is just there."

"Why did she have to die?"

"Life is only a ceilidh, Una. The trees and stones last longer than we do. We are just visitors."

"What are we going to do? I miss Mammy, Aunt Emer."

"I know you do. But we have to think of Nan and the baby. Keep busy, Una, I need you to help me. Your father is lost Una, lost, so we have to pull together. I can't manage without you. Promise me you'll help."

"Of course I will, I want to help you."

"I know that, dear."

Tearfully, Una went with Emer to the dairy. They poured milk into the big brown crock for the family and filled the steel can for the creamery cart in the morning. Then they sadly and slowly walked across to the house. As soon as Emer entered the kitchen she noticed Nan was missing.

"Where's Nan?" she asked.

Peadar got up and took a lamp and walked into the girls' bedroom. He came back quickly. "She's not there," he said his face pale, alarmed, "she's gone." Una and Emer followed him into the yard.

"Nan, where are you?" they cried. "Nan, Nan! Come here."

Una grabbed a lantern from the porch. She and Emer searched the pigsty and the byre. Una didn't think Nan was there, she didn't like the pigs, but she could have followed them when they went to milk. They ran to the chicken run and the hen house, disturbing the fowl roosting for the night. The hens flew up, squawking and fluttering. Peadar searched the dairy and the stable, ran along the sides of the farm buildings and behind the hay stacks in the haggard, holding the lantern aloft and praying to see her tiny figure running into the light. Una and Emer ran behind the dairy and checked the paddock. The gate was closed. The pony, startled by the light, galloped away, snorting.

"Nan, Nan, where are you?" they called.

"My God! The river," cried Emer and they ran along the path. The neighbours, gathered now, followed, stumbling and bumping into each other in the dark. "Nan, Nan," called Emer.

"Please Nan, come out, where are you, please come here," Una cried, tears running down her face.

The lanterns cast jumping rings of light. Beyond and above the light, darkness mocked them. When they reached the river, Peadar jumped into the stream holding the light high and splashed along the brambly banks, back and forth. His dog swam after him. He sank knee-deep in mud, staggered to the edge and ploughed through the rushes. Emer waded to the far bank, breast high in muddy water, and Una tried to follow.

"Go back Una, go back, you'll drown too."

Terrified, Una turned away and frantically searched the reeds and shallows, her legs trembling with shock and cold. The river seemed broader than in daytime, black expanses of muddy water appearing as the lanterns were held aloft. More men arrived. They formed a chain with some of the younger women and, holding hands, they trolled the dark water, moving slowly in a line down toward the falls. Younger men came carrying bullrushes they had dipped in paraffin and lighted. They held the torches aloft and searched down to the bottom of the falls and beyond the bend in the river.

"No sign of her here," they yelled back to her father, "no sign at all."

One lad dropped his torch near the bank. The dried brambles caught fire, the flames ran along the edge, leaped up and then died, hissing in the water. All stopped, stared at the flames and crossed themselves as at an omen.

The men and young women searched till they were exhausted. At last Peadar climbed out of the water onto the bank and put down the lantern. His clothes were soaked up to his chest, his hands shook as if he were an old man.

"It's no use. If she came here she's lost, we will never find her now," he whispered hopelessly.

Tom Plunkett put a hand on his shoulder, "We'll try again lad, when we get the daylight."

Worn out, Emer waded across to take his hand, and as she clambered up on the near bank a water rat ran over her foot.

"Oh my God almighty," she screamed and ran sobbing back to the house, her wet skirts dragging her down. Una ran after her.

The others walked back slow and broken, holding to each other, brambles catching their faces and startled birds flying up out of the hedges.

"Holy Mother, take her to heaven, Lord have mercy on her." The women prayed and clung together, keening.

Emer raced on, stumbling and tripping on the uneven path, maddened by shock and remorse. Una slowed, too broken-hearted to run any more. My God, they were all lost. If only she had watched Nan, or asked someone else to watch her.

On the porch Emer paused, breathless, and wrung out her skirt, then went into the kitchen. The fire was dying down and the old woman was dosing beside the infant asleep in his cradle.

She pushed open the door of the death room and stood riveted on the transom. Nan lay asleep on her side, snuggled against the dead body of her mother, her little legs bent, her thumb in her mouth. Emer snatched her up and ran outside shouting, "She's here, I've got her, she's here." Una shrunk back against the door as at an apparition. The people surged forward to see her, to touch her.

"Thanks be to God," they cried. "Thanks be to God…Thanks be to God."

Peadar took Nan and hugged her and tears almost overflowed his dark eyes. The mourners crowded round the little girl. "Isn't she lovely," they said, ruffling her black curls. Nan rubbed her eyes sleepily in the lantern light and buried her face in her father's shoulder.

Relief at finding the lost child seemed to somehow lessen the tragedy of Angela's death. The stunned mourners showed a new liveliness. They built up the fire and the women laid out the food. Una swung the big kettle over the flames to boil for tea. Emer put out a box of tobacco, some clay pipes and a small bowl of snuff.

But Peadar sat desolate, Nan against his shoulder, staring into the fire. She was sleeping peacefully. Her small arms were round his neck, her black, curly head rested under his chin, her soft breath on his arm and her little knees tucked into his chest. Bran, his dog, lay across his feet. Steam rose from his wet clothes.

With the long fall day's work in the fields over, the rest of the men of the townland began to arrive to spend the wake night with him. They came forward one by one, shaking his hand and then quietly sitting for a while among their neighbours.

Whiskey passed round and the women sipped it. Lizzie Scanlon whispered, "I heard the banshee last night," and helped herself to a pinch of snuff.

Margaret Smith, a stout hard-faced farm labourer's wife, contradicted her sharply, "It was cats you heard, the banshee don't cry for that family!"

"But she could start crying for them, couldn't she?"

"God knows there's reason enough to cry," said Cassie Plunkett her plain round face pale with sorrow and shock.

"I know what I heard," Lizzie insisted stubbornly, and sneezed.

"The priest says there's no such thing as the 'shee," Margaret told her.

"What does he know?" Lizzie scoffed, whiskey loosening her tongue, "I heard the Banshee, I saw her too, sitting there in the thorn tree, a little woman, her hair in tatters. It never fails," she continued, "didn't I hear her the past Lent crying her heart out and next thing the priest is reading prayers for the crowd that died in the big ship."

"What ship?"

"The Toytonic, sure it couldn't have luck, it was built by Protestants up in Belfast."

"Well, there was lots of Catholics drowned in it too, Lizzie," Cassie reminded her.

"Sure that's what I'm telling you, that's the reason I heard the banshee. She was crying for the Catholics."

"Stop that talk Lizzie, we have to thank God the child is safe."

"I'll say nothing about that poor child's prospects, who knows what's before her," Lizzie said ominously, "wasn't she wanting to be with her dead mother?"

"Don't mention such a thing. Sure, God is good," Margaret said devoutly, crossing herself.

"And the devil's not bad, either," retorted Lizzie. She quickly pulled her shawl round herself with her thin knobby hands and got up to fill her pipe. "Sure life's only a ceilidh," she said, "we should enjoy it while we're in it."

Out in the yard, the young men sat around, arguing about the Land League, their voices getting louder and louder.

Pat McGee, a little white-headed old fellow told them, "there's too much loud talk here for a wake. You ought to stop now and again to see if you could hear the *Coiste Bodhar*, it's lucky to hear it."

The young lads were amused.

"There's no ghost coach. That's all a load of rubbish about the *Coiste Bodhar*."

"Why wouldn't there be? I've heard it myself and seen it, too."

"*Mor dhea*, as if anyone ever saw it," they mocked.

"That sort of blather has the Irish ruined," said John Slowey, a small sturdy little farmer. "You should sit with the old women if you want to tell stories like the *seanacee*."

Silenced for the moment, Pat puffed hard on his pipe and sent clouds of defiant smoke up over his head. He was over seventy now, a widower, living in a ramshackle cottage down where the lane turned towards the road and the village.

"Well, we have the chance to have our own land now and we should forget that old nonsense," another man said.

"You should be thanking that dead woman's father for that," Pat jumped into the fray again. "He's the man kept the Land League goin' when the rest of you were *plamasin* and bowing and scrapin' to the landlords."

"What good is it when everything is decided in London still?" Liam Shanahan wondered.

People drifted in from the yard to the kitchen for food and to light their pipes. Peadar's dog came out on the step and surveyed the scene, then lay down, his head on his paws, his eyes turned up watchful. The moon began to rise above the beech trees, a clear, late August moon, and filled the yard with pure silver light so bright the stars drew back. The young boys lit a fire near the paddock gate to dry their clothes. The men brought an oak barrel on a cart and set it on a box beside the dairy, the murmur went round that they were tapping the barrel. They took their mugs, held them under the flowing tap, then drank the foaming porter.

After a while someone said, "Give us a bar or two," and, as the fiddle started up, they encouraged the fiddler, shoulders swaying, feet tapping.

"Sure you've never lost it, Pete."

Then the fiddler changed the beat, and the slow note of an old love song from the days before famine scattered the people rose in the night air. It silenced the crowd. A woman's voice took it high and plaintive.

"Who in the song so sweet.
Aileen aroon.
Who in the dance so neat.
Aileen aroon."

And the deep voices of the men joined in.

"Dear were her charms to me
Dearer her laughter free
Dearest her constancy
Aileen aroon."

And the singing rose and rolled in waves over the moonlit fields yellowing with oats and barley, mingled with the barking of foxes in the hedges and the distant faint rumble of a train miles away. Singing together in pain and grief for the dead, gratitude and joy that little Nan was safe from the river.

At the kitchen hearth, Emer sat with the infant in her arms. She dipped her little finger into a bowl of warm milk Una held, then put her finger in the baby's mouth and he sucked it. She took the bottle from Una and put the nipple in his mouth. "You see Una, he's hungry! Come on, you try." She passed the baby over.

Una noticed the baby seemed to be watching her with his dark blue eyes. His eyelids drooped and he began to suck. "Look, Aunt Emer, he is drinking, I thought he would die like Mammy."

"No, my dear," said Lizzie, lighting her pipe from a coal held on the end of the tongs "an infant comes out of the dark, and wants to stay in the light."

Tears welled in Una's pale, red-rimmed eyes, and she held her little brother tighter, struggling to control her weeping, unable to summon the grown-up, composed Una. Emer noticed her pale exhausted face, took the baby and gave him to Lizzie to hold. "Una, come and lie down for a little while."

In the bedroom Emer helped Una remove her clothes and tucked the bedclothes round her. They lay together on the bed. Una thought she would never sleep, but she did.

Emer left her sleeping and returned to the kitchen. Des the carpenter came up as she sat at the fire, and crouched down beside her.

"You'll be needing a coffin."

"Yes."

"Should I measure her?" he asked.

Emer raised her head sharply. "There'll be no measuring done here! Angela is five feet, just up to my shoulder."

"I was only just asking," he told her and then said, "and what kind of wood would you be wanting?"

"The best you have, and I'll pay for it."

Dismissed, Des sat on the dairy step and smoked . He thought for a while, then remarked quietly to Liam Shanahan, "Peadar's sister must have a few pounds saved from when she was in America."

"She has her Confirmation money still, I wouldn't doubt."

"And her First Communion shilling, too," said Des thoughtfully.

Under the beech trees John Slowey said, "It looks like a good harvest."

"It does indeed, I have a few hard days ahead to save it," Tom Plunkett agreed.

"And we will have to have a *meitheall* of men to get poor Peadar's in for him."

"You can count me in for that Tom," Jim Lever assured him. "Did they send word to her brother?"

"They did, they sent one of those telegraphs from the town."

"He'll be here for the funeral, so."

Tomorrow they would work all day in the fields and in the evening they would take the dead woman's body to the church, past farmhouses with drawn blinds and the shuttered shops of the village, carrying the coffin on their shoulders, and leave her there. She would stay a long night alone before they carried her to her final resting place in the old graveyard at Knockmore, five miles away. No one mentioned that awful end.

They drank their porter, raising their mugs to the dead woman. "Sure, poor Angela, she's in heaven," they said, "God be good to her."

"Ah sure, she was beautiful," said Pat McGee, "I remember well the great wedding she had. She was just a slip of a girl, her face was like new milk and her cheeks red like the haws."

They were quiet for a minute, remembering the lovely Angela, now cold and stiffening, stretched out in her wedding dress between lighted candles, the small lively woman who till a few hours before had been busy in her house and yard. Then the talk started up anew, the buzz of conversation grew louder and their cigarettes and pipes glowed in the shadows.

The fiddle began again and a couple of tin whistles joined in. The spoons started a hard metallic clanging. The bones began a ghostly other-worldly clicking. Young men and girls stood and formed a set to dance, circling and whirling on the hard-beaten earth of the yard. As they swung and spun, their shadows jumped in a frenzied, leaping ring and the nails in their boots sparked on the flagstones. The dog raced round them yelping furiously, and another in the distance answered, and then another and another, howling and barking in the night. The fiddler bent forward, the music faster and faster, the ring of watchers clapping and stomping in rhythm. The moon sailed on between wisps of clouds, the great firmament seemed to shift; yesterday and tomorrow were one with wild music, stomping feet, moonlight and wind rising and blowing over the little drumlins.

Una stirred in her sleep as Emer laid Nan beside her. She had been dreaming, making bread with her mother. The kitchen filled with golden light from the turf fire, Angela's arms snowy to the elbows. She winged her flour-filled hand over the board and whitened it, turned a broad slab of bubbly dough over on itself and punched it flat, then with the side of her hand measured off a portion for Una, and they worked together kneading the bread. No matter how Una tried to shape the dough, it turned into a baby. Half asleep, she heard music and dancers feet. She turned and took Nan lovingly in her arms.

Una opened her eyes, immediately awake. Her father was watching her. He was slumped in the chair beside her bed. She saw strange creases in the skin around his mouth and his stubbled face had no colour. "Did you sleep, Una?"

"I did a little."

She realized it was morning and her mother was gone. The light from the window was weak and dull. The house deathly quiet. Where was everyone?

"Una, like a good girl, I want you to go down and stay with your aunt, and take Nan with you. This is no place for you."

Nan sat up beside Una and rubbed her eyes. Her father reached over and lifted her in his arms. Nan put her thumb in her mouth and with her other hand grasped her father's ear. She closed her eyes and sucked her thumb.

"Get dressed Una, like a good girl, then we'll go down to Emer's."

Peadar carried Nan out to the kitchen and Una got out of bed. She picked up her shift off the chair and then put it down again and sat on her bed, then picked up her dress, put it aside, mechanically took the shift again and began to dress herself. Her father looked strange. What if he began to cry, like Una had yesterday? How shameful that would be. She knew he wouldn't. Men didn't cry. It would be too embarrassing.

The kitchen was empty, the hearth black and cold. The door to her mother's room was half open. Through the half door to the yard she saw her father talking to Tom Plunkett. Peadar set Nan on the dairy steps beside the cat and came back in.

"We'll go now Una, I'll bring your things down later."

"Where's Granny?"

"Tom left her home in the trap early this morning. She needs to rest."

He looked closely at her, as if to reassure himself that she was still as she had always been.

"Before we leave, would you like to see your mother again?"

Una understood this would be the last time: she nodded, and her father took her hand and led her into the room. Two black shawled figures, Mary McDermott and Carmel Horan kept watch by the bed. They stood up when Una and Peadar entered. Her father motioned them to sit. The curtains were closed, the room in half light. Una stood at the foot of the bed looking at the corpse, the small still hands, the immobile face that seemed to have the colour and consistency of wax candles dripped down to untidy stumps. That thing wasn't her mother, it was some display, a pretense. She dipped her finger in the holy water, crossed herself and walked away, out to the yard. She fought back tears at the sight of her mother's yard boots tidied away under the form beneath the kitchen window. Her father followed her. He took a shawl from the back of the kitchen door and wrapped Nan in it. The fog was turning into drenching rain. They began to run down the lane toward Emer's house.

"I don't know what I'd do without Tom Plunkett. He's meeting Joseph's train for me."

They were sitting at the dinner table. Nan was taking her afternoon nap in Emer's bed. The baby stirred in his cradle and she picked him up and rested him on her shoulder. "We'll wait till he comes to take her to the chapel," Peadar continued.

"I'll not go, Peadar," Emer said, "I'll stay here with the children."

"There's no need of you going, you'll be at the funeral tomorrow, that's enough."

"Am I going, Daddy?" Una wondered if she would go when they took her mother's coffin to the chapel. She wanted to show her father and Uncle Joseph that she was valiant and strong, a heroic and brave girl.

"No Una, I don't think you should be there, it's no place for you. Stay here with your aunt."

"Una, your father is right, stay here and help me. Your father and Uncle Joseph will come back here after."

"Am I going to the funeral?"

"Una, you are too young. Mary McDermott will come tomorrow to stay with you."

Peadar got up and walked over to the open door and looked out at the rain.

"But I could go Daddy, I'll not cry, I promise I won't. I'm big enough."

"Maybe she should go, Peadar," said Emer, "I think she would be alright to go."

Peadar turned back from the door, "I don't want her there, the people may talk but it's no place for a child."

"I went to my grandfather Maguire's funeral."

"No! No need of you going. You stay here with Nan and the baby."

"But Daddy, you needn't be worried on my account."

"It's not on your account dear, not at all, it's because your mother wouldn't wish it, she wouldn't like you at her funeral. She didn't like funerals, it's on her account."

Una knew then how much he had loved her and did still. Angela was a presence in his mind and in all their minds. She would remain so, long after they picked up the ordinary work of the days and weeks after summer holidays ended and Una returned to school: skimming the cream and churning it for butter, cooking and carrying the food to the fields for the men who came to save the harvest, twisting the straw ropes to tie the sheaves, and planting the stooks in the tough stubble, the shortening days hurrying them on. Angela was present in memory, and would be, for as long as they lived.

WITHOUT LAND

LIZZIE FELT THE PRESENCE of the Nameless One in the crimson morning darkness and said silently, "You're there! Sure that's grand, now come round me like the sun."

It was Saturday quiet, no clatter of bottles or rumble of barrels from next door, no voices, not even a bird song. Yesterday she had run out of tea and was forced to buy a half pound at Mahon's next door. She was sure Mrs. Mahon left her short in the change. Tea was a shilling a pound and Lizzie had proffered a half crown.

"The ould rip," Lizzie fumed. "She gave me such a clather of pennies and thrupenny bits that I didn't know what I had. I like the round shilling, easy to count. That's one thing about Jany Fenton, the priest's housekeeper, she paid the round shilling. Emer Maguire, too, when I went two days to help her after the funeral. Poor girl with a baby to manage."

But the crowd next door were no better than tinkers. Last night Lizzie had gone to the door to investigate a rumpus in the street. Two young fellows, Paddy Mullins and Seamus Nannery, drunk as lords, were arguing with Liam, Mahon's shop boy.

"Ah, if it's not Lizzie the Cabbage," Seamus mocked, "how many skirts are you wearing?"

"Don't mind that fella, Miss Scanlon," Liam admonished. Lizzie slammed the door in his face.

Tramps, no manners at all, sometimes when they were drunk they urinated against the wall outside her door. Lizzie was used to the village boys sneering at her for wearing several skirts, one over the other, as the weather grew colder. She was nobody's fool. She knew her nickname in Mahon's pub was Lizzie the Cabbage. And her name wasn't even Scanlon, it was McCann. She'd only been brought up by Fergus and May Scanlon from the age of five. Fergus was the village blacksmith and his trade died with him, because apart from Lizzie they had no children. Now smithing was done in Ballynamon, three miles away. Lizzie had loved to hang around the hitching post, a little out from the door of the forge, and watch Fergus raise the red hot iron from the fire, holding it aloft a minute before hammering it into shape on the anvil, showers of sparks rising and falling back in the gloom, a strange sharp smell of falling sparks on his leather apron, a pungent stench when he fitted the hot shoe to the hoof. A thousand times she had watched. She could have shod the horse herself, if such a thing were not unthinkable. The horse owner would stand at the animal's head, talking in low, soothing tones. Fergus crouched with his back to the horse, knees bent, sitting on air. He'd take the horse's leg, cradle the hoof in his cupped hand and nail the shoe. Lizzie held her breath till the shoe was in place, and trimmed with the long iron file, Fergus caressed the horse's foreleg and placed the shod foot gently on the ground. She would then sigh deeply, and watch him work the bellows at the glowing fire to fashion another shoe.

A horse liked to be shod, Fergus explained. "If I didn't trim his hooves they'd grow a foot long, now wouldn't that hobble him at his work, and a horse likes nothing better than working."

The forge was the center of village gossip, talk of prices and rents and sometimes of revolution. But Fergus quelled that kind of talk. "My forge is no place for that kind of tomfoolery."

"Wasn't I lucky," Lizzie often said to the Nameless One. "Those were great days."

Lizzie's world was formed by the talk of men in the forge, and by her foster mother's endless tales of banshees and fairies, Fenian glory and tragedy. May Scanlon had a fine contempt for men. "Sure the crowd that's about now, they're no good, *spalpeens* that's all, the best of them is in America." All this Lizzie hoarded in memory, yet behind those sweet remembrances she sometimes felt a distant memory of pain, a crushing blow, a shadow that menaced. She quickly brushed it aside and then felt unaccountably bleak and guilty.

Lizzie opened her eyes. The dim light from a tiny window revealed the white-washed walls and her clothes heaped on a chair. She stretched a little, sat up, felt around with her toes for her boots, gingerly eased her feet in and stood. Then, wrapping her shawl around her, she tottered out to the kitchen. Her little doorless bedroom was tucked behind the big kitchen hearth. The black cat, sleeping before the fireplace, sat up and stretched. Lizzie crouched down painfully, lifted the tongs, raked and stirred the tiny live coals amongst the grey ashes. From the turf box beside the fire she took hard dry sods, stood them on end around the coals, then knelt and puffed a lung full of breath on the fire. The dry peat caught and flamed courageously. The cat darted away across the kitchen. Lizzie blew again on the fire, a long, sighing expiration, her ribs stretching and then sucking in with the effort. The turf reddened and glowed. Outside, the rooster crowed.

Lizzie filled the black iron kettle from the pail and hung it over the fire, then went back to her bedroom, and removed her red flannel nightdress and pulled her blouse and woolen gansey over her head. Her long plat of grey hair stuck in the neck of her blouse. She freed it, stretched her bent arms up toward the roof and rolled her shoulders back to ease the morning stiffness. Moving slowly, but still a little painfully, she stepped into her petticoats and skirt. The balls of her hip bones ached and creaked in their sockets. "You see how the years are walking over me?" she told the Nameless One. "Their feet have me marked."

Stiff and sore, Lizzie walked to the kitchen door. The cat followed and scooted out when she opened it. The village of Slanabaille was enveloped in early October fog, the seven houses across the street shuttered and silent. To her right she could just see where the road rose gently and left the village; one fork looping past the church, between thick hedges and over little hills to the hamlet of Ballynamon, the other fork to the market town of Obanbeg.

There were three houses on Lizzie's side of the street, Lizzie's at one end, Brady, the cooper, at the other end, and J.J. Mahon's in the middle. Between Mahon's and the bridge, Lizzie's acre sloped to the water. Further east, the river tumbled over little falls and sometimes overflowed in a soggy bottom at the end of Lizzie's land. Close to the stream, rushes, ferns and reeds grew in clumps and brambles; blackberries spread themselves out. Corncrake and snipe nested. Higher on the slope, where a thorn bush exploded into glorious white flower every spring, Lizzie's two goats grazed, and beside the cottage her potato ridges were fenced with chicken wire to protect them from the hens.

Lizzie had the largest hen house in Slanabaille. Originally it had been the forge. Hens nested on the low, stone platform where the smithy had tended his fire and worked at the anvil hammering horseshoes. Her turf was stacked beside the hen house.

She couldn't see her goats in the field. The sun was weak yet, the thorn bush ghostly in the mist. "Where are they now?" she asked the Nameless One, longing for the first taste of morning tea. The days had shortened, the long, dark winter nights coming; crops were in, potatoes saved and stored in the pit. Time's a trollop, Lizzie thought, you have to pay her rent every day of your life. And she passed her hands over her still aching hips.

She returned to the house, took the kettle off the hook over the fire, wrapped herself in her white knitted shawl and went to look for her goats. She took the road to her left over the little bridge, up a short way and passed through high iron gates that stood wide open. On the huge piers that held the gates, the words "Darling House" cut into the grey limestone. From the gates, a high stone wall ran down to the river, to the right it curved into the distance and was lost in the mist. The sun was winning a little over the fog except in the low land by the river. Its slanting light jeweled drops of mist in serried lines on the grass. Here and there, sleepy birds began twittering. Lizzie's stiffness and pain had eased. To her left, she could see the tiny stream crossed by the little footbridge. The stream drained an ornamental lake further in on the estate. Old elms and limes stood in clumps by the stream. Striding now across the grassy lawn Lizzie trod over evenly spaced furrows, between low ridges that stretched on either side of the gravel drive. "Just look at that, the ridges are still there," she told the Nameless One as she peered through the mist looking for her two goats. She spied them resting on the damp grass a hundred yards further on. They looked like old, bearded men staring solemnly through the fog. "You'll be the death of me," she told them as she strode over. "And aren't you as wise as Christians knowing where Darling's sweet grass is. It's a great wonder that you wouldn't know when is milking time."

She stood for a minute, watching the mist rising from the river. The river spread out in a shallow pool thick with green slime and mud. Lizzie stooped and picked up the two ends of rope that looped round her goats' necks then noticed that a little further away the animals had defecated on the grass. "And why wouldn't you," she laughed.

Head lowered, leading the goats over the ridged lawn, she suddenly halted, her eye catching a gloved hand holding leather reins, and a booted leg. Her gaze travelled up to the heavy body and pale face of the horseman. He sat solid on a huge chestnut mare, staring down at Lizzie. She shrunk back. They eyed each other for a minute, then the landlord touched the horse's side with his heels and rode away. She stood quivering with resentment and rage, her lean wrinkled face flushed. "God whither your heart and stop your blood," she muttered viciously. "And bad luck to you and all belonging to you."

Wild, searing hunger passed through her, convulsing her belly, trembling her legs. She wanted to feel her stomach full, tight against the waistband of her skirt. She craved thick rashers of bacon and mottled fried potato bread, soppy yellow-eyed fried eggs with lacy whites.

"Come on you, the good of the day is gone and my fast is not broken yet." Lizzie rushed for home, dragging the animals after her. Near her home she slowed, short of breath, her heart pounding, her left side aching. As she led them in at the side of her house J.J. Mahon, the red-faced tavern keeper, was hauling porter barrels out of the shop for the brewery dray.

"God bless the work," she told him.

"And yourself Lizzie."

"That fellow's too sweet to be wholesome," she reminded the

Nameless One. "Wasn't he wanting to buy my place years ago? A land grabber, full of himself, thinks he has the run of the country."

Above the frosted glass doors, yellow writing on the green shop front proclaimed, *J.J. Mahon Publican.* And below, in smaller gold lettering, *Licensed to Sell Beer Wine Spirits and Tobacco, Seven Day License.* One shop window displayed an amazing variety of merchandise on tiered shelves. Pens, squat bottles of blue ink, writing tablets, candles, paraffin oil lamps and curved glass baby bottles. The other window held a cardboard sign reading *Powers Whiskey*, the lettering surrounded by stars, the sign itself propped on a porter barrel.

J.J. Mahon was not a talkative man. Years behind the bar at the back of the shop, listening to men arguing, had left him with little to say. In the front of the shop, his wife sold everything a household might need, from treacle and molasses to iron cooking pots, from Ricketts Blue to worm powders. Her domain, a short low counter, was backed by shelves of tobacco in glass jars, packets of cigarettes, boxes of wax candles. The floor in front had an untidy collection of wooden tea chests and barrels of sugar. Beneath the counter Mahon kept two ledgers where the credit accounts were stored. Most small farmers had a bill at Mahon's shop which they discharged when they sold an animal on the Fair Day. Lizzie never owed him a penny. "That gombeen man, a robber, overcharging for meal in July when the potatoes are gone," she told the Nameless One, "and greedy for my bit of land, wanting to grab it to get a way to the river for his two scrawny cows, and watching me, waiting for me to drop out of my standin'."

The first bite of warm, doughy, fried potato bread watered Lizzie's mouth and she pressed it upward, flavour and solace spreading through teeth, nose and sinuses, her hungry brain seizing the taste. She closed her eyes, soft eggs running down her throat, elbows resting on the table. Mug cupped in her chapped brown hands, she slurped the hot, sweet, milky tea. A sweat broke through her pores and soaked her hair and face. "I'm a greedy gut," she told the Nameless One. "What's come over me? It's because I've walked on hungry grass, but still there's nothing like a good healthy feed." And she loosened her skirt, tidied its folds around her legs and sat at ease over the remains of her meal.

A timid knock roused Lizzie from her bloated stupor. "Are you from this world or the next?" she called out, half joking.

"Ah, sure it's only me," answered Des Donoghue, and sidled in the door, one shoulder ahead of the other, hands in his pockets. He shut the half door carefully after him.

"Good man yourself, Des, sure you must've smelled the tea."

"No, no, no, Lizzie, I had my breakfast."

"A drop of tea won't kill you," she said, rising to get a mug from the dresser.

Des' brown curly hair parted in the middle and grew over his ears, a big droopy mustache gave his face a mournful look that belied his twenty-three years. His vigilant eyes took in the remains of the meal, her flushed face, the frying pan sitting on its stand in the ashes.

"You're late with your breakfast."

"I had to follow the goats, they went up to Darling's place, bad luck to him, he left the gates open."

"Ah, sure there's no harm in them going there, although you'd be tired running after them, wouldn't you," he said soothingly, accepting the mug of tea from her hand.

Lizzie reached behind her and took a piece of knitting from a cloth bag that hung on the knob of her chair and began to knit furiously, fingers moving the needles by touch alone.

"Sure you're the one that's handy with the needles," Des flattered her.

"Not like I was Des, not like I was, the years are walking over me. I mind the time that I could make fancy lace."

"Sure you're not seventy, nor near it."

"I'd have to ask the priest to know for sure, he has it written above in the book. I used to know my age but I forgot. I have enough counting to watch my little bit of money never mind counting my age."

From his pocket Des produced a small, round bottle wrapped in brown paper and placed it on the table.

"A Baby Power for you Lizzie, when you feel like a little drop."

"Sure that's grand Des, did you get a packet from America?"

"No, Emer paid for the making of Angela's coffin."

"Ah Angela, poor Angela, she was too good-looking. It's always the beauties that's taken."

Des let Lizzie ramble on, watching her face closely for every shadow of emotion.

"I was up to see Emer a week ago Sunday," she told him, "I got a yellow letter from America, from my cousin, John, he writes the very odd time, he's all I got in the world now, and Emer read it for me and wrote a few lines in return."

"Sure Lizzie dear, any time you want reading or writing done I'll do it for you, any time at all. And I was thinking," he added, all the time studying her expression, "about what we talked about, how your cousin doesn't want your place. I've a bit of money put by."

"I'll not sell when I'm alive," she said quickly. "You're nothing without land."

"I know, I know," Des agreed with her, "sure I was only wondering, but we could come to an arrangement, you remember Lizzie, the arrangement we talked about."

"Oh, I remember well, I'm not likely to forget."

"Sure we're old friends Lizzie, you and me, there's no hurry," Des was saying now, "there's no hurry at all; this is just between us two."

"I'd need to sit down and study meself," she told him.

"Ah, you would, wouldn't you," he said gently, "I know you would, sure I was only just asking."

Lizzie knitted away, bone needles flying. The cat, crouched in front of the hearth, blinked her green eyes sleepily. After a short pause Des ventured, "I hear tell Peadar Maguire sold three cows last Fair Day. I wonder what's up with him?"

"Ah sure, he just doesn't want to feed them in the winter."

"I don't know about that, but I was wondering if Peadar was short of money."

"Not Peadar," Lizzie told him, "he could always get a bit from Patrick in America and Emer has a bit."

"There's a lot of talk they're leaving the devil a long time in that child. He's not baptized yet, it's a wonder the priest stands for it. People say it's a scandal, what if something happened to him."

"Well," said Lizzie, "they'll christen him tomorrow after the Month's Mind Mass for poor Angela. Anyhow he's a fine healthy child as far as I could see."

"They say it's some sort of an American notion Emer has."

"Ah Des, sure Emer's a grand girl."

"Ah sure, of course she is. They say the priest has a great notion of her."

"And why wouldn't he, Des, you nearly couldn't blame him."

"Well, there's people that'd fault him. Like the parish priest over in Ballynamon, or the bishop himself. He might be giving him a good belt of the crozier."

"Ah, what he doesn't know won't sicken him."

"You're right, Lizzie."

Des stood up to leave. "You'll think over what we talked about Lizzie?"

"Ah, I need time, Des."

"Oh, of course you do, Lizzie. Of course."

"I'll think about it, I do want you to have it."

"I know that Lizzie, just think it over."

"Ah, you know I will."

"I'll go so."

When Des left, Lizzie stood leaning on the half door looking after him. He turned in to Mahon's next door. He was always in Mahon's, that's where the men gathered. Sure why wouldn't he, that's where he'd hear all the news.

The racket from there was starting up. Barrels rolled on the cobblestones, bottles clattered and Mahon's son Jack shouted at Liam, the helper who bottled the stout in the back shed.

She stood looking at herself in the cracked brown-tinged looking-glass beside the door. Her fierce, black eyes set in fine wrinkles, her thin, brown face with deep furrows each side of the thin-lipped mouth. She folded the thick, grey plat of hair up on top of her head. She looked younger now, different. "Who do I belong to at all?" she asked the Nameless One. The cat jumped on the half door, distracting her. When she glanced back at her reflection, a face looked over her shoulder. There for a second and then gone. Lizzie shivered. Pisherogs, superstition, she was seeing things.

She picked up the cat and went out to the hen house to collect the eggs, the cat riding on her shoulder. Motes danced in the sunlight that streamed in the door. Twelve nests. Only seven eggs. Had a rat been about, or a weasel? She crouched down and looked for broken egg shells. Nothing. The hens were pecking in the grass. "You're a mean stingy lot," she told them. Maybe they needed meal twice a day now. The sedge and grass were thinning out, not much to eat outside to supplement the table scraps. The days were shorter and it was cooler. She would have to part with another four shillings to J.J. Mahon for meal. Bad luck to him, she thought, I hate to give that miser a penny.

Lizzie brought the eggs into the house and put them in a bowl on the dresser. She was going to bake. Three cakes of soda bread, two for Emer for the dinner after the Month's Mind Mass tomorrow, and one for herself. Angela was dead a month. God be good to her. Lizzie piled up the fire with turf and went to replenish the turf box. She stacked five turf on her left arm, three, two, one in a pyramid and carried them into the kitchen. She once owned a strip of peat bog, left to her by her foster father. In memory she was footing turf with Fergus and May one Easter. They were stacking wet, buttery sods in pyramids to catch the wind, you had to catch the wind to dry the sods Fergus said. You have to catch the wind! Birds nesting in the bog, snipe and grouse and corncrakes. Curlews crying from the whin bushes and bog larks soaring high above the earth singing and singing, white clouds flying in the square pool of black water that formed where Fergus cut the turf. She never went near the edge of the bog hole. Fergus marked off neat rectangles of peat and sliced them clean with the wing-tipped slane. He cut steps into the bank. "Always leave steps, in case you fall in," he warned her.

"That's what Saint Columba said," he told her, "he fell in one time, and the faeries pulled him out and he cursed the bogs." The bog was a strange place. At night faery lights flared there. The bog surface shook and squelched like a green and purple mass of jelly quivering under her feet. Fergus laid branches across it to step on.

"You got to leave steps," Lizzie remembered.

She sat looking into the fire. Ten years ago, Lizzie sold her strip of peat bog to Tom Plunkett for forty pounds and four loads of turf every June as long as she lived. Tom was good as his promise. He never missed delivering the turf and stacking it beside the hen house. Lizzie still thought of the bog as her own. It kept her warm every winter. Tom had drawn up the paper and Lizzie had placed her mark where he had shown her. He counted out the pounds, more than she'd ever seen. And he drove her into Obanbeg to the Bank of Ireland, in his trap.

Tom had bought the trap at an auction. It was the first time Lizzie had driven in one. How strange it was to look down on the horse's back, and see him toss his head and the wind separate his flowing mane, his loose feet sure on the white rough road. They drove past the county workhouse, like a prison it was. A few old men sat outside on a bench. They stared as the trap drove past. One old fellow in rags shook his stick at them. Lizzie turned away and watched the quivering hindquarters of the horse, his nodding head and alert ears, the road disappearing, slipping away under the shiny frame of the trap as they jogged along. Up the hill and down the long slope, past the white cottages, tumble-down stone row houses and ragged children rolling hoops in the street.

And the crowds in the town! Knots of people standing about. Had they no homes to go to, standing around in the middle of the day, talking. The bank as big as a church, a fellow in a uniform polished the brass on the front door and held it open for them. They put the money in the bank. A fellow behind a high counter wrote it out. Lizzie added twelve shillings saved from what she had earned washing clothes and cleaning for the schoolteacher and the priest's housekeeper.

The bank manager wore a high collar and a long coat. He had a waistcoat as fine as Darlings, bad luck to him. He shook her hand. "That's a tidy sum, Miss McCann," he said and Lizzie stared at him. Miss McCann!

"Thank you kindly, sir."

And the tidy sum she had. A woman with money in the bank. She minded herself. Never owed a penny. That was her way. She was going to arrange for her funeral soon, Des would help her. She imagined her wake, lying among her neighbours. Des speaking well of her. No workhouse for me; I never want to darken the poorhouse door, she told the Nameless One. "When my time is up I'll know. Just give me the whole of my health till then, I know I shouldn't be huckstering with you, but still…."

Lizzie went to her bedroom and dragged a battered, green, tin biscuit box from under her bed. She sat at the kitchen table and pried the lid off with a knife. Her thin, wrinkled hands leafed through the yellow papers. The flimsy paper was the one she had marked for Tom. In a way, Des was proposing the same thing. He'd give her one hundred pounds and she'd put her mark on a paper. She'd live out her life in her cottage, when she died Des would have it. Maybe he'd find some good girl and children would play on the green slope. Lizzie liked that. A hundred pounds was far less than the place was worth, she knew that. Her land was the best plot in the village, but Des was young and hadn't much money. He supported his old mother, and carpentry work was not steady. He'd told her some of the money had come to his mother from a cousin in New York. Maybe she'd tell Des tomorrow that she would put her mark on that paper. Des would be at the Month's Mind Mass and the dinner after. Des was a grand fellow.

AT MASS, Lizzie knelt behind Una, Emer and Maura, Angela's mother. "Ah, Maura's coming back to herself, she's very thin, still she looks more alive, sure I thought she'd never recover, never be the same again," Lizzie told the Nameless One. Emer held her infant nephew against her shoulder. Little Nan leaned her head out of the pew, watching the priest at the altar. The men knelt on the other side of the aisle, Peadar and Angela's brother Joseph. Behind them were their neighbours, men on the right side of the aisle, women on the left.

At Angela's funeral, Peadar's face seemed to have lost all expression, except the white mask of grief and exhaustion. Yesterday, Des returned from Mahon's pub to tell Lizzie the news. Peadar was going to America. "Ah well," she told the Nameless One, "he'll forget all about her there. That's the men for you, he'll meet some disheen of a one, some ornament of a woman in America, that's what men always do, they always suit themselves. He'll marry again before she's cold in her grave."

"*Et lux in tenebris*," and the light shines in darkness. The priest was finishing the mass, "*unigenita Patre plenum gratiea et veritatis,*" the only begotten of the Father, full of grace and truth.

"*Deo Gratias,*" thanks be to God.

Not one word had Lizzie understood. She was wrapped in the aura of the guttering candles and fragrant incense, gazing at stained glass windows with their apocalyptic figures of Saint Michael and Lucifer in mortal combat, Saint Patrick in a green cloak, banishing the snakes forever, the Virgin in blue, her foot crushing the serpent, lilies held in her slender hands.

Most of the congregation streamed out. The men stood outside smoking under yellow and red leafed maples and elms. Shawled women walked on in clumps of three or four, talking.

In the gloomy church porch the little group waited for the priest. He came, followed by the two scrubbed altar boys. Emer held the infant. Joseph was beside her. They were to be the little boy's godparents. The altar boy's candle dripped wax.

Emer wore a high-necked white blouse with a lace collar, cameo brooch at the throat and a loose wool jacket over her black skirt. Nothing like a bit of style, thought Lizzie. "Of course, the priest has the fanciest dress of the lot," she told the Nameless One, laughing and eyeing his white lace surplice over the flowing, black, pleated soutane.

Father Dillon made the sign of the cross on the baby's forehead, on his little breast and on his right hand. He touched his ears, nose and mouth with oil. Then a fingertip of salt in his mouth. "Be gone Satan." The baby opened his dark eyes and his tiny tongue licked his lips. Emer held him over the font, Joseph stood with her, his green eyes in deep black shadows. The baby's tiny face, framed by his white shawl, composed again in the sweet innocence of sleep. The priest droned on, then scooped a little water and dripped it on the tiny head. "I baptize thee, Patrick Donagh, in the name of the Father and of the Son and of the Holy Ghost."

Lizzie looked at Una, at her blue serge dress and polished black boots, her pale, sad face and thin, red hands holding her prayer book and felt her old heart expand with sympathy for the motherless girl. Only time, thought Lizzie, cures sorrow. Maybe distance, too. Maybe that's why Peadar is leaving, leaving his two little girls and his baby son. They filed out under gently tossing trees.

Lizzie could not have expressed it in words, but it seemed a page was turned. They stepped out into a new beginning. The Maguires, who had been frozen in shock, halted by grief and loss, were now finding their step again. "Ah, they're coming back to themselves," she told the Nameless One. "And aren't they prosperous, with two traps, no less, Maura's as well as Peadar's."

Emer sat on one side of the trap with the baby and Nan, Peadar on the other side with Una. The pony walked on. Peadar gave Una the reins. Joseph followed in another trap, driving his mother, Lizzie, and Cassie. He halted the trap as they passed a group of men walking.

"Sit up with us Pat," he offered to Pat McGee, who had trouble walking.

"Ah, I'll walk with the lads."

"What about you, Tom?"

"I'll see you up there."

The traps rolled along the road and up the lane. The trees and bushes were in mid-autumn flame, stubble pale gold in the light. From high in the trap they could see the river gleam beyond its border of trees. Blue smoke rose in the soft damp air from the farmhouse chimneys. There was a pungent scent of coming rain and autumn.

"So Peadar's emigrating," said Cassie.

"He thinks it's the best way, but he'll come back, please God, when he has his money made," Maura told her.

"People do come back now," Cassie agreed, "not like the old days."

Lizzie surveyed Joseph's big shoulders and red hair. He had

ruddy cheeks and Angela's green eyes, but his were bold and confident. Angela's had been soft and gentle. "That fellow'll sweep all before him," she told the Nameless One.

In Peadar's yard the men stood about, smoking. The dog rose from the front step and came head bent, tail wagging, craving Peadar's approval. Nan was swinging on the paddock gate, hanging on with one arm. Under the other she held a little wooden pony on wheels, painted black eyes with big dramatic whites. Its nose was a black streak and its flowing mane and tail were real pony hair, threaded through holes in the curved neck and round rump. She held it up for Des to see.

"Tell me this much, what's the name of the horse?" asked Des.

"It's a pony!"

"Ah, right enough, a pony."

Nan jumped off the gate and ran to her father. A misty rain began.

Maura had brought a table and linen from her own house, and when she lined it up with the kitchen table there was space for all to sit. Una helped Lizzie and Emer mash turnips and parsnips and slice soda bread and roast goose. Maura turned out the potatoes on to a dish on the table.

"Call the men, Una," said Emer.

They drifted in, Peadar carrying Nan. Maura took charge, "You sit here Peadar, at the head of the table."

"Where O'Neill sits!" said Peadar.

"Is the head of the table," responded Una quickly.

"Good girl, Una," applauded her Uncle Joseph.

They smiled subversively at the thought of Shane O'Neill's haughty response to the English Queen's invitation to sit with her at the head of her table.

Joseph said the old blessing.

"Great giver of the open hand,
We stand to thank you for our meat
A hundred praises, Christ 'tis meet,
For all we drink, and all we eat."

They crossed themselves and took their seats.

"I wouldn't know you, Joseph, that ever I saw you," said Cassie, "you're so tall."

Maura glowed with pride at this compliment to her only son.

"How tall are you at all?" Cassie asked.

"Six feet," he told her, helping himself to roast goose.

"There's no one six feet exactly," pontificated Pat McGee, "you're either a quarter of an inch over or an eight of an inch less, no one is six feet except Christ, and He was exactly six feet."

Emer rolled her eyes at another of Pat's sermons and parables. Sitting beside Una, Joseph saw her and smiled.

"Well, tell me this much Peadar," said Des, "when did you make up your mind to go to America?"

"Just before the Fair Day. I sold the cows except one, that's enough for Emer to have to milk, and the pigs, except one I killed for the winter."

"Joseph, what about those women starving themselves in Dublin Jail because they won't be let vote?" asked Cassie.

Before Joseph could answer Pat told her, "Women voting would cause fights in families, the priests are agin it."

"The priest should mind his own business," said Lizzie.

"It is his business."

"No, it's not."

"I tell you everything connected with the people is his business, isn't it?"

"He'd be better to just stick to his prayers."

"What do you think, Emer?" asked Joseph.

"Women should have the vote, of course, that's only fair," she answered, "but I wouldn't starve for it."

"I couldn't starve for anything," vowed Lizzie, "nothing worse than hunger."

"Many's the one starves. In Dublin they starve, God help us," said Maura.

"That's just poverty not want of food."

"Home Rule, Maura, that's what we need, then we might get somewhere," Tom told her.

"And we would have too," Pat jumped into the argument, "if it wasn't for Carson, big mouth from the North."

"Carson, you know, is a Dublin man," Joseph corrected.

"Ah, sure he is too," Pat agreed, not wishing to contradict the schoolmaster.

"Sure, it's a Cavan man you need," said Des, encouraging Pat.

"Right enough," Pat agreed, "Joe Biggar, there's the fellow for talk, I mind the time he kept the House of Commons up all night talking and they couldn't get a thing done nor stop him talking."

"That crowd is all talk," Lizzie told him, "there's not one of them cares about the people."

"I think that fellow Connolly does," said Tom.

"The way I see it, them fellows talk rubbish about liberty and where does it get us," Pat warmed to his subject, "the poor farmer has to work till he drops no matter who's driving the train."

"Still and all it makes a difference who's in Westminster," Peadar said.

"What difference, tell me that, will you, what difference?" Pat was looking for an argument.

"Pat," declared Joseph, "Home Rule will come, it's a sure thing, the only question is when. The Parliament Act they passed last year means that the Lords can no longer call the tune, it's the Commons has the power and what we have to do is put the right men in the Commons."

"Aye," Pat persisted, "if they were to be had."

"When are you leaving us, Peadar?" asked Cassie, to turn the talk from politics.

"Tomorrow, I'll go with Joseph to Dublin and then across to Liverpool. I'll get a White Star from there to New York."

"You made up your mind very quick," Des commented.

"I did, but you know, you don't want to be on the Atlantic too late in the season."

"Nor too early either," said Tom.

A sudden quiet fell on the kitchen, nothing but the steady tick of the clock and an ember falling in the fireplace. Pat's hand halted, the dinner fork held aloft, the others sat staring at their plates. It was as if they saw that picture again, hawked at every market since the previous April, the huge ship, one half plunged in the black ocean, the other end reared, all lights blazing.

Cassie at last broke the silence. "Sure, America's just the next parish."

Nan slid off her father's knee. She pulled at Una's dress. "Can I go to the river?"

"No miss, you can do no such thing," Emer said firmly.

"Wait now, Nan," Maura promised, "we'll have seed cake."

Una poured tea, Maura sliced cake and served baked apples and clotted cream. Outside it darkened and began to rain heavily. Emer fed the baby. Peadar and Tom were talking about America. Pat shaved his quid of tobacco, rubbing the grains between his gnarled fingers, sifting them from one hand to another, then packed his pipe carefully.

"Any matchmaking, Lizzie?" asked Des.

"Not a one this year," said Lizzie, "unless I make yours," and she looked at Emer, at the sweet curve of her neck where the chignon clung, the serene expression, the soft darkness of her grey eyes. Des was years younger, but what odds about that, lots of matches like that were made, often the best matches. She imagined them living in her little house, though of course Emer had her own house, and now it looked like she would be taking over Peadar's.

"You're such a great matchmaker, it's a wonder you never made your own," Des was telling her now.

"I had me chances, lots of chances, but somehow none of them was ever right," and as she said it she knew that wasn't true. Years and years ago there had been a young, fair-haired lad with blue eyes who went to Australia. What had she been waiting for, what sign or signal, what someone to tell her everything was alright? So many years ago she couldn't remember. She hadn't even let him speak to Fergus!

"Ah, there's more married than is content," she told Des.

"Never a truer word was said, Lizzie. Sure you're always right about the likes of that."

"And how are you getting on Una?" Lizzie asked, as Una refilled her cup.

"I'm alright. I'm back at school. But when Daddy leaves and

Uncle Joseph goes back the house will be so empty. I dread an empty house."

"People will come to visit, Una, you never know who might turn up to keep you company."

"Uncle Joseph brought me some books when he came this time. Reading is company for me."

"Sure that's grand. I never learned myself. But sure I haven't much need of it."

Emer settled the infant in his cradle at the hearth. Maura filled small glasses with whiskey.

Peadar rose,"I give you Donagh, long life to him." And they stood to salute the baby.

"And good health to him," said Tom.

Joseph raised his glass, "Donny, lad, long life," he paused a minute, "merriment in season, peace always. Your thoughts your own," he paused again,"and always a friend awake for you in the night."

They drank to little Donny, and he slept on, firelight a halo round his little black head. Una lit two oil lamps and placed them on either side of the mantelpiece. Maura cleared the table, and milked the cow; Una shut the hens up for the night. The men began to play cards and the women moved to the fireside. All settled in for a night's play and talk. Pete the fiddler arrived and some of Peadar's neighbours. They stood behind the card players, commenting on the ebb and flow of luck as they waited their turn with the cards.

Nan fell asleep in her grandmother's arms.

The good food and the whiskey spread warmth through Lizzie and, as was expected, she began a story. Des, who had temporarily yielded his place at the card table, encouraged her. "Tell the one about the card player, Lizzie."

"Do Lizzie!" Maura coaxed.

"One time," Lizzie began, "there was a young fellow from Granard drinking in a tavern. He was a wild drinker, so he was, and what was better, he was the best card player in the country, none to match him, he was that good at the cards." Lizzie wiped the flat of her hand up over her forehead and through her heavy hair, as if she was thinking deeply. The benign light of the oil lamp softened the harsh lines of her face; the firelight played over the listeners waiting, as in a trance, for the tale to unfold. The exclamations of the card players came to them as from a distance and the friendly scent of peat smoke and tobacco and whiskey wafted over them. Lizzie scanned the faces to see the effect of her telling on her audience. Though they had heard the story, in several variations, many times before, they were attentive. "There was lots wouldn't play with him too," she went on, "for fear he'd best them, and then there was them that wanted to play with him, that were mad for a game with him."

Lizzie took her clay pipe and her little tin of tobacco out of her skirt pocket. She filled the pipe, examined her handiwork closely for a minute, then continued. "Anyway, that night a tall well-dressed gentleman sat beside him and stood him a drink. 'We're short a hand at cards,' he says, 'will you join in?'

"'Why wouldn't I?' said the Granard man, 'sure I never refuse, and there's no one to beat me at cards.'"

"I wish I could say that for myself," Des interrupted.

"Let Lizzie tell it," said Maura.

"So they went by the back roads," Lizzie resumed, "and after a bit they came to a sheebeen, and there was a crowd playing cards."

Lizzie paused, grasped an ember on the end of the tongs and held it over the bowl of her pipe. She sucked hard on the pipe, the tobacco in its mouth glowed and lit her sharp nose and fierce dark eyes. Satisfied she replaced the tongs and went on. "So the Granard man joined the play. The gentleman did too, he sat beside him. They were winning all round them, the two of them. That fellow from Granard was raking in the money." She took another draw of her pipe, "as sure as I'm here it wasn't natural the way he won money. Not natural at all!" Lizzie looked around to see the effect of this statement, and then continued. "There's them that has the knack of money."

"I wouldn't mind having that!" Des told her.

"You're better off without it, there's them that has money and no luck."

"And aren't you right, Lizzie," Des agreed.

"Anyhow," she resumed the story, "just at the stroke of twelve, midnight, didn't he happen to drop a card on the floor. He stooped down to pick it up. And what do you think he saw?"

"You tell it Lizzie."

"A cloven foot! A goat's hoof. The devil's feet on the gentleman. Imagine that. A devil's foot he had. The worst thing you could see." Lizzie glanced around again, and paused dramatically, studying the faces, then said, "the Granard fellow, the fret came over him, terrified he was. He scattered the cards and ran for his life." Lizzie took a satisfied draw of her pipe. "I heard tell he never drank again."

"The way I heard the story first," said Des, "it was a young girl that met the beautiful man at a dance."

"Yes," said Maura, "and as she walked off with him in the moonlight she looked down and saw that he had cloven feet."

"That's just another of the old yarns they tell to frighten girls, I'd pay no heed to that," said Emer decisively, picking up the baby, who had begun to whimper.

Una added turf to the fire, and the bright sparks flew up the chimney. Maura put Nan on a blanket on the floor near the hearth, then refilled the whiskey glasses. Nan curled up asleep and sucked her thumb.

"That child would sleep anywhere," Des remarked.

"Don't we know that," Maura agreed.

Emer was telling Lizzie she needed winter woollens knitted for the children. "Una is the worst off, she has outgrown everything."

"I'll give you a good price," Lizzie assured her.

"I'd like to knit my own stockings," said Una, "but I haven't learnt yet."

"You will," said Lizzie, "sure I'll teach you."

"I'll get wool when I go to Obanbeg tomorrow and Una'll bring it down to you."

Pipe smoke hung in the air, the turf fire blazed. Maura put Nan to bed. The card players swung between winning and losing. Outside the rain eased a little.

Near midnight Des stood to leave. "It's well for farmers with nothing to do now with the crops in. I got to go to a job in Ballynamon tomorrow."

"I'll walk home with you Des," said Lizzie rising and taking her shawl from the back of her chair.

They shook hands with Peadar.

"Godspeed you and bring you back," Lizzie told him.

"Goodbye, Lizzie."

"Godspeed, Peadar."

"Thanks, Des."

As they passed out of the circle of light thrown through Peadar's windows and into the lane they heard the first notes of the fiddle start up. Peadar's American wake would last till morning. A gloomy, wet night shrouded the little hills and they made their way between the hedges. Their eyes adjusted to the darkness and they could distinguish familiar outhouses and trees. Lizzie pulled her shawl up over her head. Des took her arm. Lizzie was steady enough on her feet, despite her age, but she liked that he was considerate of her.

"I'm glad we're together Des, I don't like to be on my own if the lights are on the bog way over yonder."

"Ah, no fear of that tonight, you never see them if it's a wet night," he reassured her.

She wanted to be at home by her own fire. The bargain she had made with Tom was a great one, she always had plenty of turf and a blazing fire. They could distinguish the outlines of Emer's house, crouched among the sycamores.

"I wonder what she'll do with the house and land now, Lizzie?"

"She told me she'll keep the house up, set the odd fire in it in the winter. Sure Peadar intends to come back."

"What about the land? It's a nice few acres."

"Oh, that'll be let, the bit of rent will pay the rates."

"It'll do more than that."

A plot began to form in Lizzie's mind. "I hardly knew Emer at all till Angela died, and she started to give me a few days work helping with the wash. She's a wonderful girl, Des."

"Ah, sure she is of course, Lizzie, but she got a right job now, three children to manage."

"But she's well able to manage them Des."

"Ah, sure she is of course, she is, good luck to her."

Something dismissive in Des' tone, as if he was not interested in Emer, warned Lizzie, and she put the thought of a match between them aside. She'd come back to it. They went past Tom Plunkett's place and then Pat McGee's little hovel of a cottage, and on down the hill into the village. Streams of light from J.J. Mahon's window stained the wet, cobblestone street. The rest was in darkness.

"Mahon is up late, Des."

"He does his account books on Sunday night, Lizzie."

"Well, I'll have no account with him, that fellow made his money on the poor, overcharging. Bad luck to him!"

Des made no response, and they parted at Lizzie's door.

"Des, bring that paper we talked about over on Saturday. I might as well put my mark on it."

"Ah good Lizzie, you won't be sorry."

"I know I won't."

"So, next Saturday, Lizzie."

"Without fail, Des."

"Goodnight, so."

"Safe home, Des."

The goats were waiting, standing at the side of the house, heavy with milk. She'd have to get a lantern and milk them. She was tired and her knees and hips began to ache a little.

Goats milked, Lizzie built up her fire and sat with a mug of tea, looking at the flames and thinking about the day. "That Joseph is a bit of a lad," she told the Nameless One, "and Peadar, he has a long journey ahead of him." She saw him on the train being carried away from Slanabaille and into the city, which she could only imagine as a huge collection of buildings, a fantastic, even dangerous, place. She'd seen a newspaper photograph of a city once. High dark buildings, wires like clotheslines in the sky. Dark figures in the streets. And carriages without horses. She thought of Peadar on a ship surrounded by towering waves. Lizzie shivered despite the big fire. "Keep him safe," she told the Nameless One.

Tomorrow she had a job washing clothes for the priest's housekeeper. "Ah," she told the Nameless One, "sure I'll have a smoke to finish the day," and she packed the tobacco from her little, round tin into the bowl of the pipe and lighted it with a tiny ember from the fire on the end of the tongs.

"Peadar, good luck to him."

The cat jumped up on her lap, she stroked his head. The fire-light glinted on the two fancy tea caddies on the dresser where Lizzie kept her money. She loved to look at the beautiful pale women in blue dresses painted on them. She made money scrubbing and washing, or knitting. She no longer made lace, but she had saved the last lace shawl she had made, packed away in the old wooden trunk. Des would take her to Obanbeg when they made the bargain and she would put the money in the bank. With Tom's money and the bit she put in before, she'd be well off. She would never see the inside of the workhouse.

"I'll sleep on the settle bed," she told the Nameless One.

Lizzie's was a big kitchen. In the alcove facing the fire was an old settle bed where she had slept all her young life. It was heaped with quilts May had made, and a spread Lizzie knitted. When Fergus died and May grew old, Lizzie yielded the settle bed to May so she could sleep nearer the fire. Then she'd taken the bedroom door off so she could hear the slightest sound from the old woman. After May died, Lizzie never replaced the door. From her bedroom she could watch the fire shadows leaping on the kitchen wall. She settled herself under the quilts. Tonight, she wanted to lie looking into the flames and feel Fergus and May near, for Lizzie knew they hovered still around their house. They would like Des, he was a great fellow, a grand lad. Sleep crept round her and she felt the Nameless One near. Sure that was grand.

On Saturday, after Des left, Lizzie climbed on a stool and took down the two sheets of paper he had hid behind the big blue platter on the top shelf of the dresser.

"Leave me on me own for a bit," she had told him, "I want to think, to study meself, before I make me mark."

"All right so, Lizzie," he had agreed, "I'll be back after a while."

"Come this evening Des, and we'll have our tea together."

And so he left, maybe for home, half an hour's walk up the lane to the right beyond Darling's, or maybe next door to Mahon's for any news being talked about.

Lizzie squinted at the heavy black writing. Even lines on the creamy paper. Des had left a pen and a little bottle of blue ink. She filled the kettle and hung it over the fire. She'd have a cup of tea and think about it. Sensing someone at the half door she looked up. Una was there.

"Come in, come in, and sit down," Lizzie said, forgetting about the paper.

Una carried a basket with twenty skeins of wool and a slab of butter wrapped in cabbage leaves. She put the basket on the floor and sat down at the table.

"You're just in time," Lizzie told her, "I was just thinking of having a cup of tea, and I have seed cake, too, that I made yesterday."

She poked the fire under the hanging kettle hard and then put two mugs on the table. Una handed her the butter.

"Aunt Emer churned yesterday and we have lots to spare."

"Ah sure, Emer's butter's always sweet," said Lizzie, unwrapping the muslin from the seed cake and beginning to slice it.

Una was always hungry, for words and for books. Her eye involuntarily followed the lines on the top sheet of paper. Some sort of legal document. What was it doing there? Lizzie couldn't read or write.

The kettle began to boil, steam pouring from the spout. Lizzie spooned tea into the old metal teapot then poured the boiling water over it. Una read the first few lines again and flushed guiltily, realizing Lizzie was watching her.

"I didn't mean to read it, Lizzie."

"Sure, why wouldn't you read it, seeing as you can read, it's a great thing to have a bit of schooling. It's me will, I'm making it at last, at long last, I'm leaving me cottage and land, after my day, to Des Donoghue. Sure no one deserves it more than Des. There'd days when if he didn't drop in I'd never see a soul."

Lizzie set the sugar bowl on the table and poured milk into

the two mugs. "I like to put the milk in first," she said. And then she caught the child's stare. "Is anything wrong, Una?"

"Lizzie," said Una, "I think there's a mistake in the paper."

Lizzie snatched it up, "What mistake, what's written there? What's there Una? Read it for me." Her vehemence surprised Una a little.

"The name written there isn't Des's."

"Whose name's there child?"

"John Joseph Mahon," Una told her, frightened now by Lizzie's stern face.

"What name?" Lizzie's face was white like a bedsheet.

"John Joseph Mahon, Lizzie, that's the name, that's the name on the paper."

"My God!" The words came in one expiration and she stood rooted on the spot, shocked into immobility.

"What's wrong, Lizzie?" Una stood up and stepped away from the table

"The goddamn lying sleeveen," she screamed and dropped the pot of scalding tea. Una started in fright.

"What did Mahon give him that he'd steal my land for him? The bastard. The bastard. The thieving lying bastard!" Lizzie collapsed on the chair, chest heaving, knees shaking up and down, her heavy skirts trembling, the spilled tea steaming at her feet. She leaned forward, elbows on her quaking knees to steady them, head in hands. Silent tears of rage began to overflow her black eyes and course down her thin face.

Una cowered against the dresser. After a few minutes she said pleadingly, "Please don't cry, Lizzie. Please! Please don't cry."

Lizzie noticed Una's terrified face. She dabbed at her eyes with the corner of her apron, I'm grand now, I'm grand, she told herself.

"Una astore, I'm all right. My good teapot."

The teapot had a big dent. Leaves and tea puddled on the stone floor. Una picked it up and took a rag and basin from the table under the window and cleaned up the floor. Then seeing Lizzie more composed she said, "I must go Lizzie, Aunt Emer will be worrying."

"Sure, sure child," Lizzie pulled herself together. "Let me see that wool." She separated the skeins on the table into three bundles, one large and two small one. "So it's a gansey for you and stockings for yourself and Nan. Tell Emer that'll be five shillings."

"Lizzie make mine big, Aunt Emer makes me take Parrish's Food every day so that I'll get fat."

"Sure you're growing, we'd need to put a stone on your head to stop you" Lizzie forced herself to be hearty to reassure the girl.

When Una left Lizzie mechanically filled the kettle, then sat down again, overcome by shame and anger. What a fool she'd been, let herself be deceived and used. All these past months, as she and Des had talked over their bargain, he had been acting as an agent for the grasping tavern keeper next door. Everyone knew she'd never sell to Mahon, or his ignorant son. She'd refused him years ago, and they laughed and jeered at her. She was selling to Des for a pittance. She had wanted him to have her land. She knew he was often at Mahon's but that was where the men gathered. What a fool. She saw now that she had loved him like a son. At the thought of his betrayal sobs shook her thin frame. She was old, weak, helpless. She despised her enjoyment of his company, a silly girl who let him coax her with whiskey, sweet talk and flattery, pretending she was a great one!

Lizzie dried her tears, stood and then sat again, looking at the fire, remembering her hard life, her struggle to be independent. She had betrayed Fergus and May, forgot all they had taught her, every caution, every warning about the treachery of the world. How could she have done that? Let herself be taken in by that sly bastard!

The fire blazed in a sudden flash. Lizzie stared into the flames. Sadness and pain, fears long suppressed, lost hopes long forgotten, tumbled over one another. Lizzie closed her aching eyes. Trembling wraiths appeared, thin spectres of women and children walking on stick legs, searching for something to eat, walking in the rain to famine graves. Blackened faces of hanged men returned, the sweet, sick stench of rotting potatoes filled her nostrils. Men on horseback cursing. A voice raised in a long keen, furniture and bedding in the roadway, a thatched roof blazing, timbers crack like gunfire, flames roar and belch against a lowering sky. A woman screams, higher and higher over the awful thump, thump, thump, of crowbars smashing cottage walls.

Lizzie lay in a trench. A bundle of rags propped against a mattress of ferns and branches moaned, blackened legs jutted out from tattered skirts. The legs jerked, the mass shuddered and then was still. A mane of long dark hair hung from the shrunken head, in the swollen purple face a mad smile. Bloody gums held the terrible black-toothed grin of the dead. A voice was calling, calling her, "Come away, Elizabeth. Come back here, don't touch her. Don't touch your mother, you'll catch the fever."

Lizzie sobbed in terror. Sour bile rose in her throat, choking her. Shivering, she slid off the chair on to the floor. That voice as familiar as her very own, her father's voice, so dear, so far away. Lizzie lay on the floor and wept. Hot salt tears trickled down her cheeks and neck to soak the collar of her blouse. She stuffed her fingers in her ears, still she heard the awful silence of the deserted fields.

She lay before the dying fire and did not hear Emer and Cassie enter, nor feel their presence till they lifted her in their arms.

Emer took Lizzie home. In the days that followed Lizzie was sometimes tearful, weeping tears unshed for years. Sometimes she raged against Des. When Emer gently suggested that Des was young and foolish, and probably meant her no harm, she raged against Mahon. "Lizzie, that was something concocted in Mahon's pub, they forget you may outlive the lot of them," Emer comforted her.

Lizzie helped Emer in the kitchen and the dairy. They grew close to each other, the old woman and the younger one, closer than Lizzie had been to another person since May died. It was late autumn and they walked through the fields while Una was at school. Emer carried Donny. Lizzie helped Nan pick flowers. Michealmas daisies and thistles with purple crowns, and the goldenrod. They went to Maura's orchard one evening and picked apples. The baby lay in his basket on the ground beneath the trees. Una and Emer stood on ladders filling cloth bags, with Boland's Flour Mills in red letters printed on them, and handed them to Lizzie to be packed in the barrel. Some of the apple trees were so old they yielded little fruit. Maura said when Joseph came again for the weekend she'd have him cut down those trees. "Apple wood makes a great fire when it dries; in the spring, please God, I'll have another half dozen put in," she promised. They jogged home in the cart through the dusk, Una holding the baby, Nan on the floor of the cart eating an apple, the old iron clad wheels of the cart rumbling through the ruts in the road.

"I'm not going to use that cart again," Emer vowed, unharnessing the pony, "if I can't take the trap I'll stay at home."

There was little outside work to do, beyond feeding the fowl and pig and gathering the eggs, so they had time to talk. Peadar's children distracted Lizzie. She spoiled Nan and fed little Donny goat's milk.

"It's the best for him. The strongest are reared on it." Nan spat the goat's milk out. "You don't know what's good for you! If you'd drink goat's milk you wouldn't be needing that Parrish's food Emer buys for you!"

In the afternoons, Lizzie rocked Donny and sang in her hoarse old creaky voice

"O had you seen the Coolun, the Coolun, the Coolun,
O had you seen the Coolun,
Walking down cuckoo street.
And the dew of the meadow shining, shining,
And the dew of the meadow shining
on her milk white twinkling feet."

Nan paraded around the kitchen, her curls rising and falling with every step, "shining, shining, shining," she chanted.

"Lizzie," said Emer, "you have such long hair, you could be a Coolun."

"Ah, I had lovely hair in my day."

Nan banged a spoon on a poringer, "shining, shining, shining."

"Nan! Lizzie is trying to get the baby to take a nap. Come and sit on my knee."

Una wanted to learn to knit. Lizzie showed her how to cast the yarn in stitches on the needles. "Curl both hands over the needles in the same way Una, that's how May taught me to do it."

"Don't you miss May?"

"It's a strange thing, when she died all I could feel was that she was gone, gone, nothing to be done. That was for about a year. Gone! That's what was in my brain all day long, I'd say for a year or more."

"And then did it go away?"

"Well, she came back. That feeling of her gone went away, you know, and it seemed that she was around me all the time, always there and Fergus, too."

"How do you mean, Lizzie?"

"Well, I live in their place and when I go about my work I remember that we used to be together. I mind things they used to say."

"Is that not very sad, Lizzie?"

"No. It's nice. Its grand! It's my bit of company. Now, try not to look at your hands or the needles Una. Feel the needles, don't look. That's it, that's the way!"

Each day was shorter than the one before. Lizzie began to tire of walking home twice a day to tend her hens and goats. She missed her cat. She'd been away a fortnight and ought to go home. As content as she was with Angela's children, the river and her own place called her. One day, as she sat with Emer plucking chickens, Lizzie said, "The spirit that always used to be round me is gone, He's left me."

"What spirit Lizzie?"

"I put no name on Him, he was always there."

"Like God?"

"Maybe, or maybe the fellow that owns the sun, but He's gone."

"He's not gone, God doesn't change like that. It's because your whole mind is taken up with Des and J.J. Mahon, Lizzie, there's no room for anything else. Forget about them. Des has no sense, he's only a boy. It was Mahon's doing. You know that."

"Bad luck to him," Lizzie cursed, "there'll not be one of his seed or breed left in the place, trying to get my bit of land for half nothing. And lying about it! I should have the law on them. They'll never have a day's luck! Never a day's peace or ease, bad cess to them. Not one of their seed breed or generation will be there. Not one Mahon will be left there. Not a single one!"

"Don't talk like that. What need you care, Lizzie? You still have your place."

"That's right, I needn't darken his door if I don't want to."

One day she brought the tin box from under her bed back with her. When the children were in bed she and Emer spread the papers from it on the kitchen table. Lizzie put aside the papers she had marked for Tom, all the letters with stamps of the old queen's head and the newer one with the king's head she had got from the bank, and handed the remaining two pages to Emer. "Read these for me like a good girl."

Emer took up a heavy yellow page and read, "*For Elizabeth McCann, my daughter because of the new law all is sold up to Darling and our house is tumbled. Attracta your mother is dead of the fever I leave you in the care of Fergus and May Scanlon and the mercy of God I will send for you from America when I am settled. This statement was given by Liam McCann and was taken down by Turlogh Murphy. 11th Day of August 1849.*"

"Lizzie, that is sixty-three years ago. How old were you then?"

"I don't know, I must have been Nan's age or a bit more. I mind my mother, I forgot her, but lately I remember her."

"Do you remember your father, Lizzie?" said Emer gently.

"Sometimes, I mind his voice."

"Did May not tell you about them?"

"I thought May was my mother, and you know Emer, the starvation was never never mentioned, people were ashamed of it."

"I do know that. It's never talked about, even yet."

"Emer, what law was that he wrote about in the letter?"

"The Encumbered Estates Act, Lizzie. The landlords had such debt that their estates were sold to pay it."

Emer was reading the other paper.

"Lizzie, this seems to be from someone named Anthony to Fergus. He is writing from America at Christmas 1849 to say that your father was very sick when they reached New York and that he went on to Boston and your father never followed him and he lost touch with your father."

"Anthony was my father's cousin. His son John sometimes sends me a letter."

"Yes, I've read his letters for you. Your father must have had land on that estate before it was sold to Darling's grandfather."

"I think maybe I always knew that."

"Your mother's name was Attracta."

"I know Emer, it's not a name you hear round about Slanabaille."

"Would you like to know where she came from? We could ask the priest to look in the register."

"I don't think I'll bother."

"Saint Attracta was the saint of the long hair Lizzie," Emer was gently teasing her, "they say she harnessed deer with her hair."

"A Coolun with long hair, that's a fine story, Emer."

"It is Lizzie."

"I think I'll move back home Emer. I'm ready now."

"Are you sure, Lizzie?"

"I am Emer. Thank you," Lizzie said simply.

The next evening, when Una came from school, Emer left her in charge of the two little ones and drove Lizzie home in the trap. She brought her tin box with her. They swept out the kitchen and lighted the fire. When Emer left, Lizzie imagined Fergus and May near her. Shadowy images of her mother were in her mind, a young woman with curly black hair.

Lizzie milked her goats and fed the hens and shut them up for the night, then sat on a stump beside the forge and looked down over her acre to the water. The cat jumped on her lap. She loosed her braid of long grey hair and combed it out with her fingers. The river was swollen now by the autumn rains, darkness was rising from the earth. Her currant and thorn bushes were in shadow but the western sky still held its light, touched the surface of the brimming water with gold. The cold air was on her hands and face, the purple and brown of the grasses at her feet filled her eyes. The first star came out in the twilight sky. A lone swan sailed down the river serene and confident. Lizzie wondered again where his mate was, in Spring there had been a pair. She liked that swan, knew him well, remembered his strong snake head and savage beak. The rumble of a homeward cart on the cobblestones, the bolting of hen-house doors, familiar sounds of the village settling down for the night were in her ears. She began to feel the Nameless One near. "Ah, I knew you'd come back. Sure, I knew you'd find me," she said. "Stay with me now, stay."

Two Months in Spring

"I WOULDN'T HAVE believed it if Lizzie hadn't told me herself," said Cassie Plunkett.

"I thought Des would never darken her door again after the sneaky thing over her land. But given he was for enlisting, I expect they decided to do the decent thing and made up."

At fifty, Cassie was stout and vigorous, a sensible woman. She sat over the remains of evening tea in Emer Maguire's kitchen, talking to Emer and Joseph.

"I think Des enlisted," Emer said, "because the world and his wife knew about the land grab. He was ashamed about it."

"And then you know," Cassie reasoned, "when his mother, God rest her soul, went, there wasn't the same reason to stay."

It was a Friday evening in March. Joseph had ridden over from the local railway station in Obanbeg, having traveled from Dublin with a ladies bicycle in the baggage compartment. A ladies bicycle for Emer, and it had arrived with a great commotion. Fourteen-year-old Una wheeled it around the yard with Nan, now seven, perched on the saddle, holding her shoulder.

"Are the recruiting fellows having much success here?" Joseph wanted to know.

"Colonel Darling joined first, nearly two years ago, you know that," said Emer.

"He had no choice but to join his regiment, the paper said that it was Princess Victoria's Royal Irish Fusiliers," Cassie added.

"Royal Irish, goddamn Redmonite nonsense!"

"Joseph! Mind what you say! Donny is listening," Emer warned. But Donny was lining up his wooden soldiers in front of the hearth.

"What about the lads round here, are many of them joining up?"

"More than you'd expect," Cassie told him, "Soldiers' Dependants Allowances, that's the real reason. No one believes that rubbish about saving Belgium and Serbia. With money so hard to come by, who could blame them. After the conscription law passed in January, people thought it was only a matter of time till they had to join up anyway."

"Conscription will never apply to Ireland," Joseph said. "The people won't stand for it."

"Since when, Joseph, did the Irish have a choice?"

"They have a choice now, Cassie. You know what they say, England's trouble is always Ireland's opportunity."

"But they say if we support England now we'll have Home Rule when peace comes."

"I believed that myself once, Cassie, but I believe it no longer."

The two women exchanged surprised glances. Joseph was seldom so serious. They had seen the recruiting posters in Obanbeg, *Irishmen Enlist Today. For Small Nations, And For Ireland*. But still, Emer thought, it's for the money they enlist.

"It must be three years at least since the row about Lizzie's land," Cassie said.

"Four years October, just after Peadar went to America," Emer said. "Anyway, it wasn't all Des' fault, J.J. Mahon put him up to it, he wanted the land for himself. Because Lizzie can't read he thought he'd fool her."

"Ha, see what a mistake we made letting women learn to read," Joseph's remark was directed at Emer. She looked sternly back at his mocking green eyes. I'll pay that no mind, she thought, he's just looking for notice.

His eyes were so like his dead sister's, except his were always full of merriment, while Angela's had carried a gentle, compliant expression, as if she had already acquiesced to her own demise. Emer had no notion of encouraging him this evening. She had expected him for Saint Patrick's Day, Thursday next. He would have a holiday from teaching that day, and Nan was making her First Communion. Instead he had arrived today, a full week ahead of time at six o'clock, just as they sat down to tea. Cassie had watched him pass on the bicycle, and had come up to see it.

And now he'd warned he might not be able to come to Nan's First Communion. Joseph, who'd been like a father to his dead sister's children, not coming to Nan's First Communion! And couldn't promise to come for Easter either, five weeks away. Emer could hardly believe he might not be home for Easter. He'd come to Slanabaille most weekends since she'd undertaken the upbringing of her two nieces and her little nephew. Why not now? She wondered if he had a sweetheart in Dublin, then felt angry and resentful. Waves of irritation and frustration swept over her. He must have a girl in Dublin. It could be nothing else. Could he not be at Nan's First Communion, at least?

Joseph stood and hoisted little Donny in his arms."Come on, Donny lad, let's see how your sisters are getting along with your aunt's bicycle."

When he left, Cassie said "You're not very happy with Joseph!"

"I'm furious. He may not be here for Nan's First Communion. And the children have so little family left in Ireland. Just him and me, now that his mother is gone. Has he any idea what it's like to be a woman alone rearing up children?"

"Well Emer, you took on a great deal when Peadar went to America. Remember we told you that at the time. And you answered, what's to be done that you couldn't do?" Cassie's round plain face shone with approval. "Now look at how well off you are, we all are. Lashings of money, prices for eggs and butter and beef and pork never better, we're feeding England. They're rioting for food in Birmingham."

"There's lots of hunger in Dublin too, Cassie, always was, and no one caring about it."

"That's not want of food, that's poverty. No money to buy it."

"I know. At least here we always have what we can grow ourselves."

"I never thought Joseph was interested in politics, Emer."

"Nor I. But this war has everyone discontented. Some think it will bring us Home Rule and others say you can't trust England."

"Tom thinks we'll get Home Rule all right, but that it won't make any difference. He says what counts is what price we get for our cattle and pigs."

"He's right there, Cassie," said Emer. She reached for *The Independent* Joseph had brought and spread it on the table between them. "Look here Cassie, the Brown Thomas advertisement, the women's skirts are narrow now, and well above the ankle, as much as four inches."

Cassie examined the pictures of women. Skirts, shorter than they had ever been, revealing trim ankles and shoes with narrow straps over arched insteps.

"I'm going to get busy and alter all my summer skirts," Emer told her. "I'm so tired of bulky winter clothes."

"You're such a great seamstress," said Cassie, "the two girls always look so neat, everyone says they are a credit to you, and yourself, clothes always look so well on you."

It was true. Emer would be thirty-eight in October, but youth lingered defiantly in her slim, tall figure and sure, vigorous walk. Her night black hair, now rolled up on her head in the fashion of the day, showed a few streaks of white and there were sunbursts of fine lines around her large grey eyes. But her face, with its habitual grave expression, was beautiful. The contrast with her rough rural surroundings heightened the impression of loveliness.

Cassie was Emer's best friend. She and Tom had no children of their own. They had a foster son, Stephen, an orphan they adopted from the poorhouse. He was twenty now, and Cassie, who had with all her heart wanted children of her own, lavished affection on the three children Emer was raising. Her encouragement matched Emer's desire to be told she was doing the right thing, she was managing the children well. That desire was the cause of her disappointment with Joseph's news. His arrival from Dublin on Fridays seemed to confirm all she and the children had done the preceding week, to approve everything, provide assurance that all was well. I'm like a child, thought Emer, I want praise all the time. But it wasn't that. She loved the children and needed to be told their happy, healthy appearance was not only in her own fond eye, others saw it too.

Squeals of excitement could be heard from outside. Joseph was riding the bicycle with Nan in his arms. The dog rose from the hearth and stood at the half door, waiting to be let out. Bran was getting old and stiff.

"I think Bran misses Peadar," Emer remarked, as she went to the door to open it for him.

"A dog will miss a person," said Cassie as she prepared to leave. "So, I can take *The Independent?*"

"You can and welcome."

"Safe home, Cassie," Joseph called after her as she went down the lane.

"It's almost dark, time to come inside," Emer ordered from the half door. "Una you shut up the hens. Nan, the turf creel is almost empty!" That Joseph would stay out all night.

Una cleared the table and washed the dishes. Emer went out to milk the cow. Joseph told Nan and Donny a story about the pooka.

"Most of the time the pooka looks like a goat, but what do you think this one looked like Nan?"

"A fox."

"No."

"A dog."

"No, a dog is never a trickster."

"You tell me."

"Alright, he was a weasel. A little fat whistling weasel! Anyway, one time there was a schoolmaster who annoyed this pooka."

"How did he annoy him, Uncle Joseph?" Nan asked.

"Well, he didn't believe in him, and no one likes to not be believed in. Anyhow, before the master had time to bless himself, the pooka was in his head and up to his mischief."

"What did he do, Uncle Joseph?"

"He hid in the turf creel in the school, every time the master opened his mouth to teach, the pooka made him sing a song,

Oh, Mrs. McGrath the sergeant said
Would you like to make a soldier
Out of your son Ted?

"You know that old song Nan! And the master, seeing he was losing the run of himself, clapped his hand over his mouth like this, Donny," and Joseph put his palm over Donny's mouth, "but that pooka wasn't in the ha'penny place when it comes to brains, so what do you think he did next, he made the master's legs dance like this, Nan." He pulled her up to dance around the kitchen, demonstrating the antics of the demented schoolmaster. His tall, lanky figure and gesticulating arms and legs filled the kitchen. Straight red hair fell forward over his freckled face. Donny laughed, his irrepressible toddler's laugh, rocking back and forth on the floor, face turned up to Joseph in adoration. Una stopped working at her lessons at the kitchen table to watch. Friday and Saturday nights were great fun. The children never wanted Joseph to go back to Dublin on Sundays.

It'll take a very long time to get the children to bed tonight, Emer thought, coming in from milking. She unhooked the falling table from the wall. Might as well get her ironing started. She took the box iron from the mantelpiece above the fire and settled the block that fitted inside it to redden in the hot embers of the fire glowing in the mouth of the big hearth. Because there was no school next day, Emer allowed the children a treat, mugs of hot Fry's cocoa with lots of sugar. Only Una and herself were allowed to swing the crane that hung in the fireplace forward and remove the big black kettle. In September, Una would go to the convent of the Sisters of the Cross and Resurrection in Obanbeg and Emer would miss her. Sending Una to the convent school was causing lots of talk in the Slanabaille.

"You pay no heed to that talk," Emer had told Una when she reported what Margaret Smith had said: "Wouldn't the National School be enough for you, what do you want with the convent? And them nuns have a big strap."

Joseph said "You'll love the conven school Una, there'll be lots of girls to talk to and your Aunt Emer will be there every visiting day bringing you fancy cakes."

The children dawled over the cocoa. Nan and Donny wanted another story but Emer said no it was getting too late.

With the children finally settled and the ironing finished, Emer sat down at the fire opposite Joseph, and as she had done many Friday nights for more than three years, she told him about the children. The dog stood resting his head on Joseph's knee.

Little Donny was always the first in their thoughts. Joseph was saying that they should be using his proper name, Donagh, so that when he went to school next year it would be the name he was called.

"Well, you're the worst offender yourself," Emer told him, "you were the one who started calling him Donny, don't you remember that? And furthermore, I don't think he will be ready for school next year, he'll hardly be five, he's just a baby yet. Anyway, we teach him at home."

"He needs to go to school, he's with women all the time, you and Una mollycoddle him," Joseph fussed, "if we don't look out he'll be a proper sissy."

Donny was the favourite with both of them, their godchild, and his happy disposition and sweet baby ways charmed everyone.

"He'll be top of the class when he does go to school," Emer boasted, "he talks in full sentences and he's not four yet."

"Ah, he's blessed among you women!" Joseph was teasing again, but he was giving in. Donny would be home with Emer till he was six.

Donny would miss Una in September, and so would Nan, but above all Una must get an education. Maybe she would be a teacher or a nurse. It was not to be thought of that she would stay in Slanabaille, such an out-of-the-way place, the back of beyond, where there was nothing for young girls but to marry some small farmer, if one was to be had, and work their fingers to the bone, or emigrate. Emer had decided she wanted better than that for her girls.

"The girls expect you for Nan's First Communion, Joseph, you know how disappointed they'll be."

"I can't promise Emer. For the next couple of months, till June anyway, things are uncertain for me. I can't promise, but I'll be here when I can."

"A couple of months? The children will be lost without you. Is it your work Joseph, is it something at the school?"

"No, it's not my work."

"Well, what is it then?"

"I can't tell you yet."

"What's so secret you can't talk about it, Joseph?"

"I don't want you to ask me about it. You know I would be here if I could. I'll come when I can, any time I have a chance, and I will be here in the summer holidays."

Emer could hardly bear it.

"Not till summer holidays," she exclaimed, "all that time. What's so important that's keeping you in Dublin?" She savoured her resentment to the dregs.

"I'm just very busy for the next while, I can't help it."

"What are you so busy with you can't come to Nan's Communion?"

"I can't tell you just now."

"Why not?"

"Well, it's a private matter."

Emer flushed with embarrassment. "I don't mean to pry."

"It's all right, Emer. I promise I'll be here the whole summer, and I might come. It's not definite that I won't be here."

"Well, I can't believe you'll miss that day."

"Emer, I just don't want to talk about it. Some day we will talk about it. Not now."

He has a sweetheart in the city, Emer concluded. Just like a man. He'd found a girl and nothing else mattered.

Then as she often did, she took down the bank-book and the notebook where she wrote her household accounts and they discussed what the children needed and what money their father was sending from New York.

"Peadar still writes every other week, he never forgets," she told Joseph, by way of reminding him of his own failures.

Peadar's land was let, and so was the farm her father had left her. "Sure, you're rollin' in land yourself," Joseph would tease her. But this spring she meant to keep back the two big fields nearest the old house and buy six young cattle to fatten for the autumn cattle fair. She had planned this with Joseph at Christmas.

"You'll be a woman with cattle! Nothing like a bit of cattle jobbin'." Joseph joked about everything. She might make thirty pounds, maybe more, if the price of beef kept rising. Enough for Una's school fees and then some. Emer sold eggs, and now the egg man came every week, calling around the farms, so she needn't bring them to Obanbeg herself. She had only one cow now, so there was no milk to spare to sell to the creamery; in fact, in the winter Emer had to get cow's milk from Tom Plunkett and goat's milk from Lizzie Scanlon.

And as if he read her thoughts Joseph said, "How is Lizzie now, Emer? I haven't seen her for a while."

"In good form for over seventy. Tom Plunkett still keeps her in turf. She has her goats and her garden, and she still comes to me and to the schoolmaster's wife for wash day. You know Donny is her favourite."

Then, as if talk of old Lizzie reminded him of something Joseph said, "The children should be learning Irish."

"What? There's no teacher at the school qualified to teach it. What use would that be, to fill their heads with a lot of old forgotten words? Their lives will be hard enough without putting that on them."

Emer spoke vehemently and Joseph said no more. Emer had heard him talking that nonsense before, maintaining that every people should remember the *Sceal Fein*, their own story, in their own language, that people lost something when they lost their own language, in the end that was all they had. At the Christian Brothers school, where Joseph taught, students could learn Irish if they chose. It's the latest fad in Dublin, Emer thought. Joseph and his friend Pat O'Flathery were in the Gaelic League, that's where that idea came from. Emer had no use for that, she had lived in New York. Gaelic League nonsense, all of a piece with sentimental songs sung by half drunk Irishmen on Saturday nights, standing on the sawdust floors of smoke-filled taverns on the Lower East Side. Times were good and getting better, why bring up that old idea now? That wasn't the way to get on in the world. And above all, Emer wanted them to get on.

"Their father wouldn't hold with that," she said now.

"Their father's in America, Ireland is changing, we don't know what he'd want if he were here."

"Joseph, you must be daft, I never heard such foolishness. I don't want to hear any more about it."

Emer was more vehement than usual. She was angry with Joseph and looking for something to disagree with him about. This would be her last word on that subject. Times were good for farmers, and after the war Ireland would have Home Rule. Joseph was living in a dream. Must be the new sweetheart in Dublin. She had turned his head.

Then Emer told him she was thinking about putting an extension on the house, a bedroom for Donny and a parlour and an iron stove for the kitchen. Cooking on the open fire was hard work. Of course, it wouldn't be easy to get men to do the work. Des Donoghue was the best local carpenter, but he'd joined the British army.

"A bicycle and an iron stove! Two great articles altogether! You'd spend money to a marching band Emer," Joseph teased.

She ignored that, he was just as anxious for the children to be comfortable as she was. And he often laughed about how careful she was with money. Una needed school uniforms, Donny, still in skirts, would soon need proper little boy's clothes. Joseph worried about Una, as did Emer. It seemed to them that the loss of her mother had ended her childhood, made her serious beyond her years.

"She still sleeps with a lighted candle. What will she do in the convent school?"

"I spoke to the House Mother about it and there is always a light burning under the statue of the Virgin Mary. They'll give Una a cubicle near the statue. Anyhow, there's always a nun sleeping in the dormitory."

"She should be all right, so."

As they talked Joseph sat watching her, his head back against the big chair, his green eyes half closed. Gradually Emer's resentment subsided. He had been diligent in visiting the children for three and a half years. Almost every Friday he'd arrive, and she'd meet the train. If he couldn't come he'd write.

At eleven o'clock Joseph stood up and stretched. "I'll go so," he said, meaning down the lane to spend the night in the empty house where Emer and her two brothers had grown up. He lit a lantern, took a burning sod from the fire and put it in a galvanized bucket. He'd light a fire in the old hearth and sleep in front of it on the settle bed.

Emer stood at the open door as he went down the lane.

"Beanacth lath, bless you," he called back and she watched the bobbing light of the lantern growing fainter till it disappeared in the darkness. The old house would be damp. He'd need the fire, though the air was soft for March. The dark landscape was silent as the grave. Through the open window of the children's bedroom Emer could hear the reassuring sound of Donny snoring. There was a quarter moon, glittering stars climbed the sky. A wood pigeon fluttered in the hedge at the side of the house. She smelled turf fire, sweet dried earth burning, rising up through the chimney into the night and was suddenly filled with restlessness. She was not in the least tired.

Emer sat looking into the fire and thinking about the evening. It occurred to her that other women in the world were bringing up children on their own. That's how it was for many whose husbands were fighting in France. The difference was she was bringing up her brother's children, not her own. How strange life was.

Six years ago she had been still working as a maid and seamstress in New York. When Emer thought about her days polishing and dusting and her evenings sewing, it seemed a life lived by someone else, a dream. It had an unreal quality about it, life in another century. It was 1894 when she started to work in that big mansion. Just sixteen, another raw, lonely, Irish girl working for a wealthy American family.

The mistress of that big house was born to wealth, the habits of money, of a place in the world, the right to command servants and disregard the servant's wishes, moods, feelings, even humanity. How Emer resented that. Being ordered about, bossed around by the older maids, assigned the hardest tasks, the slops, scrubbing and laundry. Restless, noisy New York, the smell of wet dust and locomotives and garbage. And Eamonn, what of him? Eamonn O'Reilly who had walked with her on spring evenings as the maples came in bloom and their flowers carpeted the pavement like tiny green downed swallows. She'd said goodbye to him in 1910, to come back to Ireland because her father had written to say her mother was dying. When Emer's ship was just two days out of New York, her mother died. She arrived home to kneel at her mother's grave, where the fresh mound of earth was already settling, and weep in Peadar's arms. Her little brother, grown to be a man while she was away, married to Angela and a father of two children. Nan had been an infant then. How much had changed while she had been away.

Three weeks after she arrived home a letter came from Eamonn to say he was going out west. There was money to be made there, lots of money, the mines were opening up and everyone was going. He would write to her when he got settled.

No letter came. Every day she watched for the postman and was disappointed. When Emer looked back on weeks spent watching and waiting for a letter, despair almost overwhelming her, the only emotion she had was fierce pride in her endurance, a confidence in the good sense that sustained her. Over and over she had told herself, feeding her father's hens and pigs, and milking his cows, I will not let this hurt me, I'll get over it, and when I'm over it, I'll go back to America. But her father was so lost and alone. Being a widower was something he had never imagined.

"I always thought I'd be the first to go, Emer," he said, "I never thought I'd be left like this."

The hurt, slightly lopsided look on his face, his appreciation of every meal she cooked, his comfort in her company, touched her deeply. He was bereft without his wife. Her big, dependable, decent father. So proud to wait for her at the gate in the trap, as he had for her mother every Sunday for thirty-eight years, to drive her to mass.

The landscape slowly began to delight her, its very smallness, its little green hedgerows, gentle hills, narrow winding roads and lanes, its familiarity. It seemed created on a more human scale, possessing a greater civility than the clang and rush of New York.

Then her father had a stroke and was dead in a week. It was late August. Emer did a man's work, helping Peadar save the hay and oats her father had planted. By the time the harvest was in, Emer had made up her mind to stay in Ireland. Her older brother, Patrick, had long before written that he would stay in America. She'd run the farm herself.

When she remembered Angela's death, the shifts and shallows of her thoughts disturbed Emer. The awful tragedy of that life ending so suddenly, so early, so needlessly, sometimes threw a faint shadow over the present, over what was for Emer a happy sequel, a joyful life's work, the raising of Angela's children. So Emer tried to never think of Angela. Instead, she delighted in Donny's dark hair and grey eyes. The Maguire looks. His father, Peadar, all over again.

She understood very well what drove Peadar to emigrate. The soft mists and hare-haunted hills that soothed her soul were for him a constant reminder of his own personal pain, his Calvary. He had run away to America, the escape route for Irishmen. He couldn't face the future without Angela. And with Emer there, he could go. It wasn't the money. They would have managed. And although Peadar had said his girls would get an education as Angela would have wanted, they would have managed that, too. Joseph would have helped, and Emer had money.

Though Cassie told her how wonderful it was that she shouldered such a responsibility, the truth was, Emer recognized, going to check on the sleeping children, the responsibility overtook her. Fate handed her an undertaking that was all the sweeter for having been purchased at such a terrible price. She liked to run things, to be in charge, to have a hand in how things turned out. And the children, she couldn't have loved them more if they were her own. Tall, fair, quiet Una: how she had grown this past year! Busy little Nan. And Donny, who seemed truly her own. She had taught him his first words, watched his first steps.

The years chased each other, slipping one after another over the edge of the future. Busy, successful years. Happy crowded years.

They flew past. Again she felt her own restlessness. It was the spring that was making her a little discontented, she decided. She longed to shed her heavy winter clothes. Starting Monday, she'd begin her summer sewing but first, before she did anything else, she would cut Una's First Communion dress to fit Nan.

On Sunday evening, when she took Joseph to catch the ten to six train for Dublin, Emer was thinking again about summer sewing. Day-long rain had eased to a light drizzle. Joseph held the reins in his long bony hands, folded like shiny brown ribbons. The pony's haunches shone slick and the wet drops dulled the brass harness fittings. They sat opposite each other on the edge of their seats to take advantage of the umbrella Emer held over their heads. The pony trotted along. Wheels swished through puddles. Joseph was in excellent spirits, whistling a little tune and encouraging the pony.

As they rounded the corner into the station yard, Darlings' motorcar, driven by their workman, was coming out. The pony shied. Joseph was forced to pull him up fast and into the side of the road to let it pass. "God damn it, does he have to take the two sides of the road?"

In the station yard, Emer saw Lady Darling walking to the first class carriage at the front of the train, narrow skirt well above her trim ankles and exquisitely gloved hand holding her umbrella above her high-feathered hat. In a flash, Emer determined that she would write to Brown Thomas and order just such a dress for herself, or maybe to Clery's. Brown Thomas was always more expensive. Still she liked the Brown Thomas style. Blue poplin, that's what she'd like. A deep blue. Perfect for summer. Why wouldn't she? She hadn't anything new for ages.

Joseph halted the pony close to the track and handed her the reins. He stood to get his bag from behind the seat. Suddenly he stooped under the umbrella and kissed her cheek. "*Slan leath*, Emer." Goodbye.

Dumbfounded, Emer stared after him. The flush from her cheek spread over her face and neck. He was striding toward the train, his tall figure bare-headed in his Sunday clothes, dark brown trousers and a brown tweed jacket with a half belt at the back.

What had come over Joseph? Saucy brat! He mightn't be back for a while. Why had he kissed her? What did that kiss mean? How would she face him again? What was he doing, kissing her like that?

The pony snorted and stamped his hoof. Emer stayed there, under the umbrella in the misty spring drizzle and watched while the train shunted and steamed away, gathering speed, rounding the turn in the track, and disappeared to send back sailing swirls of smoke that hung in the rain. Still she sat there, trying to understand what had changed. Her face still flamed. What a nerve he had. Losing the run of himself, he was. The Angelus bell rang out through the mist. Six o'clock! She had to get home to the children. The pony tossed his head and the harness jingled. She pulled the rein and turned him for home. Damn him anyway. What was he thinking about? She was left to tell the children that he wouldn't be coming home so often, those poor children. She flicked the pony's haunch with the whip and he broke into a trot. The children were expecting her, it was getting dark.

Stephen Plunkett was sitting on the dairy steps when Emer drove the pony into the yard

"Will I unharness the pony for you, Emer?"

"That would be a big help, Stephen," she said, stepping down to enter the house. The children were busy. The kitchen lamp was lighted and Una had already milked the cow and used up the last of the buttermilk mixing scones on the falling table for a late Sunday tea. With the back of a spoon she was making a hollow in the top of each biscuit to fill with jam.

"Stephen came up to see if we need any help," Una told her.

Nan was carefully cleaning eggs and packing them into the squares in the egg boxes for the egg collector on Monday. What great little women her girls were. Una could manage a home.

"How many eggs this week, Nan?"

"I've three dozen packed already, and there's one dozen and fourteen still in the basket."

"That's two dozen and two Nan, five dozen in all."

Donny was stretched on the floor his little wooden soldiers lined up for battle.

"Will you play with me, Aunt Emer?"

So while the girls prepared the tea, Emer stretched on the floor beside Donny and he assigned her the command of a line of soldiers. He had built a little wall with his wooden blocks.

"Those are your men," he said, and she was again struck by how well he spoke, little Donny, whose mother died when he was born, who had instead half a dozen mothers. He was growing up indulged by his adoring sisters, and spoiled by Cassie and Lizzie Scanlon and Emer.

"I gave the pony water and a basin of oats. Is there anything else you want done, Emer?" Stephen was standing at the half door.

"Thanks, Stephen. Do you want to stay to tea?"

"No. My mother'll have my tea ready. Thanks just the same."

"I think Stephen is lonely, do you Una?" asked Emer when he had left.

"I never noticed."

"Charge, Aunt Emer," Donny protested, "your men have to charge, they have to run. Make them run!" Emer was forced to give up her musing about Stephen and pay attention to the battle.

ALTERING UNA's Communion dress for Nan was not easy. It taxed her patience and ingenuity. The dress, linen, with a lace yoke, had yellowed from seven years in a box on top of the press in Emer's bedroom. The neckline was too wide for Nan, the dress slipped off the little girl's shoulders. The child fidgeted through every fitting session. In the end, Emer undid all the seams, and using material from the wide gathered skirt made Nan a narrower and shorter dress, copying dresses from advertisements in *The Independent*. All Tuesday afternoon she pedaled the sewing machine. On Wednesday, she did the finishing by hand, and when the children came from school she was still sitting upright at the kitchen table, her right hand moving in quick circles, stitching. Finally, it was finished. Once it had been carefully ironed she stood Nan on a chair and dropped the dress over her head. Lifted it a touch off her shoulders, and let it settle.

"It's nice, but it's very plain Aunt Emer," said Una.

"No, simple is the word, but wait till her veil is in place."

She fitted the yellowed lace veil with the seed pearl trimming on Nan's curls.

"Not so plain now, you look lovely, Nan."

A letter had arrived from Joseph with a present for Nan, a little Celtic cross on a thin chain. So he wasn't coming! Such an expensive gift, was Joseph trying to make up for not being there? Emer wasn't impressed. He should have come.

Next day, kneeling in the little stone church a few rows behind the First Communion girls, Emer wished he were there to see Nan and tormented herself imagining how he might be spending Saint Patrick's Day, in Bewley's or some such café, maybe in the evening at the Gaiety Theatre or walking in the mountains. Perhaps his friend O'Flaherty was with him. Maybe he had a girl, too. But if Joseph had a girl why had he kissed her? And if the kiss meant what Emer thought it meant, how could he not have come?

The priest droned on through the mass. Emer looked up at the beams in the vaulted roof and the light streaming through stained glass windows with their images of the Virgin and Saint Patrick. She recalled the first Christmas after Angela died. Una cried and cried. Joseph had taken her for a walk and talked to her. They went together to midnight mass while Emer remained home with baby Donagh and Nan. That awful lonely first Christmas, how glad she was to have Joseph there. It began snowing on the afternoon of Christmas day and for two days it snowed steadily. Not even the Wren Boys called to sing and dance at the door and collect treats. Just themselves, with Cassie and Tom and Stephen. Lizzie didn't arrive till the snow eased up, and then came stomping up the steps. "Freezing Emer, I never saw the like at Christmas. Sure the holy water froze in the press!"

More than three years ago that was. Emer went over in her mind the Saturday nights when they sat by the fire, each with a mug of tea, and talked about the children. He had said once how like her mother Nan was, except she did not have Angela's masses of red hair. Nan's hair was jet black like the Maguires, her father's people. Like Emer's. Still, he'd said, Angela would never be gone while Nan had those huge green eyes. He'd said Emer was doing a great job with the children. The girls were growing up lovely but they would never be as lovely as their mother had been, God be good to her, or as herself, Emer was. Remembering that compliment, warmth spread through Emer. Her face flushed under her spring hat. Now, I'm losing the run of myself, she thought. Why am I like this? At my age, I ought to have sense. She forced herself to concentrate on the mass.

Donny, sitting between Emer and Una, was bored and stood up on the seat. Una took him down gently and gave him her prayer book to look at. The somber austerity of Lent was set aside for this day, the altar a brave show of daffodils and candles. The priest in a green chasuble, green for hope and for Saint Patrick. Everyone had a spray of shamrock. In the sermon the priest again recounted the story of Saint Patrick's convincing the pagan Irish of the possibility of the Blessed Trinity. "And he stooped and plucked the shamrock and held it up before them, Three in One. One in Three."

Five little girls in white sat prim and straight. Across the aisle, on the men's side, the boy communicants shuffled their feet and pinched and elbowed each other when the teacher's eye was not on them.

It's a good thing, Emer thought resentfully, it's not Donny's communion. He'd be over there without a relative to kneel behind him. She would not think of Joseph for the rest of the day. The Offertory bell was ringing, the priest knelt and raised the white circle of the Host above his head. Again the bell rang, he lowered the Host, then once more the bell was heard and he raised the chalice. Emer bowed her head. In a few minutes the children would line up for communion.

Shepherded by their teachers, they filed up to the altar rail, boys at one end, girls at the other. Emer watched Nan. The altar boy held the patten under her chin and the priest placed the Host on her tongue.

How sweet Nan looked, quiet and serious for once. Her hair had grown over the winter and in her little strapped shoes and Communion veil, she was the loveliest of the five little girls in the ceremony. The long, wide gathered skirts of the others looked old fashioned. Emer wished she could have had a photograph made to keep and to send to Peadar in New York. The children walked back with the bowed heads as they had rehearsed, again and again, in the previous weeks. There was a heavy shuffle of boots as everyone stood for the last gospel. Two of the little girl communicants whispered behind their lifted prayer books. The teacher leaned over and slapped their arms with her missal. They straightened up guiltily.

"*Ite Missa Est,*" the mass is ended, intoned the priest. The response was drowned by the old harmonium emitting a high squeaking note. The choir sang.

"*Hail glorious Saint Patrick, dear saint of our Isle,*
On Erin's dear children, bestow your sweet smile."

The congregation stood talking in groups of two or three. If it was Saint Patrick's Day, winter must be over. The children, released from all restraint, ran between the knots of adults. Communion sixpences and three-penny pieces were slipped into eager little hands. Nan ran up to Emer. "Mr. Mahon gave me a trupence and Mr. Plunkett gave me a tanner."

"Don't use that word Nan, it's a sixpence. I hope you said thank you."

"Her uncle in Dublin didn't come?" said Margaret Smith, pulling her black shawl round her ample shoulders and eyeing Emer's clothes.

"He couldn't," Emer told her, "he's too busy, he'll be here for the summer."

Why was she feeling the need to justify his absence to Margaret Smith? Margaret was such a gossip.

But Margaret just said, "Ah, they're always busy in Dublin, and sure the half of them is joined up."

Did she mean Joseph was enlisting? Never.

"I'll be up for tea," said Lizzie, kissing Donny, "and I'll have something for Nan's money box."

The groups were dispersing, hungry for breakfast. Una and Donny were already walking toward the trap.

"Come along, Nan," Emer heard her own voice shrill and sharp, "It's time to go."

Emer sat across from Nan in the trap admiring her dress, pleased with her work. She had started to alter her own dresses to match the new style, with little progress. Brown Thomas had not yet responded to her order, but when her new blue poplin dress arrived she would make a paper pattern of it to guide her in her sewing. She craved a new outfit. Not one stitch, she thought, have I bought for myself in five years.

TWO DAYS LATER, on Saturday, when she rode her bicycle in to Obanbeg for the first time she realized why skirts were shorter and narrower that Spring. Her heavy serge skirt was cumbersome and slowed her progress, even though she had pinned it up. Still, she made the journey in just under an hour. What a convenience to get tea, and seed for cake, Pears fancy soap, a length of cotton to make dresses for the girls and *The Independent*, all without the work of harnessing the pony. The prices were lower than in J.J. Mahon's shop, and there was more variety, too.

Maybe she'd sell the pony. She'd talk to Joseph about that if he ever came back. What was he spending his time at? With the Dublin sweetheart? But what about that kiss at the railway station? Hardly honourable if he had a girl. Yet she was sure that only a girl could have kept him away. If Joseph had a girl, why did she feel that it was a tragedy and wish it wasn't so, tossing and turning in bed, thinking about him, asking herself if he really had kissed her or did she imagine it? The days were longer now and she was home well before tea. She had bought a barnbrack for a special treat. Donny ate three slices.

"Donny is a piglet! Donny is a piglet!" sang Nan.

Donny's food-stained face broke into a grin. They lingered over the tea. Una read the paper aloud. A U-boat had sunk a merchant ship in the North Atlantic.

"Why is it called a U-boat?" Nan asked.

"Because it hides under the waves," Una told her.

"I can hide under the river in the summer," Nan boasted.

"You are not to go to the river, ever, without someone going with you," Emer warned, wiping blackberry jam off Donny's face and hands and looking stern.

"Why do they call them *Hun*s?" Una wondered aloud, still reading the paper.

"I don't know," Emer answered absent-mindedly, "I forget why."

"The parade of the Irish Volunteers and the Citizen Army up Sackville Street on Saint Patrick's Day was the first time these two groups have marched together," read Una.

Emer looked over her shoulder at the fuzzy photograph.

"What's a volunteer?" Nan wanted to know.

"Nothing that need concern us," Emer told her. "Look on the inside page Una, I want to see the styles."

A strange uneasiness came over her, Saint Patrick's Day, when Nan had made her First Communion. She shivered a little, as if a small chill wind had blown into the kitchen. Saint Patrick's Day? She shrugged it off. Couldn't be. Dublin was sixty miles away. Who cared what they were at, they were always at something in Dublin. Some group was always play-acting at revolution up there. And she had no response from Brown Thomas to her order. She had been looking forward to something new for Easter.

"This year is the tri-centenary of Shakespeare's death." Una was still perusing the newspaper.

"What's tri-centenary, Aunt Emer?"

"I think it's three hundred years since he died."

EMER SEWED dresses for the two girls for Easter. She cut the skirts straight, hems falling a few inches below their knees, and made Donny his first pair of short little boys' trousers and a white sailor shirt. If only Joseph would come and see them. How grown up they were, how smart her little family would be for Easter Sunday.

"Is Uncle Joseph coming for Easter?" Nan asked.

"He might, if he isn't too busy."

"I miss him, he never comes any more."

"I know Nan, we all miss him. But we have Aunt Emer and ourselves, and maybe he will come," Una said.

On Maundy Thursday the postman brought a notice that her order from Brown Thomas was in the post office. Emer craved something new. All her clothes seemed stale, dowdy, worn. She would go to Obanbeg Easter Saturday and pick it up, have her new dress for Easter. A bit of style. Perhaps it wasn't warm enough for poplin yet, but still, with an extra petticoat!

EASTER SATURDAY morning Emer and Una baked, then Emer planned to go to Obanbeg. She'd take Donny with her. Nan and Una set off down to the village to take a seed cake to Lizzie for Easter. Emer changed her clothes and had just finished dressing Donny when she heard the clop of hooves in the yard. She went to the half door and saw J.J. Mahon, the tavern keeper, pull up, step down from the trap and loop the reins over the paddock gate. What on earth could he want? She'd never seen him away from his shop except at mass. His stubby body waddled over, his red face looking determined.

"Good day, Miss Maguire."

"Good day to you, won't you come in?"

J.J. sat at the kitchen table and looked around at the whitewashed walls, the high dresser shining with dishes, the sides of bacon and smoked ham suspended on hooks above the fireplace.

"Fine place you have here."

"Well, it suits us," said Emer and thought, he knows I have land to let, that's why he's here. That's it, he wants to rent the land.

"You'll have a cup of tea?" she asked, hanging the kettle over the fire.

"I will indeed, if you're making it."

He's here because it's Easter Saturday and the pub is empty, the priest is hearing confessions for the stragglers who left their Easter confession till the last minute. I won't be going to Obanbeg now, she thought, spreading the tablecloth. But the letting of the land was important, very important. The dress could wait till Tuesday.

Donny stared at him, his thumb in his mouth.

"That's a fine lad you have there," J.J. told her, "very like your side, very like his father."

"Yes, he is like Peadar."

Would the man ever come to the point? She decided to ask plenty for her land, the price of beef cattle was rising, he probably wanted the land to fatten up cattle.

"Donny, here's your slate and chalk, you can sit on the step outside, draw me a cat, and watch for Una and Nan." She opened the half door and put Donny out on the step.

J.J. drank his tea and ate seed cake, his pale eyes darting glances about. Emer sipped her tea. She could see J.J. was in no hurry. At last he mopped his face with his red handkerchief, blessed himself and pushed back his chair. He crossed his legs and folded his arms.

"I have an offer for you, Miss Maguire."

"Oh, you have?"

"Well, you know trade is good. The shop full all the time, in fact. The missus and myself have in mind to take on more help."

"I'm glad to hear it," Emer answered, putting down her cup.

"Sure it's a great chance for a young person to serve their time in a bar and grocery isn't it, Miss Maguire?"

"It is," Emer agreed politely. Was the man never going to bring up the letting of the land?

"So, we've decided to make an offer to yourself, Miss Maguire."

That's more like the thing, thought Emer.

"Yes," he went on, "we'll take on your oldest, Una, to train to the trade."

Taken completely by surprise Emer stared at him for a minute, then her mouth settled into a hard line.

"Mr. Mahon, Una is not yet fourteen, not till August, and she is going to the convent school in September, that's decided."

"Sure, that's a big expense, to send her there, think of the chances she'd have at our place."

"No. That's all settled, it's settled, and there'll be no change."

Emer was curt and a little hostile. Then, afraid she would lose her temper and say something she might regret, she rose and walked to the half door to check on Donny. She turned back, "Mr. Mahon, haven't you lots of help there with Liam and your own son, he's a fine lad."

Mahon's face tightened in a flat stiff contraction. It was as if she had struck him and the blow had altered his face completely.

"He joined up, my son did, joined up last Wednesday, so he did."

Suddenly she felt very sorry for him. "I'm sure the whole thing will be over soon and you'll have him back home, everyone says it will be over by Christmas."

"That's what they said about last Christmas," he answered bitterly.

"It has to be over soon. It can't last much longer."

"His mother's heart is broke, that's all I know." J.J. got up to leave. "Good day to you, Miss Maguire."

"Goodbye now. I'm sure you'll get someone to help in the shop."

As he drove out he passed Una and Nan coming in.

"Lizzie said Mr. Mahon's son is taking the Saxon shilling," Nan reported, and Emer had to smile hearing the old expression of Irish contempt for British army pay.

"She said he had a row with his mother because he was walking out with Greta Smith and his mother doesn't like her," Nan added. "Mrs Mahon said she was a skivvy."

"That need not concern us Nan and don't repeat that word. Greta is a lovely girl."

"What did he want, Aunt Emer?" Una asked.

"Nothing really, nothing we could help him with, he's looking for help in the shop, he delayed me, and I never did get to the post office. It's too late now, it'll be closed, I'll go on Tuesday."

"Can I go with you?" Nan wanted to know. "We have no school that day."

"Maybe, if it's a fine day, but now we have to get busy. There's ironing to do and shoes to polish. Tomorrow is Easter Sunday."

"Is Uncle Joseph coming for Easter?"

"I don't know, Una. He should be here. I expected him on Maundy Thursday. He must be busy."

"I want him to come," Nan said.

"Maybe he will," Una told her.

"There's no one on the road, Aunt Emer, only ourselves." Tuesday morning, Nan was sitting up very straight in the trap opposite her aunt.

"It's spring, Nan, April 25th today. Everyone is busy with farm work, look over there." Emer pointed toward a field a few hundred yards from the road. The bowed neck of a horse patiently turned at the end of the field and a ploughman stepped lamely, one foot in the furrow. Flocks of crows swooped after him, scavenging in the trenches of fresh turned earth. "He's very late with his ploughing. The farmers are working dark to dark now. Listen Nan, did you hear it? The cuckoo."

"No."

"Listen again, ah, there he is. He's back. He's early this year."

"I heard it that time."

The air was soft and fragrant, the green hedges snowed here and there with whitethorn blossom. Near the poorhouse gate lilac trees were coming in bloom. How delicious an early morning outing in spring.

Climbing the long slope outside the town the pony crossed the road from side to side. Emer let him take his own pace. They had the way to themselves. Then they crested the hill, and began the descent past the cottages and tumbledown row houses, into the town. Emer held the reins tightly, thin, barefoot boys were kicking around a blown up pig's bladder in the street. Some of the boys had shaved heads, crusted with scabs. Lice, Emer thought grimly, it's the season. She'd have to check Nan's hair.

Women hung out of windows and stood outside the doors of the shabby, old stone houses gossiping, but the main street was quiet. People were standing outside the post office. Nan sat up straight, her ankles crossed primly, her big green eyes shining.

"We'll leave the pony in the railway station yard Nan, there's always fresh water in the trough there, then we'll go back to the shops."

The station yard was empty, deserted. Quiet after the Easter holiday, Emer thought. They went back along the street, past the Railway Hotel, Mercers Bakery, The Arcade Drapery. The dozen or so people standing at the post office were talking in loud voices. A notice was nailed to the door.

Closed until further notice due to an insurrectionary rising in the City of Dublin. The authorities have taken active and energetic measures to cope with the situation which is proceeding favourably.

Emer read it again word by word. A rising. My God, Joseph. If he were connected with that! A cold river of dread flooded Emer. She stared at the notice and then at the faces in the crowd. A rising against the Crown? In growing fear and alarm she listened to what was being said.

"That's *the Volunteers*," a big burly fellow was saying.

"Na, it's *the Republicans*, *the Brotherhood*," said another man, "them's a bad crowd."

"Well," said a woman, "my man was here when the telegraph came to shut the place up, and they said it was the *Sinn Fein*."

"What the hell is *Sinn Fein?*" asked a shop man with a red face and big blue apron.

"Aw cute hoors," said a fat little fellow in a long black coat, "cute hoors."

"That's all a right cod about *Sinn Fein*" said the first speaker emphatically, "it's the *Volunteers*."

"That's Dublin for you," insisted a small man with his hands in his pockets, "things are going along grand, but nothing would do that crowd but to start a rising, they should be all sent to the Front."

"Proper order I say, a holiday in France is what they want," said a well-dressed man who had just joined the group. The woman who had first mentioned *Sinn Fein* shrugged, and with a ruffled, insulted gesture she pulled her shawl up over her head and walked away. A rough-looking labourer shouldered his way to the front and read the notice.

"Fools," he said and turned aside to spit in the gutter.

"Still and all," said a big, shawled, red-headed woman, "I bet they put up a fight."

"I hope it doesn't stop our allowances," muttered a good-looking girl of about twenty. She had two starved-looking children by the hand.

Emer could listen no more. Frightened, she lurched away, back along the street, dragging Nan, making for the station yard and the trap. Good God, if Joseph was part of that! Could he be?

"What's the matter, Aunt Emer? What's wrong?"

"Nothing, nothing, the Post Office is closed, that's all."

"I wanted to post my letter to Uncle Joseph."

"We'll post it tomorrow."

Emer looked down at Nan's worried little face. There were tears of disappointment standing in the little girl's green eyes. The child had sensed the change that had come over Emer. The excitement of the happy holiday had gone. Her aunt had turned into a panic-stricken stranger hurrying away before they had even visited the shops. Emer crouched down beside Nan. One big tear escaped and rolled down Nan's cheek. Emer blotted it away with her handkerchief.

"You and I, Nan, will have our dinner. Wouldn't you like that?"

Nan nodded twice. They hurried on and turned in at the side door of the Railway Hotel. Emer had to calm herself. What had come over her? Where did she get the idea Joseph was involved in anything clandestine? He was too sensible for that. It was just that Gaelic League he and that little man O'Flaherty were involved with. When Joseph brought O'Flaherty home for a visit, Emer thought him a vague, dreamy sort of fellow. His head full of the folklore revival; harmless plays and dancing. That's what wrong with me, I'm jealous of the dancing. I need to settle my mind, she told herself, looking down at Nan's shining, eager face. It was the children she had to think of.

They were early. The dining room was empty, but from the bar, across the dark hallway came the sound of men's voices raised in argument. They sat at a table near the big window.

"What can I get you, Mam?" asked the little bandy-legged waiter when he was not quite as far as their table.

Emer waited till he reached the table. "I'll have a glass of port, please."

"And for the young lady?"

"A glass of peppermint."

"Certainly, at once," and he scuttled away.

"Will we go to the shops after, Aunt Emer?"

"Yes, and you will spend your First Communion money."

"Sandeman's Four Star, Mam," the waiter put their drinks in front of them. "The servant girl will wait on you. I'm run off me feet in the bar. No trains today you know, I've a crowd of commercial travellers stranded. That's Griffith's lot, hooligans, and the country at war."

"Thank you," Emer said coldly.

When the waiter was gone Nan asked, "Is there a war on?"

"He means there is a war over in France, Nan, not here, it really is nothing for us to worry about."

Men's heads could be seen passing above the heavy brass rail and lace curtain that covered the lower half of the window. Business in the bar would be brisk.

Then four men came in and sat at a table near the fireplace. Emer noticed, as she had many times before, how Nan's lively little figure and tossing black curls always caught the strangers' eyes. Her sweet little Nan.

The servant girl was a tired woman about Emer's age.

"We have nice spring lamb, Mam, nice chops and fried potatoes."

"We'll have that."

Emer picked at her food, her thoughts rushing and whirling. She didn't dare ask but she needed to find out more about the rising. Of course, if Joseph hadn't been involved in it what did it matter? It seemed to be a small thing, nothing really. The notice at the post office said things were under control. Surely Joseph wasn't mixed up in anything illegal. Or was he? The memory of that kiss came to her again.

"I want to buy something for Una and Donny," said Nan, breaking into her thoughts.

"Oh, what do you think Una would like?"

"A lace collar for her green dress."

"That might be very dear, Nan."

"How much would I have to spend?"

"Maybe two shillings, maybe half a crown."

"I have nine shillings."

"Yes, but you mustn't spend it all. You have to save some. What will you get for Donny?"

"A top, I think."

"He's a little young to spin a top. What about a story book, and you could read to him."

"How much would that be?"

"Maybe sixpence, or a shilling."

"THAT'S THE NICEST dinner I've ever eaten," said Nan as they walked to the shops. In the Arcade she hesitated between two lace collars, her fat little dimpled hands turning them over.

"The creamy one is best for Una, I think," said Emer, trying to hurry her along. Everyone was talking about the rising in Dublin. People said the schools wouldn't reopen the next day, after Easter holidays. At the news agents, the owner looked at them over his spectacles.

"No *Independent*, no trains, some caper in Dublin. The Castle won't be long putting a stop to that gallop."

Emer said nothing. Nan bought a book of stories for Donny.

I have no evidence Joseph was with those men, Emer told herself, watching the road beyond the pony's tossing mane. Ahead the way was pitted with holes from recent rains. She slowed the pony. No sense having him cast a shoe. If she bought another bicycle, one for Una, she wouldn't need the pony. Not with the land let. Tom Plunkett would lend her his horse when she needed the cart. The pony was a lot of work. She'd talk it over with Joseph. She flushed thinking of him. How did she get like this, like a silly young girl? Those feelings should be over, behind her. Sure he and O'Flaherty were only in the Gaelic League, just a drama club, poetry and plays. He probably met a woman there. A love affair was keeping him away. Her whole being flooded with jealousy. My God, what was she coming to?

"I'll read Donny a story tonight."

"Yes dear, if he's not too sleepy."

In the evening, having told all that had happened to Cassie, Emer went home to milk. After supper she kissed Donny and lifted him into his cot. Nan tugged at her sleeve. "Aunt Emer, can I come to town with you tomorrow and post my letter?"

"You have school, dear. It's almost time for bed."

Emer was weary, the long day, the trip to town and the storm of her emotions had tired her. When Una had taken her candle and book and said goodnight, Emer went and lay on her bed.

Still thinking about the news she had heard in the town, she fell asleep. While she slept, that Tuesday night, a startling thing, which had never occurred before, happened: artillery started to shell Dublin. Applying the hard experience of the western front, the British army brought the gunboat *Helga* up the river Liffey, positioned machine guns in the center of Dublin and began to blast it into ruins.

The 1916 Rising against the British, a rebellion of dreamers and idealists, had caught the authorities off guard. They had taken none of the groups agitating for freedom, The Irish Volunteers, The Irish Citizen Army or The Irish Republican Brotherhood, seriously. And because the revolutionaries were considered a joke, the city was poorly defended. But Dublin Castle reacted quickly. By Tuesday troop reinforcements had begun to arrive in the city. While Emer slept, Dublin was pounded.

WEDNESDAY MORNING, as the girls were getting dressed for school, Cassie appeared at the half door. "The school's closed today, Emer. Tom heard it in Mahon's last night. The ruckus in Dublin is not over yet."

"Oh Cassie, don't tell me that. I can't believe it's still going on."

"There mayn't be much more to it you know, Emer. A small upset I'm sure, but I thought I'd tell you about the school."

"Thanks, Cassie"

"I have to go Emer, I've no milking done yet."

Emer stood on the step watching her friend hurrying down the lane. Something stirred beneath the surface of her mind and it slowly dawned on her that Joseph's kiss at the railway station was a farewell kiss. The kiss of a man about to undertake something dangerous, a last goodbye. There had been only goodwill and friend-ship and farewell in it, nothing more. Feelings which had ram-paged through her since that day were ridiculous, laughable, built on nothing. She had betrayed her own good sense and was ashamed of herself. She'd fallen in love like a silly girl. She had more impor-tant things to do than brood and break her heart over him. She had a family to raise. When he came again she would be as she had always been. For now, she would forget him.

And she did, in the daytime. But at night there was no escape from longing. Emer lay under the open window thinking about Joseph, racked by desire, her arms tight around her pillow. An oc-casional sound filtered through on the early summer air, the pony slamming against his stall when he shifted position; the screech of an owl; small animals scampering about. When sleep came she dreamed about him, strange anxious dreams. Once she dreamed he was waving to her across a river. She started swimming towards him but the current took her farther away, his figure fading out of her sight. Just when she lost sight of him she woke up to find her-self weeping. In the morning, exhausted, she swore again not to think of him.

School remained closed the rest of the week. There was no postman. In Dublin only one paper, *The Irish Times*, published and it was heavily censored. Rumours ran through the ruined city that the Germans had invaded. In Slanabaille, there was no news at all.

Una missed school. It rained steadily and Emer delayed going to town.

"When do you think the school will open again, Aunt Emer?"

"Probably Monday," said Emer and broke a length of thread for the button she was sewing on Nan's coat.

"I wonder if Uncle Joseph had a holiday from school, too."

"Probably."

"I miss him."

"I know Nan."

"Why doesn't he come to see us?"

"The trains are not running regularly."

Donny hit his tower of wooden blocks hard with his fist and they scattered on the floor. "I wish he'd come to see us."

"He will Donny, he's busy just now."

"When will he come?" asked Nan

"In June for certain, that's the summer holidays."

"That's a long time away."

"Not that long, Monday next is the first of May. Nan, why don't you lay the table for tea."

THE GIRLS WORKED away on their lessons as if the school was open. No word came from Joseph. On Saturday evening, Una wrote an English composition about what she would be when she grew up, and Emer sewed. Nan read to Donny.

"*Once upon a time there was an old sow who had three little pigs, and because she had nothing to give them she sent them out to seek their fortune.*"

"Just like this house, we have three children," Emer said, getting up to light the lamp. The kitchen was getting dark.

"Where did they go?" asked Donny.

"Wait and listen for the next bit," Nan tended to be bossy.

"Una, your penmanship is excellent," Emer was looking over her shoulder.

"When I'm finished with this I'm going to write to my father."

"I'll write a bit at the end of your letter," Nan offered.

"You should write your own letter to Daddy. You never write to him."

"I never can think of anything to write."

"Una, where's your father's old gun he used to shoot rabbits with?"

"It's hanging over the fireplace in your old house, Aunt Emer."

"When did you last see it there?"

"I don't remember, it was always there."

"Was it there yesterday, Una?"

"I didn't notice, I don't know. Do you think someone took it? The door is always locked."

They had been down at the old place the day before to fodder the six young cattle Tom Plunkett had bought for Emer at the April cattle fair, something Joseph had promised to do. Emer couldn't remember seeing the gun. When had she last seen it? Maybe months ago. Joseph had taken it. Only he could have taken it. If it was gone, he was definitely in that trouble in Dublin. And if he was in that trouble he could be in jail.

Emer stood up quickly. It was already dusk. She didn't want to alarm the children. "Una, I'm going for a walk, I won't be long."

"Can I go?"

"No Nan, stay and read to Donny."

She forced herself to walk till she was out of earshot of the girls, then raced down the lane in the gathering dark, her heart beating very fast. Her hands trembled as she fumbled for the key under the stone at the side of the door and fitted it into the old lock. The door swung open, and in the faint light of the rising moon she saw the gun in its place above the hearth. She sank down on the settle bed exhausted, her arms round her trembling knees. His absence filled the room. All those nights he had slept in front of this fireplace, on this settle bed. She rested her forehead on her knees and a great well of emptiness opened in her. She had been making up crazy stories in her head like a madwoman. Joseph was gone. She was completely alone. Even if he were in danger she couldn't help him. She could hardly help herself. Scalding tears soaked into the cotton of her skirt, the sound of her sobbing was lost in the empty house. At last she prayed: Help me Lord, help me to keep going, just to keep on.

She stayed a long time in the dark kitchen, then locked the door again and went round to the back of the house to check on her new cattle. The sight gladdened her heart. The moon, a few days off full, had now climbed above the hill; her cattle were outlined in its light. They grazed, feeling with strong rough tongues for luscious dew-chilled grass, walking and cropping as they went. Mindlessly they fed and walked, their sturdy hooves deep in dewy clover, their tails flicking back and forth, their shadows moving after them.

Standing in the moonlight, watching and listening to her cattle, peace began to fall over Emer. The children were thriving, her own heart mending. They were going to be fine. She turned for home, immensely satisfied with her investment. The cattle would fetch a fine price in the autumn. Suddenly she heard footsteps on the stones. Someone was coming up the lane. Cassie, walking up for a Saturday evening visit and a cup of tea. Emer waited for her.

"Lovely evening, Emer."

"It is."

They linked arms companionably and went slowly up toward the house.

"Cassie, for a while I thought Joseph might be mixed up in that rising in Dublin."

"What? Please God he's not. What made you think that?"

"He hasn't been home for over a month."

"I thought you said he must have a sweetheart who was keeping him in Dublin."

"Yes that's it, that's what it is, and the trains haven't been running."

"That's true," said her friend, "but say nothing about it. Tom thinks it was a bad business. They say they got help from Germany, and you know what Dublin Castle will think of that. Say nothing about it! Say nothing till we hear more, Emer. There'll be news at mass tomorrow."

Sunday was cool and wet. Low Sunday, the first after Easter. They went to late mass. Donny was sleepy, it was almost his nap time. Emer took the little boy in her arms. When she stood for the first Gospel his head dropped onto her shoulder. She held her missal up in her left hand and followed along as the priest read.

"The Gospel according to John. *Then the same day, at evening, being the first day of the week, when the doors were shut where the disciples were assembled for fear of the authorities, came Jesus and stood in the midst, and saith unto them, Peace be unto you.*"

Emer held Donny tighter.

After mass, she was glad of the rain. She could not bear to talk. If anyone should engage her in conversation she was sure to weep, but everyone was hurrying home out of the rain She clutched Donny in her arms. "Hurry on Una, take Nan's hand, its starting to rain." Emer went quickly over to the trap.

MONDAY, THE school reopened and the postman came. He brought a notice that there was a special American letter that had to be signed for at the post office. Money from Peadar. On Tuesday, Emer left Donny with Lizzie and started for Obanbeg, on her bicycle, to pick up the parcel from Brown Thomas and her letter. It was a week since she'd been to town with Nan. She'd get the paper and find out what had happened in Dublin, pick up her new dress and put Peadar's money in the bank. Emer pedaled furiously away from Lizzie's, back up through the village and on to the main road. The money Peadar sent every month meant a great deal to Emer. Added to what she got for the land she let, it kept the little family very comfortable. What she saved from it would one day enable Peadar to come home. She sang under her breath. She had her own little store of money too, in the bank, saved, pound after pound by her mother, from the money Emer herself sent home during the years she worked in New York. And she knew very well that the comfort they lived in caused jealousy in Slanabaille. People said the Maguires thought too much of themselves, that they were proud, always getting above themselves.

Thinking about Peadar, she crested the hill above the town and was brought up short by the sight of a lorry placed across the road. Four soldiers leaned against it smoking, two policemen were searching a farmer's cart. Sacks of seed potatoes in the cart had been slit open and the potatoes spilled around the farmer's feet. He sat silent and sullen on a plank laid across the cart.

Emer's first instinct was to turn back, but then she thought the better of it. It might look strange if she did. The metal on the rifles in the soldiers' hands glinted, the wooden stocks shone like polished mahogany. Their casual stance was unnerving.

"Where are you going?" the younger of the two policemen asked as the other one waved the farmer on.

"Into the town."

"And what business have you there?"

"There's a package for me at the post office. I'd like to get it if the post office is open."

"Everything is open. Everything is as usual, the same as it always is. Off you go, my girl."

Emer cycled on, her back very straight. She felt the soldiers' eyes on her and was conscious of the weapons they carried. She did not so much as glance at the farmer as she passed. She thought she knew the policeman, but she wasn't sure.

Soldiers hung around the hotel and there was a line of people at the post office. They were strangely quiet. Emer took her package and letter from the tight-lipped postmaster and signed the proffered record. The package and letter had been opened and re-sealed. She crossed the street to the bank. She had just enough time to make the deposit before the bank closed at half-past eleven. She did no shopping. As she cycled out of the town she noticed the lorry and the soldiers had left the road. She raced on for Slanabaille. When she reached Lizzie's place she jumped off her bicycle, snatched up Donny and hugged him.

"The town was full of police and soldiers, Lizzie."

"Ah, they won't come this way, not out here at the back of God's speed. Anyway there's never any trouble in Slanabaille. The devil looks after his own. And I hear it's all over in Dublin, the poor lads are in jail, they surrendered, what's left of them. They're guests of the king now, bad luck to him."

Jail! Joseph in prison? Please God not jail, anything but that. "Lizzie, that's terrible."

"Well, at least they're not dead. Nothing so bad that it couldn't be worse!"

"And there's nothing to be done but wait for more news," Emer concluded.

"Sure," Lizzie continued, "we'll just go on with what we're at. Keep working like we always do."

"I've done no spring cleaning, Lizzie. Can you come tomorrow and Thursday to help me?"

"I will, you know I'm always here if you want me."

Emer flung herself into the cleaning. She scrubbed the floors and the tables with Sunlight soap. She and Lizzie whitewashed the house and aired the mattresses in the early sunshine. Emer turned the bedsheets, ripping them down the worn center and sewing the outer edges together. Lizzie washed the winter blankets, her sleeves rolled up above her elbows, her sinewy hands twisting and wringing the heavy, wet laundry. Once again Emer was struck by Lizzie's strength and vigour. Lizzie into her seventies. "I hope I'll have your years and health," she told her when they stopped for tea.

"Sure, why wouldn't you?"

"Well, I hope I do."

"No one knows what's fornenst us, Emer, but it's all decided. I put up with such hunger when I was small that it hardened me, toughened me so that often I wonder at myself. It killed all my people, but sure it just made me all the stronger."

Lizzie complained of aching joints and rubbed Sloan's liniment on her arms and legs, but she did the work of two. As they pinned the washing on the clothesline in the strong breeze, Emer told her about J.J. Mahon's offer to employ Una in his bar.

"Ah the auld hawk, Emer, he knows how to pick a worker. The country is crawling with girls looking for work but he had to go for the best girl in the parish. My girl, Una! The cheek of him! The bloody cheek of him! I hope you gave him the back of your hand."

Emer thought of Una's departure for school in September and felt the years were flying. Soon Nan would go, too. To cheer herself Emer tried on the new dress. It fitted perfectly. It was so light and summery. The scooped-out neckline showed off her strong, white throat. Narrow, easy sleeves and a bias cut skirt that flared from her slim waist. None of the old heavy gathers. Oh, the cost of it! Two pounds five shillings. Money bought nothing. Good job they lived in the country and grew their own food. Of course, Ireland was doing well out of the war. England bought every ounce of farm produce available. She turned around in front of Angela's old looking-glass. A very different look it was! So much more natural, like the dresses in the *Ladies' Home Journal* Peadar sometimes sent her from America. Very nice! She felt a different person in it. Younger, smarter. Tomorrow she would show it to Cassie. What would Joseph think of it? She longed to show it to him. Would he like it? She flushed at the thought, then became embarrassed and angry at her own foolishness, her feelings a tangle of desire. She had promised herself not to harbour those feelings, not to think of him this way. But where was Joseph? When would she see him again? She forced him out of her mind and concentrated on the dress.

With the girls back in school, Emer lavished attention on Donny. The farm and house she now tended with such care would be his one day. Her darling little boy. He got himself very dirty playing in the clay when she turned over the earth on her potatoes. His deft sticky hands found and wrecked the jewelled gossamer spider webs in the cabbages. He toddled along as she fed the hens and gathered the eggs. Together they counted the eggs.

"Look Donny, one, two, three, four, and the brown one?"

"Five."

"Good boy, and the speckled one?"

"Six."

"Excellent, that's a half dozen Donny. Let's see what's in the next nest."

Friday morning, they went for a walk along the path that ran down to the river from the side of the house. Emer had not come that way for a very long time. Last year's fallen leaves were soggy under their feet and the hedges were summer-thick and fragrant. The old dog followed them a few yards and then turned back.

"You never go down to the river by yourself, Donny, you know that, you're too small."

"But I could go to school!"

"When you're older, when you're six, yes, you'll go to school."

His soft little hand held hers in perfect trust. Suddenly Emer saw the lovely fan of a pheasant jut out from the undergrowth.

"Look Donny," she whispered, "look at his tail."

Silently, stealthily the pheasant slid under the hedge and disturbed not a leaf in his passing.

"It was a pheasant, Donny, did you see his tail?"

He shook his little black curls and looked at her in wonder.

"Let's see if we can make him fly out."

She clapped her hands loudly and stamped her foot. No sound came from the tiered green curtains of the hedge, no sudden throb of wings. Emer crouched down to talk to the child. "He's hiding, Donny. He's afraid. He won't come out now. I bet he has a wife there, a mother pheasant. They pair off in the spring you know. She'll lay eggs and they will hatch out and there'll be baby pheasants. Just like the baby chickens we have. Let's go on to the river."

They walked on and Emer thought again about Joseph. Where on earth was he? Please God he was safe. All she wanted now was for him to be safe. To come back and see the children. She thought of sending him a telegraph, but a combination of fear and pride deterred her. She now clearly understood how much he meant to her, how his visits framed the weeks. Even if he felt nothing at all for her, she still longed to see him. If he were involved in the trouble in Dublin, a telegraph might be a mistake. Informers were everywhere. She wished she had a newspaper. Tomorrow was Saturday. Una would be home from school. Emer would leave her in charge and cycle to Obanbeg for a newspaper. Or Cassie might have news tomorrow, or they'd hear something at mass on Sunday. Still the whole uproar seemed over. Could he be in jail? Why didn't he write? Maybe he was embarrassed by that kiss at the railway station. So long ago that was. If she didn't hear from him soon, she would write to him. It must be seven weeks at least, since he was home. The weekend before Saint Patrick's Day. And it was now almost a fortnight since Easter. It seemed like years.

The children were long asleep, Emer was putting a piece of bacon to soak for Saturday's dinner and listening to the wind raging round the house. The dog got up from the hearth, limped over, and stood at the door. Emer heard a footfall and a knock. Her heart jumped, a wild zigzag. Emer opened the door and in stepped Joseph. He stood leaning against the door. His breath came in gasps. His red hair blown about his head.

"Joseph! How did you get here?"

"On the train and by the fields."

He leaned back against the closed door, hair falling over his eyes. He brushed it away, stretched out his hands and placed them on her shoulders. At arms length they stood and gazed at each other in complete and perfect understanding. Then Emer took a step forward. She felt the rough tweed of his jacket against her cheek, smelled his sweat-soaked shirt. They held each other for a long time without speaking.

Joseph finally spoke. "Emer, have you any whiskey?"

He hung his jacket on a chair and sat at the table. Emer fetched the whiskey bottle from its place high on the dresser behind Angela's big willow pattern platter, and filled a small glass. She sat across from Joseph and watched him while he sipped. His long slender fingers holding the glass, his big shoulders slumped. Her heart beat very fast and she felt all the days since Peadar had left, all the times Joseph had spent home with them in Slanabaille, gather in one skein of memory behind them. A boundary between them had been crossed, they were poised to plunge into an unknown future. He was thinner than she'd ever seen him. Freckles stood out from the pallor of his face. He raised pain-haunted eyes.

"They're all dead Emer, all dead, Tom Clarke, McDonagh, Pat Pearce, and yesterday, Willie Pearce and Joe Plunkett, all shot. Shot Emer. Shot like you would a thieving fox."

She sat staring at him, trying to absorb this news. The names were not familiar to her. "My God! Joseph, we never knew, how could it happen so quickly?"

"Even in Dublin, Emer, we heard nothing, not a word till Wednesday and then we heard they were shot. It was in the paper. An announcement from the Castle. Like lightening, Maxwell struck them down."

"Lord have mercy on them, Joseph"

"Yes. The city's a pile of rubble, Emer. And thousands are being rounded up for jail."

"Are you on the run, Joseph?"

"No."

It was quiet then in the kitchen. No sound but the clock ticking and an ember falling into the hearth. Emer thought she saw it all then in her mind's eye, the half-forgotten images from the past, the skirmishes and fights, the house burnings, murders, all the violence of risings she'd heard about, from long ago. Some essential restraint between them, some reserve was gone. Yet these were Joseph's politics, not hers.

"Joseph, you were one of them?"

"I was. Did you know that, Emer?"

"I guessed. How did you get away?"

"I missed it! I missed it all. By a fluke, by a crazy fluke. I was in the Republican Brotherhood, and the Rising was set for Easter Sunday. We called it manoeuvers, that was the code name. We were expecting a shipment of arms and it didn't come, so Eoin Mac Neil, our chief, called it off. We needed the guns, you see. He put an advertisement in *The Independent* that the manoeuvers were off. So O'Flaherty and myself went off camping in the Wicklow mountains. Off on a lark, an Easter jaunt, a holiday. Imagine that!"

His green eyes had a rueful expression, as if he reproached himself. He went on, "We were in Wicklow when Pearse and Connolly went ahead. On Easter Monday. They went ahead with the rising."

Again those unfamiliar names. Except Connolly, she knew who Connolly was, the labour leader. She sat listening as if she knew them all.

"When we tried to get back into the city on Easter Monday night we couldn't get in, neither the trains nor the trams were running. We heard the city was in flames. No one could get in or out, so we stayed in Wicklow for a week, till Sunday. It was foolish, mad! And now they're all dead."

"Connolly, too?"

"I don't know, he was shot in the fighting. Taken prisoner."

He took a sip of whiskey and rubbed his tired eyes. She noticed faint trace of red beard.

"I can hardly believe it Emer, so fast everything changed, not much more than a week and they're all gone."

She didn't know how to answer, how to distract him from his grief. The noise of the wind in the chimney ceased momentarily. In the heavy air she waited for it to start again, to fill up the interval of silence. "The children will be happy to see you," she ventured at last.

"And I to see them."

At the thought of the children she asked, "Won't the police and the army come looking for you?"

"You needn't worry about that. Myself and O'Flaherty have always been very quiet about our activities. The school wouldn't stand for it if they knew."

"But Joseph, there are informers everywhere."

He smiled at her, his old slow mocking smile transforming his tired face. "I have a few friends in the police, Emer."

"It's all over now, isn't it?"

"No, it's not all over. It is for a while, everyone is in jail. But some day they'll get out, and we'll get help from America."

"Joseph, no one around here supported the rising."

"That will change Emer, it will all change."

She was afraid then, a nameless dread of the future.

"You can't go back to that, you have to stop it, Joseph. You must stop it. The children need you! Please give it up. You must give up that life."

She was pleading with him.

"Oh, I'll lie low for a while, a year or so. Nothing else to be done! Everyone is in jail."

"You must give it up altogether, Joseph. What about the children? We need you. I need you. I have been crazy with worry. Think of us, Joseph."

"You have nothing to worry about, Emer."

She saw it was hopeless, this was not the time to persuade him but still she said, "You can't be putting yourself in danger."

"I'm not in any danger, Emer. What I am is tired."

He stood and stretched then walked round the table to where she sat. "I think I'll go down to the old house to bed." He was looking down at her, smiling.

She put out her hand and touched his arm. "Don't go down there tonight. Stay here, Joseph. Stay here with me."

He stooped then and kissed her. She tasted the whiskey on his tongue and stood up from the chair, put her arms around him and held him as tightly as ever she could.

SPECIAL INTENTIONS

WIDE AWAKE, Una watched the wavering shadows on the ceiling of the junior dormitory. The flame of the votive candle in the blue bowl in front of the statue of the Virgin trembled in the draft from beneath the door. The wick had almost burned down. Not a sound but the breathing of sleeping girls. Una looked over at Eilish curled up on the narrow iron bed in the opposite cubicle. The white counterpane was folded at the foot of her bed. The papery whisper of Sister Agatha's morning feet came closer. Una pulled the sheet over her head till the nun passed.

Over in the convent, the nuns were rising for prayers, flocking to the dark chapel where three lamps burned, one suspended from the ceiling at the main altar, and one at each side altar. Siobhan Byrne, whose sister was a nun in Dublin, told Una that the nuns lay on the floor for these offerings. Una imagined a flock of shot crows, prostrate on the cold tiles, praying silently to thank the Almighty for rest and the coming day.

Far away, Una heard the convent clock strike four. She closed her eyes and pictured her whitewashed bedroom at home, the warmth of Nan beside her and Donny in his cot beneath the window, snoring. Una wondered if Nan missed her, then fell back asleep and didn't hear Sister Agatha pass again like a black shadow, rosary on her thick belt clicking softly, turtle-neck protruding from the white wimple; head, hooked nose, bulbous eyes and pursed mouth, checking, right, left, right left as she passed each bed. Back then for another hour's rest before the bell clanged half past six and she rose to light the gas lamp at the end of the dormitory.

When the bell did ring, Una was dreaming. She couldn't remember the dream, but woke with a start thinking she had made some promise, agreed to something. Morning sounds, beds creaking and girls yawning, then the swish of the curtains at the end of the cubicles being closed, water splashed in basins. Twenty-three sleepy first-year girls started another day. Una stood on the mat, poured frigid water into the basin and slipped her nightgown down over her shoulders. Trembling with cold, she wiped her face, neck, and breasts with the icy sponge. At home, Aunt Emer would have a roaring fire and a hot kettle. At home! Una slipped on the thick, tight, modesty vest and fastened it under her arms, her fingers clumsy. She had no breasts to speak of but the nuns insisted she wear it. Once Una had pulled on the long-sleeved shift and fastened the towel round her hips she stepped out of her nightgown and finished washing. "A good child of Mary is never completely undressed," Sister Cecelia taught the girls. "Nor does she ever touch herself under her clothes."

The bell rang again, fifteen minutes to mass. Sister Agatha marched up and down between the cubicles, "Hurry girls, hurry!"

They filed out, each dipping a hand in the holy water font beside the door. Una caught sight of herself in the long mirror at the end of the dormitory, a tall thin figure in a navy school uniform. Her head faded out. Only the dress had any materiality. She was transparent, as if missing something crucial and essential, something she lost in this cold, crowded barracks.

Last into the chapel, yawning and dopey, the first-year girls knelt in the two rows nearest the door. Sister Agatha came after them, lifting the rosary beads hanging from her belt as she genuflected toward the altar. She stationed herself, like a watchful hawk, behind her charges, to note whose back was straight, who paid attention.

Up in front on the epistle side, behind the lattice screen and under the sharp eye of the mistress of novices, the postulants knelt. They seemed little different from the third and fourth year students kneeling behind them. They were often seen walking together in the convent garden after tea, chattering to each other the way Una and Siobhan and Eilish did. Their grey dresses ended well above their laced boots, some of them even had long hair pinned back under the band of their short veils. The hair gave them individuality, black or blond, curly or straight. Siobhan Byrne said that the night before they made their final vows, the mistress of novices cut all their hair off and they renounced all vanity. That was the biggest sacrifice of all, she said, bigger than never going home again or never seeing their family except on special visiting days. "Never to admire yourself in a looking-glass, or buy new clothes or see the new styles, that," Siobhan insisted, "for some girls, is the worst thing about becoming a nun."

"What do you think is the worst, Eilish?"

"It's all one worse than another, the awful food and fasting and never getting married and being locked up."

"You have to pick one bad thing."

"Being locked up."

"What about you, Una?"

"Not seeing my sister and my little brother."

"You'd get used to that," Eilish said. "I have two older brothers and I never see much of them anyway. The youngest one is in the army in France, and my two sisters, Helen and Jane, are in America"

When she started convent school, Una hoped she'd feel grown up. Instead she was useless and lonely, as if she'd left her substance behind in the long low whitewashed house where she was the eldest, and Aunt Emer's closest companion. Thinking of Aunt Emer started tears in Una's light blue eyes. Then she reminded herself she had Eilish. Eilish was her friend, her first friend of her own age, and made the convent tolerable.

Una forced her attention back to the mass. They stood for the gospel. Monday meant awful shop bread for breakfast and tea with bits of leaves floating in it. She longed for a mouthful of Emer's homemade soda bread, chewy and sweet. First class was English, Sister Saint Mathew. Una tried to remember the lines she'd been assigned, lines 105 to 109 from the endless poem *Paradise Lost*. It didn't even rhyme. *What though the field be lost all is not lost the unconquered will.* That wasn't it, it was the conquerable will, or was it the conquered will? Una knew she'd have to rush to the classroom after breakfast and go over it again, and if Sister Saint Mathew caught her cramming she would know she hadn't learned it and would be sure to ask her. Learning poetry by heart made no sense.

Siobhan Byrne told Una and Eilish that everything had to be learned by heart so they'd do well in the examinations.

"Board of Commissioners gives a grant of money to the school if we do well. Poor examination results, no grant."

"My father gets a bill for my fees every three months, so what do the nuns need with more?"

"That's for extras like religious instruction, or music, or your room and board."

"In your eye!" Eilish hooted, "I should send the nuns a bill for staying in this dump of a cubicle and eating their rotten food, and for learning the rubbish of poetry Sister Saint Mathew gives us. What use is it?"

Eilish was a small curvy girl with dark brown wavy hair and bold brown eyes. Una thought her very pretty. Sometimes she'd have a pimple on the side of her nose or on her chin and she'd rub at it with a soapy sponge and complain, "It's the disgusting food we have to eat in this jail, Una."

Eilish was the first girl Una met the day she arrived at the convent, the previous September. Aunt Emer, Donny and Nan had driven her over in the trap and left her, Nan with a lot of tears and Emer with admonitions to take care of herself and write if she needed anything. The prefects were showing the new girls around. When the prefect took Una to the dormitory and found her cubicle, Eilish was sitting on the opposite bed, her back to the wall, legs straight out.

"No sitting on the beds," said the prefect.

Eilish got off very slowly, and when the prefect left she sat back up on the bed.

"My name's Eilish, what's yours?"

"Una."

Eilish jumped off the bed, crouched on the floor, slid a tin box from under the bed, and invited Una to have a piece of chocolate. The box held sweets, cake, and a box of raisins. Una hadn't been hungry that day. But often since she and Eilish shared tuck. They were supposed to bring the food to the refectory and have it at tea time, but no one did. In the break, after classes and before tea, they'd sit on Eilish's bed and munch on biscuits and cake. Una provided Aunt Emer's fruit cake, Marsh's biscuits or apples from Maura's old orchard that was now Uncle Joseph's. The nuns would be over in the chapel then, and if they heard the prefect coming, Eilish shoved the tuck box under her bed and Una tiptoed over to her own cubicle. They were busy tidying up the shelf or cupboard in their respective cubicles when the prefect looked in. Una felt a little guilty about the deception but Eilish always said, "What odds about it, are we supposed to starve? It's our own food. Everyone does it." Eilish was so assured, so confident. If she would take her lessons seriously, Una thought, she'd be the perfect friend.

In Slanabaille, Una had never made a friend. By the time she was ten and in fourth class she was the only girl in the little one room school who attended consistently. Most days Miss Clarke, the schoolmistress, would leave Una in charge of one of the junior classes at the back of the room while she taught the older classes. Una would supervise the first and second class pupils as they practiced penmanship, copying, *The sleeping fox catches no poultry*, over and over. Some days only twenty of the fifty children registered would be in school. Uncle Joseph said it was shameful people didn't send their children to school.

Eilish had gone to a large town school yet was no further ahead in her lessons than Una. She never studied, but Una thought she knew plenty about the world. She was from a big town, Athlone, where her parents owned a bar and grocery shop. Once Eilish had to stay in while the rest of the school went for a walk, and write a whole poem on the blackboard because she hadn't learned it for class. Una had offered to stay with her, but Sister Saint Mathew said no.

Today, in the second half of class Sister Saint Mathew might ask for lines from the play. Una knew them better than the poem. She could imagine the man or the woman who said them. Still they never seemed to get to the end in class, only as far as the long speeches, where you had to learn lines by heart. There was a story in it though. At the front of the book, opposite the page that said *The Works of William Shakespeare, Volume V*, was a picture of a lady in a white dress with black hair loose down around her shoulders. It reminded Una of her Aunt Emer, that night three years ago, when Una had awakened and felt her mother in the room beside her. She knew her mother's ghost was there. She heard it tap at the window. She felt the foul breath of the grave, smelled it, ripe, damp and rank as the breath of a cow when you loosed her neck chain to let her out to pasture. It was pitch dark and the ghost was beside her, hovering at the head of her bed, waiting for her to move. "Aunt Emer!" Una yelled but her ears heard no sound. She kept her eyes shut tight and screamed and screamed, louder and louder, soon reassured by her own voice, by the power to scream. When she opened her eyes Emer was standing by her bed.

"Shush Una, you'll wake Nan and Donny."

The candle she carried lit the upper part of her body strangely, a trunk, a white face, and a head with long black flowing hair, floating in the dark. She stooped and was Emer again, setting the candle on a chair and sitting on the bed. Nan was still asleep curled over at the wall.

"What's wrong Una? You frightened the life out of me, screaming like that."

"There's something in the room."

"Like a mouse or something, I'll bring in the cat."

"No, Aunt Emer, it's a ghost, I heard it tap at the window."

"It's windy tonight dear. It was just a branch hitting the pane you heard."

"I felt its breath. It was here beside me," Una sobbed.

"Nonsense, you were dreaming. There's no ghost. What would a ghost be doing here? You have Nan there with you and Donny and me in the other room."

"Aunt Emer, I think it was Mammy come back."

Emer put her arms round her. "Oh, I see. And why do you think that?"

"At school Greta Smith talks about the poor restless souls wandering about in the month of November and I thought Mammy might be restless and come back here. She was so small when she was dead, I knew her soul was gone somewhere else. Don't you remember how small she was?"

Aunt Emer just went on holding her for a long long time. Then she said "Una, your mother's spirit was too big to be sneaking in here. It was much bigger than her body, much bigger than we could ever see. It fills up the whole townland, it's that big. She's around all the time Una, like she always was, not skulking in here in the dark. When we bake bread, or we milk, or we walk to the river, she's there, like the wind blowing the clothes on the line, or the leaves falling, the rain or the blackberries we pick for jam. That's where she is. Remember that. Never forget that. She's all around. Not some silly ghost coming here in the dark. Not something to be afraid of."

"Can I talk to her?"

"Why wouldn't you, if you want to?"

Aunt Emer lay on the bed beside her and they dozed till Donny started to cry.

"I'll leave the candle, Una." Emer kissed her and left.

Una never did try talking to her mother, nor did she tell anyone else about that night, and Aunt Emer never mentioned it. But she remembered what Emer said. After a while she stopped weeping when she thought of her mother or when anyone mentioned her. She put her mother's death away in the back of her memory and began to picture her mother not exactly as she used to be, but as a big idea made up of hundreds and hundreds of small ideas, things she remembered her mother saying or doing or laughing at. Una had puzzled it out and weak tears, childish tears, didn't overwhelm her now when anyone talked of death. When she heard a lark, she remembered a July day when she was about seven. They had brought her father's dinner to him in the field. On the way back her mother spread her shawl on the hill, they lay on it and watched the gyring lark rise up, up in the blue sky, singing as it rose.

"Next month," her mother said, "you won't hear him at all. Too busy with his family."

There was the warm sun, the silence, the sharp strum of her father's whetstone as he sharpened his scythe three fields away, the furrow they left in the long grass at the side of the field coming and going, the wheaten colour of her mother's knitted summer shawl and the lumpy feel as Una lay on it.

Una wondered if Uncle Joseph thought about Angela. When her Grandmother Maura died two years ago, Una was intending to tell Uncle Joseph about the dead being an idea, but his face was so sad she didn't dare. Maura's feet and hands swelled up before she died, she couldn't put a foot out of bed, could hardly move or speak. Her face was brown and mottled, tight like the belly cats showed when they were full of milk and slept by the fire. Margaret Smith stayed with Maura when she was sick. Una heard her say to Lizzie "Sure that swelling, that's the coffin maker!" Una shivered. A coffin maker! But the day of the Month's Mind Mass Uncle Joseph said, "Ah, she's better off, she got out of it handy enough," and seemed to be himself again, so Una never told him her theory of the dead becoming an idea. Joseph certainly didn't cry, like Una used to, if anyone mentioned death. Sometimes he'd laugh! Last year after they all had measles Nan had put black ink spots all over her doll and pretended it was very sick and died. She had a funeral in the kitchen and Nan herself was the priest. She put a long dress on Donny and bossed him about, made him carry a candle and be the altar boy. She put the doll in a boot box and shook water on it. "Ashes to ashes, dust to dust, if God doesn't take you, the devil must," Nan intoned.

Uncle Joseph laughed very hard at that and said, "It's a good job girls can't be priests, Nan, you'd be great competition for the clerical students at the college in Maynooth!"

He looked at Aunt Emer but she pretended not to hear him. Sometimes Aunt Emer did that to Uncle Joseph. Ignored him deliberately. Aunt Emer! Again she was smothered in a black scalding anxiety. Aunt Emer! And she prayed hard for her intention. "Dear Mother of God grant my special intention."

Eilish, kneeling beside her, sat up on the seat. If Sister Agatha said anything about her not kneeling Eilish would pretend she was sick. "Oh Sister, I have such cramps, I have my monthly," she'd say. Sister Agatha would blush. "Don't mention that," she'd say, "it's unladylike to talk like that."

Eilish would giggle about it later. "The nuns, Una, are a bunch of old clucking hens."

Una was shocked at Eilish's talk. What if Siobhan Byrne told the nuns about it? Siobhan was a nun's pet, a stout round-faced girl with thick black eyebrows and long black hair tied in a black ribbon. She knew all about praying for things and doing novenas.

"If you do something nine times, like say the rosary nine days in a row at the same time, that prayer is always answered."

"How long do you have to wait for an answer, Siobhan?"

"Oh, maybe a long time. God makes you wait sometimes. Look at me I'm praying for the last three years at least for God to make my father stop drinking."

"I'll pray too, Siobhan."

"I wish you would. When he is on the batter we all tiptoe round the house. We don't say a word because he'd get in a rage and hit anyone who gets in his way. My mother's praying Seamus, the baby, or one of the other two lads, will be a priest. That'll make up for father's drinking."

If it was a very serious problem you prayed to Saint Jude, who was the saint of hopeless cases. Una was praying to Saint Jude for her own special intention. Now the priest was beginning the Agnus Dei. Mass would soon be over.

Every night before she went to bed Una knelt and said the rosary and a prayer to Saint Jude. She meant to do it for nine nights but had lost count. It was a lot more than nine. She'd started when she came back from Christmas holidays and now it was the first week of March. Last night, Sister Agatha told her to get into bed or she'd catch cold, so she finished the rosary in bed.

After mass, as they streamed downstairs on their way to the basement for breakfast, Una saw Sister Saint Mathew, her thick, black shawl clutched around her shoulders, her books held to her chest, heading for the classroom. Sister Saint Mathew was always cold. Just a little sparrow of a woman, she even wore her shawl on spring days. There would be no time now before class to learn the lines, *the unconquerable will, and the study of revenge.* That was it, she knew it. The trouble was, if you got one word wrong all was lost, you couldn't remember anything, stuck there in front of the whole class, trying.

When they stood behind their chairs waiting for grace Eilish whispered, "I saw old Mattie with her books, did you learn the lines, Una?"

Sister Agatha rapped her ring on the edge of the raised table in front of the room, "No talking before grace."

"Bless us, Oh Lord , and these thy gifts."

"Now you may be seated."

"Did she know I was talking Una? That one has it in for me."

"I don't think so."

"Do you know the bloody lines?"

"Yes, I think so."

Sister Saint Mathew didn't ask Una to recite that day. She asked a small, quiet girl named Elizabeth. Then they did another scene from the play. There was a ghost in the play but it was, Sister Saint Mathew said, just a dramatic device to start the action of the play and used in a later scene, when Hamlet was talking to his mother. Sister said if it were today, Shakespeare would probably use another device, maybe a dream, but Shakespeare liked to play to the crowd and in his day they believed in ghosts. So, Sister Saint Mathew didn't believe in ghosts either. Sister Saint Mathew said Hamlet was the most quoted play in the world. Una couldn't imagine herself quoting it. What could she quote? It was just a lot of words. She knew most of the speeches in the play. You had to know them for the examination. The speech in Act One where Hamlet wished he was dead, the lecture the old man gave his son about how he should behave in France, and the one Sister Mathew liked, *To be or not to be.* Just three to learn. She could manage that, and as Eilish said, "after the examination you could forget all about them."

Then it was mathematics with Sister Anne. Una liked mathematics, it made so much sense. She could always work it out. And it was about real things, money and the dimensions of land. And algebra and geometry were puzzles and riddles, there was always a solution and the answer was always an application of a rule. If you knew the rule you always got the answer. Sister Anne said she had a head for math. Una always got top marks and that made her very happy, because it would make Emer happy.

"GOOD CATHOLIC girls always are pure in thought, word, and deed. In mind and body."

Sister Cecelia was well launched into her Friday afternoon religious instruction. Last class of the week and she was having difficulty getting the girls' full attention. The lenses of her gold-rimmed spectacles caught the light and flashed as she turned her head to survey the first and second year students.

"God sees our thoughts, our inmost desires. Nothing is hidden from Him. A good girl abhors," and her voice dropped to a growl for emphasis, "abhors, all occasions of sin. This means, girls, this means that you must always, always, keep a safe and virtuous distance from boys."

There was a sudden quietness, then a squirmy, fidgety restlessness in the room. Listening, Una froze in horror, her throat closed over in panic. Aunt Emer! There was a mortal sin on Aunt Emer's soul. She would go straight to hell and burn in the fire. She was committing a mortal sin not once, but over and over again, and God saw.

Sister Cecelia said the souls of sinners in hell cried out day and night for even the smallest drop of water to ease their burning tongues. When they tried to climb from the fire pit, they were pushed back into the flames by devils with pitchforks. The fire didn't kill them, they stayed alive, burning for all eternity. Poor Emer. And Uncle Joseph too. Una thought they would grow to loathe each other in the flames. They would be filled with guilt and remorse and burn forever. That was the punishment for sins against chastity. Of course, sinners could repent. But Emer wasn't repenting. To indulge in the grossness of the flesh was a mortal sin. That's what the nuns taught. Only the holy sacrament of marriage made it acceptable.

Una hadn't really noticed when it began, she didn't notice until Christmas. When Uncle Joseph was visiting from Dublin, Aunt Emer went down the lane with him to the old house and Uncle

Joseph walked back with her late in the night. At first Una thought Emer was just going for a walk, to talk to Joseph, or to see her cattle. But the cattle were sold in October. One night at Christmas, after Donny and Nan were asleep, Una waited up to talk to Emer. Sitting at the window, she saw them come into the yard. Joseph had his arm around Emer. The moon shone straight down on them as they came up to the house. Una felt herself rigid with excitement watching what was forbidden. Joseph took Emer in his arms and kissed her. Una couldn't move. My God, that was a sin. Una stayed very still. With a rush of resentment she saw they had deceived her. How stupid of her not to notice before. All summer long they had been spending time together in the old house. She ran to her bedroom and hid under the bedclothes. When Aunt Emer looked in, she pretended to be asleep but she couldn't sleep, couldn't wipe that scene of Emer in Joseph's arms out of her mind.

Two days later, Christmas break was over. Indignant at their behavior and terrified for their souls, Una was almost glad to come back to school. There she could pray for them every day at mass and offer up novenas asking for one special intention: that Uncle Joseph and Aunt Emer stop their terrible sins, or get married and be excused. They must get married, for she knew they would never give it up.

"Our Lady blushes, blushes with shame, girls," Sister Cecelia continued, "blushes if a Child Of Mary transgresses against modesty, or commits a sin against holy purity."

Una felt herself flush scarlet and then grow very cold. If Sister Cecelia knew about her aunt she would surely tell the Reverend Mother and the other nuns and they'd think Una was a sinner too, from a bad breed, a family of sinners. Now Sister Cecelia wrote on the blackboard *Motherhood*, and, below that *Vocation for the Religious Life*.

"These are the two great callings for good Catholics, for children of Mary. The greatest gift you can give to God is to offer yourself as a nun in his service." She looked up to heaven for emphasis. "There is no greater honour or joy than this, girls. No greater honour than to renounce the world. Many girls have a vocation and are not aware of it." She lowered her head and looked over her spectacles at the class. There was an uncomfortable, expectant, stillness as if she might suddenly single some girl out. "I know there are girls here who have the call. God needs nuns to do His work. Pray, pray daily, or twice a day, for the gift of a vocation." The end of the word vocation was drowned in the ringing of the class bell, the shuffling of feet and the opening and closing of desks.

"Girls, girls, we will continue next week. Girls, please leave in an orderly fashion, quietly, no running!"

Eilish waited for her in the corridor outside the classroom. "What's wrong Una? You look like you're going to cry."

"Oh, nothing at all, nothing."

"Come on up to the dorm, I got a parcel from home."

Una followed her miserably. They sat on her bed. Una still had Christmas cake and nuts left, but she wasn't hungry.

"I thought the bell would never ring, that Cecelia going on and on about holy purity. What she wants is for us all to be nuns, Una. That's all, turn us into nuns." Eilish was unwrapping a package of McVittie and Price biscuits. "And you've got a face as long as a wet week. What's the matter?"

"Oh Eilish, I'm so worried," and her voice was flat and dull, so cleaned of all expression that Eilish stopped rummaging in her tuck box and sat on the bed beside her.

"My God, Una, what's wrong?"

"It's my Aunt Emer and Uncle Joseph. I can't sleep, worrying about them. They are committing mortal sin. They spend hours at night together down in the old house, and Eilish, I've seen them kissing."

"Sure what odds about that, they're married, they're entitled."

"They're not married."

"What? Are they brother and sister then? Oh My God! Jesus Mary and Joseph, Una, that's the world's worst mortal sin, that's incest."

"No, they're not, they're not," Una defended them hotly, tears starting in her eyes. "They're not. Aunt Emer is my father's sister and Uncle Joseph is my mother's brother!"

"Oh, well, that's nothing then."

"It's a sin. Sister Cecelia says it's a mortal sin if the couple are not married."

"That's just old nun's talk. You didn't tell her about them, did you?"

"No. I was going to but I was afraid of what she might say. She would say their souls are damned."

"Well, don't tell her. She's always trying to scare us. Pay her no mind. When my mother talked to me about boys she never said anything about sin, not one word, only that a girl could be cheap and disgrace herself."

Una watched her with wary eyes. What was she going to say next? Eilish held out the biscuit package. Una shook her head. "I'm not hungry."

"Come on skinny, have a biscuit." Una took the proffered treat and Eilish continued. "Una, I was so completely disgusted by the whole business and what my mother was telling me, I told her she never never had to worry. Didn't you think it was grotesque when you heard it first?"

"No, not really. When you live on a farm you know all about it from the animals."

"Well, I'm never doing it, Una."

"Neither am I."

"Who told you about it?"

"Aunt Emer talked to me."

"Did she say it was a sin?"

"No, I don't remember her saying anything about sin, only that I had to wait till I was married in case I had a baby. And if I had a baby, and I was not married, people would treat me badly, say I was a tramp, and look down on me. Anyway, I'm never doing that. And I'm never getting married, either."

"See Una, what did I tell you? She never mentioned sin, there's no sin. And in the play Sister Saint Mathew never mentions sin, it's all about Hamlet being a prince and so not marrying that one Ophelia because she's not a princess. And anyway, he's going crazy, right off his head. And her old dodderer of a father never mentions sin either. Just talks about playing hard to get. If it was a question of sin, Mattie would have said so. The nuns never miss a chance to talk about sin. There's no sin."

"Sister Cecelia says there is, unless you're married."

"Rubbish. What does she expect, that we're nuns?"

"She said it was an occasion of sin to even be with boys, that all contact with men was a sin unless you're married."

Eilish stopped eating. "So marriage makes a sin all right! That's nonsense. How can that be? What about murder? What if the nuns had a ceremony that made murder alright? Murder would be a sin unless you had the ceremony first."

"Well, in a way it is like that Eilish, murder is not a sin if you are at the front."

A hurt look crossed Eilish's face. Una realized she was thinking of her brother and cringed at her own thoughtlessness.

"Oh, Eilish! I didn't mean anything by that, I'm sorry, what I meant was there's all sorts of rules."

"Well, the rules are all so that girls won't get pregnant before they are married."

Una,clapped her hands over her face.

"Una, what's wrong?"

"My God, what if Emer gets pregnant?"

"So! If she does she will get married in one big hurry, I promise you that, and you'll have a double cousin."

"She could die having a baby, that would be horrible," her voice broke a little and she turned her face away like a sad penitent child. "That's how my mother died."

Eilish put her arms around her. "Oh Una, Una, don't be so sad. I can't bear it when you're upset. It's awful about your mother. I know that. I'm so sorry about it, I know that was terrible, but your aunt won't die I promise you, you couldn't have that much bad luck. No one could."

"Well, I'm praying so hard, every day, that they will get married."

"I'll pray, too."

"Maybe if I gave up something for Lent."

"Maybe, anyway we have to give up tuck. The nuns won't let us have parcels in Lent."

"I'd give anything if they would get married."

"Una, do you remember your mother?"

"Of course, I was ten when she died."

"Do you look like her?"

"Not at all. She had red hair, curly red hair and she was not tall like me. She was beautiful. My grandmother said when she got ready to go to a dance she would have every candle in the house up in her bedroom while she put up her hair and tried on dresses. Lizzie Scanlon, an old woman at home, told me the men were all dying about her but she only wanted my father."

"It must have been awful, Una, when she died."

"It was. As time went on it got better. But sometimes I'd see something and think it was nice, and then I'd think but Mammy's dead, and I couldn't enjoy it. But I'm over that now."

"Still and all you must miss her a lot."

"Not so much any more, not like in the beginning. In the beginning I wanted to die too, I cried if I even thought of her. I wanted us all to die and be together again. I'm over that for a long time now, and I don't cry any more like I used to. I like to talk about her sometimes, but I can't at home in case I make Nan sad. Nan doesn't remember her."

"You can talk to me."

"Yes, Eilish I know that, that's the one nice thing about being here at school. I can talk to you."

"Have you the English lines by heart for Monday?"

"I think so, we have to read on in the play too, as far as the end of Scene Four. I haven't done that yet. Have you?"

"Oh, I went over it, more old rigmarole. She's going to do it in class because I said last week it was boring old rubbish. She didn't get mad at me though. If it was Sister Anne I'd have been put to stand outside the door."

"If she's going to do it in class I won't bother to read it, I have math to do, and I have to learn the history notes yet, that bit about the Third Estate."

They heard footsteps, other girls up to the dormitory for a break and a snack. Eilish shoved the tuck box under the bed. Music drifted up from the senior study hall. The senior girls were playing records on the big oak gramophone. Una was fascinated by the music from the gramophone. She had never heard such a thing. She wished she had taken music as a subject, but had declined because it would have meant paying an extra fee. "Eilish, let's go down to the hall and listen to the music on the gramophone."

In the hall the chairs and desks were pushed back against the back wall and the gramophone was playing a Strauss tune. Some girls were up waltzing. Josephine Murphy, a small black-haired girl, was dancing with Eithne Heffernan. Eithne was a prefect. Josephine was Sister Anne's special pet. She cleaned off the blackboard for Sister Anne and when the math exercise books were to be collected Josephine jumped up to do it and then to carry them for her. When the first and second year girls went for a walk, Josephine walked with Sister Anne and the other nun at the back of the line. Eilish said anyone who hung around nuns like that was a gom. Still, lots of girls attached themselves to a particular nun or senior girl. Sometimes when she had first come to the school Una had been envious because she wasn't a nun's or some senior's favourite, but then she reminded herself she had Eilish.

"Come on, Una, we'll dance."

"I don't know how. I've only danced sets, Eilish, like *The Walls of Limerick*, you know how they do in the country."

"Come on, let's have a waltz, I'll show you," and she pulled Una up on the floor.

Una was stiff and clumsy, head and shoulders taller than Eilish and they bumped into other couples.

"Look down at my feet Una, it's easy, this way, one two, three, one two three. That's it, one two three. It's really very easy."

After a few minutes, Una had learned the steps and they circled around the floor.

"Now Una, stop looking at your feet, if a fellow asks you to dance, you want to talk to him, not look at your feet."

Una stiffened and missed a step, then recovered. Dance like this with a boy? She couldn't imagine it. It would be an occasion of sin. Eilish was so smart, there was nothing she didn't know. Una's serge uniform and lisle stockings were heavy and warm, but they kept waltzing. The gramophone began to wind down. When the music stopped Eilish asked, "Did you ever kiss a boy?"

Una froze. This was wrong, forbidden, a sin, maybe even a mortal sin. Sister Cecelia would say it was a mortal sin. What was Eilish asking?

"No, never."

"Never Una, never, not even once?" She made it sound like Una was lying. "Was there no likely lad at home?"

"No."

"I did."

"Did you Eilish? Who?"

"The fellow who works behind the bar at home."

This was secret, exciting, and dangerous. Had Eilish told that sin to the priest in confession? If she had, what did the priest say? What would Sister Cecelia say?

"I'm never going to kiss a boy."

"Don't be daft, Una. It was great. I felt as if everything in the world stopped and waited when we kissed. Next day I wanted to do it again. That's why they sent me here. They thought I was getting too wild."

There were clearly depths to Eilish of which Una had never dreamed. "Were you getting wild?"

"No, it's just that they were afraid I'd get into trouble, but I wouldn't. I was just kissing him for fun."

How worldly and grown up Eilish was. She knew about everything, could joke and laugh about anything, not like Una, whose whole world had darkened, narrowed with worry and dread. If only she could talk to Emer about it, but she couldn't. Emer and Joseph were looming shadows of anxiety. If only they would just get married. Or if Nan was old enough to talk to. Maybe if she had never come to school in Obanbeg, Emer would not be committing sin.

"Eilish, did you mind coming here?"

"Not really, I'm sixteen you know. I spent more than a year helping in the shop after National School. I was going to be a shop assistant. I'm the only one left to do it, with Terry in France and Declan training for a teacher. My sisters are in New York."

"Why didn't you stay at it?"

"They hired another lad to help in the bar and sent me here. I was fed up in the shop anyway. I wasn't ready to settle into that."

"Why did you do it, did they make you?"

"No, I felt a bit sorry for my father after Terry joined up. He didn't want him to, but Terry hated the shop. He wanted to get away. When the recruiting officers came to Athlone he signed up. He was only eighteen. Once you sign up there's nothing to be done. You have to go and you can't get out of the army till the war is over. My mother says the rosary twice a day that he'll be safe." Eilish's voice sounded sad, and Una thought how unusual it was for her spunky friend to be anything but cheerful.

"I'm sure he will. I'll pray too."

The gramophone started up again, but before anyone had a chance to dance the tea bell rang.

"Friday. Bloody eggs. It's a good job I had tuck," Eilish declared. "I love tuck, nothing like tuck," she sang, "Don't you think I should've been in the Gilbert and Sullivan concert at Christmas, Una? I love tuck, wonderful tuck."

As they turned at the bottom of the stairs they saw Sister Agatha standing in the corner, her hands hidden in the folds of her big loose sleeves. "Eilish, come here!"

When she rejoined Una at tea she whispered, "The old rip, I have to stay home from the morning walk on Sunday for singing out in line. And I was dying for a walk. Maybe it'll be raining and there'll be no walk. Anyway, I'll get the English lines learned."

After tea Sister Agatha gave out the post. The girls crowded round. Una wasn't expecting letters. Aoife O'Keefe, a timid little girl who was only twelve, pulled at the nun's sleeve. "Sister is there no letter for me?"

The nun pushed her away roughly. "Don't touch the holy habit, Aoife."

Aoife walked away.

Eilish drove her elbow into Una. "The old hag, holy habit my eye," she muttered.

"Eilish," Una whispered, "be quiet, she'll hear you."

IT DIDN'T RAIN on Sunday and Una walked with Siobhan Byrne. Una told Siobhan she had a very special intention, a private intention, a secret.

Siobhan said one way to get a special intention was to make a promise, strike a bargain with God. "You could promise something," Siobhan told her, "like to make a pilgrimage to Loch Dearg."

On Sunday afternoon, Aunt Emer and Uncle Joseph came for visiting day. When Una went to the parlour she peeked in at the side of the lace curtain that covered the glass in the parlour door. Uncle Joseph was sitting on the sofa, close to Aunt Emer. They weren't holding hands or anything. He on his way back to Dublin after spending the weekend with Emer and the children. Una knocked politely and went in. Aunt Emer hugged her. Uncle Joseph shook hands. He asked Una what she was learning. She told him about not liking English, that Irish wasn't too bad, the nuns didn't emphasize it much, and how well she did in mathematics. "Good girl, but English is very important. You'll get to like it after a while."

"I don't like learning it by heart."

"I know, but that's the way it's set up Una. Later on you'll be glad you know poetry by heart."

Aunt Emer brought her a cake.

"I don't know about the cake, Aunt Emer. Maybe you should take it back. Sister Cecelia said we must mortify ourselves for Lent. Lent starts in two weeks.

"Well, that doesn't mean you're not to eat. If you don't eat you'll get sick. As it is you're very thin."

At the other end of the parlour two senior students were talking to their visitors. Una was afraid they might hear and think her aunt's words implied some criticism of the nuns.

Emer had a letter that had come from her father for Una to read. Her father wrote such short letters, one page in his heavy, careful handwriting, with no news. "Is Daddy thinking of coming home, Aunt Emer?"

"He hasn't mentioned it lately."

"I'd like to see him."

"It's not that safe for him to come now, ships are not safe in the North Atlantic, there's a submarine war on," Joseph told her.

Emer looked closely at Una. She seemed remote, as if she were preoccupied. Maybe Una was lonely. "It's not long to the Easter holidays. Nan is counting the days."

"And then," said Joseph, "it's the short term. No time till you're home for the summer."

"In the summer, Una, I'm going to get some work done on the house, get a stove put in."

"Will we have water from the pump brought into the kitchen?"

"Yes, we will."

"Your aunt will have more amenities than the Shelbourne Hotel," Joseph teased.

Emer ignored him.

Una looked hard at them. She felt distant from Emer. Had Emer gone down to the old house with Joseph on the weekend? They looked the same. If only they would get married. If her father came home he'd make them get married. He'd have a good serious talk with them. Three years ago Mary Devoy's father discovered her in the hay shed with Patrick Brady and made them get married. With Mary's uncle he went down to J.J. Mahon's where Patrick was drinking, dragged him out of the pub and shouted at him. "You have my daughter ruined, if you don't do right by her I'll knock the head off you, I'll kill you." The whole townland talked about it. Lizzie said Mary's father was perfectly right. Of course, Aunt Emer didn't look ruined, she looked radiant. Her pink wool dress had a pleated skirt, white collar and cuffs.

"Your dress is lovely, Aunt Emer."

"Thank you, Una. At Easter, we'll have to get you some new clothes. You've outgrown everything. It would be nice for you to have something stylish. I'll leave you *The Independent* so you can see the styles," and looking at Joseph she added, "at least it's not the *Roscommon Herald*."

"Ah Emer, I'll make a Republican of you yet."

Una couldn't believe it. They were flirting. Had they no shame? Now she was sure they had gone down to the old house together on Saturday. She wondered if Lizzie knew Joseph and Emer spent all that time down in the old house. Maybe Lizzie would talk to them.

"Una, are you all right? You don't look yourself somehow."

"I'm fine, Aunt Emer."

It was time for Joseph to leave to catch his train. She kissed her aunt goodbye, shook hands with her uncle, and went slowly and miserably back to the dormitory with her cake, deciding as she went that the only thing to do was pray harder and promise a great and terrible sacrifice so God would make them get married.

On Monday, Sister Saint Mathew didn't ask anyone to recite. Instead she wanted to know if they were reading the play.

"Elizabeth, for whom was safe passage through Denmark requested by messengers of the king of Norway?"

"For Fortinbras."

"Correct. Very good, Elizabeth."

"Who informed Hamlet that the players were on their way to Elsinore? Siobhan?"

"Rosencrantz."

"Very good, Siobhan."

"To this point does the Queen suspect her husband has murdered his brother?"

Several hands went up.

"Joan."

"No, Sister."

Una's pale face turned even paler and she slid down a bit in her seat. If Sister Saint Mathew kept up this questioning she knew her turn would come and she hadn't read the play, had just looked it over lightly. She'd spent all her time learning the assigned lines. I detest English, she thought, all these long speeches. Eilish is right, it's a complete waste of time. If she asks me a question I'll die.

Sister Saint Mathew went in a different direction. "Now girls, we come to this weeks assigned scenes. We have seen that Hamlet, bidden by his father's ghost to revenge his murder, is assailed by doubts, considers suicide, rejects Ophelia and insults her and devises a strategy to confirm the King's guilt by observing his reaction to a play." She paused and looked around the class.

"Elizabeth, when Hamlet has an opportunity to kill the King why does he not kill him?"

"Because the King is praying."

"Joan, do you think the King suspects Hamlet is plotting against him?"

"Yes, Sister."

"How do you know that?"

"Because he orders him to go to England."

"Correct."

"Girls, would you agree that Hamlet is a mystery, Joan?"

"Yes, Sister."

"Why?"

"I don't know."

"Oh! Una?"

Una was stuck. "Is it because he is always acting, he acts differently with different people?"

"Very good, Una, that's a big part of it, but it's also because we really never know why he does anything. Like all humans he's mysterious. And of course, he was a superb actor. Remember his address to the players!"

Una felt a wave of satisfaction flow over her. She'd known the answer. She wasn't sure how she knew it, but she did. Sister Saint Mathew was going on with the lesson. "Why Hamlet defers his revenge is a question that has been debated by scholars for three centuries. We won't debate it here. All we know is that Hamlet faced a great decision, a crisis, a crossroads. We might wonder if Horatio had been a different character, would Hamlet have behaved differently? What Shakespeare meant is a great enigma. To this point, Hamlet has not raised his arm against anyone, he is blameless in action but not in thought. Not in thought! Everything has occurred in his mind. The tension in the play heightens as he plans his revenge, there's so much happening we don't notice the time. Did you not find when you read it that there was a world of action taking place?"

No one offered an opinion on this. Una had barely skimmed the scenes, in all honesty she couldn't say she had read it.

"Well girls, if you saw it performed on the stage you would know there was a world of action going on: war, intrigue, theatrics. The play is more than half over when Hamlet confronts his mother," she spread her hands, "and the ghost, his father's ghost, reappears."

Una felt the teacher's eyes on her. What question was coming?

"At the end of that scene is Hamlet still blameless, Una?

"No, Sister."

"Correct Una, he will be a murderer, won't he? Now Elizabeth you begin at *What wilt thou do? Thou wilt not murder me?*"

"*Thou wilt not murder me? Help Help Ho,*" Elizabeth droned.

"Elizabeth! Think! Think! You have to plead with him, his mother is terrified, can't you see that?"

Elizabeth tried again.

"That's a little better. Now your turn Siobhan!"

"Polonius, *what, ho, help, help, help.*"

"Siobhan, shout it, the man is terrified."

"*What ho, help help help,*" Siobhan screamed. The class erupted in laughter. The nun ignored the laughing.

"Now that's better Siobhan! You're next Joan."

"Hamlet, *How now a rat, dead for a ducat, dead.*"

"Joan, give it some feeling. He's stabbing him. This is murder, murder!" and the dumpy little nun made several vicious backward slashes with her pencil, demonstrating the stabbing. Her shawl slid to the floor. Una watched. So this was what it was, this was how it was done! Why hadn't she seen it before? There was giggling from the back of the class. The nun went on as before.

"Continue Siobhan!"

"*Oh, I am slain.*"

"Siobhan, the man is wounded. Dying, groan Siobhan, groan, drag it out, make us believe he's drawing his last breath. Like this Siobhan. "*I am slain,*" she shrieked. The class broke into nervous laughter. Una listened and watched very closely as the tiny woman put life to the dialogue. What a world of feeling and action she was showing them.

The class continued with Sister Saint Mathew now playing Hamlet, now Gertrude, now the Ghost. Finally, as Hamlet prepares to leave and take the dead Polonius with him, she stooped, and bent almost in two, and slowly walking backwards lifted and dragged her shawl along the floor, as if it had the weight of a dead man. "*I'll lug the guts into the neighbour room,*" she grunted glee-fully.

Una was transfixed. The antic spectacle of the old nun, jump-ing and cavorting about, impersonating a young man committing murder, was as astounding as if the sun had come up out of the west and shone a light through the mist. Una fell in love, forever, with words and with plays, with Shakespeare and the English lan-guage.

"Wasn't it marvelous Eilish? Didn't you love it? The way she acted the murder!"

"Ah Mattie, she's a right old actress."

"But, wasn't she great?"

"Well, there's a bit of life in her anyway, not like that old rip Agatha who never opens her mouth except to give someone a bad mark."

They were on their way to dinner. "Listen Eilish, listen, the choir is practicing *Stabat Matar dolorosa*. Isn't it lovely and so sad?"

"It is. They're getting ready for Easter, tomorrow is Shrove Tuesday you know, pancakes, and we have to finish our tuck. No tuck in Lent, Una. Old fish and porridge and tapioca pudding. I hate that stuff. It's like frog spawn."

LENT DRAGGED ON. Outside the days lengthened, shafts of spring sunlight pierced the gloom of the classroom, fading out the chalk on the blackboard. Sometimes Una looked out through the win-dows and thought of Nan at home. She would have her skipping rope out. There was no after-class break, only Stations of the Cross in the chapel. The food was even worse than before, fish for dinner Wednesday as well as Friday. Monday and Thursday was mutton stew. This Lenten fare added to Una's lack of appetite. The stew, in particular, was tasteless and greasy.

"Bloody lucky dip," said Eilish, scooping up a fork-full of the grey slop, and letting it drip back on the plate. "You never know what you might find in it, maybe a pound note."

Una sliced a grey looking potato, not really intending to eat it.

"Una don't look so glum. Lent won't last forever."

On Friday, Sister Cecelia again exhorted the girls to pray for the grace of a vocation. "The greatest gift we can give God, girls, is to offer our lives up as a sister in His service. No greater honour or sacrifice girls, no greater joy." She held up her hands in the big loose sleeves for emphasis. She looked theatrical in her black pleated habit as she lifted her arms, a thick leather belt tight around her young waist, her laced shoes and slim, elegant ankles a sudden, secular surprise under her heavy skirt.

The girls whispered Eithne Heffernan had a vocation, and that two other girls had talked to Sister Cecelia about vocations.

Aunt Emer wrote to say Donny had a bad chest cold so she wouldn't be visiting for a few weeks. It rained incessantly for almost a week, afternoon walks were cancelled. Una looked out the study hall window, the view obscured by the heavy rain, and thought of Emer warming camphorated oil in a pot of hot water and sitting before the warm fire with Donny on her knee. She imagined the pungent smell as Emer uncorked the oil and rubbed it on his little white chest. She remembered Donny's high thin shoulders. When there was illness in the little family routines were relaxed and they all drew closer together in a cosy intimacy. For a few minutes, she forgot how angry she was with Emer.

The second Thursday in March the sun came out, and they lined up after dinner for a walk, two by two in a long crocodile, senior girls first, two nuns bringing up the rear. In the convent vegetable garden lay sisters were digging, their skirts pinned up, hands red and raw from wind.

"I think they have the worst of it," Una remarked.

Eilish didn't agree. "If you want to really live a humble life that's the one Una. That's a real sacrifice, scrubbing and cooking and working on the farm and praying. Sure the nuns that teach have it easy, never a hand's turn in the kitchen or on the land, just boss us around and do the odd bit of praying."

"Which one would you like to be, Eilish?"

"Me? You must be joking! None of them. It's the Kerry order for me. You know Una, that order?" Eilish linked arms with her. "That order, where you have two heads on one pillow and two pairs of shoes under the bed. That's the one for me! But you'd make a good nun, the nuns would love to get you." Two heads on one pillow; something caught her breath, something hot, forbidden, a bad thing. Emer and Joseph.

"Eilish, you said you were never getting married!"

"I can change my mind. It all depends, depends if I meet a nice lad."

The line straggled out beyond the big black iron gates and along the Dublin road. The chattering of the students floated up to where telegraph lines penciled long loops against the sky and disturbed the flocks of gossiping sparrows in the sycamores. Last year's nests still hung in branches budding with leaf, left behind like lonely remnants of desertion or signs of something lost. Restless rooks and crows congregated at the tops of trees, cawing hoarsely, changing tree perches and cawing again. In the farm fields, the ploughed earth stank of manure.

"I wish it was Easter Una, I'm sick of school and Lent."

"It's not long now. It's early this year. Easter Sunday is April eighth. That's not long Eilish, and we go home the Wednesday before Easter. That's just three weeks away."

The line moved closer to the edge of the road as two lorries crowded with soldiers lumbered by in a cloud of dust. The men stared down at the line of girls, their young faces grinning. The girls looked up at the line of bristling guns. There was a hard March brightness to the day.

"Those lads are probably on their way to France," Siobhan said behind them.

"No, Siobhan," Eilish turned round to disagree with her. "They're just from the barracks, if they were going to France they would be going the other direction, towards Dublin." Hearing Siobhan corrected for once was very satisfying to Una.

"I can't wait for Easter and a decent meal," sighed Eilish.

Una, too, was weary of the monotonous round of class and prayers; after the walk there would be French and then Geography. No break before tea, Stations of the Cross instead. No tuck, and after tea, endless study in the big hall.

"No TALKING, GIRLS. No whispering." Sister Cecelia was taking junior study hall. She glared over her gold-rimmed glasses at the fifty girls sitting in five rows of desks. Two students in the back row, who had been talking, assumed studious expressions. For a few minutes, all was still. No rustle of paper, no shuffling of feet. Then the scrape of nibs on paper, the hiss of the gas lights along the wall, an occasional cough. It was dark outside, the windows tall black holes. The grate in the big coal stove in the middle of the room glowed red.

Eilish, whose desk was closest to the stove, put up her hand.

"What is it, Eilish?"

"Please Sister, can I move my desk, I'm roasted to death."

"No, Eilish, you must learn patience, that is a small thing to bear, to be too hot." Eilish's brown eyes flashed anger. Una could almost hear her think: "the old rip."

There was a knock on the door. Everyone stopped working and looked up. Eithne Heffernan entered. She had a whispered conversation with Sister Cecelia. The nun got up from her desk and went outside with her, closing the door. Immediately the room exploded in talk. The door opened again and the nun came back. She did not remark on the talking but walked straight to Eilish. They whispered together. Una, sitting behind, thought she heard her say something about the Mother Superior's office. Eilish went out with the nun and Eithne Heffernan sat at the nun's desk.

"Please, everyone go on with your work."

"Where's Eilish gone?" a girl in the front row asked.

"I don't know, she has a visitor in the parlor."

A visitor on a Thursday, and so late in the evening? Then the bell clanged and there was shuffling of feet and the squeak of desktop hinges as the girls stood up.

"Line up girls, line up."

"I wonder what's up with Eilish," Siobhan whispered.

"I don't know."

"No talking in line, girls."

They filed out two by two, down the broad stairs to the basement refectory for cocoa. As they passed the second study hall, the line was joined by intermediate and senior girls.

They took their places, standing behind their chairs, at the long tables. Sister Agatha stood on the raised platform at the head of the refectory to say the grace.

Bless us, oh Lord, and these thy gifts…

"You may be seated. Mother Superior wishes to have a word with you."

Una hadn't noticed the Mother standing beside the dais. She was conscious of Eilish's empty chair beside her. The nun stood up on the platform and pushed back her veil impatiently.

"Girls, I have very sad news to tell you. Eilish Hoolihan's brother is missing in France. Eilish has gone home to be with her parents. I want you all to offer special prayers for Eilish and her family. When you have finished your cocoa, we will have prayers in the chapel."

Someone drew a loud intake of breath like a sob. Elizabeth, across the table from Una, began to cry softly. Tears, threatening to overflow, stung Una's eyes. Terry, Eilish's big brother, just nineteen and joined up for fun, to see the world, to get away from home.

Siobhan left her place and came up beside her. "That's awful, Una. It's terrible. It means he's dead, when they are missing they are always dead. Poor Eilish."

"Maybe not, maybe not, maybe he's just wounded."

"Then they'd say he was wounded."

The girls filed out silently. Una felt guilty about her conversation with Eilish earlier, on their walk. Why didn't I remember he was in France? She thought poor Eilish, if only I had known. Today, when we were walking and talking and the soldiers passed he was already dead. And those soldiers, they were so young. Maybe Eilish was wrong, maybe they were going to France.

Because it was Lent, statues in the chapel were shrouded with black cloths. In front of them lamps threw only faint light. At the side of the communion rails, small votive candles flickered. The rest was in shadow. The mutter of the rosary droned on and on. Una wanted to go to the dormitory, to be alone and quiet and think about that place in France, the Somme, where Colonel Darling had been killed in July and Uncle Joseph said was a slaughterhouse. Where Terry, Eilish's brother, was now lost. Was he forgotten, in some wet trench? Or a straggler who couldn't catch up? Maybe he was still alive, hiding in some ditch. Or stiff dead on some road. How cruel and terrifying the war was. Suddenly everything changed. When she next saw Eilish, Eilish would be the girl whose brother was killed. Una would be the one who had made a great promise to God. She knew now the promise she had made that morning in the chapel at mass was a perfect solution to all her worries. Looking at the postulants, so calm and devout, Una had promised God that she would become a nun and enter the Sisters of the Cross and Resurrection if God made Emer and Joseph get married. There had been no private time with Eilish to tell her about it. She had intended to tell her tonight. Now, maybe her promise would be something good to share with Eilish when she came back, to distract her in her grief. To leave the awful world where young men were slaughtered would not be such a sacrifice Una thought. The convent would be far from war.

She lay curled up in bed, wakeful and sad, her heart contracted with worry. She looked over at Eilish's empty bed, longing to see her, talk to her, be the one with whom Eilish shared all her sadness. She could tell Eilish how her brother might one day become an idea, a part of everything, of the meaning of things, just as Una's mother was to her, so that when Una considered something it was in a different light because of Angela, because of what Angela had said or done or might have done. Strange that when she thought about being a nun she couldn't imagine what Angela would say. Why was that? Una remembered again the walk in the afternoon, how long ago that seemed, the soldiers on the road. Those soldiers were no longer something vaguely frightening, but boys who might be struck by bullets, who might tumble and bounce back dead in the mud of some field, left for dogs and foxes to rend and chew. Una desperately wished she had told Eilish the promise she had made to God.

No one knew when Eilish would return. Sister Saint Mathew said probably not till after Easter. In English class, in poetry, Una felt the sweep of it. In *Paradise Lost* Satan was plotting war, stirring up his troops. In drama class, Sister Saint Mathew said Shakespeare was never wrong about tragedy, that before the play was over eight people would die, and all because no one was able to understand how their own mind worked. No one was able to pull back from the edge of disaster. Pride, vanity, blind arrogance, drove them on.

Now Una studied English, she didn't just learn the lines. Sister Saint Mathew frequently called on her to read to the class and when she had to leave for any reason, left Una in charge. Una would sit up at the teacher's raised desk, tall, thin, and pale, her long, heavy plat of coarse blonde hair and light blue eyes in her square serious face. She would look over the heads of the other students and think to herself, when I am a teaching nun this is where I'll sit. And when I teach English I'll teach just like Sister Saint Mathew, I will make it real for my students, as real as if they lived it.

On Friday, Sister Cecelia was absent and the junior girls sat at the back of the seniors' religion class. Most of the junior girls read their English texts or did math assignments. Una listened because it was Sister Saint Mathew. She didn't teach, she didn't talk at all. She wrote on the blackboard, *to be detached is to care nothing for what others say or think about us but to go about our own work because it is our duty.*

The senior girls talked about it. Was Jesus detached? Could you be rich and successful and be detached? What it seemed to mean was that you did what you thought right, no matter what anyone else thought. Was that a bit like Emer? Did she think it all right to spend all that time down in the old house with Uncle Joseph? But, it was a mortal sin. Did Aunt Emer tell the priest in confession? What if she died before she repented? No one knew when they might die. She looked at the faces around her. Had anyone else the same worry? Did anyone else have a sister or brother or aunt committing mortal sin, in danger of dying with a sin on their soul? How sure of themselves the seniors were! They advanced their opinions and spoke up in class. Sister Saint Mathew said nothing at all. What a strange way of teaching. When the bell rang, Una wished the class would begin again.

If Eilish were here they could talk about it. Siobhan had missed it, she'd been allowed out with her brother who was emigrating to Australia. She had tea in the hotel and was full of news. It was said there would be conscription and that old men, as old as fifty, might have to fight. Some Republicans had been sent to jail. There had been an election in Roscommon and the Sinn Fein candidate won. His name was Plunkett. Una wondered if he was a relation of Tom and Cassie. She'd ask Emer.

Emer wrote, Donny was much better and she'd probably come to visit the next Sunday. The first Sunday in April. That was April Fool's Day! Una didn't really expect her. Term was almost over. Siobhan said it was now against the law to sing Republican songs. But in the pubs people sang them anyway. War songs were alright, like *It's A Long Way To Tipperary*. Una wondered if customers sang in Eilish's father's pub in Athlone.

On Friday evening, one of the senior girls thumped the piano in the senior study hall. Una hated the song, it was so cruel, so full of hate she wanted to stuff her ears. Didn't the girls know Eilish's brother had probably being killed in a trench?

"If you were the only Boch in the trench
And I had the only bomb,
Nothing else would matter in the world that day,
I could blow you up into eternity.
Chamber of horrors just made for two,
With nothing to spoil our fun."

The door opened and Sister Cecelia stepped in. "Girls, I'm shocked. You know you are not to sing that song! Close that piano, Bridget. I'm surprised at you. And Holy Week so close. You should be ashamed of yourselves. You should be praying for the dead in the war."

Sister Cecelia was pale as a lily, her cheeks hollow and wan. Her eyes had grown huge and glittered behind her spectacles The big leather belt was slipping from her waist on to her hips. She is fasting thought Una, mortifying the flesh, fasting for Lent. Next year she herself might already be a postulant fasting and praying in the convent. It depended on Emer and Joseph, if God made them get married. Wednesday, the Easter holidays would start and maybe during the holidays God would make them get married.

SATURDAY, JUST before tea she heard the prefect call from the door of the dormitory, "Una Maguire, you have visitors in the parlour."

Visitors on a Saturday? Una ran down and paused at the parlor door to peep in at the side of the curtains. She saw Joseph standing, his back to the door, examining the big painting *The Stag At Bay*.

She didn't see Emer. A lady in green was sitting with her back to the door, head bent forward, exposing short, bobbed hair and a white neck. Wondering who she was visiting, Una knocked softly and opened the door. The lady stood up and turned around. It was Emer. Emer with her all her hair cut off!

"Aunt Emer, you cut your hair."

"I thought I'd like a change. Do you like it Una?" Una stared at her. She looked so much younger, like a different person.

"I'm not sure. It looks very different."

Joseph came over to shake hands. "Sit here on this sofa with me. You look pale, Una."

"I'm all right."

"Well, the holidays are here soon, we'll fatten you up."

Una told them about Eilish, how her brother was missing and probably killed. "Eilish was sent for, to go home."

Her aunt looked sad. "Poor lad, and his poor family"

"It's not going well for the Brits," said Joseph. "Well, the Yanks will soon be in it, and that'll finish it up."

Then Emer said, "We have news for you Una. I'll let Joseph tell you."

Joseph took Una's hands. He seemed a little nervous. "Una, your aunt and myself have decided to get married."

Una sighed deeply, involuntarily, and her eyes filled with tears. She clenched her teeth to stop them, but she couldn't. She felt so weak and helpless, like a big baby, the tears poured down her pale face and into the hollow of her neck.

"Oh Una, Una," Joseph put his arm around her and wiped her tears with his handkerchief. She couldn't stop weeping.

"It's nothing to cry about Una. Aren't you glad?" Emer dabbed a little at her own eyes.

"I'm not crying. I'm just very very glad, very happy. I wish I could tell Eilish, that's all."

"Well, maybe you will, you can write to her, maybe even go and see her. Wouldn't you like that?"

"Yes, I would. When are you getting married?"

"Una dear, we have the priest's permission to get married in Joseph's parish. It's Easter Monday. So Easter Sunday we'll go to Dublin for a few days, that's if you will agree to be home with Nan and Donny."

"Of course. Does Nan know?"

"No one knows yet, except you and the priest, and I've written to Peadar. I'll tell Cassie tonight. Tomorrow the priest will read the bans, then the whole country will know."

"Lizzie will stay with you while we are away, and Cassie and Tom are just down the road," Joseph said.

"I could manage myself, I've stayed by myself before."

"Not overnight. I know you could manage, but it's better to have someone with you. We will only be away for a few days."

Una wiped her eyes. "Aunt Emer, your suit is lovely."

"Thank you, dear."

The bell rang for tea. "I have to go, Aunt Emer."

"I will call for you on Wednesday Una, I'll be coming to meet Joseph's train."

Her prayers were answered. No more sin. Joseph and Emer would make their confession for Easter and their souls would wash white as snow. How simple it was. God had answered her prayers. The relief of having everything settled. The sheer joy of it. If only Eilish were back, she would tell her. Una would be a nun. What name would she take? How to go about it. Sister Cecelia would know. She must talk to her quickly. She would be so happy, her face would light up and she would clasp her hands together and look up to heaven the way she did when she talked about giving yourself to God. What an achievement for Sister Cecelia. A vocation in her first year at the convent, common enough, but still. The first vocation of 1917! That's what she'd say! What would Emer wear? Would Joseph still live in Dublin? Would they all move there, or would he just come home on weekends? And what if her father came home? Would they all live together, or would Aunt Emer want to go back to her old house down the lane, or Maura's old house where the chimney had fallen in because no one lit the fire there since Maura died.

A nun! God had given her what she wanted. Maybe being a lay sister was best. But she wanted to teach, to be working with words and ideas like Sister Saint Mathew was. She had promised and her prayers were answered. Was it possible that she, Una, had a gift for praying? Knew how to persuade God, had the secret of getting things through prayer? If only Eilish were back. Oh, to talk to Eilish, to sit on her bed and munch cake and apples and talk and talk. Of course, it was Lent and they weren't supposed to have tuck, but still they could talk. Eilish would be excited for her, she had said once that Una would make a great nun.

She wouldn't tell Siobhan. Siobhan couldn't keep a secret. And she would boss Una around with her superior knowledge of nuns and the convent. When you became a nun did you swear to something, or was it like confirmation where the bishop said a prayer over you and struck you on the cheek to remind you to be a soldier of Christ? There was something about final vows. That must be when you swear. What did the postulants do? Did they study to be nuns, and if you weren't good enough did they send you away? Where did the nuns sleep? Had they cubicles over in the convent like the one Sister Agatha had in the first year dormitory, with a big crucifix on the wall over the bed? Sister Cecelia would know. Una did know that when she was fifteen she could enter the convent as a postulant. She would be fifteen soon. She would wait for Sister Cecelia after mass on Sunday and tell her the news, then she would tell Emer at Easter. She waited impatiently to tell Sister Cecelia.

But Sister Cecelia was not at mass on Sunday. Una watched at the glass door connecting the school to the convent but Sister Cecelia didn't come out. She always took Monday's senior study hall. Monday evening, as soon as her own study hall was over, Una ran to the senior hall and stood at the door as the students filed out. Then she went in, but Sister Anne was sitting at the teacher's desk.

"What do you want, Una?"

"I thought Sister Cecelia was here."

"Sister Cecelia is in bed with a very bad cold. Is there anything I can help with?"

"No thank you, Sister."

"Well, hurry on, you'll be late."

At night, Una stared over at Eilish's empty bed. If only Eilish were back. One more day and Easter holidays would begin. The school was strangely quiet, half empty, the halls echoing. Many students had gone home early.

Emer picked her up first on Wednesday and they went to the station to meet Joseph. He kissed Aunt Emer. It was alright, he was going to marry her. Emer stopped for a cake at Mercer's Bakery and she bought *The Irish Times* at the news agents, to see the styles.

"I wouldn't take that paper if I got it for nothing," said Joseph, when they got back to the trap. "That's for colonials."

Emer ignored him. "Una, if we were having a wedding party you would have been my bridesmaid, as it is, you will have to wait for your own wedding, or Nan's."

"Ah," thought Una, "you don't know it yet, but I'll never be married. I'm going to be a nun, that's my secret. I'll be a postulant by the end of the year." But she would keep her secret, tell no one till she had planned it all with Sister Cecelia. Then she would announce the great news.

The house looked smaller, as it did when she arrived home at Christmas, smaller than she remembered it and the beech trees taller. Donny had a boy's haircut. He looked like a shorn lamb, his head bare and cold, his baby curls gone.

"We're going to be by ourselves for four days," Nan announced wanting, as usual, to be first with the news, "Aunt Emer and Uncle Joseph are going away to get married."

"I know Nan, but we won't be alone, Lizzie will stay with us."

After mass on Easter Sunday people stood around, the men smoking, as they always did. They shook Joseph's hand. Lizzie teased Emer, "You're the one to put manners on that wild Joseph. Even if I didn't make the match, it's a good one."

There was a tremendous air of excitement. America had joined the war. It was rumoured that a big American fleet was coming to Cork to blow the U-boats out of the water. Una wondered what Sister Saint Mathew would say about that. In class, when they talked about Hamlet, she said that man was a murderous creature by his very nature, that men loved to kill, they were excited by battle. How impossible that seemed, gentle men like Joseph?

Lizzie said Emer and Joseph were like two youngsters when they left for the station in Tom's trap on Easter Sunday evening. After Donny went to sleep, she and Nan listened to Lizzie gossip. Lady Darling had gone to live in England with her two children. That's where she came from. The big house was shut up. Just one old man and a young lad there, and Greta Smith to look after the place. It would go to wrack and ruin, every perch of it.

Then Una and Nan stayed awake talking and it was as if Una had never been away. She felt, so safe and comfortable at home, she realized how much she hated the cold, bleak dormitory. Nan asked a lot of questions. Imagine having twenty-three girls in your class.

"Twenty-three is not that many Nan, some classes have twenty-eight or more."

"Twenty-eight, imagine! Do the nuns hit you, Una?"

"No, I don't think so. Not unless you do something very bad. I've never seen anyone get the strap in my class yet, but they do have a strap. You get a bad mark if you do something wrong and then you are not allowed to go for a walk or to the hall for music or games."

Una told her about the gramophone and about learning to waltz. Nan said she couldn't wait to be fourteen and go to the convent school.

"I wish you were at school with me, sometimes I'm lonesome."

"Really Una, even with all the other girls?"

"Well, yes, even with a lot of other girls, but you remember I told you at Christmas about my two friends, Eilish and Siobhan. Eilish is my very best friend now."

She didn't tell Nan about Eilish's brother, thinking it would frighten her. Una was back in the old round of life at home. They played with Donny, sliding down the hay ricks in the haggard; they played hop scotch in the yard, and lined up for *O'Grady Says*. Nan was bossy as ever, always wanting to be O'Grady. They giggled at Donny's efforts to play, to follow O'Grady. Nan cheated, peeking before she turned round to make sure Donny adopted the right pose and wasn't out. They gathered the eggs, fed the pig and hens, and milked the cow. Lizzie cooked and Nan helped her. Cassie sent Stephen to fodder this year's new cattle Emer was fattening at the old house.

"I could have done that myself," Una told Stephen.

"You could, could you now? Since you went to the convent sure you've turned into a real worker." He grinned at her in a funny way. She looked straight back at him, as tall as he was. For no reason in the world she thought about Eilish kissing the lad behind the bar.

"For your information, Stephen Plunkett, I was always a worker."

The whole country was talking about the marriage. On Tuesday evening, when they went down to Lizzie's to milk her goats, they met Margaret Smith coming out of J.J. Mahon's. Margaret's sharp sloe eyes looked Una up and down. "That's a great match your uncle and aunt made but," she added slyly, "it's a terror what talk there is, what some people say. They're all talking, hinting that Emer robbed the cradle. At Mahon's they said last night that she could be his mother, that it's not before time they got married."

Nan stared at her. Una blushed for Emer then, she remembered how Sister Saint Mathew had said you paid no attention to what people thought, you did what you knew was right. "Of course," Margaret added piously, pursing her fat lips, "I give no heed to that sort of talk."

"Well, Margaret," said Lizzie, "there's some peoples' tongues too long for their mouths."

When Margaret walked on she banged her stick on the ground. "It's jealous they are, long-tongued begrudgers. Say nothing about it."

Una warned Nan. "Don't tell Aunt Emer what she said."

"Why?"

"Because it would upset her, that's why."

Lizzie brought a lace shawl from her house for Emer. "The last one I made, Una, before my eyes got too weak. I used to make fancy lace, as good as the nuns in Carrickmacross."

"It's lovely, Lizzie."

Cassie came in the evening to see how they were getting along. She brought a tablecloth for Emer. "Saturday night we'll have a bit of a ceilidh, though Emer doesn't want a fuss. But, I want to have a bit of a party for her. It's only once in a lifetime."

Emer returned with presents. When she opened the brown paper packages, the wide, gold band gleamed on the ring finger of her work-reddened left hand. New short trousers for Donny, and a tin whistle from McNeill's in Capel Street; dresses for the girls from Clerys. The first dress Una ever had from a shop! Emer made her walk up and down the kitchen modeling it. "You look just beautiful Una. Red is your colour. Raspberry red it is." She loosed Una's plat of hair and spread it on her shoulders. "Now, walk to the door again. Beautiful! What do you think Joseph?"

Joseph lowered the newspaper. "*Ah cailin deas*. Lovely!"

The dress clung loosely to her waist and flowed over her hips. It was so light and delicate, Una felt wonderful in it, so grown up, so in charge of herself, no longer the overgrown, clumsy girl with big feet and hands. She wanted to dance, to lift her arms and waltz, to twirl, and feel the light airy material flare out around her. If Eilish was there she'd dance with her. Poor Eilish.

"Those shoes and stockings won't do," said Emer, "we'll have to see what they have in Obanbeg."

Obanbeg! She had forgotten about school, about her promise to be a nun, renounce pretty clothes and dressing up. How could she have done such a thing?

"Now, let's see your dress Nan."

It was a pink dress with a wide coppery sash around the hips. Nan flounced about.

"Stand a minute. I think I'll have to shorten it a bit."

"I'll grow into it."

"Not the way you grow! But it's very pretty. What do you think, Joseph?"

"She looks just grand."

"It's beautiful on you, Nan. You look very nice," said Una.

"Not as nice as you, you look like the pictures in Donny's book with your hair loose."

"I don't have curls like you, mine's like a horse's tail."

"I'll shorten your dress for Saturday, Nan. Una, you'll have to wear a pair of my shoes."

Emer had said she did not want a fuss, but Cassie told her, "It's just a few of us, Emer."

Cassie arranged for Pete and his fiddle and sent Stephen to fetch whiskey and stout from J.J. Mahon's. She invited Greta Smith because Greta needed cheering up, needed to get away from that fortress she worked in. Pete sat in the corner tuning up his fiddle. Pat McGee had already been drinking at J.J. Mahon's when Stephen fetched him in the trap. It seemed to Una the older and more feeble he got the more argumentative he was. He sat at the fire and started a fierce debate with John Slowey. "America in the war, Dough Boys how are you! What the soldiers ought to do is stop fighting, just stop, that's all, stop altogether."

"That would be mutiny, Pat," John puffed his pipe complacently.

"And proper order, too," Pat shouted, "then what could Lloyd George do, and Haig, and that Unionist Carson, looking for heroes. Some hero he is!" His face was flushed and his bloodshot eyes bulged. "Tell me that now, if the lads mutiny, what could they do?" And he thumped the floor with one of his two sticks.

"I hear the French lads might be giving up," John added.

"And proper order too, I say, proper order," Pat declared again, and seemingly satisfied at having made his point, he threw down one of his sticks. It fell with a clatter and he rooted in his pocket for his pipe and tobacco.

Cassie crouched down beside him. "Pat! Pat, you'll have an attack or something. You're not so young any more you know. Go easy. You're drinking too much."

"I'm not drinking half enough," he stormed and banged his stick against the floor again.

Cassie handed him a mug of tea. "Drink that up, Pat."

She motioned to Pete to start playing. He began a three-hand reel. She pulled Stephen and Greta up to dance. "Come on, you too, Nan!"

Una watched the dancers footing it in a circle. They seemed countrified, lumpish, and simple. They danced around the kitchen looping arms raised in an arch, stooping under, round again, lifting their knees high, then following each other in a circle straight like soldiers. Pat was silent now, puffed his pipe and kept time with his stick. The dancers grew flushed and over-heated, but kept stepping away, till Pete at last drew down his bow in one long stroke and the music stopped.

"Nice work, Stephen! Very nice stepping, girls," Cassie praised, and began refilling glasses and tea mugs. Una got up to help her. Donny was underfoot, playing with his whistle, blowing loud, piercing notes. A few more neighbours arrived and sat with their backs to the wall. Cassie served them drinks. Joseph was talking to Tom about the war.

"Ah, give us the Bard there," Pat shouted.

"Yes," said John, "let's hear that auld one."

"Ah yes, the Bard," sighed Lizzie, "the Bard."

Stephen blew a few notes on the tin whistle and Pete raised his bow in agreement and, tentatively at first, then resolutely, their notes combined into the old song. The listeners sitting around the walls hummed and swayed. Una shivered a little. When she last heard that song, the singer had been her father. Her father, she had to write now and tell him she was going to be a nun! How would he take that news? Would he be proud of her? Would he say, "good girl," the way he always used to? Or would he think she was too young, or that she was doing something strange? He had been gone five years. Suddenly she longed to see him, to talk to him. How a song brought back a moment, an occasion! Music, for Una, always evoked memories. More than anything else, a note on the fiddle or a few bars of a song stirred imagination, marking for her what was happening and what had happened. It had been so unusual for her quiet, sensible father to sing. That was one of the few times she had heard him, very late on the night before he left for America. She was half asleep in her chair, and could see him standing so tall in front of the hearth, his dark head held up to the lamp, a glass in his hand.

"How I long for to muse on the days of my boyhood,
Though four score and three years have flitted since then,
Still it gives sweet reflection as every young joy should,
That merry-hearted boys make the best of old men."

Joseph crossed to where Emer was sitting and took her hand. They danced the old lilting waltz, her blue dress wafting out, her shawl slipping half off her shoulder, straight bobbed black hair shifting and shining in the lamplight, round and round, each step taking momentum from the one before, the sedate, decorous old dance. To Una it was as if her aunt had danced without clothes, wanton, shameless. She checked the faces of the others. Pat and Lizzie swayed in time, their eyes closed. John whistled the tune. Cassie laid down her teapot and she and Tom danced. Nan pulled Donny up off the floor and dragged him, unwilling, about, and when Una looked again Emer was talking animatedly to Joseph, his head bent to hear her. They broke apart and Joseph came and took her hand.

"Any place on your dance card for your old uncle?" Una took his hand and stepped out with him on the flagstone floor.

"Back to school tomorrow, Una."

"And you to Dublin."

"I am, but I'm watching for a school about here. Your aunt wants me to talk to the priest about a vacancy that's coming up in Kilderry."

He held her firmly and she followed his lead, her borrowed shoes a little loose, and Joseph sang softly,

"Whilst all the pretty maidens around me assembled,
Loved bold Phelim Brady, the Bard of Armagh."

It was different dancing with a man. Joseph was taller than her, and danced sure-footed and strong. It was nicer than dancing with Eilish. Poor, poor Eilish. Dancing couldn't be a sin. Una felt she could dance for hours and hours, the music carrying her away, her pleasure in her neat precise steps and in the lilt of the music was her very own, independent of any other person, dancing forever, waltzing, and turning to the music for hours and hours.

The moon was setting when Joseph roused Pat from his doze at the fire, gripped him under the arms and hoisted him into Stephen's trap beside Lizzie. The last of the stragglers, Cassie and Tom, set off down the lane. Donny was long asleep. Una slid in beside Nan.

"Isn't Aunt Emer beautiful, Una?"

"She is, I wish Daddy were here."

"I barely remember him, is he like Uncle Joseph?"

"No, he looks like Emer, she's his sister you know, don't you remember?"

"Oh, I forgot. Can I blow out the candle, Una?"

"Yes, I don't need a light any more."

The crowing cock woke them on Sunday morning.

"That's the bird of dawning, Nan."

"Who calls him that?"

"Marcellus."

"Who's that?"

"A soldier in the play we are learning."

"You know a lot of people since you went to that school, Una."

"He's just in a play, but when I look about me everything reminds me of something in that play."

Back to school, Una thought, stepping out of bed. Back to her promise to enter the convent, like going past a barred gate into a dark tunnel never to come out again. Never to dance, sway to music playing, or give a saucy answer to the likes of Stephen. And never to come home to Slanabaille. Nuns were only allowed home if there was a death in the family. To do everything by rule, never to depart from the routine not even once, no matter how much you wanted to. And not even Eilish to talk to.

"We have to hurry, we're a bit late," Emer said, rushing in and lifting Donny from his cot. The little boy was sleepy.

"I'll bring you to Joseph, he'll dress you, Donny."

She was back in a minute fussing with Nan, brushing out her hair. Nan complained, "Aunt Emer, that hurts, you're pulling my hair."

"I'm finished now, Nan."

They were almost late. Last into the chapel, they took their places just as the sarcristy door swung open and the priest and altar boys paraded out. In unison, the line genuflected to the altar and then the priest turned and faced the congregation.

"This mass, and all masses today, are offered for the soul of John Mahon of this parish who was killed fighting in France on Easter Monday." Una felt Emer's sharp intake of breath and the shock that swept the crowd. The priest turned back and began mass, "*Interibo altara Dei*, I will go onto the altar of God, to God who giveth joy to my youth."

Jack Mahon, Jack with his open freckled face and wide grin, his thick, bare muscled arms loading porter barrels on a cart. Was that face blown away now? Greta's sweetheart. How was it possible? How could God allow that? Why hadn't they heard before? And yesterday, Mahon's shop was open, Mr. Mahon pouring glasses of Bass and Guinness and fumbling for change in the till, people drinking and smoking and talking and singing there. Stephen said the shop was full when he went to pick up Pat McGee. And she remembered Greta dancing. Poor Greta!

After mass, people stood around looking as if they were unsure of what to do next, their faces alarmed, distressed, even the shawled country women, who always hurried home, stayed to talk.

"It will kill his mother," said Cassie.

Someone said a telegraph had come late on Saturday, just before the telegraph office closed, and the telegraph boy had come over on his bicycle with it.

"But Uncle Joseph, the priest said he was killed last Monday."

"There's a fierce battle going on over there, Una dear, it's still going on, they call it the Nivelle Offensive. There's a General Nivelle leading the charge, but I read that the Germans are giving as good as they get. I'm sure there are so many casualties they can't keep count. It's a real shame, the poor lad, *ar deis De go raibh se.*"

"Yes," said Emer, "he's at God's right hand."

Neither the Mahon's nor Lizzie were at mass. Lizzie didn't go out as much now. People said the years had begun to catch up with her.

"This will upset Lizzie, too," said Joseph as he turned the pony for home.

"Not to mention Greta, and his poor mother who fought with him about Greta. I'll call down to see Lizzie this evening."

"But Lizzie hated them. She cursed them once."

"That's what your aunt means. That's why she'll be upset."

Joseph looked grim. Nan sat up close to Joseph. Donny looked around anxiously, as if he knew something was wrong. Emer put her arm around Donny, bent her head and spoke softly. "Listen," she told him, "do you hear that blackbird, you know what he says, he's saying, wet your feet, wet your feet. Listen Donny, he's talking to you."

At home, Una packed her case for school. Stephen was going to drive Joseph to the train and drop Una at school on the way. When he came to get them he took Una's case and put it carefully under the seat in the trap, as if it were tucked away finally and forever. He was very proud of his new mare. "You can hold her halter if you like, Una."

Una held her while Stephen talked to Emer and Joseph. The mare shook herself violently and the harness jerked and shuddered. Una moved her grip on the bridle, closer to the bit. Behind her blinkers, the animal's brown bulbous eyes floated in a purple film and she looked wild, as if she was terrified, didn't want to be in harness, and might suddenly bolt. Stephen's voice carried from the step. "Arras, that's the name of the place where he was killed. Arras, someplace in France. Poor lad."

Arras, where Hamlet killed Polonius, behind the arras. How strange words were, one reminding you of another, sending your thoughts tumbling and racing in a hundred directions. Back to school today, to see Eilish again. Poor Eilish. What would she be like, would she be in tears? Would she be weeping all the time? What would she think when she heard Una was going to enter the convent? Una hadn't told Emer yet, she'd wait till she'd told Sister

Cecelia. Then it would be clearer. She'd recover the conviction she'd lost since she came home. Sister Cecelia would say it was the influence of the world. The world and the flesh! And the devil, that's who went about the world distracting girls from their vocation, tempting them with worldly things, with frivolity, making them forget their duty to God and His holy church. That unseen and sneaky devil.

Una's promise lay on her mind like a dread, and she felt guilty. Guilty about how heartsick she was thinking of shutting out Nan and Donny; guilty about regretting her compact with God. What had come over her since she came home? Had she forgotten God had granted her wish? Maybe Emer and Joseph would have married anyway. Still, she had promised. What was wrong with her? Something had changed in her since Easter. She needed to get back to the convent to renew her promise, needed to forget how deprived she felt at leaving the world behind. But, how could she possibly renounce pleasures she had only just discovered? Dancing, pretty clothes, company and games, the beat of life at home and above all, beyond all else, this new feeling she had now, that streamed and bubbled under all other feelings, that somewhere, there were wonderful things just waiting to happen to her.

Emer came over to her. "Una dear, you know you're very pale, are you alright?"

"It's just from last night. We were all up so late, I'll be fine when I get back to school. And I'll see Eilish." Suddenly Una wanted to tell her that she was going to be a nun, she almost did, but Donny ran under the mare's belly and she stooped quickly to snatch him up.

"Don't do that Donny, ever."

"Uncle Joseph does it."

"That's different, he just stoops to fasten the belly strap, you are not to do that, you are never to run under a horse, it's very dangerous."

"We have to go or I'll miss my train," Joseph said, hastily kissing Emer and Nan.

The road was Sunday afternoon quiet. The middle of April, soft air, and the trees already burst in bloom, the hawthorn and lilac white and mauve, at the workhouse gate. Joseph and Stephen talked about Home Rule. "Lloyd George does lots of promising," Stephen declared.

"Ah, the yanks are pushing him. He's beholden to them now, without America, they're done for."

"I think so, too. They say the lads in France are at the end of their rope."

France! Eilish would be back! Una gripped the edge of the trap impatiently. They were almost at the outskirts of Obanbeg. If only Stephen would hurry the mare, she wanted so badly to see Eilish and tell her everything. They trotted on at an even pace, cresting the hill, down the slope and through the town and in the convent gates.

"Here you are, Una," said Stephen.

There was a line of traps in the drive. Everyone was arriving back, back for one more term. Eilish had probably come on the noon train from Athlone. At the school door, she grabbed her case. "Goodbye, Uncle Joseph. Thanks, Stephen." Una raced up to the dormitory.

"No running, walk like a lady," Sister Anne cautioned, at the top of the stairs.

Una walked the last few yards. No Eilish, and none of her belongings in the cubicle either. An empty seat beside her at tea. "Eilish is not back, Siobhan, do you think it's just that she is late?"

"I don't know. Sure, she mightn't come at all."

That night Una tossed and turned. She stared anxiously across at Eilish's empty bed. She tried to pray, but every time her mind wandered off, thinking about home, about Aunt Emer dancing. How could she ever be a nun if she were lonesome like this, if she couldn't pray, if her mind was full of schemes for beautiful clothes while fiddle music and waltzes lilted through her head? Was there some sort of order where you could go home for visits? Sister Cecelia would know. She would ask her tomorrow. Sister Cecelia always said, "Work, work, girls, work and pray." Did she want to be a nun even in a convent where you could go home on weekends? But she had promised God. God had granted her wish and she must keep her promise, because Sister Cecelia said God is not mocked. It seemed so hard, such a sacrifice. She knew she was wavering in her vocation and God saw her and was waiting to see if she kept her promise. She couldn't fail Him.

Wretched and lonely, Una knew she would never get to sleep. She lay hour after hour listening to the other girls breathing and watching shadows move on the dormitory ceiling. When Sister Agatha slid past, going to morning prayers, Una stuck her head under the bedclothes and pretended to sleep.

She waited after mass for a few minutes, but Sister Cecelia didn't come out. "Hurry on Una, you'll be late for grace," warned Sister Agatha. At breakfast Una couldn't eat, her head ached, and there was a hissing in her ears from lack of sleep. Everyone was excited, talking at once, the first day back and so much to tell. Una wanted to stuff her ears or run away. What had she to tell? That life at home was over? Siobhan said this term would be tough, very tough, they must work extremely hard because examinations were in June, and the questions were already being planned by the devious examiners of the Intermediate Education Board.

If only Eilish were back, Una could pour out her heart to her. Eilish would understand, would encourage her, as she always did. "Go on girl, you know you can do it!" Eilish had said Una would be a great nun. She had to see Sister Cecelia about her promise. She would ask for her at the convent door in the break after dinner. If she waited longer, her resolve would weaken and God would be mocked. If only Eilish were here, even if she was still sad about her brother's death, they could talk. When would Eilish be back? If only I could confide in someone, Una thought sadly, sitting exhausted and listless in English class. When Sister Saint Mathew turned her back to write on the blackboard Joan whispered, "Una are you sick? You look awful!"

The nun turned around to see who was talking then returned to her writing. Una read the words indistinctly, mistily, through the unshed tears in her tired red rimmed eyes. *What is Fortinbras' function in the last scene?*

Una couldn't think. She couldn't remember, was it to make things normal again, to wake everyone from the nightmare of death, to close the play? She was numb and stupid, unable to concentrate. Suddenly, it didn't seem important what the play said or what it meant, or what mark she got in the examinations. She promised herself that as soon as classes were over she would find Sister Cecelia and settle her mind about entering the convent. Then to the dormitory and lie down and try to sleep.

When the bell rang Sister Saint Mathew said, "You stay back please, Una, I want a word with you."

The students left; another class was lined up waiting for the room.

"Come along, Una."

Dejected and weary, Una followed the old nun along the corridor toward the convent. She looked down on top of the short woman's head, at the black topped straight pin which held her veil. They went through the glass doors and into the nuns' sitting room.

"Sit down, Una." Una sat on the edge of a high-backed chair. "What's the matter? Are you ill?"

The nun had a shrewd look in her old brown eyes.

"No Sister, I'm fine."

"There's nothing wrong?"

"Nothing, Sister." Sister Saint Mathew's boots needed mending. What small feet she had.

"Is everything alright at home?"

"Yes, Sister."

"Look at me Una," she lifted Una's chin. "What's the matter Una? Tell me, what's wrong?"

Una could hold back her tears no longer. "Oh Sister," she wept, "I'm so miserable!" Suddenly she wanted to tell her everything, how home had been so joyful and normal, so wonderfully ordinary, how happy Emer and Joseph were, how poor Jack Mahon had been killed in the war, how lovely Greta was, with her dark straight hair falling from a center parting, how she couldn't bear not to ever dance again, how she didn't want to be a nun at all. But all she said was, "Oh Sister, I promised I'd be a nun if I got something I prayed for and now I've gotten it."

"And you're not sure you can keep your end of the bargain?" Sister Saint Mathew sounded slightly amused.

"I want to," Una sobbed, "but I'm not sure I'm holy enough, I'm not sure I could stick it."

Sister Saint Mathew sat down on the a chair across from Una.

"How old are you, Una?"

"Fifteen in August, Sister."

"Have you talked this over with your parents?"

"My mother is dead and my father is in America. My aunt brought me up."

"Oh yes, Una, I forgot. So you haven't talked to your aunt about this?"

"No, Sister."

"You know, God always leaves us with our free will."

Una pondered this for a minute. Free will? "When I promised, it was with free will."

The nun's face took on a determined look. "Una, listen to me, you're far too young. I know lots of girls enter at fifteen, but it's too young."

"But I promised God," Una sobbed, "if I got my special intention, I'd enter the convent."

"God doesn't make bargains like that. What kind of God would that be, bartering and trading that way?"

"But, I really promised." Una wanted to be reassured, she could hardly believe there might be a way out, she might get away with not entering the convent.

"You didn't think about whether you were suited to be a nun before you made the promise, and you're convinced you made some irrevocable promise. Am I right?"

Una nodded childishly, her eyes aching with tears.

"If you have been paying attention in English drama you know what thinking like that can get you. Remember Hamlet, he thought himself into murder."

"Sister Cecelia says God is not mocked."

"Well, that's all fine," persisted the nun, a little impatiently, "but He would be surely mocked if you became a nun and did not have a true vocation, if you didn't have the temperament for it, if it became a sad life for you. I've seen girls in the convent that shouldn't be there, nuns that should never have entered."

"I don't think I'm suited to it."

"Then you're not! One enters the religious life because it is a particular individual's best chance at happiness. If being a nun is not the best life for you, then you shouldn't even consider it." Una stared at the nun's earnest face, incredulous. Sister Saint Mathew continued, "If it wouldn't be a joyful life for you, how could you ever influence anyone else to be good?"

Joyful, what was joyful about the convent? Maybe English class, maybe hymns at Benediction, that was all.

"Sister, how would I know if I had a vocation?"

"You would know! You would have no doubts, you would be full of joy and happiness. When you have a vocation you'll know. Do you know what kind of work you want to do?"

"I know I want to be a teacher."

"No doubts about that, Una?"

"No."

"You see, you do know what you want. Concentrate on your studies, Una, pray for light to see the way. I can assure you, if you're to be a nun you need to be a lot more sure than you are now. You don't want to take the wrong turn in the road because you made some sort of vow when you were under duress."

"What about my promise?"

"Was that a free promise, Una? People make promises like that when they are upset. Forget it till you're finished school."

"I think about it all the time."

"You see Una, that's where the discipline comes in, to manage your thinking."

"Thank you, Sister."

"And anytime you are worried, I want you to come and talk to me. I'll give you a note for Sister Anne, you're very late for class." Una got up to leave. Sister Saint Mathew was bent over at the table writing a note. "And Una," she didn't lift her head when she said it, "no need to mention this to Sister Cecelia." Then she handed her the note and looked straight at her. "Understood?"

Una nodded, "Yes. Thank you, Sister."

Una flew back along the corridor to math class. She wanted to lift her arms and sing and dance, but she walked decorously, as befitted a good convent girl. How simple it was, how clear Sister Saint Mathew's thinking was. A nun telling her to be joyful, to do what she wanted! Now she was glad she had not been able to meet with Sister Cecelia. Somehow she knew Sister Cecelia would never have talked with her as Sister Saint Mathew had. Sister Cecelia would have leaped at the chance of another vocation and then there would have been no way out, matter how many doubts Una had. She was reprieved, free again. Years and years of endless choice opened before her. She sat in math class watching Sister Anne writing fractions on the blackboard, knowing the figures on the board were not so important after all. The important thing was her freedom. She was like a caged bird let loose in May.

Una hadn't eaten any breakfast. At dinner, she'd been too excited and relieved to eat. By four, she was starving. As soon as class was over she went to the dormitory to get a snack, climbing the wide stairs slowly, feeling as though with each step she was climbing towards a new happiness.

Eilish was sitting on her bed. "Eilish, you're back! I'm so glad to see you. Oh Eilish, I am so, so sorry about your brother."

Eilish held up her hands palms facing out. "Please Una, please. I don't want to talk about him, I don't even want him mentioned."

"Why, Eilish?"

"Because I just don't."

Her friend's appearance was a shock to Una. Eilish was pale, her eyes sunk in shadows, her expression subdued.

"All right, Eilish, I understand. I won't say anything."

They went down to tea without a word between them. When grace was said Siobhan left her seat and came round the table to talk to Eilish.

"Oh Eilish, was it awful?"

"Please Siobhan, I don't want it mentioned." Siobhan looked nonplussed. The other girls at the table stared at Eilish in silence. In study hall, Eilish kept her head down in her books. She didn't speak as they took their cocoa before prayers, never even commented on the weak, purplish drink. Eilish had become a stranger, silent, like a stone, her face shaved of all feeling. When they were ready to sleep, Eilish jerked back the curtain at the end of her cubicle and climbed into bed. She never even said goodnight. If only she would talk to me, Una thought, I'm sure I could help her. I want her to be the old Eilish again. Before Una fell asleep she asked God to help Eilish, to take away the awful pained look from her face, to make Eilish herself again.

Sometime in the night Una awoke and heard her friend sobbing. She slipped out of bed and crept in beside her. Eilish was so small compared to Una. Just as she would with Nan, she took her in her arms and whispered, "Don't cry Eilish, dear, don't cry, it will be alright, don't cry dear, I hate it when you cry." She mopped her friend's wet face with the corner of the sheet and they held each other till they were both asleep.

Una snapped awake. The bedclothes were flung back. Sister Agatha dragged her out of bed. Slap after slap stung Una's shocked face. In a rage, Sister Agatha pummelled Una's arms and shoulders. Una turned away. The nun punched her back.

"Brazen brat, crawling in another girl's bed. How dare you do such a thing." She gave Una a tremendous shove towards her own bed. "You are not to speak to Eilish Houlihan again and as long as I run this dormitory you are never, never to go in another girl's bed or to lie with another girl like that. You are a disgrace." She turned sharply on her heel and strode off to prayers. Una sensed everyone in the dormitory awake, listening. Her hot face stung and she felt her shoulders aching from the blows. Eilish crept over.

"The old bitch, she's crazy. Are you all right, Una?"

"Yes, I wouldn't cry to please her," she whispered. "I wouldn't satisfy her."

"Good girl. Go back to bed Una, she'll be back."

She lay shuddering under the clothes and pulled the sheet over her burning face. Her shoulders and upper arms hurt dreadfully.

The unfairness of it, the injustice, what was she accusing her of? All she'd done was comfort Eilish. What rule had she broken? She wanted to go home. She wanted to talk to Emer. Emer would listen. It wasn't so far, ten miles. She could walk. Maybe she would get a lift in a cart. She'd be up, dressed and gone before Sister Agatha came back from prayers. She'd never come back to this awful place. Una sat up and put her feet on the floor. She would have to hurry. Then she thought about what running away would mean. People in Slanabaille would talk, the Maguire's were a queer lot, they had no luck, the mother dead and the father skidaddled off to America. Una was well aware of how the gossip would be. Running away would expose them all to vicious, malevolent talk. She couldn't. She'd stay till the end of term, then she'd see. If only she hadn't fallen sleep, if only she had gone back to her own bed. Suddenly a storm of hate and anger flooded through her. She wanted to put her hands tight around that nun's raddled turtleneck, squeeze and twist it till her head sagged like the heads of chickens when their necks were wrung. And then she thought, I'm murderous too. She heard Sister Agatha returning from prayers and concentrated on pretending to be asleep.

Coming from morning mass and at breakfast students stared at Una, at the marks on her cheeks. Humiliated, she kept her head down in class. She felt everyone whispering. Everyone knew she had done something awful. But why was it awful?

After dinner Sister Agatha beckoned to her. "I've moved you to the cubicle up beside mine. You are not to talk to Eilish Hoolihan again."

Una stood with her eyes downcast, her whole mind resisting, her heart rebellious. She'd done nothing wrong.

"Did you hear what I said, Una?"

"Yes."

"Is that how you address a nun?"

"Yes, Sister."

"That's better."

Una walked to her classroom with her eyes cast down. She sat at the back of the room and as the other students entered their looks were full of curiosity. Una kept her eyes on her book. Eilish sat in front of the class. As soon as classes were finished, Una slipped out and went up to the dormitory. Her things had been moved. Her tuck box was sitting on the top of her bed and her clothes and laundry bag were dumped on the chair. She began to put them away. Eilish peeked around the corner of the cubicle.

"I'm not supposed to talk to you."

"Ha! In your eye! You're not going to mind that old rip."

"I don't want to get in any more trouble."

"She doesn't have to know. She's not God!"

Eilish was still pale but she sounded like her old scornful self again. She sat on Una's bed. "Are you going to tell your people? I would!"

"No, not now anyway. I don't want to upset Joseph and Emer. Anyway, this is the last term this year. I'll see how I do in the June exams. Maybe I won't come back here." She felt very decisive as she said that, very content with herself. Her mind was made up.

"Una! Have you lost your five wits or what? And you wanting to be a teacher. You're so smart and work so hard. You could win an exhibition, a scholarship. I certainly wouldn't let that old hag change my plans."

"Eilish, she's changed them already. I thought I might be a nun, now I know I never will be."

"You a nun, have a titter of wit in your head, you're not cut out for that."

"Why not?"

"You're always romancing, that's why. Joseph this and Emer that. Little Donny this and Nan the other. You couldn't leave them."

"You said once I'd make a great nun!"

"Oh Una, I was just teasing, don't you know yet when I'm teasing you?"

"Mattie had sort of talked me out of it."

"Well, Mattie has more sense than the lot of them put together! You should go talk to her about that old targer beating you."

"But Eilish, I hate it here, everyone is staring at me all the time."

"So! Don't mind them. They'll soon get tired of that. Only yesterday they were staring at me because my brother was killed, now they're staring at you. I'll give them something to stare at."

Una sat down on the bed beside Eilish.

"Eilish, my aunt and uncle got married."

"Marvelous! When?"

"At Easter."

"See, I knew they would. Didn't I tell you they would? Were you a bridesmaid?"

"No, they got married in Dublin. A friend of Joseph's and his sweetheart were their witnesses. But we had a ceilidh at home when they got back. I waltzed a lot."

"Good job I taught you to waltz!" Eilish put her arms around her and gave her waist a tight squeeze.

"We are not supposed to talk to each other."

"Don't mind them, Una! What they won't know won't sicken them. We don't have to tell them. And next year you'll be in a different dormitory. You won't have to put up with Agatha. From now till June it's cram, cram, for exams anyway. My mother said for you to come and visit us in the summer."

"I'd love that. Aunt Emer suggested it too."

"Oh Una, I missed you. I couldn't wait to come back, I wanted so badly to talk to you. All over Easter I missed you. Swear we'll be friends forever."

"Eilish, of course we will. I thought I'd die if you didn't come back."

"Oh, I wanted to come back. It was just awful at home, my father so quiet, my mother crying all the time. She stands behind the counter and if anyone she knows comes in she begins to weep."

"Poor woman!"

"I know! I know! But Terry's gone. I want to forget about him for now. It's the only thing I can do. My sisters are coming home from America."

"Even with the war on?"

"Well, now they can come in a convoy, it's supposed to be safer with the American fleet that's coming to Cork on the watch, but it might be months and months before they get a passage. They'll probably stay at home then. Declan doesn't want to work in the shop."

"Do you want to go back to it, Eilish?"

"I don't think so. I want to be independent of it, you know, to get away from home, maybe to live in Dublin. Lots of girls live and work away from home nowadays. Why wouldn't I do it, too? I just can't stand to think of being stuck at home. I know I should be home with my mother, but if my sisters come home she'll have them. I would like to work in Dublin."

"I think I'd like that, too."

"Una you're clever. The smartest one in the class. You could be anything you wanted."

"Well, I'll settle for being a teacher."

"Una, you didn't swear we'd be always friends."

"Of course, Eilish, I swear."

"Forever, Una?"

"Yes, forever."

"Say it Una, I swear we will be friends forever."

"I swear, we will be friends forever Eilish, no matter what, for always."

They sat there, arms around each other, and Una thought it was only a day since Sister Saint Mathew had freed her from a terrible burden and now Eilish was back.

There was the sound of voices and feet in the corridor, other girls coming to the dormitory. Eilish slipped back to her own cubicle. Una rose to put her belongings away.

Walking After Curfew

Dublin was under curfew. After dark people stayed inside their homes, their doors locked. Uncle Joseph predicted there would soon be a truce, that even in England people were calling for peace. Still, there was no let-up of the raids and skirmishes.

When Una told Eilish what Joseph said, Eilish declared, "It can't come too soon for me. I hear them in the pub at home saying when the men came home from the war they expected a better life, expected Home Rule and when they didn't get it they all turned Republican. Of course, my poor brother didn't come home. I often think if he had, he'd be following Michael Collins."

Two Saturdays ago, Una had accompanied Eilish to see a cousin of her mother, a widow who lived on a war pension in an upper flat of a house in Lower Leeson Street.

"It's a duty call, Una. My mother expects it. I promised her I'd visit."

"We'll go a bit early, Eilish. We need to be home before dark."

"Well, round here there's never any bother. We'll be all right."

Mrs. Fitzsimons had bristling hair cut in a bob and a short stout figure, still in mourning black. Her two daughters were nuns in the Poor Clares Convent in Cavan. Eilish said they had entered one after another two years earlier, just sixteen and seventeen.

"Some people suit the convent and for some it's a refuge," Eilish said the night before, when they were planning the visit.

Mrs. Fitzsimons' only son was in South Africa, a British civil servant. Eilish had said any mention of the fighting would upset

Mrs. Fitzsimons, who considered herself loyal to England. Her husband had been killed in France, just like Eilish's brother, Terry.

A round tea table sat in the bay window, tall candles and the white tablecloth starched to a shine. Outside, early November winds blew leaves about. Eilish's cousin served them cold Denny's ham, potato salad and pickled beets, trifle for a sweet.

"Eat up Una, you're too thin." Mrs. Fitzsimons fussed and mothered.

"Not really thin. It's just that I'm tall."

"Well, you've a fine figure. Clothes sit well on you, but I don't know where a man with height to match it will be found."

Mrs. Fitzsimons passed the bread and butter. On the sideboard was a photograph of her husband in his British army officer's uniform. "I had it taken in Glenns, over in Grafton Street, on his last leave. Easter '15. He didn't want to be bothered with it, but I'm glad I insisted. It's all I'll ever have of him now."

"I'm sorry, Mrs. Fitzsimons."

"I know dear," Mrs. Fitzsimons filled Una's cup. "I always buy Lipton's tea. That was always Gerry's favourite."

"Everything is delicious, Mrs.Fitzsimons."

Dusk gathered in the corners of the room. Una sat between the wavering candlelight and the steady red glow of the coal fire. It was clear Mrs Fitzsimons was enjoying their company. Una wondered what it was like to be a widow alone with memories, surviving on a war pension, helping out in the local church to pass the time. Una thought she could never be alone, could never come home every night to an empty flat.

"We can't stay late," Eilish warned, "you know, the curfew."

"Yes," sighed their hostess, "I never thought I'd speak against the King, but I'm speaking now. Between the night raids and the work stoppages this country's at its wit's end! As far as I'm concerned, the English should get out and take their Black and Tan police with them. Of course, I find no fault with the King. It's that Lloyd George I blame."

Eilish's jaw dropped in surprise.

"Many people feel like that," Una said.

"Everyone feels like that," Mrs. Fitzsimons affirmed. "Even Loyalists like myself. And I don't like that DORA, I've never liked it, doesn't seem proper or just. They arrest people for nothing."

"Yes," agreed Eilish, "everyone detests the *Defense Of The Realm Act*. The idea of just arresting people, and jailing them without trial. It's not fair."

Una looked across at the sorrowful red poppy that decorated Gerry's photograph. "But the Black and Tans don't raid this side of the Liffey, Mrs. Fitzsimons."

"Not yet they haven't," said Eilish, "which is not to say they won't start."

"It's not just between the Republicans and the Black and Tans," said Mrs Fitzsimons, "it's getting harder and harder to go about your business. Last Friday week I went over to Mary Street to a dressmaker for a fitting of a dress she's making me for the winter, and I had to walk all the way to Church Street to cross back over the river. The traffic was held up and the Capel Street Bridge was closed. They said the police had a house surrounded, that there were Republicans hiding there. I looked in the paper next day and there was no mention of it."

"Half the time," said Eilish, "they raid and burn a house and it's the wrong house."

"Nice carry on," said Mrs. Fizsimons, "they make a mistake, small comfort to the people burned out!"

It was not quite dark when they left.

"Well, there's a rib broke in the devil!" Eilish said in her best Athlone accent when they were in the street, "you could have knocked me over with a feather when I heard her say that about the English getting out."

"Emer says that too, Eilish, and you know how much she is against any kind of resistance, any sort of protest, even a work stoppage."

"Come on, we have to be quick. We're not supposed to be out."

It was dark with the sudden blackness of November evenings, and they hurried along. When they left Hatch Street and turned south on Earlsfort Terrace footsteps sounded behind them. "Should we run?" Una whispered.

"No, don't be silly, it's just someone walking home. There's two of us."

They passed under a gas lamp. The steps came nearer. It was a man. "Well, the curfew doesn't keep you ladies at home."

They spun round. It was their neighbour, Brian O'Donnell. He had a bed sitting room opposite theirs in 24 Mullagh Street. Brian dropped into step beside them, a slight young man, not quite as tall as Una, with easy, graceful manners.

"You're out late yourself, Brian," said Eilish.

"Ah, it makes no difference in this part of the town. It's always quiet around here."

They turned south on Harcourt Street and east to the South Circular Road. Black as pitch, no moon, just the bright stars and hazy street lamps throwing small pools of light. The houses shuttered and dark. Their footsteps echoed on the pavement.

"Not a soul on the street," said Eilish.

"Law abiding citizens in this neigbourhood," said Brian. "Keeping the curfew."

"The curfew is a nuisance."

"It is Eilish, but they say it will be lifted soon. Probably by Christmas. Business people complaining."

There was no one else about. An armoured car could thunder up at any time, soldiers jump off and surround them. Una was glad of Brian's company. Then the street lamps ended. In the silent darkness, with only starlight, the mundane journey began to feel perilous and exciting. On Mullagh Street the overhanging trees had an air of concealed menace, as if someone watched from behind the trees or from dark windows of the houses. They entered number 24 quiet as thieves. The landlady's light showed under the parlour door. The gas light on the stairs was lit. On the landing, Brian bowed mockingly. "It's been my pleasure to escort you ladies in safety."

"In your eye, Brian," Eilish retorted. "More like we escorted you."

"Eilish don't talk so loud," Una admonished.

"Goodnight, Brian."

"Goodnight."

Now Una was thinking about Brian, as she looked over her classroom. Brian and his laconic mocking bow. Sometimes he reminded her a little of Joseph, always cheerful and friendly, but he was young and more handsome. Ten minutes to afternoon recess. She looked at the calendar, five weeks till Christmas holidays. Her High Infant class at St. Brendan's National School was practicing their numbers. Eighteen six-year-olds copying lessons off the blackboard on slates, $2+1=3$, $2+2=4$. Rubbing out mistakes with their sleeves and starting over. Chalk squeaked on slates. Lily Mullin in the front row worked with her tongue curled up over her upper lip. She was her teacher's favourite, although Una never demonstrated favouritism. The child's black curly hair reminded Una of Nan. Lily rubbed her nose with her sleeve. Chalk from her sleeve clung to her nose. Lily sneezed.

"Bless you, Lily."

Lily smiled shyly up at Miss Maguire.

In the open space under the window Una had drawn a wide chalk semi-circle on the dusty wooden floorboards. The First Class pupils stood toes to the circle, each holding The First English Reader. Kathleen was reading, hesitating over long words, following lines with her index finger.

The door at the back of the classroom opened and Sister Mary Patrick floated in like a ship in full sail, veil flapping behind her.

"Miss Maguire," she announced, "Reverend Mother wants classes to finish early today. You can dismiss them before recess." She looked around at the children. "Class will be let out early, children." She dropped her voice to a whisper, "Reverend Mother is afraid of some trouble in the streets, Miss Maguire."

The High Infants were already on their feet chattering, "We're getting out early, we're getting out early."

Una clapped her hands. "Children, not so much noise. Put your slates and chalk away and line up."

The children lined up in two rows. "Walk quietly to the cloakroom. And everybody go straight home."

They filed out jostling and pushing each other. Una and the nun walked after them. In the cloakroom, Una helped the smallest ones with their coats. The other six classrooms were emptying out, pupils streaming across the schoolyard, up the footpath and on to the South Circular Road. Una and the nun stood at the door watching. Some of the older girls held hands with the little ones. Una remembered taking Nan's hand in just that way long ago in Slanabaille as they walked from school. She turned back toward her classroom. "Are there rumours of trouble about Sister?"

"There are always rumours. Reverend Mother is nervous, getting on for the weekend."

"But Sister, we never have any trouble around here."

"Well, you never know. Things seem a bit unsettled. It's because of that execution, the hanging of that poor Barry lad. God help us all! The children are better to go home early. You go, too."

Una nodded, "I'll be off soon. See you on Monday. Goodbye, Sister."

The nuns had certainly changed, Una mused, tidying up her classroom before setting off.

At the Cross and Resurrection Convent the nuns had appeared to be oblivious of the outside world. The only hint of war in Europe had been the mention of the dead among those to be prayed for. But at Carysfort Training College, where Una had trained to be a teacher, the long sporadic fight for independence dominated every conversation. The girls saved pictures and prayer cards of the executed leaders. The nuns followed every move of Eamon De Valera, now First Minister of the Dail, as the unofficial government was called. Eilish laughed about that. "He was elected on April Fools' Day Una, sure that's a sham of an election. A crowd of chancers, the lot of them, Dev's the biggest chancer of the lot. Over in America he's claiming to be the president of Ireland."

"Uncle Joseph thinks he's a great leader."

"Nothing to lead. Like the admiral of a Swiss fleet."

Although the British government was, as the newspapers said, the lawful government, the Dail and Sinn Fein behaved as if the Dail were the government. Dev had taught mathematics at Carysfort College until he had gone to jail after the Rising in 1916, and by the time Una had arrived at Carysfort in 1918, the nuns had elevated him to position of saint. Stories about his teaching days were told and retold till they attained the flavour of myth.

Una was now a junior teacher at St Brendan's Girls National School. Next year she would have her permanent certificate. She had won an exhibition at the end of her second year in the convent school, and proceeded to Carysfort with a grant of thirty pounds for each of her two years there. Emer was so pleased, so proud. Una believed she had worked very hard to please Emer, and her father, and never guessed how much her success was due to Eilish's unfailing belief that Una could succeed. It was impossible for Una to ever be discouraged with Eilish around. "Go on Una, you know you can knock spots off any of the girls."

The street seemed a little quiet for Friday afternoon as Una walked along toward the turn for Mullagh Street and home. In the distance she heard a tram rumble along. First a motorcar passed then a horse-drawn cab. A hint of rain on the air and the heavy light of November lay over the city. Then two army lorries sped past, breaking the quiet. Despite what the nun had said, Una wasn't nervous. Military cars and lorries were a common sight in Dublin in 1920. There had been no disturbance on her particular street, or in her neighbourhood, although raids and arrests were all too frequent in other parts of the city. Uncle Joseph insisted it couldn't last much longer. That wasn't what Emer thought. "The British should leave, but don't depend on it. Carry on with living the best you can," she said "that's all ordinary people can do. Don't be waiting for the emergency to be over. You could wait forever."

Emer and Joseph disagreed about the Irish Republican Army. Emer maintained that the IRA was war crazy. "Their whole campaign is not worth one life lost."

"Ah Emer, talking and politics hasn't worked, you need to show the gun."

But there was little talk of revolution at Emer's table. She absolutely banned it, and Joseph always ended by letting her have her way. Still, the long war was wearing cruelly on the people. Even in Slanabaille there were hints of trouble. In August, the Black and Tans burned down the creamery in Ballynamon, and the very next night Sinn Fein burned Bellview House near Obanbeg in a spectacular blaze. Joseph said that the owner of Darling House, a Major Nugent, was minding his manners in case he would be burned out too. "Anyhow," Joseph added, "the army will stop burning creameries when they see big property owners burned out as a result."

Una turned down her street, thinking of home in Slanabaille, about Christmas and Emer's good cooking. At the near end of Mullagh Street two rows of tall, three-story houses faced each other across black iron railings enclosing small front gardens of speckled laurel and bare lilac bushes.

Una pushed in the letter slot in the door of 24 Mullagh Street, felt around with her first two fingers, found the key string, pulled it through and inserted the key in the lock.

"Is that you, Una? You're early!" The landlady called from the kitchen at the back of the house. "Come in a minute, Una!"

Una dropped her handbag on the hall table and walked through the dark hall to the kitchen.

"School was let out early, Mrs. Quill."

Mrs. Quill, as usual, was stationed in her wide, wooden chair beside the big black range. The smallness of the firebox added to the fierceness of the glowing coals. A black iron teapot steamed gently on the back of the stove. Mrs. Quill's bulk filled the chair. She was wearing her best dress and boots.

"Sit a minute, Una. Would you like a cup of tea?"

"No thanks, when Eilish comes home we'll have our tea." She wasn't about to accept an offer of the strong, stewed black tea that had probably sat on the range since noon.

"Una, you're not thinking of going home for the weekend."

"No, Mrs. Quill, I don't think I'll go home till Christmas, the trains are so uncertain. You never know when they are running. Why do you ask?"

"I have to go home to Mullingar. My nephew wrote to say my sister is poorly."

"Oh, I'm sorry to hear it."

Una looked at her landlady, the heavy, sallow face and sharp, calculating blue eyes. She hadn't known Mrs. Quill was from Mullingar. She had a Dublin accent.

"Well, if anything happens to her, things will be in a right mess and no mistake. That nephew of mine's head is full of the Sinn

Fein, and not a blind bit of notice does he take of the shop or the house, although his wife is sensible enough." Una made no comment on the landlady's estimation of her relations, and Mrs. Quill continued. "Una, would you ever feed Lloyd George his saucer of milk twice a day when I'm gone?"

"Of course, I will. When are you leaving?"

"On the train at a quarter to five. I've my bag packed, all I have to do is to catch the tram."

"Don't worry about the cat, Mrs. Quill, I'll look after him," Una promised.

"Well, you're the only one I'd ask," Mrs. Quill stood up stiffly. She took the teapot and emptied it into the sink, then went into the hall and began to put on her coat.

"Goodbye, Mrs. Quill," said Una as she picked up her handbag and mounted the stairs, "I hope your sister is better."

The front door opened, letting a wedge of light into the dark hall, illuminating the mirror, table, and coat pegs. It closed again behind Mrs. Quill, the key on the string jangling. Off the hall to the right of the front door was the landlady's parlour, with its round table of dark wood, horse-hair stuffed chairs and the wind-up gramophone on a side table. Pictures of Pope Pius X and St. Patrick framed either side of the window that looked out onto a strip of a lane and the next house. Beyond the parlour, on one side of the kitchen, was Mrs. Quill's bedroom.

There were two bed-sitting rooms on the second level. The one in front, which had a bow window, was rented by Miss Breen, a quiet woman of forty who worked in the almoner's office at Holles Street Hospital. The back one was rented by a student, Michael Gallagher, a sandy-haired freckled boy who attended college in St.Stephen's Green. Between these two was situated the room with the communal facilities, an great claw-footed bathtub, a lavatory with an overhead cistern and a chain with a dangling china tag reading "Pull".

When Una turned at the top of the stairs on the third floor, Brian O'Donnell came out of his room at the back of the house. "Well, Una, finished for the week?"

"Yes, Brian, I am."

"Great life teachers have."

"You should take it up, Brian," Una shot back saucily.

"Ah Una, sure you'd need brains for that."

He passed her and went down the stairs. She heard the door close after him. In the window of the landing, smoke from the chimneys rose above the dark slate roofs and spires of Dublin and met the clouded sky. She watched Brian walk up towards South Circular Road. What a good-looking lad he was, his black hair falling forward on his forehead. She liked the way he jerked his head to toss it back out of his eyes. His fine, upright figure gave the impression of greater height than he in fact had. What had he been doing at home? Odd hours he kept. She knew he worked for a firm of wine importers at Ormond Quay. Did he have a day's holiday? She remembered hearing him leave his room on the previous day just after she had arrived home from school, about ten to four. She felt herself wanting to know more about him. Last Sunday, he had tea with Eilish and Una. He brought them a bottle of sherry. It was still on the chimney-piece, waiting for the proper occasion.

Still thinking of Brian, she went into her own and Eilish's bed-sitter at the front, hung her coat in the wardrobe and put a match to the fire. It was a big room, half the floor. The two-hooded dormer window faced the street. Under the windows there was a gas ring, a sink and cupboard for their supplies, and between the windows and the fireplace, a table and chairs. In an alcove at the far side of the room were two single beds, side by side.

Una sat for a few minutes in one of the chairs in front of the fire, then rose and lit the gaslights on either side of the chimney-piece. The fire was blazing up now, warming the damp air. She filled the kettle and set it on the small gas ring to boil. Then, she went down the stairs through the kitchen and out to the yard to retrieve her bottle of milk and a bowl of eggs from the food safe. It was built as a lean-to against the rear wall of the house, a square sturdy cupboard with fine mesh sides that allowed cool air to flow through. No sign of the big grey cat in the back garden. Inside the kitchen, Una left him a saucer of milk. He'd cry for admittance at the back door when he was hungry.

Upstairs, Una laid the table. Preparing the evening meal was her responsibility. Eilish, who left the house before seven for a firm of solicitors on the other side of the Liffey, usually made breakfast. The house was very still. The couple who occupied the floor above, Mr. and Mrs. Rourke, were so quiet one hardly knew they were in the house. Mrs. Rourke was head housekeeper in the Shamrock Hotel down off Sackville Street, her husband was the night porter in the same establishment. Mrs. Rourke would very soon creep up the stairs, home from work. A few hours afterwards, her husband would depart in the same way, for his night's work.

"Good, you have the tea ready," said Eilish, shaking rain off her coat and spreading it over a chair in front of the fire. "It's been a long week. If it weren't raining, and if it weren't for the damn curfew, we could go out to the pictures or for a walk."

"Oh Eilish, I have letters to write, and it's too wet anyway, so even without the curfew I'd stay home. Let's go tomorrow."

"We could go tomorrow afternoon, it's Saturday, remember. Maybe finances would stretch to tea in Bewleys." Eilish helped herself to hard boiled eggs. "What time did you get home?"

"Early, just after three. Mother Superior let school out early, she thought there might be trouble."

"So, there's always some sort of trouble, but not out here."

Una spread gooseberry jam on her bread. "Mrs. Quill's gone home for a few days, her sister is sick. Did you know she was from Mullingar, Eilish?"

"No, I didn't. Just goes to show how little you know of anyone in the city."

"And Brian, he was on his way out when I came in. Unusual hours he keeps."

"Ah, so you're keeping an eye on him Una. I think you fancy him. Admit it. You do."

"He is nice Eilish, and very good-looking."

"See Una, you're doing better, growing up. Two years ago you would never have admitted you liked a fellow."

"I would so."

"No you wouldn't, you'd have blushed and denied you were interested. You'd have thought it was a sin."

"Oh Eilish, you always exaggerate."

"I'm not exaggerating."

"Well, I do like him."

Eilish looked at her sharply, "Una, just don't get any notions about him."

"Why not? He's very handsome, and very polite."

"Una, he's no good for you. A streel like that! Working in a wine shop. Just don't get any serious ideas."

"I'm not," said Una defensively, "I just think he's very nice, that's all."

"Nice alright, but a bit of a lad, too."

"Eilish, how can you say that? You don't know him."

"Neither of us do. Sure he's only been here a month. I just think he's too sweet to be wholesome. I wouldn't trust him from here to Nelson's Pillar."

Eilish got up and drew the curtains against the night. After they had washed the dishes, Una sat at the table and wrote letters while Eilish read. They could hear the rain gently washing against the window. By ten o'clock they were both sleepy. They heard Brian O'Donnell's door close, and Miss Breen go to the lavatory.

"I'm going to put the bolts on the front door."

Una went downstairs and shot the bolts home, then went through the kitchen and opened the back door; she looked out into the dark drizzle. "Kitty, kitty! Where are you?"

There was no sign of the cat. Una bolted the door, put a shovel of slack from the scuttle into the firebox and closed the damper. She went back up.

"The cat's not out there, Eilish," she said as she began to ready for bed.

"Oh, he'll come home when he's good and ready."

"I'm going to bed, Eilish."

"And I will too, just when I finish this chapter."

Una lighted the candle that stood on the table between the beds and quenched the gaslights. She got into bed and lay with her arms behind her head, staring up at the ceiling. They heard the student on the second floor walk from the bathroom to his door.

The house was settling down for the night. Eilish got into bed and blew out the candle. "Goodnight, Una."

"Goodnight, Eilish."

HOURS LATER, Una woke to the chugging, dragging sound of an armoured car somewhere in the distance. It seemed to be coming from South Circular Road.

"Eilish! Are you awake?"

"Yes, I hear it. It won't come this way, it's up on the main road."

The noise came nearer and lights swept the windows sending their beams into the room. Eilish shot up in bed. "Una, they're on our street."

Una sprang out of bed and fumbled for matches to light the candle. The car halted outside, motor idling. Una ran across the room and peeped out at the side of the blind. The vehicle was stopped in front of number 24, its headlights shining on the wet garden and the gate.

"Eilish, it's a raid. Get up, get up."

Rifle butts thumped the front door.

"My God Una, the buggers."

"Eilish hurry. Quick, put on your coat. We must open the door!"

Una shoved her arms into the sleeves of her coat and ran for the stairs. "I'm coming, I'm coming," she yelled, sounding a lot calmer and braver than she was feeling. "Don't break the door."

Miss Breen, pale as death, was hanging over the banister on the second floor landing. Michael Gallagher opened his door and seeing Una, followed her down. Weak-kneed, she struggled to draw back the heavy bolts. Michael stepped in front of her and pulled them back as the door was shoved in. A soldier grabbed him by his hair and stared at him for a second, then shoved him roughly aside and rushed past Una. Two others followed. One carried a lantern. They pounded into the kitchen and she could hear them slamming cupboard doors. Eilish came running down the stairs and stood beside her. The lights of the armored car shone into the hall. The engine was left running. An officer stood in the doorway slapping his baton against his leg.

"No one in the first floor bedroom sir," a man called out.

"That's the landlady's bed," Una called back. "She's gone to Mullingar. There's illness in the family."

Miss Breen came down holding on to the rail as if her legs might give way. She shrunk in behind Michael. The men rushed past again and thundered up the stairs. The women shivered in the hall listening to the soldiers pounding on doors and stomping through the house. Michael stood back at the kitchen doorway seething with resentment, freckles standing out in his pale face. The officer walked up and down the hall, to the kitchen and back. The men could be heard questioning Mrs. Rourke, her quiet voice answering. "I'm on my own here, just a woman on my own. The fellow in that room is a porter at the Shamrock. He's on the night shift. You know the Shamrock? Just off Sackville Street."

After a while she crept down the stairs and stood with the others in the hall. The curling papers that furred her head gave her the look of an angry cat while the wind from the door twisted her nightdress around her legs. From upstairs they heard men loudly cursing. "The wrong damn house again! I knew it. On a bloody wild goose chase. I tell you mate, the Paddy's are all liars."

Una shrunk against the wall, terrified of the violence in their voices. The officer stopped at the bottom of the stairs and looked at her closely, her pale face illuminated by the candle. The candle flame fluttered. The hand she had curved around it trembled. He walked back and shut the door.

"Are you English?" he asked her. "You look like an English girl."

"No sir, I'm Irish."

"You don't look Irish! You remind me very much of my sister, with that blonde hair. You're very like her."

"Well, if she's any relation of yours she's not worth much," Eilish blurted out defiantly.

"Please excuse her, sir," Una apologized quickly. "She doesn't really mean that. She's just upset."

The officer strolled over to the parlour door and back. The men came clobbering down the stairs.

"Nothing sir, no sign of him," the lead one reported. "We must have got taken in again, wrong information, deliberately, the wrong bloody place."

"Let's move it along then, look sharp."

"We have the wrong house, the wrong district. Completely mislead," the man behind said. He was carrying the bottle of sherry from Eilish and Una's chimney piece.

"Give me that!"

The officer grabbed the bottle and handed it to Una. The men clattered past him and out. "Goodnight, miss," he said, touched his cap and was gone, pulling the door shut behind him.

The little group in the hall stood silent, stunned, looking at the closed door, the key swinging on its string. The flame of the candle quivered and shadows leaped on the walls. They listened hard to the sounds of the armoured car backing up and turning. Then it lumbered up the street the way it had come, lights and noise fading away toward Dolphin's Barn.

"Eilish!" Una shrieked, when the noise ceased, "you could have had us all shot. Are you crazy? To say that?"

"Oh, please excuse her sir, sweet little Una, good little Una," Eilish danced around, mocking Una. "*Mor dhea*, as if you meant a word of it."

"Eilish, what made you do such a thing?"

"Oh Una, you should be on the stage."

Una found herself laughing hysterically. She sat on the stairs and held the bottle against her chest. "Well, I fooled him, didn't I? Didn't I? But I was very frightened, I really was. He believed me though, didn't he?"

"I think," pronounced Miss Breen, taking the candle from Una's shaking hand and putting it on the hall table, "I think you saved us."

"Yes Una, you did very well," Michael said, bolting the door. "We could have been killed."

Mrs. Rourke looked out through the curtains in Mrs. Quill's

parlour. "Not a sound or light on the street," she reported, coming back to the hall.

"Well, no one is going to as much as open their door tonight," Michael said.

"Now's the time to drink that sherry," Eilish cried wildly, relieving Una of the bottle.

"Where's Brian?" asked Una. "I'm sure I heard him come in earlier."

"They asked me who was in that front room," declared Mrs. Rourke proudly, "I gave them my husband's name. I pretended I lived alone in our flat. I told them he was on night shift at the Shamrock Hotel."

The cat could be heard crying at the back door. "Oh, I forgot about Lloyd George, and it's raining too."

Una took the candle, went through the kitchen and opened the back door. The cat rubbed his wet fur against her legs. "Una," said a voice in a whisper, "Una!" The voice came from the top of the food safe. She raised the candle.

"Brian! What are you doing up there? You almost frightened me to death. Don't you know we were raided?"

Brian jumped lightly to the ground "I know Una. They were looking for me."

Ice inched along Una's spine. "For you? For what, Brian? For what?"

"For DORA my dear," he said a little ruefully.

"What? You could have got us all in terrible trouble. We could have been arrested, maybe even shot."

"I know." He bowed with exaggerated ceremony. "I'd never want to get you in trouble, Una."

"You can't stay here Brian! Not if they're looking for you! You know that. You have to get out. Now! They might come back."

"Not tonight they won't, and tomorrow before the sun is up I'll be on my way. I promise. I've business elsewhere on Sunday, Una."

"How do you know they won't come back?"

"I know them. They won't be back! Did you not hear what they said, Una? I heard them say they had the wrong house, the wrong neighbourhood. They're off somewhere else. Probably to the North side. And soon it'll be daylight and they'll be back in the Portobello Barracks."

He was shivering, his clothes soaking.

"Come in then and get dry. But you have to leave by morning."

Everyone crowded into the kitchen. Brian hung his coat on a chair in front of the range. Michael shoveled coal in the firebox and opened the damper. Eilish took glasses from Mrs. Quill's cupboard and began to pour and pass the sherry.

"You first, Brian. Sure you're drowned from sitting out there in the wet."

They clinked glasses high. *"Slainte."*

They lit the gaslights in Mrs. Quill's parlour and sat around her table sipping the sherry, feeling like truant children up long past their bedtime. Then Michael opened the gramophone. He wound it vigorously, set the needle in place, and John McCormack's voice soared through the house. *"Oh believe me if all those endearing young charms…"*

"May I have the pleasure, Una?" Brian stood and executed what was by now his trade mark bow.

Una rose and took his hand, "Why not?"

"which I gazed on so fondly today…"

Barefoot, she danced with him out into the hall, up into the kitchen, and back again. Even without her shoes she was just slightly taller than he was. Eilish and Michael followed, executing elaborate fantastic steps. The singer's voice climbed to a high unfaltering sweet crescendo, *"were to fade by tomorrow and fleet in my arms…"*

Mrs. Rourke, quite carried away, pirouetted, the sherry glass held aloft. Her nightgown fanned out, like a child dancing in the wind. The singing slid lower, *"like faery gifts fading away."*

"There's no one like John McCormack," sighed Mrs. Rourke as she danced.

Miss Breen poured herself another sherry and called out, "How did you get out onto the food safe, Brian?"

"Oh, Mrs. Rourke let me out her window and I climbed down the spout," he called back, not missing one beat of the waltz.

"Really, Brian?" asked Una.

"Yes, Una. She did."

Quiet mousy little Mrs. Rourke, now twirling to the music. It was unbelievable, preposterous, thought Una, as she circled round the kitchen in Brian's arms. But then so was the night and its terror, now somehow turned into a celebration of their escape of Brian evading capture, their triumph in deceiving the police. The gramophone wound down. Miss Breen chose another record, re-wound it, set the needle and the dancers changed partners and were off again. Mrs. Rourke sat down breathless and Miss Breen refilled her glass.

"Those blackguards of soldiers put the heart cross ways in me," confided Miss Breen.

"They're not really soldiers, you know. They're police, paid ten shillings a day to terrorize the people," Mrs. Rourke answered, sipping her sherry.

"I wonder they can get anyone to do it. You did well to talk up to them," Miss Breen raised her glass in acknowledgment of the other woman's prescience and together they watched the two waltzing couples with benevolent, almost maternal indulgence as the clock on the shelf over the kitchen stove ticked toward morning. When they remembered to look it was almost half-past six. It would soon be sunrise.

Brian checked his coat. Not quite dry. He put it on anyway.

"Must be off!"

The cold dawn was rising over the city. They all stood at the door to say goodbye to Brian O'Donnell. Miss Breen a little tipsy from the sherry, Eilish and Una subdued. Smoke from morning fires rose into the grey sky. The rain had ceased, laurels and the bare lilacs dripped somberly, weak light spreading in the east held the chimney pots and roofs of Dublin in sulky silhouette. When he took her hand, a sad, empty feeling came over Una. She knew he had to go. They might not ever see each other again.

"Goodbye, Una," he bowed.

"*Slan leat* Brian, goodbye."

"So long, Eilish."

"Goodbye."

He shook hands with everyone. "Goodbye Mrs. Rourke."

"God keep you."

They watched him walk quickly toward South Circular Road. He didn't look back; he carried nothing with him.

"Una, you reminded me of nothing so much as your Aunt Emer, when you talked to that officer, plamasin and making apologies."

"What else could I do Eilish? He had a gun."

"I know. You're right. My tongue's too long for my mouth. I don't know what came over me. I could have got us arrested."

"We should go to bed."

"I'm not in the least sleepy. I'm hungry, though."

"I'll make breakfast," offered Mrs. Rourke. "Come on up to my place."

"I'll get bacon from the safe," said Una.

"And I've sausages out there," said Miss Breen. "Bring them, Una."

"Alright."

"Brian should have waited for breakfast."

"I don't think he wanted to, Miss Breen."

"It's better he's gone," Mrs. Rourke said firmly, "we'll see no more of him."

"Is that what you think?"

"It is, Una dear. He's better away. Better for him and for us. Come on up and we'll all have something to eat."

Away, thought Una, going out to the food safe. It sounded so lonesome.

They were still tired on Sunday. The morning was cold and damp. "It's supposed to be a day of rest anyway," Eilish reasoned as they walked home from early mass. "I'm going to laze about for the day!"

The day passed quietly. They tidied the flat and Una wrote to her father.

"Watch what you write to him, Una. Some post is opened you know."

"I wouldn't mention the raid. It would worry him."

It was almost dark at four o'clock. "I keep thinking about Brian.

I wonder where he is?" Una was sitting on the fender drying her hair in the heat from the fire.

"God only knows."

"I hope he's alright."

"He's well able to look after himself."

"I wish Mrs. Quill were back."

"She'll be back before the end of the month. You know, to collect the rent."

"I've a mind to cut my hair," said Una, standing up and shaking her head. Her heavy blond hair swung around her face.

"Leave your hair alone. It's grand."

MONDAY MORNING, as usual, Eilish was up before seven. She lit the gas and moved quietly about so as not to wake Una. When she was ready to leave she touched her shoulder. "Una! It's twenty-five to eight. I left your tea on the table."

"Thanks, Eilish."

Eilish turned down the gas and was gone. Una heard Miss Breen leave and then Michael. Grey morning light seeped into the room. Sleepily, Una sat up in bed. She stepped out, padded over to the table, and poured herself a cup of tea. The start of another week. In Slanabaille, Donny and Joseph and Nan would be setting out for school. She added milk to her cup. I mustn't forget the cat's milk, she thought.

She was pinning up her hair when she heard the front door open and someone running up the stairs. Eilish burst in the door "Una! Una!"

"My God! What's wrong?"

"Una, there's British officers murdered. When I got to the tram the newsboys were shouting. I couldn't get a paper with so many crowded round. But I saw the headline. Ten murdered yesterday. All shot!"

"Ten shot? My God!" Una sunk down on her bed. A flutter of fear ran along her spine and she tensed as if she expected a blow. "Brian? Do you think he had something to do with it?"

"I'm not sure. But it's strange, very strange. The way he left."

"My God, Eilish! You remember he said something about business elsewhere on Sunday? Could it be him?" A heavy strand of hair slid out of its pins on to her shoulder. She pushed it back in place with a shaky hand. She felt herself flooded with dread; the raid, the police with the guns. Brian walking away in the empty dawn. Men shot like vermin. Eilish sat beside her and put her arm around her.

"Will this ever end, Eilish?

"Of course, it'll have to end. Everyone says so. It can't go on like this."

"Eilish, I can't believe it. If Brian was part of it we were in real danger, we were dancing with a gunman, with a killer."

"We may have been. Did you not think he was very odd?"

"I liked him Eilish," Una stood up and walked over to the window. The street was quiet. "Do you think anyone will connect him with this house?"

"No, I don't. I've been thinking about that. We'd nothing to do with it. Nothing! They didn't even think he was here. And what did we know? He was just another tenant. And he wasn't here long. If he was one of Collins' men he's away, to the west, to Galway or Mayo. Hiding out. A cute crowd, Collins' lads. Work in the dark, never get caught."

They heard Miss Breen shut the door of her room and go downstairs. A little later Michael left.

Una heaved a deep, heavy sigh, "I have to go to school."

"I bet there's no school."

"Are you going to work, Eilish?"

"I certainly am. I'll be late but that's understandable. The trams are slow but they're running. It's best to act normal, you know."

"Then I'll go up to the school."

School went ahead but many pupils stayed home. Only six of the eighteen children in the High Infants Class were present and just ten in the First Class. Distracted, thinking about Brian, she wrote the first four letters of the alphabet on the blackboard and set the High Infants to work on forming their letters. The First Class copied addition exercises from *Standard Arithmetic Book 1* onto their slates. It was unusually quiet, the children feeling something was wrong.

"Miss, my father said Britishers were murdered yesterday," said Molly Conroy.

"That was far away from here, Molly. They're in heaven. Now go on with your work."

A few minutes before eleven o'clock recess Sister Mary Patrick barged into Una's classroom. "There'll be prayers in the church at twelve, Miss Maguire," she announced.

At ten minutes to twelve Una lined up her pupils, and with all the classes from St. Brendan's, they walked west toward Adelaide Road. On the other footpath a line of bobbing green caps with the lettering CBS in gold, and fluttering blue and gold scarves, moved in the same direction. The boys from the Christian Brothers School. The noon Angelus rang as the two lines converged at the church door. They filled the first ten rows of seats in the dusky interior, boys on the right and girls on the left. The advent candle threw an uncertain light in the gloom. When the shuffling and coughing ceased, Mother Superior led off with the first sorrowfull mystery of the rosary.

In the evening, the little group gathered in Mrs. Quill's kitchen.

"We mustn't mention Brian to outsiders," Mrs Rourke warned. "You never know who you might be talking to."

"That's right. We'll need to keep our mouths shut," Eilish agreed.

The papers were full of speculation about the murderers. People went nervously about their business, looking over their shoulders for gunmen hiding in the shadows. Police seemed to be everywhere but they did not return to 24 Mullagh Street and Mrs. Quill's boarders relaxed their guard. But Una thought about Brian O'Donnell constantly with a mixture of fear, horror and sadness. So young, so full of fun, so handsome and perhaps ruthless, too. Halfway through writing something on the blackboard or helping some child with a problem, her mind would circle back to the previous Friday night when they were dancing. Is Brian safe? Where did he go? Was he hiding somewhere, on the run from the law?

Early Thursday evening Mrs. Quill arrived home, just as Una was beginning to prepare tea. She went down stairs to meet her.

"Well, Una, I hear Collins' boyos had a bit of target practice while I was away!"

"Mrs.Quill it's been awful. Shootings and raids."

"I know Una, I heard. It's terrible. God between us and all harm! This was the first day I could get a train."

"How is your sister?"

"On the mend, thank God. I think she might have had that influenza you know. Lots of rest and lots of beef tea. She'll be all right."

"Mrs.Quill, we were raided."

"What? Out here?" Mrs Quill sank slowly into her chair.

"Last Friday night. The Black and Tans came."

"God Almighty, no place is safe! What were they after?"

Una told her about Brian and they went up to his room. The bed hadn't been slept in and the wardrobe had just a shirt and an old pair of trousers.

"Well, I don't know," sighed Mrs Quill anxiously, "there's no end of trouble. He might be one of Collins' lads and he might not. Tomorrow, I'll go round to his work and enquire. If he was a Republican they won't tell me anything. But say nothing about it. I don't want the police coming around here, or that other shower, the Black and Tans."

"But do you not know where he's from, Mrs.Quill?"

"Well, I know he's from Clare. But I didn't ask questions. For me the principal concern was that he had a job and paid his rent, and he did, he's paid up to the end of the month. If he's not coming back, I might as well rent the room. This time I want a girl or a woman. No more lads for me. I've had enough."

When Mrs. Quill returned from her talk with Brian's employers, she told Una and Eilish they knew as little as she did.

"They said he was a good worker, but they hadn't seen him in two weeks. He'd sent them a note he was sick."

"In your eye he was sick! Up to no good he was."

"Eilish, we don't know that."

"Well," said Mrs. Quill, "we're better off without him. If

anyone asks, say you know nothing. They say a crowd that was shot last Sunday were all informers. That's some price to pay for being too long in the tongue."

Una still couldn't stop thinking about him. If they had had a chance to become friends things might have been different, he might have given up violence. The more she thought about him, the more convinced she was that he was part of some unlawful activity. She imagined herself meeting him again, talking to him. She rehearsed what she would say to convince him to change.

"Ah sure, he must have got away. That's the main thing," Eilish decided.

Una hoped he had, but she still wanted to see him again. If only she had stopped him. How ridiculous dancing like that if he was plotting murder. If she just knew where he was. He could have been arrested and they would never know. Eilish said she was tired of Una's white, woebegone face. "Una, you know you're moping about. I don't know what to do with you."

"Well, I'm afraid he's shot, or in jail. I told him he couldn't stay here. I was too frightened. Now I wish we'd stopped him."

"Stop him? Sure no one could stop him if that's what he wanted. There was always something strange about him. Something wild. I'll tell you what you should do, take the train down on Saturday and talk to Mattie about it. You know you always listen to her."

"If the trains are running."

"I bet they will be. Even the Black and Tans take the train sometimes."

The curfew was lifted the following week. On Saturday, she took the train to Obanbeg. "Give Mattie my best," Eilish called from the door as Una set off.

The train was half empty. Only herself and a middle-aged couple in the second class carriage. It was early December, foggy and damp. The trees leafless. Walking up the drive of her old school Una passed the students out for their Saturday walk. Light chattering voices drifted back on the cold misty air. How young they seemed. A little over two years ago she had been walking with Eilish in the same long straggling line. She felt different now. What was it that was different? How had she changed? She looked up at the tall windows behind which she had studied, pictured the green shiny maps and the blackboards on the classroom wall, the ink turning thick and grainy in the inkwells. The convent still smelled of Mansion floor polish and wax candles.

Nothing could restrain Sister Saint Mathew's joy at seeing her favorite old girl. She kissed Una smartly on both cheeks. "How wonderful that you came for a visit, Una!"

In the nuns' parlour a lay sister served tea in the convent's best Beleek china. Scones and clotted cream and damson jam. Sister Saint Mathew filled their cups while Una told her story. "I think I might have stopped him if only I had known, Sister. I know he liked me."

Mattie turned her teacup round in her hands, studying the raised basketwork pattern, thinking.

"It's tragic Una, tragic now, for his family, whoever they are, for you and for him, for everyone, if he's a murderer." She looked up at Una, searching her face. "But in the end, it doesn't matter, Una. In eternity it won't matter. He did what he wanted to do, or what he was told to do, and he may have got away, to England, or America."

"Will you pray that he is safe?"

"Well, Una," her face took on one of her stern looks and she fingered her beads at her waist, "some of that is up to him you know. But let's both pray that whatever happens to him he is strong, has peace and a quiet mind. And makes the right choices. That's all we can do."

"Do you think he has made bad choices up to now, Sister?"

"How would I know, Una? Sometimes people believe they must take certain actions. They lose all faith in the way the affairs of the country are being run. And then feel they must take matters in their own hands. All is not well or happy in Ireland. Are the Republicans right, Una? Only time will tell. Just pray he's at peace."

Mattie was never as you expected her to be. Maybe that was the way to remember him, to ease her conscience, to stop her thinking every waking minute of what she might have done, of what they might have become to each other. To pray that he would have a quiet mind, make good choices. Would she be able to do that?

And not worry if he was in jail, or shot? And not think about him constantly with a horrid hollow feeling, as if starving for something she couldn't identify.

"And how is your teaching going? Before you know it you'll have your Certificate."

"Oh, I love it, Sister. It was the right choice for me."

They talked about what Una was doing, earning her living, sharing a flat with Eilish, going home to Slanabaille when she could, and teaching the very youngest at St Brendan's.

"Eilish is a good friend for you my dear, she has lots of good sense."

Remembering Eilish's outburst during the raid Una wasn't so sure. Of course, everyone was so resentful, so weary of the whole business, the raids, and the curfews.

Una told her about Nan. She would be coming to the convent school in two years. "I think she will fit in well, Sister. I was the first to leave home and I was lonesome at first."

"She'll have big shoes to fill, Una, following you."

"Thank you, Sister."

"Thank you, Una, for coming to visit. Come soon again."

When Sister Saint Mathew stood up to walk to the door with Una, her shawl slid on the floor. Una picked it up. Una was about to remind Mattie of how she had once dragged her shawl across the floor to demonstrate Hamlet dragging the dead Polonius. Then she decided not to. Mattie would think she was silly. How did someone decide to kill? Was he really a killer? Maybe he hadn't pulled the trigger. Maybe he just carried messages. If only she knew.

The third Saturday after the raid, Una and Eilish went to Grafton Street to shop. There were police everywhere, in twos and threes, parading up and down. Still, people were in the shops. Una chose a long black silk scarf with a beaded fringe, a Christmas present for Emer.

"Isn't it lovely, Eilish. It's more than I intended to spend, but it will go so well with her green winter coat."

"If you think she'll like it, get it. Next Saturday it might be gone, or the shops might be shut."

"I'd like to go to the bookshops on the quays too," Una said, as the shop assistant wrapped the scarf.

They walked down the slight slope of Grafton Street and when they came to Bernardos Furs they stopped to look in the window. "I'd love a fur, but I'll never afford one," said Eilish, admiring the only garment on display, a leopard skin coat fanned out to fill the entire recess of the window.

"It's hardly ever cold enough in Dublin for a fur, Eilish."

"Oh, but the luxury, Una. The style!"

They turned away and crossed the street. As they walked along the curved iron railing of Trinity College Una thought she spied Brian O'Donnell. His slight figure moved in and out through the crowd, then disappeared through the domed door that led into Front Square. "Eilish look! There's Brian."

"Where?"

"Over there under that arch."

But he had disappeared. There was no one but a few students and the uniformed guard at the gate.

"Una, you're cracked! That wasn't him. He's gone, forget him, Una. And stop romancing about him."

"I'm not romancing."

"You are Una! You're always romancing about something. Forget about him. He wouldn't be at Trinity, never. He was a Catholic! And he wasn't that smart! He'd never be there, not even as a skip or a servant. Come on, let's do our shopping and then I'll stand you coffee and biscuit." She pulled Una along toward the bridge over the river.

Una picked through the books looking for something for Joseph. She turned over a slim, dark green volume. "Look at this Eilish. *Songs Of The Fields*. Joseph'll love this. It's only one and threepence."

"Get it for him, then."

"You know, Eilish, Lizzie Scanlon, God rest her, told me Joseph was in the Republican Brotherhood and Emer made him give it up."

"And so you think you could make Brian O'Donnell give up the gun, too?"

"I'm not saying that exactly, but I could try."

"There's two chances of that, Una," Eilish said grimly, "little and none! Come on, I'm getting chilly. Let's have that coffee."

Una scarcely heeded Eilish. She looked for Brian whenever they were out in the streets. The Saturday before she went home for Christmas they were out shopping again and she saw him standing at a stall in Moore Street, buying a bunch of holly. It was early evening and almost dark. He tossed back his lock of black hair as he pocketed his change. Una rushed forward. He moved ahead through the crowd and she followed as he disappeared round a corner. She ran after him and when she reached the corner he was gone. She stood in the December dusk feeling like a fool. Maybe it wasn't him. Maybe she imagined it. Eilish walked up quickly. "What's wrong, Una?"

"I thought that was Brian, the fellow buying the holly."

"That wasn't him."

"It looked like him. I was sure it was him."

"Una, you're seeing things. It's a good thing you're going home next Saturday. That fellow's in Canada or Australia by now. Remember what Mattie told you to do. Put Brian O'Donnell right out of your head."

"She didn't say forget him Eilish, she said pray he would have a quiet mind."

"It's your own mind, Una, needs to be quiet."

SHE PLANNED TO take the eleven o'clock train Saturday. At Amiens Street Station, a squadron of Black and Tans were stopping travelers at the barrier, questioning and searching some of the men. Even some first class passengers were questioned. She was not stopped but the train was an hour late. In her railway carriage, two men groused and cursed the police and the delay. Two others sulked behind their newspapers. An older woman in the corner sat silent. Una concentrated on her book.

Joseph was in Obanbeg station to meet her, wrapped in his big coat and muffler. It was sunny and very cold. Bundles of fleecy clouds piled up in an icy blue sky. He took her suitcase. "Great to have you back, Una." They walked over to where he had tied the pony. "The train was very late."

"The police delayed it. They searched some of the men."

"Oh, I'm not surprised. You weren't bothered?"

"No. I'm sorry you had to wait Uncle Joseph."

"Oh, that's nothing. You're here, that's the main thing. I was getting worried. We'll start straight away."

In the trap she wrapped the rug around herself. Joseph turned the pony for home. "You came on your own, Uncle Joseph?"

"Oh, they're all waiting for you. Emer and Nan busy with Christmas cooking."

"How is Donny?"

"Donny has a little cold, not a bad one. He wanted to come but Emer thought it better for him to stay home. It's well he didn't come, the train being late and it being so cold. He's dying to see you."

"I brought him a little model airplane."

"He'll like that. Ever since the two fellows from Newfoundland flew across the Atlantic last year he's mad about airplanes."

The town was busy, horse carts and traps lined up before the shops, country people buying their Christmas supplies. The shop windows were trimmed with holly and lighted candles.

"It's cold, Joseph, colder than in Dublin. I hope we have snow for Christmas."

"That's what Nan's hoping for. It's cold enough for snow, but I see no sign of it."

The pony, winter shod, trotted through the town, then slowed his pace going up the slope, breathing clouds of vapour in the frost. Near the top they passed the gapped ruins of two burnt-out houses side by side. Only the gables were left, brown-stained from fire and rain. Una stared at them.

"The Tans' work."

"Joseph, people in Dublin say there'll be a truce soon."

"I expect it, maybe by summer. The British themselves have no stomach for it anymore."

"How do you mean?"

"They can only hold it by more violence, more atrocity. They're losing their taste for that."

"Joseph, the Black and Tans came to search our digs."

"What?" He pulled the pony up short. "Your place was raided?"

They were near the workhouse gate and he guided the pony off the roadway towards the margin. The pony laid his ears back, protesting this unusual halt in the journey. Joseph looked at her, alarmed. "When, Una?"

"A month ago."

"And you never told us?"

"I wasn't home since. The officer in charge seemed to be nice."

"Sometimes they're like that, to get you to talk. Una, we had no idea about this. We thought that was a safe place, that the land-lady was reliable. And Eilish's been there two years."

"Well, the fellow they were after got away, anyway."

"I don't care about that. What about you?"

"Oh, I was alright. Eilish was cheeky to the officer."

"She was? That wasn't smart. What was there, that brought on the raid?"

He looked serious as she told him about Brian O'Donnell, that he'd only lived there a short time and how he'd got away, how Mrs. Rourke had spirited him out through the window and pretended his room was rented by a porter on the night shift at the Shamrock Hotel.

"Well, anyone working in a hotel in Dublin has their wits about them. They see plenty."

"I really liked Brian O'Donnell, Joseph. He was a lovely lad."

"Una, that's no one for you to be liking. Stay as far away from those people as you possibly can."

"Joseph, how can you say that? Lizzie told me you were in the Republican Brotherhood."

His expression became very stern. "Una, these are a different class of men. Most of them have been in jail, or in the war. They're hard, hard men. We were just fools, blundering about. Only Connolly, and maybe Collins, had any idea at all about killing. These men think nothing of sacrificing girls like you and Eilish if it suits them. It was very dangerous for you to be there, to have anything at all to do with them. Very risky."

"Maybe Brian wasn't one of them."

"From what you've told me, Una, I'm sure he was."

"But, he was so friendly and nice."

"He wasn't, Una! He was a killer. Think of the state we'd be in if anything happened to you. It would kill Emer. When we read or hear of a Sinn Fein demonstration in Dublin she always says 'Thank God Una never bothers with that.' It's a worry, you so far away, you being in the city."

The pony snorted and shook his harness. Joseph sat with the reins idle in his lap watching her face. She dropped her eyes. There was such insistence in his voice it shocked her.

"Promise me Una, you're going to forget that fellow."

"It's not that easy," she said stubbornly.

"Una! You're only young, your whole life ahead of you. It's disastrous for you to be thinking like that about him. You'll ruin your life."

"Eilish said he might be in Canada."

"He might. Anyway he's a marked man. Put it behind you now."

"I'll try," she said grudgingly.

"Not just try, do it. Keep busy, Una. The teacher's union needs young people like you. Why aren't you involved with their work? And there's lots of clubs in Dublin, lots to do. Eilish would agree with me I'm sure."

She sat looking down at the green wool rug covering her knees. It was the first time Joseph had ever been severe with her. She wished she'd never told him, but she'd wanted to confide in him, to get his opinion of Brian, to dispel the uneasiness Eilish's scorn had sown in her mind. Now she had his estimation and it dismayed her. His attitude diminished Brian, made him a dubious figure. But at the same time in Joseph's emotional reaction she began, reluctantly, to see the sense in what he was saying. For a minute she wanted to weep.

"You can put that fellow out of your mind if you want to. Promise me you will, Una."

She wanted him to resume the journey, to drive on, to forget what she had said. But Joseph wasn't ready to drop the subject. "The Republicans have their own troubles Una, they don't agree among themselves. Even when the British leave there'll be problems. Lots of trouble. We've no experience in governing ourselves. It may take years to settle things. Collins has an army and there's no guarantee they'll all go home and settle down to work. Things could get nasty yet. So we'll put all this behind us now, Una?"

"Yes."

"Good girl."

He flicked the rains and turned the pony back on the road. They trotted on for home, the town chimneys smoking behind them. Out in the countryside, the farmyards were empty, everyone indoors at the fire. She pulled the rug up round her shoulders. The bare trees threw webs of black shadows, the wind shivered claw ends of thorn bushes, froze stumps of forgotten cabbages in gardens, the weak winter sun moved west striping the horizon with cinnamon and afternoon drifted into evening. Una pondered what Joseph had said. A marked man. Now she hoped Brian was in Canada. Mrs. Quill said that once the place was raided they'd never see him again, that he couldn't risk returning to the house. "Not that I'd want him," she'd maintained. "I'm looking for a steady tenant, none of that Republican shenanigans!"

The pony plodded on. Joseph huddled in his coat. Did he think less of her now? Was he afraid she'd spoil the holiday brooding? As if he read her thoughts he said "We'll have a grand Christmas, Una. Lots of company. Emer's planning a bit of a party at the New Year. Cassie and Tom'll do the honours at Little Christmas."

"I'm glad to be home, Uncle Joseph."

"Of course you are. And we're delighted to have you."

Una was silent, thinking about her sister, her little brother waiting at home. She hadn't seen them since Hallowe'en. She'd bought Nan gloves for Christmas. Black leather with rabbit fur trim at the wrists. Nan's first pair of gloves from a shop. Nan suffered from chilblains in winter and was always losing her knitted gloves. She'd be more careful with these. Una imagined Nan pulling them on, smoothing them over her plump little hands. She'd spent too much on her holiday shopping. To compensate, she and

Eilish decided not to buy each other anything. In January, she'd watch her spending, less going to the pictures, less having tea at Bewleys. But at home there might be a letter from her father awaiting and maybe a little Christmas money.

The short December day slipped toward nightfall. It was getting colder and dusk had already settled round the base of hedges and trees. She hadn't eaten since breakfast and was very hungry. They were nearing Slanabaille. Was Joseph still angry with her? Disappointed in her? "I don't want you to think, Joseph, I'm so miserable over Brian O'Donnell I'd do something foolish."

"I know you wouldn't. You're a sensible girl," he reached over and touched her hand. "We'll say nothing about this to Emer, okay?"

"Of course. I wouldn't worry her."

"Some day the two of you can talk about it. But not now. Not at Christmas."

In the twilight they turned up the lane past Pat's empty tumbledown cottage. Plunkett's windows glowed orange. Emer's old place dark. Dublin could have been a thousand miles away. Una felt like a swimmer waiting to break the surface, to breathe again, safe at home. Emer would have the table laid, the kitchen cosy, the sitting room fire going. Nearing his own stable, anticipating his basin of oats, the pony broke into a trot. She saw the lights of the house. Then they were in the yard, Nan and Donny running out, the excited dog barking and jumping about. Emer appeared at the door, her face flushed from the stove.

At Sea

THEY CLIMBED KILLINEY hill on a bright Saturday evening, the last weekend in August. Eilish, Una, Connor Dillon and Peter Gleeson following narrow paths through glistening holly and ferny woods and along the stone wall of a churchyard. The sea dropped behind them. They moved upwards in the fragrant air. The men carried their picnic basket. At the summit they turned, breathless, and looked back. Far below, the village of Bray slept in the sun. They could see tiny figures of children playing on the crescent beach under Bray Head, and in the distance, the navy blue Sugar Loaf Mountains capped in rain clouds. This was their first outing together. Two weeks earlier, the girls had been introduced to Connor at an Irish language class. Una was now required to teach Irish at St. Brendan's and was enrolled in evening classes. Eilish enrolled too. "A good chance to meet lads, Una."

The following Saturday, they saw Connor again in Bewley's, sitting alone at the far wall when they came in. He left his table and came to speak to them.

"Do you mind if I join you?"

"Not at all, please do," Eilish answered for them both.

"I'm expecting a friend, Peter Gleeson," Connor explained. "There he is." He waved at a small, dark-haired man standing at the door, looking about. The man wove his way through the tables toward them. Connor introduced the girls.

Something about the atmosphere of Bewley's Oriental Tea Room encouraged conversation. Peter had intense blue eyes in a tanned face and a teasing grin. He worked in the accounts office of Johnson, Mooney and O'Brien in Ballsbridge.

"Johnson Mooney and O'Brien
Bought a horse for one and nine."

Eilish flirted, chanting the old Dublin skipping song softly, her brown eyes flashing,

"And when the horse began to trot,
Johnson Mooney bought a shop…."

"They'll make no foolish purchases while Peter is watching the accounts," said Connor.

Connor worked in the Department of Posts and Telegraphs. The two men had been at school together in Cork, just as Eilish and Una had become friends at the Convent of the Cross and Resurrection. They were avid cyclists. Peter proposed a cycling trip to Shankill the following Saturday.

"Not on your life!" Eilish told him. "It's too far to cycle and the roads are too busy on weekends. I vote we take the tram and climb Killiney. That's enough exercise."

"What did I tell you?" Eilish said now as they spread their coats on the ground at the top of Killiney Hill. "My legs are aching like I walked twenty miles, and you lads were for cycling all the way to Shankill. Far better to take the tram."

"And look at the fine view we have," Peter said, looking around. "The best view in Ireland. Wasn't it well worth the climb?"

"It was Peter, worth every step." Una said.

"My idea!" Eilish boasted.

Below, in the plain, the city stretched out toward the sea. Here and there the spires of churches rose above the low suburbs. A fat hare scampered past. Peter threw a dock leaf after it. It scuttled under a yellow whin bush.

"If the day was clear and a fellow had field glasses, he could see the Welsh mountains," Connor declared.

Una stared dreamily out over the sea. Beyond England was Europe, Paris! Some day, she promised herself, she'd go there.

"The summer holidays are soon over Una," Connor said, breaking in on her thoughts. "You'll be in Dublin all the time, not escaping home to Slanabaille every week."

"I'm happy to stay in Dublin. I love teaching."

"I wish I could say the same for myself," Eilish declared, "I'm sick of being private secretary to the great Mr. Henderson of Henderson and Murray, Solicitors. A glorified waitress, that's what I am. I'll never know why I killed myself learning Gregg shorthand. The old fool never gives dictation. Just make me this appointment and that appointment, and Miss Houlihan, would you mind bringing tea for the four o'clock client?"

"So we'll be seeing more of you, Una?" Connor persisted. He was a tall, broad-shouldered man with a wealth of black curly hair and an open, frank expression.

"You might," countered Eilish, answering for Una, "but don't be too sure of yourself."

"Winter's coming, and there'll be dances and parties. We're having a Hallowe'en dance in my department. I can get tickets for us all."

"I'm game," said Peter, chewing on a blade of grass, "if Eilish will do me the honor."

"Well, I'll have to consider it," Eilish responded archly and then laughed. "Of course I'm game."

"I might need a few lessons," Peter warned. "The Redemptorist Brothers didn't include dancing in the curriculum."

"Oh, you'll acquit yourself well enough, Gleeson," Connor teased. "I never saw you put a foot wrong yet."

"Or yourself either."

"It's almost seven o'clock. I'm starving. Time for a scoff," Eilish announced.

The men gathered twigs and lit a fire to boil their tea kettle. Eilish spread a cloth and laid out sandwiches, cake and apples.

They sat among the yellow *buachalans* eating slowly. The climb and the sea air had given an edge to their appetites. Fat, black and white jackdaws waddled about, pecking at the crusts they tossed. The sun moved west to set over the city: at their feet the bay lay cradled between the Hill of Howth and Bray Head. Little fishing boats headed home across the crinkled water. Una lay back and closed her eyes. "I could sleep here all night."

"That I'd have to see," Eilish told her. "The first owl screech and you'd die of fright."

"I'd protect her," Connor offered.

"I bet you would if you got the chance," said Eilish and tossed an apple core at his head. Una sat up, a little embarrassed by the banter between Eilish and Connor.

Wood pigeons called to one another and doves cooed their soft persistent cry.

"You know," said Peter, "I've never actually seen a dove. The woods are so thick."

The sun slid down the other side of Killiney and they were suddenly in shade. "We should be heading back," said Connor. "Let's cross over to Dalkey Hill and go down that way."

In the dusk they gathered up the remains of their meal. Connor shook the crumbs from the cloth, joined the edges at one end, and handed them to Una, then hand over hand he folded the cloth to where she held it. There was a slightly melancholy, end-of- summer feeling to the evening. Peter carried the bag with the kettle and tea mugs. Connor and Una went first, down the narrow path. He stepped ahead, stretched his hand back to help Una down a rough steep incline. He kept her hand when the way became smoother. Una felt a little shiver of pleasure. They held hands all the way across to Dalkey Hill and down to the bottom. It was almost night when they reached the village and the stop where they waited for the tram. When it came they climbed up to the top deck among the families returning from a day at the seaside, sleepy children with sand pails and shovels, tired women in shawls. Una saw their reflection in the darkened windows. Connor was slightly taller than herself.

"DON'T GET A FALSE notion of your father's home-coming Una," Eilish advised the next day as they walked in light misty rain, arms linked, sharing an umbrella. "When my sisters came home, four years ago, it took them ages to settle in."

"How do you mean settle in, Eilish?"

"Well, they thought the place was backward, and of course

the War for Independence was going on and the Black and Tans were in Athlone, raiding every night of the week."

They'd been to mass in Saint Theresa's in Clarendon Street and now they came through Johnson's Court towards Grafton Street. The soft, moist air boomed with mass bells and a damp oyster smell drifted up from the river.

"But Eilish, things are better now. The Republican Army gave up the fight last year."

"In your eye! De Valera is raising ructions, still refusing to take a seat in the Dail, and the bloody IRA is still fighting about the Border and defying our fine Minister of Justice."

"Uncle Joseph's opinion is that my father will buy a bit of land to extend the old farm and settle here. My father loved farming, that farm was his life."

"Una, you were ten when he left, you've changed, he's changed."

"You don't even know Daddy!"

"That's right, I don't know your father, but I know you. Don't be romancing about him, Una. Time enough for that when he gets here."

Una longed to see her father. She imagined him living in the old house down the lane from Emer and Joseph's place. She remembered him as tall and handsome. Her darling father. She thought of him coming to Dublin to see her, maybe to take her to the Horse Show in Ballsbridge. Sometimes she pictured herself having a meal with him in Jury's Hotel. What was Eilish intimating?

"It's a wonder he never got married, Una. He'd be a great scoop for some war widow."

Una stood stock still. "I never considered that. It never even crossed my mind."

How stupid she had been. Of course her father might want to marry. A stepmother for Nan and Donny? At the edge of her consciousness Una sensed a pit. It made itself known at odd times, sometimes even when she was happiest, like in the train on her way home to Slanabaille. It was there now waiting to one side of her, and she might slip and slide into it. The resonance of the Sunday church bells turned ominous, the breeze flowing from the river seemed to carry unknown dread.

"Don't get down in the dumps now, Una. You disappear into yourself like a snail in his shell."

"It's just that I have this terrible fear of some catastrophe happening."

"Sure, everyone feels like that once in a while. Don't give in to it. Think about something else. Think about Connor Dillon. He's mad keen on you, Una."

"Don't be silly Eilish. We're just pals."

"In your eye you are. I've seen him look at you."

They crossed over into Grafton Street. The rain had stopped and Eilish folded the umbrella and shook it. "The weather in this country would drive you to drink."

"Yesterday was lovely."

"Yes, it was." They had arrived at the Brown Thomas window.

"Una, I'm not buying a stitch till Christmas," Eilish vowed. "Anyway, everything is an outrageous price in Brown Thomas. If I were getting anything it would be in Clery's."

Una studied the display. Autumn and winter styles. Tweed suits with three quarter coats, long lapels and narrow sleeves, collars smothered in furs.

"There's nothing here, Eilish. I'll need a new dress for the Hallowe'en dance. I'll come back next week. I've lots of time."

"Well, you should have a new dress to charm that Connor. He'd be great scoop, Una."

"Don't be ridiculous Eilish."

"I'm not ridiculous, I mean it. A job in the civil service! And your Uncle Joseph can pull the strings to get him a better one."

"You have an exaggerated idea of Joseph's influence, anyway we're just pals, and all I'm doing is looking for a new dress."

"Well, I'm wearing the green frock my sister gave me. I'll try it on when we get home. You can tell me what you think, Una."

Eilish and Una had moved up to the top flat in 24 Mullagh Street: three rooms, a combined kitchen and sitting room, and at the back, two small bedrooms. South Circular Road was a respectable area. Far from the slums and stews of the north side where the poor lived ten to a room and where children still died of hunger and tuberculosis ravaged entire families. Wages were low, women were paid less than men. A job was just till some man asked you to marry him. Often, as Una left home to catch the train for Dublin, Emer slipped a pound note or two in with the fresh farm eggs and butter.

"Emer, I don't need that, I make enough."

"Get yourself a bit of style, Una. Your uncle likes to see you dressed up."

But it wasn't Joseph, he never noticed. It was Emer who loved clothes, as much for Una and Nan as for herself. The flying clouds began to leave a gap for the sun to shine. The Sunday walkers slowed their pace to a stroll.

"Would you think of having the dressmaker run a dress up for you, Una? There's loads of time to have one made. Maybe we could go back and see what the materials in the shop windows in Westmoreland Street are like."

"No, let's go home and have something to eat. I'm hungry, and nervy too, thinking about my father out there on the Atlantic."

"Let's cut across the Green then."

They turned back to St. Stephen's Green and walked towards the gates. Although it was early morning, the park was already full of walkers.

THE VIBRATION OF the engines sang in Peadar's brain. They were moving fast. Perched behind a huge coil of rope below the stack, he smoked and watched the wash of foam and spray tossed up by the propellers, the long trailing trough of white water and the full moon very bright, sailing away from them in streams of fleecy cloud. The music from the first class deck had stopped long ago. He was a little cold, but he stayed, not eager for the stuffy, third class cabin and the snoring of his fellow occupants.

He wondered at his own lack of excitement, anticipation, or even curiosity about the end of his journey. Perhaps the ghost drifting through his memory kept his eagerness in check, the shadowy figure of Angela he carried with him always. Then again, maybe it was too early to be flooded with expectant feeling. Yet in those moments, early on in America, when he was almost overcome with longing for home, the promise of this journey had always been the remedy for loneliness. The hope of return had fueled his ambition, provided light which kept him moving on. Except those emotions were long behind him, those upheavals of his first year away.

After the first tumultuous months, Peadar had no time for loneliness. Patrick, long settled in America, got him a job in a factory, one of a grey line along the Brooklyn waterfront. It was hard, monotonous work in an airless shed, standing hour after hour working the levers of a heavy, stamping machine. There were thousands of Irish on the Lower East Side, tenements crowded with children. He had a room at the top of a tall building on a street called Murphy's Alley. The summer of 1913 was so hot he slept on the iron fire escape.

In September, Peadar quit the factory and hired on with a crew laying the foundations for a bridge. Pick and shovel work, but it was outdoors, the money was good and he knew how to handle a shovel or pick, knew the knack of letting the head of the pick do the work. There was a beauty to that, an art to balancing the shovel, so that the sand or gravel slid off it without straining his back. Then, in '17, he'd been hired on Hog Island, where the ship building industry was taking any man who applied. Driving rivets into steel was the most satisfying job in the world. To see the big ship rise from a frame of wooden scaffolds, watch it slide down into the water and wait for that tremendous drenching splash, was a luminous sight he'd never forget.

Peadar had a great sense of accomplishment there. New York was the center of things, the first place he'd made good. He was sorry to leave the city when things slowed down in 1920, but automobiles were where the work was. Ford paid five dollars a day, and he could live on less than half that. And there was always the chance of a few dollars doing a run across to Canada for a bootlegger.

Peadar didn't stay long on the monotonous assembly line. He soon found work in a furniture factory up from the waterfront, preferring the resinous smell of cedar and pine, the satisfaction of making something. Sundays, he worked as a relief conductor on a streetcar. He knew the supervisor, a man from Cork, and had hopes of being a driver when the next spot became vacant. Some evenings he worked in a bicycle shop. In his spare time, he made dollhouses and sold them to a toyshop. Working with his hands, that's what Peadar loved.

Detroit had almost as many Irish as New York, men from back home to play cards, gamble or drink with. All with the same memories of home, of farms and schools and villages and every last one of them, with a certain wistfulness, expressing their intention to go back for a visit, even to stay. For most it was just talk, they had wives and families in America, or they drank and gambled every cent they earned. Peadar liked to play cards too, but wagered only small sums. He knew he was the exception, and was aware many envied him the chance to return. What, then, was the matter with him? Where was the excitement that was his by right, after twelve years of exile? Was he afraid now to anticipate a delirious homecoming, and meet with a cruel disappointment? Peadar seemed to have lost faith in ecstatic homecomings and joyous reunions. As if he couldn't trust the possibility of joy. In three days, he would see his family again. But there would be no Angela.

Memories discounted, Peadar traveled light, just one small suitcase. Behind, in Detroit. his work clothes, his tools, and a few books were crammed in a wooden box in the corner of the landlady's cellar. She'd keep them for him, but rent his room and, if he came back, he would take his chances for work and accommodation. Used to chancing his arm, Peadar wasn't worried about getting work if he returned. And he believed in America. No better country in the world! Even in the post-war slump of '21 and '22, when wages dropped, he'd held on. Now it was 1924, things were on the upswing again, boom times were back. It was too good to give up. Even the workday was being cut, U.S. Steel cutting to eight hours. What more could anyone want? Though Emer wanted him to stay in Ireland and settle back into the life of a small farmer, he'd see how he felt when he got there.

Emer wrote often, long letters about the farm and the neighbours, and about his children. Peadar himself was no great letter writer, but never once had he forgotten to send the twice monthly money draft, and that was what mattered. His life in America was so entirely different from the sleepy little townland where he and Emer grew up that he could never put it into words. Emer herself, hadn't she worked in America when she was a girl and knew all about it? His children wrote too, frequent dutiful notes, telling him about school, or work. He was filled with pride reading those letters.

He took out his watch: two o'clock. He realized it was actually much later than that. They were two days from Liverpool but his watch was still on New York time. He'd put it ahead to Greenwich time when they landed. He looked at the watch with satisfaction. Now, that was what America was like. A solid silver hunter bought from Sears Roebuck and Co. of Chicago for four dollars. He'd bought it through his landlady who, when she had ordered twenty dollars worth of merchandise through their catalogue, got a profit-sharing certificate good for the purchase of additional items. What a country!

He'd always meant to come home. He had left first to forget, and then to gather up a grubstake in America and go back to his family. But there was the war, and the Atlantic wasn't safe, and then the years of armed struggle in Ireland, so he delayed, through '21, '22 and '23. Bad years in Ireland. Emer had been urging him to come home for nearly a year, now there was some semblance of peace. The IRA and De Valera were still stirring up trouble over the Oath of Allegiance and the border, but the long night of murder and reprisal seemed over. And she would know, married as she was to Angela's brother who, like his father before him, was mixed up in politics. Emer wrote that his children needed to see him, that Nan and Donny didn't know him, that Una was grown up; but the way he had seen it, the best he could do was to keep working, keep sending money home. His children were thriving and rising in the world.

They had Joseph's salary from teaching, and what Emer got from letting the land; though there had been a slump in farm prices, Peadar knew she had still been able to rent it, at a much lower rate. He had never failed to send home half his wages, every month.

And Emer had money from her own years in America. How connected the two countries were, the little island and the huge continent. Because Emer and Patrick had emigrated, he had been free to marry Angela when he was barely in his twenties. Because he had emigrated, his children had been able to continue at school.

Una, the first of the Maguires to go beyond National School, was a teacher now, and Nan was ensconced in the convent school. What more did they want? What need for him to come home? Waste of time and money. Well off, they were. Good schools and a warm decent house, better, by Emer's account, than he or Emer ever had. That's what Angela would have wanted, that was the pact with her, the promise he'd made twelve years ago on the Saturday before he emigrated.

He had gone to the churchyard one last time. Deserted except for jackdaws and sparrows, the hopping robins, the triangular shadows of wild geese flying overhead, a few early red and yellow October leaves blowing around. Once he would have bagged a goose for Angela to roast in the bastable. Now instead he spoke to her. He would look after the children. They should never have to work as he and Angela had done, yoked to a round of labour that yielded so little, feeding pigs and calves and fowl and milking cows, dragging buckets of water from the pump. He couldn't forgive the hard work. He believed it killed her. Married at twenty-one, dead at thirty-two.

That awful death, the sudden finality of his loss, nothing had obliterated that. Angela, his lovely lively girl, his darling, slipped away from him in a mad frantic afternoon of terror and panic. He was busy at the harvest all morning, then everything a-rushing about, fetching the nurse and while he had gone to get her mother, she left him. So quietly, so quickly, they hadn't even a chance to say goodbye to each other. And when he knelt at her grave in the cold October light that Saturday twelve years ago, he swore to her that he would never forget her, and then he wept, like a small child might cry for his mother in the night.

That was the last of his weeping. He'd finished with tears. Time, distance, change and work, that's what saved him, that and Emer, steady sensible woman, a Maguire through and through. When he had suggested he go to America for a few years and would hire a lad to help her she refused the help.

Who could have believed she'd marry Joseph? Joseph with his wild gadding about, his poetry, his Gaelic League malarkey! Involved with Sinn Fein, too. Lucky to be alive he was. Lucky he hadn't got some jail time after the Treaty! That was the safest place for anyone in that mess. Hide out in jail till it was over. Up to his neck in county politics now, he was.

Peadar had vowed he wouldn't farm again, not ever, unless he could afford to pay farm labour. And he had no intention of changing his mind about this. But he kept up with what was happening there. Farm prices were rock bottom in Ireland, anyway. And last year the weather had been the worst in living memory. Much of the harvest was lost. Farmers were selling up and leaving for America.

Despite the immigration quotas, the Irish were still coming to America and why not? Hadn't it been his salvation and Patrick's too? Paddy had been the first to emigrate, in 1892, just a lad. He remembered the gathering in the house the night before he left, his mother weeping. Paddy had never come home. He hardly wrote. He'd settled first in New York and was there to meet Emer when she arrived in 1894. Peadar never forgot his own first weeks in America, the alien feel of the place, the overwhelming noise and crowds in New York, his own terrible loneliness. Patrick had understood. But who knew where Paddy was now? The last he heard he was in Ohio, one of those Irish that left the cities and wandered from work site to work site. He'd been a quiet lad, the eldest, but lots of quiet lads took to gambling or drink. Who knew? Years ago Patrick used to send money home. That had helped himself and Angela get started. It was Patrick who paid Emer's fare to America when she went in '94. Paddy was probably worth some money now. Paying that income tax. Peadar himself paid income tax. Unbelievable, income tax, paying the government for the privilege of working.

If they'd stayed in Ireland, he and Patrick would probably have joined up during the war. Patrick kept in touch with Emer, wrote her the odd letter to say he was well or that he had moved. At least he wrote. It crossed Peadar's mind that Donagh was the last of the Maguires, by all accounts a good lad. Twelve now. Emer wrote Nan didn't remember him and, of course, he himself hardly remembered Donny, a helpless crying infant just one month old the last time Peadar saw him.

He had a photograph of them all, taken just after Emer and Joseph were married. In the picture Una looked as tall as Emer. She stood with Joseph behind Emer, who sat on a chair with Nan on her knee. Joseph held Donny in his arms. He often took the picture from the inside pocket of his jacket and looked hard at Donny. Emer had written that he had the Maguire looks, dark-haired and grey-eyed. Peadar couldn't tell; he looked like any little boy, bare knees, short trousers and a sailor shirt, dressed up to have his photograph taken.

Peadar had no real plan. He meant to see his children, stay a month, and then he'd probably go back to America. He shivered a little in the night breeze and took out his watch again. Almost three o'clock. If he stayed where he was a while longer, he'd see the dawn redden the horizon as the big ship ploughed eastward. Might as well see all that was to be seen and get value for his money.

WHILE PEADAR'S ship was riding the North Atlantic toward England, the captain having ordered full steam up to make as much headway as possible while his passengers slept, his son was waking in Slanabaille. Donagh had Peadar and Angela's old bedroom. It was a boy's room now with pictures of racehorses, winners at Punchestown and Leopardstown races, cut from *The Independent*, pinned on the wall. Under the window *The Poems of Joseph Mary Plunkett* shared the bookshelf with *Tom Brown's School Days*, Seamus MacManus' *Story of the Irish Race* and *The Complete Sherlock Holmes*. In the corner, his hurley caman and ball. Donny stretched his toes, arching his feet, then stretched his heels. His feet stuck out between the bars of his bed. It was just getting light outside.

Being an infant when his father emigrated, Donny didn't remember his father and for months together was in the habit of forgetting Peadar's existence. Now, as the day neared, his Aunt

Emer talked of nothing else. Where would his father live? It seemed the house they lived in belonged to his father and that they might have to move to the old house down the lane where Aunt Emer grazed her cattle.

"If we're moving down there," Emer declared, the previous evening, "the entire place will need an overhaul. It's not fit to spend the winter in."

"Or we could buy this place from him," Joseph said, "and let him fix up the old house to his taste. But it's early days yet, we'll see what Peadar wants to do."

Was it possible Emer and Joseph would move to the old house and leave him here with his father? His father might be a cranky old man. Maybe he'd smell like the old men at fair days with their trousers bound up with straw and their boots caked with manure. Maybe his father chewed tobacco and spat it. Or maybe he'd beat him. There were plenty of men who beat their sons. Uncle Joseph said some farmers overworked and beat everything except themselves: their children, wives, animals.

"Is my father an old fellow?"

"Indeed he is not, he's younger than me!"

"And you know, Donny," teased Joseph, "your aunt is just a girl."

"It will be just wonderful to see Peadar," Emer enthused. "It's been so long since he's gone. And wait till he sees you Donny, such a great big lad and so smart."

"I don't know whether I want to see him or not."

"That's because you don't remember him. But you'll get along fine."

Donny wasn't so sure. If they left him here in the house with his father he wouldn't stay. He'd run away. He could go to Dublin and be a newsboy. When he had gone to visit Una he'd seen the newsboys standing on a corner in College Green yelling, "*Extra! Extra! Independent or Times.*" The traffic swirled around them, trams and motorcars, jarveys driving cabs. He'd love that job. Some of them looked no older than he was.

At first, his father would have Nan's room because Nan was away at school. Emer packed Nan's dolls, Chummy books and her clothes into a trunk kept under the staircase that ran between the sitting room and the kitchen and led to Emer and Joseph's bedroom above. That part of the house was called "The Addition" which Donny considered silly. It might have been an addition when they added it, but seven years later it had become part of the house.

"My father can have my room," Donny offered, "and I'll move down to the old house. Charlie will stay with me. We'll batch it together."

"You'll do no such thing, Donagh, and I don't believe for one minute that Mrs. Lever would let Charlie stay down there with you. Your father will sleep in Nan's room, and then we'll see."

Aunt Emer always called him Donagh when she disapproved of something he suggested. Donny decided he'd talk to Charlie when he got to school.

Now he could hear Aunt Emer getting breakfast, water running and the clatter when she put the kettle to boil on the range, then the thump of the frying pan. Energized by the prospect of bacon and eggs, Donny got out of bed and ran through the kitchen to open the door for the dog.

"You shouldn't be in bare feet, Donny. You'll catch your death of cold," Emer warned, slicing rashers off a side of bacon.

The kerry blue lumbered up from the step and licked his face. "Good boy, Mooney. Good boy."

He picked up his hand ball from the step and threw it against the side of the dairy. It rebounded. He tipped it back again. It bounced again and this time he hit it hard; it sailed up on the roof, rolled diagonally, he ran sideways to catch it. The dog jumped around him barking, excited by all the activity. It was his favourite kind of morning, crisp and autumny. It reminded him of biting into an apple from the trees in the orchard at Uncle Joseph's old tumbledown place.

"Donny, come in. This minute! Your breakfast is on the table."

Joseph was already seated at the table.

"When's my father coming?"

"This Saturday."

"Can I stay home from school while he's here?"

"No Donny, you can't miss school."

"Charlie got ten days off for the harvest. Why can't I get a few days off?"

"Donny lad," said Joseph, "just be glad you're not a farmer. Prices are so low it's not worth farming."

"Do I have to bring water to the cattle?"

"No, not today. It rained enough early in the week. There's lots of water down there for them."

Donny ate slowly. He wanted to hang around to hear Emer tell Joseph about his father.

"Hurry on Donny, you'll be late."

"I am hurrying."

"You're not washed or dressed yet. You'll keep Joseph late."

Emer was packing food for them to take to school.

"Aunt Emer, pack me two cuts of that plum cake."

Donny Maguire never thought about it, but he was a lucky boy. Life laid itself out for him among fields starred with cowslips, daisies and buttercups, the mists on the river, the lowing of cows, blackbirds singing in the beech tees and sibilant swifts quartering the garden of an evening. At home, Emer presided over the kitchen and seemed even to manage the round of the seasons and the sun. At school, there was his Uncle Joseph in charge, and his best pal Charlie Lever to play handball with or sneak a few puffs of a *Sweet Afton* behind the outhouse. Sometimes the boys teased him because his uncle was the schoolmaster, but Charlie never did. And Joseph was not harsh, as many teachers were. Now his father was coming home and that would spoil everything. Who knew what changes might be in the offing? He'd give it a few days and if his father began to lord it over him he'd run off. He had almost a pound in his money box. That would get him to Dublin.

In Liverpool, Peadar was surprised to feel the ground heave slightly under him after so many days at sea. Even in that big ship! He got a night's stay a few streets up from the docks in a grimy lodging house. The bricks were black with coal dust, the green door badly needed paint, but the bedroom was clean and it was cheap. The owner, a fussy little war widow, served him tea in the parlour. Apart from a tired looking older man who seemed to be a permanent boarder, Peadar was her only customer. She spoke in sugared tones. A bit inquisitive. Peadar noticed her watching him from the kitchen. He was used to women's glances, thought he must still be a fine looking man. Although he knew he was no Douglas Fairbanks or William S. Hart, women always glanced his way. Even now, with his greying hair. His father had been a good looking man, too. Peadar believed he took after his father. That landlady was a little wren of a woman. And Peadar thought a little lustfully of the German widow he sometimes spent the night with in Detroit. For a minute he missed her and marriage with her entered his thoughts; then he decided his mind was swinging between sense and nonsense. He didn't need any woman, not for company, anyway.

"And have you a family in Ireland, Mr. Maguire?" asked the landlady.

"Yes, I have three children."

"And are they all grown up?"

"The youngest is twelve."

"That's very nice, wonderful to have a family. I have no children myself. Edward and myself were married just a week before he was called up."

To avoid her questions he went upstairs. As he passed the looking glass on the landing wall at the top of the stairs, Peadar was taken aback by a glimpse of his own face. Solemn, wide-eyed, haunted look of the exile, the wistful gaze of a lost boy, was that what women saw in him? The image left him disturbed and lonely. He dismissed it. He needed to get outside, take a long walk. He went out and closed the front door quietly behind him. He lit his second cigarette of the day. Wet leaves were heaped up, blown against the houses. The city was tired and mournful, more like October than early September. Strolling toward the business streets, Peadar realized he missed America. How much variety was there, what life pulsed in its streets, what excitement, how young it was, beating with human activity, humming with commerce. Here there was a sameness about people, a weariness. Even after six years, the funereal shadows of war still hung about.

Outside a pub, an old man was making a gallant effort to sing. He leaned back, one leg bent against the coal-blackened brick wall, a box for coins at his feet, his voice hoarse and breaking, *"If you were the only."* Peadar fumbled in his pocket for a coin.

"God bless you, sir."

He read the lettering on the cardboard sign around the man's neck, *Veteran Of Belleau-Wood.* He saw then that the man was not old, probably no older than Peadar himself. There were plenty of beggars in America, but none had shaken him as this one did. My God, a veteran, what had happened to the British Empire? And this was the country that owed America billions in war debts! This side of the Atlantic was finished, done for, Peadar decided. He wanted a drink.

The tavern was half-empty, dark, smelling of beer and cigarettes. There were men at the counter and around messy tables marked by wet glasses. Peadar noticed a lull in the conversation when he went in, then the drinkers turned back to their talk. The English left you alone, they didn't butt in on your thoughts. The drinkers just gave him an occasional sidelong glance. A dull, lifeless tavern. How different from the big basement speakeasy where he drank in Detroit, glittering with sin, a saxophone or horn player to tease the ears, sometimes a singer crooning away, and languorous women, half-naked, sashaying casually from table to table. The very air illicit and exciting. As if deals were being made, fabulous transactions planned. Always a few men there to play cards with on a Saturday night, to drink with or have a little wager, to watch the spectacle, to talk men's talk about the Harding scandals, or the unions, and sometimes to talk of home. And there always was the possibility of a raid, the rush out the back door.

The tavern began to fill up, people greeting each other, women among them, working girls, smoking and laughing. The Friday night crowd. The barman was watching him. Peadar shook his head refusing another drink, and left.

He walked past grimy brick houses and shuttered shops, beggars, another tavern. The singing beggar disturbed him. Was he getting soft, or was he on edge because he was nearing home? Peadar prided himself on his cultivated indifference to others. Only his family meant anything, its name, its prosperity. No one else was worth a minute's consideration. The rest was show, a spectacle, an entertainment, like the stories of daring robberies and murders in *The New York Daily News*. Emer had written that someone, most likely Joseph, would meet him at the boat. Tomorrow morning he would be in Dublin. Back in Ireland. He tried hard to prepare his emotions. For two cents he wouldn't go at all, he'd send Emer a telegraph and get passage back to the States. But that would be ridiculous. Peadar stepped into a fish shop. The place smelled of grease, and when the fish arrived, it was an oily grey lump, the coffee weak and grainy. On his return journey he promised himself he would go up into London and see the sights: Trafalgar Square, Westminster, and London Bridge. Turning back towards his lodging he made up his mind to stop thinking about tomorrow, to approach it as he did every other day, detached, watchful, expecting nothing wonderful, grateful if no disaster overtook him.

The landlady opened the door in response to his knock. "Had you a nice walk Mr. Maguire?"

"I did."

She stood watching him as he climbed the stairs. "Goodnight, Mr. Maguire."

"Goodnight, Mam."

How quiet the lodging was, not at all like his accommodation in Detroit, where the young lads spent half the night gathered around the crystal set in the kitchen listening to the Ever Ready Hour. It took Peadar a long time to get to sleep. He missed the rocking of the ship.

THE BIG BOAT from Liverpool was crowded, most of the men standing. Peadar leaned on the rail and watched the Irish shore approach. From the first class salon on the upper deck came the clink of glasses, and the buzz of talk and good-natured banter. It was a bright sunny Saturday morning, a little cool on the water. He was nearing home. He saw the Irish coast come up over the horizon. Then the sun glinting on the windows of the buildings along Sandymount Strand and on the Martello Tower. Behind them, the mountains cradled the bay. They passed the lighthouse, turned into the river and steamed up between the arms of the quays. It was such a short trip from England, almost before he had time to organize his thoughts they were at the North Wall, the gangway was down and the passengers streaming past an official in a green uniform who was checking papers very perfunctorily. *"Failte abaille,"* welcome home, he told Peadar, with hardly a glance at his documents. Peadar was momentarily taken aback, then a little amused; he had forgotten about the language, that Irish was now spoken by all public servants. He scanned the crowd at the dock searching for Joseph or Emer, seeing neither. Perhaps they were a bit late. Not that he minded the delay. He could wait, collect his thoughts. In a strange way, he felt as if he were still in America. He stood watching the scene. Guinness boats plied the river. He noticed a shabbiness about the docks, a backward, old-fashioned, small look to everything compared to America. Travelers, loaded down with assorted luggage and bundles, greeted friends and family, excited children ran about, porters and hawkers shouted. Peadar noticed a tall, slim girl moving along at the front of the crowd. He watched her. Even in Detroit she would have caught his eye. A honey of a gal, thought Peadar, in his American way. Shingled hair under a cloche hat pulled down over her face, the brim turned up at the back. She wore a broad-shouldered red coat, short, very short, as was the fashion, tapered to her knee and fastened with a big pearl button at the hip. She edged her way forward, he looked to either side, curious to see whom she was meeting, then looked back into a short, angled face and wide open, light blue eyes.

"Hello father, welcome home!" And she held out her hand. Peadar stood staring, holding his suitcase. "Daddy it's me! Una!"

He looked at her stupidly. Was this remarkable woman Una, his child? He searched her face for any sign of family likeness, any resemblance, any connecting thread, and was surprised by regret thickening in his throat, sorrow for the missed years.

"Una! If you hadn't spoken I wouldn't have known you."

"Oh, it's just the hat."

The travelers behind shouldered past them. Una took his arm.

"Let's go this way, we must get a hackney cab to the station. If we hurry, we'll catch the half-past ten train."

He followed her through the crowd and up to the street. Before he had time to, she hailed a cab and he sat beside her while the horse clipped-clopped along toward Amiens Street Station. She went ahead of him and purchased their train tickets while he paid the driver.

"I would have got those, Una."

"That's alright Daddy, we have to hurry."

He walked with her toward the train.

The train for Obanbeg slid out of the city, past the narrow backyards of Dublin and into the flat country. Peadar and Una shared the railway carriage with two half-drunk cattle dealers arguing and boasting about the week's transactions. Peadar sat opposite Una. This was his daughter, the too-thin, quiet, ten-year-old girl he had left behind. It was absurd, ridiculous! This was his child? He knew she would be grown up, he expected it, yet faced with it, he found himself unprepared. Who was she like at all? That pale hair and face, and those wide, light blue eyes. She asked him about his journey and for the first time in his life he found himself groping a little for the right words.

"It was faster than I expected."

She told him she lived in Dublin, that she and her friend Eilish had a flat off the South Circular Road. He had only a vague idea of where that was.

"It's south of the river, a good, quiet area."

He had known her address but nothing in her letters had given even a hint of what she was, of the young woman she had grown to be.

"Uncle Joseph will meet us in Obanbeg, then we'll go to the convent school to visit Nan, if you're not too tired."

"Oh, I'm not tired at all."

"Nan is dying to see you. She hardly remembers you."

"Is she as tall as you?"

"Nan is small like Mammy, she has Mammy's eyes. You'll see for yourself, and Donny is very tall for his age. I think he looks like you."

He could think of nothing to say, feeling himself a visitor, an outsider. His family had outstripped his idea of them. Small, she had said, like Mammy, like Angela. How casually she had said it, how matter of fact, as if losing Angela had not been a disaster that shattered him and his family, leaving everything before that shocking death a dream.

JOSEPH WAS AT the station. Grey sprinkled the red hair, he had the same lanky look to him, a little stooped, that was all. "Welcome home lad," Joseph said, holding out his hand, beaming at Peadar.

They walked over to the trap. Peadar looked around. The old market town had changed little in twelve years. It seemed antiquated despite two new pubs and a garage. Brennan's Motor Works in bold red letters. He could see a few farmers' carts in the streets and a motorcar stood outside the hotel. The post office and its mail box were painted dark green, rather than the royal red Peadar remembered. The Arcade Drapery and Mercer's Bakery each had a fresh coat of paint.

Peadar sat with his arm stretched along the top of the trap, his hand gripping the edge. He was no longer used to sitting in a swaying trap, flimsy and insubstantial under his weight. Suddenly he recognized himself, his own hand, his instruction and example, in the decisive way Una clicked her tongue at the pony, flicked the reins then shortened them, winding the strap round her right hand. The animal, as though protesting, turned his ears back showing pink insides. When they arrived at the school, Peadar stepped down to feel his feet on solid ground again.

Una ran up the steps to fetch Nan. She was waiting in the hall. "Is he here, Una? What's he like?"

"Like he always was, but he seems very tired. He didn't talk much. Come on Nan, we're going to have our dinner at the Railway."

Outside, Peadar stood beside the trap, waiting. He thought of the sleepy little girl he'd kissed goodbye that frosty October morning, so long ago. Joseph stepped down beside him and said something about the harvest, but Una was returning and Peadar's eyes were fastened on the small figure beside her, face hidden in a rampant mass of black, curly hair.

"Oh, Uncle Joseph, I thought you'd never come. Hello, Daddy."

Nan held her face up for a kiss. He stooped stiffly and kissed her and recoiled, shocked at the exquisite vulnerability of her cheek. Then he stood looking down at her. She was so small, so lively. The green eyes were Angela's. He was speechless.

"Let's go and get something to eat," Joseph suggested. "It's getting a little late for dinner over at the hotel."

Una drove round to the back of the hotel, halted the pony, looped the reins over the hook in the wall and fastened the feedbag in place. They all trooped through the side door into the dining room. Una led the way to a table across the room. Only two other tables were occupied, but the bar seemed to be doing a brisk trade.

"If you had come a little earlier Daddy, I would have still been on my summer holidays," Nan said as they sat down.

Peadar hesitated a minute, then explained, "I had to wait to book a passage."

It seemed a lame reply. He couldn't get used to talking to her, he wasn't accustomed to young people. He could not believe the girls sitting opposite, so at ease, were his daughters. The little waiter, who had watched them come in and sit down, approached.

"What will you have to drink?"

Joseph asked for a Cairne's Ale, Peadar, not sure what he wanted, asked for a Guinness.

"I'll have a Bushmills, Uncle Joseph."

Peadar was taken aback, profoundly shocked. What did Una order? Whiskey? He couldn't believe she would drink whiskey. His daughter, his little girl? Conditioned by prohibition to consider women who drank in speakeasies as morally loose, he was about to protest when he remembered his twelve-year absence had left him with no real right to interfere. The waiter returned and put their drinks in front of them. Joseph raised his glass.

"*Slainte.*"

"*Slainte,*" echoed Nan, holding up her glass of lemonade.

"Welcome home, Father," said Una.

Peadar put his glass down again without tasting the stout.

"We have beef and turnips today, sir."

He turned his head. A big, raw-boned woman in a white apron and cap was looking at him. "Beef with thin, brown gravy, sir."

"We'll have that," said Joseph.

"Yes sir. Straight away."

Although Peadar had been in the Railway Hotel on more than one occasion before he left for America, he couldn't remember the place at all: ferns in brass pots either side of the fireplace, vinegar and HP sauce bottles on the sideboard, gold-leaf trimmed mirror, a square serious face resting on a white cravat. He turned his head. The reflection was a portrait of Daniel O'Connell. It was as if he'd never set foot in the place before.

"It never changes," Joseph said seeing Peadar looking around, "once in a while they give it a lick of paint."

The waitress returned with two steaming plates and placed them in front of the girls. The waiter followed, carrying the men's food.

"Nothing missin' on that but the horns, sir," he said, as he put the plates on the table. Peadar looked at him, perplexed, not sure if the waiter was joking. The thick slab of meat was awash in juice; a mound of mashed potatoes, and dark brassy turnips almost over-flowed the plate. The waiter scurried away.

The others crossed themselves.

"I'm starved," Nan declared, picking up her knife and fork.

"That's no wonder," Una said. "One of the worst things about the convent is the food."

"*Is mait an talan and t'ocoras.* Hunger is good sauce," Joseph said.

Peadar cut a forkful of meat and ate it. It tasted strong, wild, of the fields. He tried the potatoes. Rich flavour of melted butter, yet the taste not as he remembered. Did one remember a taste?

"It's delicious, Uncle Joseph," said Nan

"Leave room for a sweet after," Una advised. "It's probably apple tart."

Mechanically, Peadar ate his meal. When he finished he felt uncomfortable, as if he'd eaten too much. When the waitress returned, she announced the sweet was bread and butter pudding.

"I don't want that," Nan objected. "That's convent food! I thought they'd have tart or trifle."

"The pudding will be nicer here, Nan," Una reminded her. "More raisins and cinnamon, a bit of whiskey in it, too."

Whiskey again, thought Peadar.

"I still don't want it. You can have my share Una," Nan offered.

They astounded him. At their age, he ate what was served him and was glad to get it. He refused the pudding but had a cup of tea. When the waiter brought the bill, Joseph took it. "I'll pay that, Joseph."

"Nonsense, lad. You're a visitor!"

"I'm full as an egg," Nan said, as they stood up to leave.

"Don't use that expression, Nan. It's very vulgar," Una admonished.

"Stop bossing me around. You're worse than Aunt Emer."

Joseph laughed.

Returning to the convent, Nan sat close beside Peadar. When they arrived, she reached up and kissed his cheek. "Goodbye, Daddy. Come and see me next Sunday. Goodbye, everybody."

He looked numbly after her as she ran up the convent steps. Her branching black hair bounced as she ran. His little girl!

The remainder of the day was like a lantern show for Peadar, slides slipping past while he sat numb and insensible, his mind uselessly reminding his heart to feel some jubilation in his return. But the day was so full of strange sensations it seemed impossible to respond to any of them. The meal, the sounds from the crowded noisy bar, his daughters sitting across from him, talking together. Nan's tiny figure waving from the convent steps, the long drive up out of town, past the tumbling stone houses and then down the slope again. Out into the country, dragging the sun after them through autumn-fattened land, the corncrake at his evening song and the stooked oats throwing shadows on the golden stubble, all scenes paraded before his jaded eyes. They went past ruined houses, nothing but gables left standing.

"Was that the British?"

"Our own did that. The Free State troops. Brother fighting brother," Joseph answered grimly.

He pointed out deserted farmhouses and Peadar realized how empty the country had become.

"Emigration, Peadar, there's as many leaving as ever," Joseph explained.

"No wonder Uncle Joseph, wages are so low."

"They'll improve, Una. Give the country time."

Just before they reached Slanabaille they turned up the lane. As they passed the old house where he grew up, Joseph broke into Peadar's thoughts.

"We keep the old place up Peadar, because in truth myself and Emer are living in your house. Would you like to stop and see the place?"

Peadar looked at the old grey farmhouse among the sycamores. He hardly recognized it. Maybe it was the evening light that made it look so shockingly small and shabby, with cracked slates on the roof and the gable window boarded up.

"Daddy is likely tired," Una interjected, "and Emer is waiting for us." She drove the pony on up the lane and into the yard. Peadar stepped down from the trap and stared at the house. Before his mind could register that this was the home he had built for Angela, a young boy came from the dairy, a dog at his heels. He held out his hand and Peadar looked into the face of his son.

"You're welcome home, father," said Donny, in his best imitation of Joseph.

"Donagh," Peadar heard his own voice, flat.

"Isn't this fellow grown to be a big lad, I bet you wouldn't know him," declared Joseph heartily.

"No, I wouldn't," Peadar said tonelessly.

His son took the bridle and led the pony away.

Then Emer came from the house with open arms. "We are so very, very happy to have you home, Peadar."

Peadar stepped up on the porch and entered the kitchen. It seemed strange, like he'd never been there before. Why did it seem so small and dark? Fading autumn light lit the dresser and shone on the dishes laid for tea. The addition Emer had put on the house changed its aspect, the kitchen opened out into a sitting room that had a bedroom above. Gone was the big hearth, replaced by an iron stove, and beyond the stove a stairs led up into gloom.

"You must be tired," said Emer.

"Maybe I am, a little."

"We'll have tea shortly," Emer said, leading him into the room beyond. She left him and Joseph came to talk. "It's good to have you home."

Peadar looked at him and said nothing. Una called them to tea.

"How was the journey, Peadar?" asked Emer handing him his cup.

"I enjoyed it. I slept so well on the boat and there was a crowd I played cards with."

"It's a far shorter trip now, Peadar, than when I took it."

"It is, the war changed shipping forever."

He noticed his son's appetite. Donny ate with total concentration and hardly said a word. When he had finished he left the table. "I'll see that the hens are in for the night, Aunt Emer."

"Good lad."

"Donny is a great help," said Emer "he even milks for me sometimes, unheard of about here."

"And why wouldn't he?" Una declared, "I've never understood why men don't do their share of milking."

"There is always so much other work they have to do," Peadar told her.

"That's no excuse," insisted his daughter. My God, where was his sweet little girl?

That night, the evening work finished, neighbours dropped in. After an initial greeting, they moved on to gossip and politics. The government was having difficulty getting the army under control. "There was a great danger the army would take over," Joseph explained for Peadar's benefit. "But last spring, Cosgrove took the ringleaders on. And Mulcahy is handling it well. First, he cut the number of officers, then reduced the troops. The officers were so mad we're lucky they didn't cause a mutiny."

"Well," maintained Tom Plunkett, putting down his glass,

"Collins, God rest his soul, had a few blackguards in his brigade, so you know they'll be difficult. Hard men, they are."

"What could you expect? It's not petticoats that win freedom," said Stephen.

"Stephen! Mind what you're saying." Una warned. "Lots of women fought in the revolution, what about Con Markieviczs?"

Stephen's broad face flushed to the roots of his sandy hair.

"Ah you see, Stephen," Joseph joked, to cover Stephen's confusion, "when you give the women the vote that's what you have to put up with."

"Oh, Joseph," cried Una exasperated, "you're impossible!"

The discussion turned to the economy and the proposed cuts in old age pensions.

"I'd hate to see them take that road! We're not that bad off," said Joseph.

Bad off, bad off bad off, bad off hummed in Peadar's head as he sat listening. It seemed the voices came from far away, behind a curtain of mist. His mind dulled, he was tired. At ten o'clock, he whispered to Emer that he wanted to go to bed. She led him to Nan's room.

His bag sat on the chair where Donny had placed it.

"Goodnight, Peadar. I hope you sleep. If you need anything, just call me."

"Goodnight, Emer."

He lay awake for a while listening to the murmur of voices from the kitchen. By eleven o'clock, he was asleep.

At mass on Sunday, people stared at him and after the service old neighbours came to shake his hand. He saw himself an actor, going through a ritual. More neighbors dropped by in the afternoon. It seemed he was a novelty, the returned exile. Stephen Plunkett came to talk to him about farming. Stephen felt that farmers had to work harder. They got used to high prices during the war and now there was a slump. But things would come back. "First, we have to produce a better class of produce," he maintained.

Joseph agreed. "I think you're right about that, Stephen."

To Peadar everything in Ireland needed to be upgraded, to become modern, even though it would never compare with America.

"Una, I'd be glad to give you a lift to the train this evening," Stephen offered.

"No thanks Stephen, Donny's going to take me."

At five o'clock, Peadar stood at the door with Emer to say goodbye. Donny was waiting with the trap. Una leaned over and kissed his cheek.

"See you Friday, Daddy."

When they drove out of the yard he regretted not going with them to the station. Una seemed to take some of the light with her when she left. It was too late to offer to go now. The trap was already disappearing down the lane.

"Peadar's very quiet," said Emer to Joseph, as she readied for bed Sunday night.

"Well Emer, he was never much of a talker."

"That's true, but you'd think he'd talk to Donny."

"Some of that lies with Donny. He's shy of his father, and why wouldn't he be."

"I'm a bit worried about it all, Joseph."

"Oh, give it time."

By eight on Monday morning Joseph had left with Donny for school in Kilderry and Judy, who came each Monday to help Emer with the wash, arrived.

"Judy, do you remember my brother Peadar?"

"I don't think I do, Mrs. O'Neill."

"Peadar, this is Judy McDermott."

Peadar held out his hand. "How are you, Judy?"

It startled Peadar, momentarily, to hear her address Emer as Mrs. O'Neill, her married name. It was the first time he had heard it used and it sounded strange to him. It reminded him that she was not only his sister but his sister-in-law. How unexpected it all was. He sat in the sitting room and looked out the window over the back garden, down to the river and the hills beyond. Emer came to sit with him and talk. She was a handsome woman still, in her country tweeds, even beautiful, with the sleek look of contentment about her. He calculated she was forty-six now, and he thought about where he would be at forty-six, in '27, three years from now. She told him about his children. "Donny wants to go to Blackrock College, Peadar."

"Won't that be very costly, Emer? Can we afford that?"

"Oh, I think we can. I've been saving part of what you send for it."

"You and Joseph have been very good to the children, Emer."

"They're like our own, Peadar."

She took down the carefully kept accounts and the bank-books and went over with him all the earnings and expenditures since he had gone to America. They were comfortable now it seemed. She had paid for the work on the house but she wanted him to approve it all.

"This is your house Peadar, Joseph and I have never forgotten that. What we hope is that we could either buy if from you or move to the old place and you could stay here."

"Emer, I'm far from worrying about houses, and if I stay I'll take the old house."

"If you stay? Surely you're not thinking of going back?"

"I've decided nothing Emer. It's too soon."

That night, Tom Plunkett came up again to see him. Peadar warmed a little to his old friend, remembering what a helpful neighbour he had been. Tom clearly expected Peadar to take up the life of a farmer.

"There's a good life to be had here now Peadar, things will pick up again, the price of farm produce will improve, and that's a nice farm of yours."

"I'm not sure Tom, I can't see myself farming."

"You can't? Maybe you need to get used to the idea again."

On Friday, Una arrived back from Dublin, with her friend Eilish, and Peadar thought what a contrast she was to Una, a small, plump merry girl against Una's tall figure and serious face. He noticed how companionably Una and Emer where, almost like sisters. Over tea, Una and Joseph began to discuss changes in the education system. It seemed the new government, a year earlier, had dismissed the boards of primary and intermediate education. Una was not happy about how the two commissioners, who had replaced the boards, were managing the system.

"It's ridiculous Joseph, the power given to those two men, and we're supposed to be a democracy. The union should object. They know nothing of local situations, they're stuck in an office in Dublin."

"Now Una," said Joseph, "the boards were full of British sympathizers, they needed to be disbanded," he paused to hand his teacup to Emer. "You know that, and we can't have colonials running the education system." Joseph spoke indulgently, his green eyes twinkling at her.

"They could have appointed commissioners that supported the government, not closed the system down," Una shot back at him, "am I not right, Eilish?"

"Well, yes, you do have a point, Una."

"Well, Eilish, you're the one that's loyal," Emer told her.

"Ah the young, Peadar, the young," Joseph protested.

"And another thing," Una persisted, "the new commissioners are men, you'd never know half the students are women."

Emer, ever the peacemaker, broke into the conversation. "Peadar, did I tell you the two teachers over in Cornafane have a motorcar now? I want Joseph to think about getting one next year. He needs it for all the County Council meetings he goes to. I believe we can afford it. I think it's time we got rid of the pony and trap."

"Ah, Emer," Joseph teased, "I should never have bought you that bicycle eight years ago, you've been trying to get rid of the pony and trap ever since."

"You didn't buy it for me Joseph, if I remember, I paid for it myself, you just brought it from Dublin."

Peadar sat there among the teacups feeling out of place, a little resentful of the effortless talk, the gossip and good-humoured banter. He had left his family peasants, Una a child, Nan a toddler of three years, and Donny an infant in his cradle; now, by some metamorphosis, they were outpacing him, moving up, almost middle-class, planning for motorcars, for professions he had never dreamed of. While his mind was glad and proud of their success, his heart couldn't feel joy in it. It wasn't that he begrudged them their comfort, they worked hard enough, but there seemed to be no one with whom he could discuss the past. Somehow he was not at home in their present, something was absent, but he couldn't grasp what it was. To hide his uneasiness he got up from the table.

"I'll take a stroll, Emer, down as far as the river."

As he left the house he saw Stephen coming up the lane. He hurried round by the side of the house and along the path toward the river. He didn't feel like talking.

UNA FELT A BARRIER between herself and her father. He seemed distant and cold, and showed no interest in her.

"Eilish," she complained, as she knelt to light the fire in the old house down the lane, "I can't get close to my father. He doesn't talk to me. Never asked me about myself. He's not like he used to be."

"How could he be Una? He's been in America twelve years."

Una stood up and stared at the flame that had begun to lick the sods of turf. "It's almost as if he's not one of our family any more."

"Una you're twenty-two. It's thinking of starting a family yourself you should be. What about Connor?"

"Oh, Eilish, I don't know how I feel about him."

"Well, he knows how he feels about you, and I think he's the one for you."

"Eilish, you're jumping to conclusions."

"I'm not, and I'm setting my cap for Peter, so you better hurry up and make up your mind or you'll be left behind."

"Setting your cap? That's not very romantic, Eilish."

"Romantic? You do enough romancing for the two of us. If you don't smarten up you'll end up an old maid."

ON SATURDAY NIGHT, the neighbours gathered to play cards. Peadar played, as always, with intense concentration, winning almost every game.

"He's a practiced card player, I'll tell you that," Joseph remarked to Emer when they were alone.

"He always was. That's the first thing I've seen him interested in since he came. I wish I knew how he's feeling. Do you think he might have a sweetheart in America?"

"You're the expert on affairs of the heart, Emer."

"In the beginning I wouldn't have wanted him to remarry, and bring a stepmother in here, but now, the children are well on their way. It might do him good."

"Well, if he's that way inclined, there's lots of single girls about the country. He could have his pick," Joseph said, punching up the pillows to plumpness and laughing. "Come on to bed, Emer."

Eilish and Una stayed the weekend, sleeping in the old house down the lane, and when they left Peadar told Emer he wanted to move down to the old place. She didn't try to dissuade him, perhaps understanding he wanted to be alone. As he set off, with a live coal from the sitting room fire in a galvanized pail, she handed him a bottle of whiskey.

"You may feel like a drink at bed time, Peadar."

"I don't think I'll need it."

"Take it anyway, Peadar."

Peadar was back in the house where he and Emer and Patrick had grown up. He lit the fire from the ember, standing the sods high around it so the flame caught their loose threads, and working the bellows, he kindled the turf. He stayed for a short while looking at the flames, remembering his mother cooking over that hearth. Then he took his candle and went to sleep in the small, whitewashed room off the kitchen, on the narrow iron bed where he had spent every night of his childhood and youth. The old place seemed to have shrunk into the ground. The sycamores towered over it. Peadar lay in the uncertain light of the flickering candle, aware of shadows hanging in the corners of the little room, conscious of holding his breath, listening for a familiar sound, but silence spread itself around him as deep as if he were at the bottom of the sea. He sat up, blew out the candle and lay in the dark.

Over and over he asked himself, what was wrong with his homecoming? Why couldn't he feel joy in it? What was wrong with him? It wasn't that he missed Angela, he believed he had long since accepted her loss. But their children, he couldn't decide what he felt for them. Pondering the confusion and turmoil of his emotions, he tumbled into a dreamless sleep.

He awoke to the distant, driving throb of a threshing machine; by his watch it was seven o'clock. He heard the clatter of buckets, stepped out of bed and went to the window. Emer's cattle were standing at the far hedge, crowded together beside their drinking pot. The trees were black outlines carved in the mist and Donny was crossing the field carrying two buckets. The kerry blue terrier followed him. The boy's long legs rose thin like the legs of a compass out of his wellington boots, and his arms stuck out from the sleeves of his jacket. Time telescoped, and it was as if Peadar watched himself, thirty years earlier, carrying drinking water to cattle on a chilly, foggy September morning before starting for school. He felt again the loose slipping of the rubber boots on his own feet and the cattle's warm presence, their heads wreathed in their own breath, the hurrying to get through the work, the rush to get to school on time. Donny seemed as familiar with the animals as if he were one of them. He saw his son, his task finished, walk back carrying both pails in his left hand, then not bothering to open the five-bar gate, climb over it out into the lane. The dog followed him, slipping through the bars. Nothing changes, Peadar realized, and yet everything had changed. And all at once he knew what had been absent at Emer's tea table, what had been missing. The knowledge came to him in a rush, followed by immense sadness. He missed the man he might have become, if he hadn't gone away.

PEADAR FELT THE three hundred and sixty souls that made up the inhabitants of the village of Slanabaille and the townland of Kilderry watching him. Through September they became accustomed to seeing the tall, silent American walk his land, his son's dog at his heels, and drink his lone pint in the pub. If they wondered whether he would be staying home or going back to America, something about his demeanor must have discouraged questions. No one mentioned going back.

He went with Emer to see Nan in the convent. He sat in the hotel dining room listening to her chatter about school.

"I know we'll come first in the a camogie championship Daddy, our team is the best."

Peadar watched her small hands plying the knife and fork, her grin when she reported who got black marks in school for various infractions. Her big green expressive eyes, the saucy toss of her head. She was so like her mother; he was speechless.

He couldn't seem to get close to his son. The boy was always away, at school, occupied with his lessons or down the village with his friends. Joseph was busy, away much of his time at political gatherings and meetings of the Irish National Teachers Organization. He felt Emer watching him too, when he sat in her sitting room.

"Have you ever considering marrying again, Peadar?"

"I have, but that's all that ever came of it."

"Was there anyone in particular?" she gently enquired.

"Emer, I've had my share of women's company in America, but remarry, never."

"Why not Peadar?"

"I've never met anyone to replace Angela, and I never will."

She left it at that and began talking about Nan's news that she wanted to go to America. "It's just because you're here and have talked about America, but Nan takes after you in one respect, she's very headstrong."

"I never considered myself headstrong."

"Then you don't know yourself."

"I'm against her ever going to America. She's far too young to be thinking like that anyway. Emigration is a hard life for girls."

"It's just because you are home, Peadar, and because you've said you might go back."

"Ah, Irish girls always look to America. Don't you remember yourself, Emer?"

"Those were very different times. It's out of the question, she's only fifteen, still a child."

"Emer, where did we get Una at all, who is she like, with that fair hair and light eyes?"

"She's like Angela's father, don't you remember? He was fair and blue-eyed."

But he didn't remember. He vaguely recalled an old man, grey and tired.

Angela was nowhere to be found, no sign or trace of her. His children seemed like someone else's offspring, as if he and Angela had not lived and loved here. Angela had been more real to him in America than she was here. Her children wiped her image from his mind; except in those fleeting seconds when Nan kissed him, or when she displayed her merry grin, then he glimpsed her mother in her eyes.

Peadar had to go to Angela's grave, but for some reason he did not himself understand, he put that visit off till the third week. Then, deciding he could wait no longer, he borrowed a bicycle from Emer and set off late one afternoon along the narrow dusty road between the sun-dazed hedges. It seemed his whole mind was waiting for this visit to be over, to complete his pilgrimage, and have done with it.

The graveyard for the parish was five miles away, by the old church in Knockmore. Peadar pedaled fast and suddenly, before he was ready for it, he saw the church spire in the distance. He slowed his pace a little then dismounted and walked up the hill. Reaching the gate, he left the bicycle lying on the side of the road. Now that he had arrived he was nervous, not quite feeling in complete command of himself. Like a sleepwalker.

Peadar knew where the grave was, but the distance from the road to the churchyard was shorter than he remembered, the graves closer together. Angela was buried beside his parents, in a plot at the back of the church. He walked round by the side of the old, grey, stone building. There were more graves than he remembered, and he read the inscriptions as he went. *Patrick McGee, 1842-1922*; poor Pat, how he loved an argument. His wife *Anne 1852-1876*. Then *Fergus Scanlon 1821-1905*. His wife *Mary 1832-1910*; their daughter *Elizabeth McCann 1843-1919*. Lizzie had lived to be a great age, he thought, then the next stone and inscription brought him up short: *John Mahon, Born 1897. Killed in action, France. April 1917*. Just a boy! Then *John Slowey 1850-1920*. Poor John. The villagers who peopled his childhood and youth had been buried here. Slowly Peadar followed the narrow path and then arrived.

His eyes avoided the granite cross Emer had found, looking instead at the low stone marking his parents' resting place. With a shock he saw they were not alone, that his grandparents were buried there and his aunts, his father's sisters, Julia and Rosie. How could he have forgotten? What else had he forgotten? He remembered his aunts, jolly women, dressmakers, and a picture entered his mind of his childish self, giddy and restless, too warm and fidgety, being fitted for trousers. Julia's mouth was full of pins, her long fingers pulled and tugged the material around his waist. They had died young, of tuberculosis, one after another in 1900. He had forgotten them completely. How reliable, then, was his memory?

At last he turned and read the inscription on the tall granite cross: *Angela Maura Maguire 1880-1912. Beloved wife of Peadar.*

This was what he had come for, yet he couldn't picture Angela in the grave. It was absurd, impossible to believe she was there. Preposterous to think of her in this place. The laughing, dancing girl he'd married. It came to him suddenly that all the years since, while he grieved for her, he had really never accepted that she was dead. She certainly wasn't here with him, nor were his parents. They were all gone. Nothing to be done about it, and he had to carry on alone.

Daisies and wild grasses grew on the graves. From there he had a view down over the little rolling hills to the lake in the distance. The same crows and sparrows as when he said goodbye to her twelve years ago. A wild lonely spot, the finality and hopelessness of the place entered his soul. Kneeling there, he felt more alone and abandoned than ever, no one knew or understood him, he knew no one either. All who knew him lay here. Peadar prayed for a moment at his parents' grave, then stoically made his way out of the lonely field of the dead.

He gripped the handlebar of the bicycle with his right hand and wheeled it along towards home, the sound of his footsteps ringing in his ears. After he had covered a mile, he mounted and pedaled furiously, determined to put the distance between the burial ground and home behind him as quickly as possible.

That evening he lingered in the sitting room, watching his son studying at the kitchen table and listening to Emer talking to Cassie Plunkett about land just south of Peadar's farm that was for sale. She urged him to buy it, to extend his own farm. "It's good land, Peadar, the best around, and good value for the price."

"I'm not ready for that yet, Emer."

He knew she wanted to tie him to home. He wanted to talk to someone about his day, about his feelings in the graveyard, but didn't know how to begin. He was tired, the visit to the cemetery and its unaccustomed exertions must have exhausted him. At ten o'clock, Peadar walked down the hill to bed. He blew out the candle, attempting to put the emotions and thoughts of the day aside, but as he tumbled into a half sleep he felt them waiting at the edge of his consciousness.

In his dreams he saw a wide field stretching to a wood. Voices were calling him, calling him back, to join them, voices so unworldly he felt rather than heard them. They surrounded him like trembling tongues of fire, a circle of flame signaling and calling out to him. His wavering heart cried at last that he did not want to go there, wouldn't endure that grief, refused to answer.

He woke with a start in the dark and fumbled for the candle and matches. The trembling flame lit his old whitewashed childhood bedroom, his clothes hung on a wooden peg at the back of the door, the whiskey bottle Emer had given him, and the glass he had brought from the kitchen, sat on the table. He was surprised to realize he was not frightened, just determined to remain in command of himself.

Peadar looked at his watch: one o'clock. He rose and filled the glass to the brim with the spirits and drank it quickly, then returned to bed, pulling the blankets closely around him. He lay perfectly still, waiting for the alcohol to work. He slept again soundly and awoke with a rush of energy, grieved still but knowing he was done with the past. It might come back in memory, but it wouldn't haunt him. He dressed quickly and went up to Emer's. As he ate his breakfast he told her of his decision. He was going back, away from that place.

"I've been living in the past, I haven't gone past the day I lost Angela."

"I know that Peadar, I've noticed it, but I hoped you'd stay, I believe that will pass in time."

"I'm going back Emer, for a while at least, to forget and to catch up. You have all moved ahead, kept going forward, but I see now I'm still back in 1912."

"What if you began to farm again, maybe you've had too much time on your hands, what about spending a while with Una in Dublin? You know she wants you to do that."

"I don't think I want that, Emer."

Una, when she came, was bitterly disappointed; she could not understand why he was leaving, she had her father back and now he was going again.

"It's so far away, Daddy. If you go back when will we ever see you again?"

He tried to explain his decision to her. "I'm not ready to be a farmer, to stay here, maybe when I'm older, Una."

"But you just came back Daddy, we all want you to stay. You haven't given it a chance. Can't you try to settle here?"

"You're all grown up now Una, you don't need me."

"We'll always need you, Daddy."

Peadar turned away, disturbed by the emotion in her voice, terrified of sentiment.

LATE SUNDAY EVENING, when Una stepped down from the train at Amiens Street Station, she was astounded to find Connor waiting for her.

"Connor! What a surprise! What prompted you to come to meet me?'

"I just thought it would be a good idea."

Connor reached for her suitcase. "Would you like to take a cab, Una?'

"No, Connor, I want to walk, a walk will do me good."

"Are you sure? It's a long way. We could take the tram."

"Yes, I'm sure. I need to walk."

"I wasn't strictly accurate Una, about whose idea it was that I meet your train. It was Eilish who suggested it. How was everything at home?"

"Oh, Connor, I'm so disappointed. My father is going back."

"Eilish suspected he might do that."

"Connor, I don't think I can bear it."

They were passing under a street lamp and he noticed tears standing in her eyes. He passed her his handkerchief. "Don't cry. He's come home once, he'll come again, Una. You'll see. It's not as if you haven't been through it all before. And you were much younger then." Connor put his arm protectively around her and they walked on.

"You know, if you feel you must go back, we're behind you all the way Peadar," Emer reassured him. "We'd really like you to stay, but we know you must do what you want."

Donny was silent, he hadn't got to know his father. The tall, too-quiet stranger was a mystery to Donny. He had never known anyone like him. Surely his father had stories to tell, things he wanted to ask Donny about, some plans besides walking the fields with the dog.

"You know, Donny," said Emer one night after Peadar had gone down to the old house, "your father is thinking about going back."

"I don't think he likes it here, Aunt Emer."

"It's just that he's been away so long, and everything changed while he was away, it has been a shock to him."

"Why can't he stay and be a farmer? He was a farmer before."

"You tell him you'd like him to stay."

The following evening at tea, Donny gathered up his courage and asked, "Would you not think of staying and farming again, Father?"

"Oh, it's a long time since I farmed, not since before you were born."

"But you haven't forgotten about it, have you?"

"No, not really."

Peadar didn't know how to tell his son that he wanted to be part of the pulsing life of America again, to feel like men do when they work together on big enterprises, to make money from his work, to have a pay packet every week, not wait to sell pigs or cattle before he saw his money, forever depending on beef prices and milk yield to know his worth. And the country was struggling, the government completely occupied with keeping order and disarming the IRA. It was different for Joseph, he had his teaching and he was a county councillor. Peadar saw no place for himself in Ireland, no future in Irish farming, and farming was what he knew. It was too backward. Maybe he'd stay in New York. He thought with excited longing of Manhattan with its fabulous skyscrapers, the East River, the ferry boats and tugs and the magnificent bridges, the Brooklyn and the Manhattan. That wondrous spectacle, that's where he wanted to be, that's where he'd stay and work.

"You know I want you to stay," Emer told him again the day before he left, "but if that's how you feel, I won't try to stop you."

So he packed his bag for America, going not as he did before into the unknown, but to familiar things. He was young yet, and strong, and had magnificent health; as long as times were good he'd stay over there.

"I won't go to the station. I'll say goodbye here," said Emer when he was leaving.

She climbed up into the trap to embrace him one more time. "God keep you, Peadar. Come back soon to us now!" Her voice was thick with tears. Joseph looked away over the pony's head.

On his way to the station they picked up Nan at the convent and had dinner once more in the Railway Hotel. Nan picked at her food.

"Daddy, I don't want you to leave. I told everyone at school my daddy was back."

Joseph consoled her. "They'll understand dear. People often change their minds."

"If you wait a year I could go with you. I'd have my Intermediate Certificate then."

"Oh, I wouldn't want you in America, it's not a place for little girls."

"I'm not a little girl, I'm fifteen."

He forced himself to ignore the tears filling Nan's eyes. He couldn't wait for the meal to be over, to get away.

"Eat up Nan," said Joseph, passing his handkerchief, "your father will come back in a year or two."

Peadar was flooded with happy anticipation of the sea journey and the prospect of picking up life in the States. But at the convent steps, when Nan stood on her toes to kiss him goodbye, her big green eyes opened a fissure in the hard kernel of his heart.

At the station he shook hands with Joseph.

"Come back again soon, Peadar."

They steamed out of the station. He'd made his pilgrimage and now he was on his way. He remembered his visit to the grave. He hadn't found Angela there. All the years since he'd left Ireland she'd been with him, in his mind, as she had been when they had lived together, constantly in his thoughts, drifting through his memory, far more real to him than their children, even though she was twelve years dead and their children were moving out into the world. Their children, his and Angela's. From the train he stared out through the rain at the flat fields. The landscape was strange and unknown and at the same time very familiar to Peadar. He was half-way to Liverpool before he knew how much he would miss them.

How's Your Father?

After much procrastination, in 1933 the Department of Posts and Telegraphs had opened a post office in Slanabaille. This great achievement was credited to Fianna Fail winning the 1932 election.

"You'd see white blackbirds before that other shower would do it," said Margaret Smith, switching her allegiance to the party that won the election.

"Well, they did it because they have their eye on the next election," Oliver Higgins told her. "Fianna Fail are cute as foxes. They're in a minority, that's why they're doing it."

The post office operated out of a green shop across from O'Brien's Bar and Grocery. It was possible to post letters, purchase post office money orders and sign for registered letters and parcels. It also served as a pension office for old age pensioners.

When Hanlon's grocery opened beside the post office, O'Briens stopped selling groceries and extended the bar into what had been the grocery-end of the premises. For a while there was hope of further enterprises starting up. Hanlon's installed a petrol pump which was a convenience for motorists, although there were few cars. The milk was still taken to the creamery in horse-drawn carts, and bread delivered by wagon. There was envy of Ballynamon, which boasted four pubs, a creamery, a medical doctor's dispensary, the guarda station and a four-room school. The post office in Ballynamon even had a telephone. For threepence the postmistress would connect you with anyone in Ballynamon who had a telephone. That this number was limited to one, the guarda station, did not lessen the wonder at this convenience. There was resentment when Donny Maguire set up his veterinary practise in Ballynamon, rejecting his home village. Some said he was a spoilt brat, and like all the Maguires, getting above himself. There was also speculation about which of the local girls he'd throw his eye on. Jessie O'Toole, the pretty, dark-haired teacher from the vocational school, was thought to have taken his fancy. Margaret Smith maintained that Emer O'Neill, Emer Maguire that was, would think no one good enough for him. "The Maguires are always full of their own importance. You couldn't keep up with them."

"Ah now, don't I remember, like yesterday, the day that lad was born," said Des Donoghue, raising mournful eyes from his pint.

It was the last Saturday in April, 1937, and Des and Margaret were the only drinkers in O'Briens. Sunlight from the two front windows held dancing motes and ran along the top of chairs and tables, picking out thick dust on the hanging lamps. It would be two hours before the first of the Saturday night crowd arrived.

"Yes," Des continued, "sure we thought the child would never survive."

"And didn't he cost his poor mother her life?" Margaret reminded him. The barman's bald head turned and nodded above the rows of spirit bottles in the mirror behind him.

"Ah, Angela, wasn't she lovely," wheezed Des who was then overcome by a violent fit of coughing. His face flushed a dark red, the lobes of his ears turned purple. He slid from the bar stool and hurried out, bent over, hand covering his mouth. Margaret looked knowingly at the barman. A moist, wheezing cough was heard through the closed door. Then the raucous sound as Des gathered the phlegm in the back of his throat and spat.

"That mustard gas," murmured the barman, grimly shaking his head and studying the glass he was polishing.

"Sure what he spits would turn your stomach," Margaret whispered, taking a mouthful of stout. "He was a great carpenter, you know. Now look at the cut of him! Idle most of his time. Good job he has the war pension."

The door opened, sending a stream of early evening light into the pub. Des returned, mopping his streaming eyes with a not-too-clean handkerchief. "A small one," he gasped.

The barman took the whiskey bottle off the shelf and held it, starred label towards the drinkers. Des nodded, still struggling for breath. "And what about yourself, Margaret?" he asked, when his breathing was easier. "Will you have a drop of Powers?"

"I'll not, Des! I'll stick to me pint."

Margaret scorned the snug, tiny cubicle off to the side of the counter where the women usually sat and sipped their whiskey or porter in modest, genteel obscurity. She always stood up to the bar and drank with the men.

"Sure, Donny could've been anything he wanted," boasted Des, taking up the conversation again when he had swallowed a mouthful of the whiskey, "and he could have played for the county if he'd stuck to the football. And he's the lad that would have them cheering in the Hogan stand."

"He'd never play county football, he's too soft. His aunt has him spoilt, gives him everything he asks for, always did."

"Ah sure, there's no harm in being a bit easy now, is there, with a nice lad like Donny?"

"Not if you fall on your feet like he did, his uncle big into politics," said Margaret waspishly.

But Des was not to be deterred from boasting. "Sure, I heard he did a great job on a horse of Nugent's that fell and hurt his leg. I heard tell that Nugent thought he might have to shoot the animal."

"Well," said Margaret, narrowing her sharp black eyes now sunk in grey wrinkles of fat, "the question is, did Nugent pay him?"

Margaret's daughter Greta still worked in the old Darling House, now renamed Nugent House, and the previous week staff wages there had been cut. She took another mouthful from her glass. "That's the thing," she declared, "will Nugent foot the bill?"

The subject of their conversation was, at that moment, driving his squat Austin motor car toward Slanabaille, on his way to tea with Emer and Joseph. He wanted Joseph's advice on a number of matters, the most pressing of which was money. It was one of those soft, late April evenings when it seems summer has arrived and will last forever. The hedges burst with wild blossom and brambles. On impulse, Donny decided he would stop by for a few minutes to see his father.

Peadar had arrived home in the spring of 1930, part of an early wave of Irish driven from America and England by depressed economies. Donny was in the last weeks of his final term at Blackrock College, studying for his Leaving Certificate and his entrance to the national university. Emer wrote to say Peadar was coming home. She said this time it was for good. She was overjoyed, but Donny saw no reason for rejoicing. He remembered the last time his father had visited. He was supposed to have stayed that time, too. For days after his departure Emer had been sad and dejected. Peadar had not settled at home as she had hoped.

When Donny had arrived for his summer holidays, his father was already settled into the old house down the lane. Donny had been given to understand Joseph had paid him some sort of compensation for the house he and Emer lived in.

His father moved in, replaced the loose slates on the roof, painted the woodwork and scythed the weeds and nettles that had overgrown the garden. He cut down some of the sycamore trees but made no effort to farm except to fatten cattle on the land. He paid Donny's school fees and when Donny asked Emer about that, she said his father had always sent money from America for his children. This only served to make Donny more uncomfortable. To think he owed so much to that cold, remote figure.

Peadar played cards Saturday nights at Emer's house or at Tom Plunkett's. He attended every fair and market and bargained hard with the cattle dealers. If he had any regrets about the years spent away from his children, he never displayed them. Once Donny had thought that behind his father's expressionless face there had to be a reserve of wisdom, or of emotion, but he had lately concluded there was nothing at all.

Donny turned from the main road into the lane, shifted down to first then stopped, his way barred by a drove of cattle. Stephen Plunkett was behind, driving them home for milking. He raised his stick in salute.

"Grand evening, Stephen."

"Tis."

Stephen leaned on the open window of the car, his foot on the running board. "Going up to see Emer?"

"I am. That's a fine herd you have there."

"Not bad. I'm not fattening many cattle this year. With this economic war it's hardly worth my while. I'll push the milk and bacon. I've switched more land to tillage. Hard work, tillage!"

"You'll get some of the tillage subsidy, so. That's all you could do," said Donny philosophically.

Stephen stepped back "Go on with you there," he shouted, and swung his stick at a cow that stood waving her head at the car. The herd crossed over the lane. Donny eyed the animals, appraising them. Good stock!

Peadar wasn't at home and the wolfhound was gone. His father was likely in one of the fields beyond the hill. The farmhouse door was locked. Only a returned American would lock his door when he was just going up a few fields. Time was, Donny thought, when Emer kept the key under the stone beside the door. Now the stone was gone, tidied away. He walked round to the back of the house. Had his father ever shown any feelings? Maybe there was nothing to show. Only once had he seen him take more than one drink, at Nan's wedding three years ago. Nan's wedding meal was held in the Railway Hotel and his father, to Donny's astonishment, had paid for it. He thought the old boy had some money socked away but never could bring himself to ask his father for help, no matter how short of money he was, not even when he was setting himself up as a veterinarian and needed capital to equip a dispensary.

The back yard was tidy as a church. His father's bicycle was propped against the back of the house. Over in the haggard he noticed the gleam of machinery and went to investigate. A brand new harvester. Was his father changing his policy? Was he going into tillage now that the government paid a subsidy for grain? He'd have to get a horse to run that machine, or hire one. What was the old boy up to?

He drove on up the lane and when Emer heard the car she

came out to greet him. "Joseph," she called over her shoulder, "Donny's here."

Joseph came behind her holding the dog's scruff. Seeing Donny's dog, Annabelle, was not with him, he loosed the terrier. "Great to see you lad!"

The dog stood in front of Donny wagging his tail, craving attention. Donny stooped and rubbed his ears.

"Come on in, Donny."

He stepped into the kitchen and took his usual seat at the scrubbed deal table, his back to the window, facing the stairs and the open door to the sitting room. Everything in Emer's kitchen had the reassuring sheen of use: the high dresser with the blue willow pattern dishes, the egg cups lined up on the middle shelf, the old pendulum clock with the Roman numerals above the black-leaded range, the blue and red tea canister. Home! Disparagingly, he thought of his narrow, shabby lodgings. He'd have to get his own place.

Emer served a country fry. Black and white puddings, sausages and fried potato bread.

"I called to see Peadar and he wasn't there. No sign of the dog either!"

"He might be in the town. He'll be here tonight for a game of cards if you'll stay."

"I can't! There's a dance in Mountnugent. I promised Charlie I'd give him a lift. I noticed a new harvester at Peadar's place. Is he going into tillage?"

"Not likely, Donny. His plan is to rent that machine out now that so many of the farmers have switched to grain."

Well, he might have known it. If there was a shilling to be made the old boy would be at it. "I hope he has more luck in getting the farmers to pay than I have."

"How's the business coming, Donny?"

"Busy enough, more work than I can handle, Emer. The hassle is to get paid."

"You have to get paid. That's the most important thing. Maybe you need help with sending out the bills."

"No, I spend a half day a week doing that. And some can well afford it. Nugent owes me thirty shillings!"

"I wouldn't stand that nonsense from him," Joseph affirmed. "He's not that hard up."

"All the farmers are slow to pay up."

"Get them at the Fair Day. That's when to talk money," Joseph advised.

Emer cleared the plates away and served rhubard tart. The men talked politics. Since there was peace she had relaxed her opposition to political talk at the table. She was thinking now that to watch Donny was to see what his father had looked like at twenty-five. The same pale skin, the dark grey eyes. Donny's face was shorter than Peadar's, and he had a slight cleft in his chin, a legacy from his mother. He was less driven, less in a hurry than his father had been, but he had the same quick movements that hinted at banked stores of energy.

"Dev made a mistake, stopping the annuity payments to England," Donny declared passing his cup to Emer for a refill. "Look at the result: high tariffs on our exports over there. We can't survive at those prices."

"I don't believe that De Valera ever meant to cancel them, he just meant to bargain them down."

"Who would ever know what that fellow meant? Anyway, it means small farmers are raising less livestock."

"Just give the country time, lad. It's young yet. Things'll get better."

At a quarter to eight Donny rose to go. "Thanks for supper, Emer."

"Don't be a stranger now," she said on the step as he was leaving. She was crouched low, holding the dog. He had a bad habit of chasing cars.

"Safe home lad," said Joseph.

They waved as Donny drove out of the yard and down the lane. He passed his father walking up toward Joseph and Emer's house, the wolfhound looping ahead. Donny geared down, slowing the car.

"Grand evening," said Peadar.

"Tis indeed," Donny agreed, and drove on. He felt as if his

father had wanted to talk. The thought made him uncomfortable. Maybe he should have delayed longer, maybe said something about the dog. The wolfhound was standing looking after the car, too dignified to chase it. It occurred to Donny that the tall dog resembled his owner. He could see how well Peadar kept the hound. The grey double coat was carefully stripped so the high shoulders and strong legs showed to advantage. That took some combing.

His sisters seemed to have penetrated Peadar's stony exterior, but he never had. He didn't know him. Joseph was his real father. The model of what a man should be. Cheerful, unfailingly himself. His memories of the years with Joseph were a sunny country, days spent fishing, at football and hurling matches, his first pint in the pub, long discussions about politics, wise counsel given and taken. Even when they had disagreed, and Donny recalled how he himself had often stormed out of the kitchen, slamming the half door and brooding sulkily on the dairy step, the rift had been soon mended. Joseph would come out and sit beside him, quiet for a while. Then he would break the silence with, "Life's too short, Donagh lad, to disagree. The dog needs a run. Why don't we walk down and look at the river?"

And they would walk together, the dog running ahead, and Joseph would remark on the weather, or the changing seasons and things would be more companionable than ever, their affection the stronger for the disagreement.

So naturally, when Donny considered setting up on his own and needed money to buy the second-hand car and rent premises for a dispensary, it was to Joseph he went. The dispensary was a room that led on to the cobblestone lane at the side of Masie O'Shea's house, up the hill from the guarda station in Ballynamon. A small sign, designed and executed by Des Donoghue, announced the service. *Donagh Maguire. Veterinary Surgeon.* It was a brave sign, anticipating professional success and prosperity. The reality was somewhat different. Although, as he had told Emer, there was no shortage of customers, prosperity was very slow in arriving.

Donny received his veterinary qualification in 1934 and spent a year in virtual slavery working as an assistant to Dr. John Curtis, the veterinary in Oldcastle. In '35 he began plotting to set up on his own. One Friday afternoon in late March his boss had sent him to Kilderry to check on a cow with mastitis. The vet loaned Donny his motorcar for the very obvious reason that he always got drunk on Fridays, and was not only not fit to drive, but hardly able to stand up from the old rolled-top desk in the dark little office. Donny had accompanied him, and had treated the cow, the day before. When Donny saw her on Friday the inflammation had greatly decreased, her udder felt soft and had lost the unnatural heat it had previously exhibited. "You need only apply the salve once a day now. I'll drop back to see her on Monday," he told the cow's owner, a wizened bandy-legged farmer with a thick, white head of hair and startling blue eyes.

"Sure God bless you. I couldn't afford to lose her. She's a great milker."

"No fear of you losing her," Donny assured him, feeling wonderfully fulfilled by the satisfaction of having, for once, acted autonomously.

"Sure, you young lads have all the brains," said the farmer following Donny out of the byre, "all the latest."

Donny drove away feeling, as he often did, that he'd do better on his own. Of course, he'd need capital to start up. Because he had the car, he drove over to see Emer. He wanted to talk to her about his plan to set up on his own. She thought he was too young, that it was too soon. "It's hard work Donny," she told him, looking anxious, "can't you give yourself a few loose years, a time when you're free of worry?"

"No, Emer, I've my fill of the old miser, I want to get clear of him."

"What about working with another vet for a while?"

"Where? They're all the same. Backward, ignorant, they're back in the horse and spring car days."

"We'll see what Joseph says. You'll stay and have your tea with us."

He'd be late back with the car but no matter. Curtis would be long asleep, passed out on the sofa in his office.

Joseph, when he came home, encouraged Donny. "The country is starting to move ahead a bit, Fianna Fail's spending money. Why wouldn't you set up on your own?"

"But Joseph," Emer objected, "what about the extra duty England has on cattle imports from Ireland? Did I not hear you say the farmers would be raising a lot less cattle?"

"I did, and it's true, still, those with good grazing land will always have livestock, and Donny's customers would be the bigger farmers. The small ones rarely call the vet."

"That's true," Donny agreed

They talked about how he might go about it. He was well-liked by the farmers. When he was sent alone to treat an animal things seemed to go well. Curtis was slowing down.

"He'll likely retire," Emer predicted.

"Drop by and talk it over with Peadar," Joseph advised as Donny was leaving. But Peadar hadn't been home and Donny didn't regret that. In the end it was Emer who told Peadar about his son's plans.

"Where's he getting the money, Emer?"

"Joseph is lending him some."

"Be sure he pays it back."

"Of course, he will."

"Well, good luck to him," was Peadar's final word.

It had begun like that, and now in '37, taken all in all, Donny was quite pleased with himself. He was his own man. If only the money came a bit faster.

MONDAY MORNING Donny was thinking of Joseph's advice on collecting debts as he drove east on Wexford Street in Obanbeg. Nugent, in particular, irritated him. He had the money. He had promised to post the fee, but a month had passed already and no sign of the cheque. Donny decided to go to the Fair Day on Friday and see how many farmers that owed him money he could approach. Farmers were usually in funds on Fair Day and paid the merchants. So Joseph was right. There was no reason why he shouldn't collect from his customers the same day the shopkeepers did.

The problem of money and uncollected accounts was driven

completely from Donny's mind by the sight of a girl walking towards him under the lush green of the early summer trees. Her fair, curly hair, back-lit by the early morning sun, haloed her head in light. He braked instinctively to get a better look, forgot the clutch and the car stalled. He tried the starter. No luck. Annabelle stood up in the back seat and stuck her head out the open window. The girl continued walking towards him. He pulled out the choke and tried again. The car juddered, the engine spluttered and died. He was still in gear, he'd forgotten the clutch. The girl walked past. Angry with himself for his carelessness, Donny put the car in neutral, engaged the handbrake, stood out and took the crank handle from under the seat. The dog was jumping about in the back, ready for a run. Donny slammed the door, walked to the front of the car, inserted the crank handle and swung it. Nothing. He swung again, and again. No result. He leant one hand on the bonnet and tried again. The engine whined, then quit.

"Can I help?"

The girl with the marvelous hair was standing on the footpath, looking down at him leaning on the car. Donny straightened up. Sweat was pouring down his face. He was about to ask how she thought she could help when she said "You're on a slope. Maybe if I steered it and you pushed, we could start it in gear."

"Fine," said Donny abruptly. He was in a fog of perspiration, flummoxed, stuck for words. She opened the door, sat in and jiggled the gear shift to check it was in neutral. Donny stationed himself behind the car. She eased up on the brake.

"Push!"

He shoved with all his strength, the car lurched forward and gathered speed on the slope. The girl shifted into first gear, the engine caught. She drove on down the hill smoke pouring from the exhaust. Donny stood there for a minute, resentful of the ease with which she had started the car and at the same time filled with admiration of her good looks. Then he ran down the hill after her. She stopped and waited for him at the bottom. He could hear the wild barking of the excited dog. When he reached the car she pulled up the hand brake, left the engine running, stepped out and held the door open for him. The dog had her front paws up on the back of the seat. She barked twice, welcoming her panting owner.

"Shut up, Annabelle."

"Good luck, now," and the girl was gone, walking back up the incline the way they had come. Donny stood looking after her. "My God," he swore at the dog, as he sat into the car. "I'm an ejit. I just made a complete and utter fool of myself!"

The dog stopped barking, put her head to one side, and regarded him with limpid eyes. Donny pushed in the clutch, eased the brake and drove off fast. The engine groaned, resisting speed in low gear; he shifted up to second and then to third, then raced along the narrow street at thirty miles an hour. A man walking a pair of greyhounds turned and stared after him shaking his head. Donny de-clutched and almost stood on the brake to stop in front of the medical hall. It was just a quarter to nine. He'd have to cool his heels for almost half an hour waiting for Sheridan, the chemist, to come and open the shop. He stepped out and stood with his back leaning against the car, his arms folded. Annabelle gazed at him reproachfully. She had hoped for a run. "No," he told her firmly, "you stay where you are."

What a stupid yahoo he was stalling the car. And he hadn't as much as said thanks, and he didn't even know her name. She'd think him a right bogtrotter. Who on earth was she? His mind pictured again the broad, freckled face, the wide blue eyes. Now I know what golden hair is, what crowning glory looks like, he mused. He was a prize clown and no mistake. He went over again all his clumsy fumbling. Stalling the car, losing his temper, shouting at the dog, slamming the door. If it weren't for bad luck he'd have no luck of any kind.

"A great day, thanks be to God," said Sheridan, hurrying to the door, the key held in his hand like a prize.

"It is," Donny agreed, and began digging in his pocket for the list of ingredients he needed for the poultices, salves and doses of his trade.

On his return journey, Donny watched for the girl, but there was no sign of her on Wexford Street. He wasted half an hour driving down the side streets, convincing himself she was surely somewhere in the vicinity. He would just say he wanted to thank her. At last, he had to give up. Duty called: he had to go five miles past Slanabaille to tend a sick sow.

EMER AND JOSEPH had loaned Donny fifty pounds, enough to buy the second-hand Austin and set himself up in Ballynamon. Slowly, very cautiously, farmers were coming to appreciate and trust him and to avail themselves of his services, instead of dosing and treating their animals themselves. He still got called to treat animals whose condition had been made considerably worse by the ministrations of their owners, but it didn't happen as frequently as in the beginning. He was getting more of Curtis' work. The word in the county was that the young vet knew his business. He hadn't paid Joseph back yet, but he wasn't worried about it. Joseph knew he had a struggle to get the practise going. And Donny felt he must know it would eventually be paid. He loved the idea of being his own boss, running his own show. His pal Charlie Lever said if he kept himself steady and didn't lose the run of himself with money, there was no reason why he couldn't be on the pig's back.

"Well, there's no fear of me losing my head over money Charlie, maybe for the want of it. The worst problem I have is getting paid."

Charlie had grown to be a burly, easy-going farmer with sandy red hair and a broad, blunt face reddened by weather. It was to Charlie Donny confided his feelings about the girl with the glorious hair. He poured out his story over a pint in O'Brien's pub in Slanabaille. They were sitting in a corner, away from the crowd at the bar.

"You're a sick man," Charlie told him derisively, "in a terrible state altogether. The best thing you can do is get drunk."

"You don't understand, I'm serious. If you met her you'd see."

"Serious about her on ten minutes acquaintance?"

"It's not like you think. She's the most beautiful girl I've ever seen."

"It's a wonder we've never seen her at any of the dances. Maybe she's just visiting."

"She didn't look like a visitor. What would a visitor be doing walking up the street at a quarter after eight in the morning? She must live in Obanbeg."

"Well, if she does you'll see her again," Charlie predicted, getting up to refill the glasses.

THE FAIR DAY WAS bright and blustery. By noon, Donny had collected seven pounds in total from eight farmers. Although five others had said they hadn't the money and could pay nothing on account, he was fairly satisfied. He'd had some success, he'd just have to keep after the farmers. Of course, others who owed him money weren't even at the fair. At least he could get through the month without asking Joseph for another loan. He didn't want to do that. He deposited most of the cash in the Ulster Bank and went back down to the fair grounds to look for Charlie.

The fair was crowded. Country lads, off school for the day, tagged along with their fathers, learning the art of pretending to be insulted by offers for their livestock which they knew were close to what the animals were worth. Loud bargaining, hand slapping, and boasting rose above the bawling of calves and the squealing of pigs. The fresh wind carried the stench of manure, tobacco and hay. In a clear space beyond the carts and livestock, three farmers were putting a horse through his paces. Donny wandered around, greeting his customers.

"Donny," yelled the owner of the horse, "come on over here and give us your word on this animal."

Donny waved at him dismissively and walked in the opposite direction. He wasn't going to get caught in that trap, giving an opinion on the merits of a horse on offer for sale. He saw his father in the distance, talking to a cattle dealer. His father nodded at him. Donny nodded back and the cattle dealer looked round to see who had caught Peadar's attention. Donny walked on past the hucksters and the gypsy women telling fortunes at the edge of the green. "Cross the palm sir, a bit o' silver. Tell your fortune, sir?"

"Not today."

He strolled on, then stopped at a stall to examine some old books. A hand fell on his shoulder. "The very man."

"Charlie!"

"I've been looking for you."

"How's the day? Made any money?"

"I sold a bullock and a half dozen pigs. Fifteen shillings the hundredweight for pork."

"Not so bad."

"Better than the bacon factory. But, I'll bring the rest of the last litter there next month, ready money."

"The crowd at the Railway must be thinning out now. I'm starving. And for once I'm in funds. Come on, we'll have a bite."

"Alright. My father took the cart home. Any chance of a lift back?"

"Of course. But first let's go up and get something to eat."

They threaded their way between the stalls, along the main street past lined-up farm carts, some with crates of hens and ducks, through knots of women chatting and shopping, and up towards the hotel.

They walked into the crowded dining room and Donny immediately saw the girl. She was sitting with an older couple and a young man at a table in front of the window. Donny and Charlie sat near the middle of the room.

"Charlie! She's here!"

"Where?"

"Shush, just behind you."

Charlie made a great production of standing up and taking off his coat and hanging it on the back of a chair, using the opportunity to get a good look at the girl.

"The fair-haired one?"

"Yes. Isn't she a smasher?"

"A looker, I grant you that."

"She's gorgeous, Charlie."

The waitress came to take their order. Donny hardly knew what he was ordering. He couldn't take his eyes off the girl. She sat with her back to the window and again the light caught her hair. His heart plunged in despair when he saw her lean forward to talk to the younger man. So, she had a man friend. Beaten before he'd started.

"Go on over and say hello."

"I don't think that would be correct. She has people with her."

"So, she's with someone else. What odds about them!"

"I won't chance it."

Their food arrived and Charlie heaped on the HP sauce and passed Donny the bottle. Donny absently poured it over his fish, then remembered he didn't like the stuff. He was so acutely aware of her presence; he could concentrate on nothing else. She was framed in light from the window. The pattern of the lace curtains was thrown by the sunlight on the shiny wooden floor by her chair. The brass curtain rail shone impossibly bright, like gold. For a minute he felt only she and himself were in the room. He looked at her neat foot, one strap clasping her high instep and a sentimental image from some song about a girl's milk-white feet came to his mind. Losing the run of himself, but he couldn't stop looking at her.

"If you're not going to eat that, I'll have it," Charlie interjected.

Donny lifted up his knife and fork and slowly began to eat. He watched her from under his lowered brows, her short yellow dress flared out from her knees, the matching cardigan, her lovely hair. He ate without being aware of the taste. When the waitress brought their tea and rice pudding, she stood between Donny and his view of the girl. When she moved, Donny's view was clear and he saw the group rising from the table. They were leaving. The girl was walking with the older woman. They passed three table-widths away and she seemed to be saying goodbye to the others. Then she was coming back. Donny's heart thumped. She stopped at their table.

"Hello."

This time he remembered his manners and stood up. She held out her hand, "I'm Victoria Mulholand."

"Donny Maguire."

She had deep dimples he hadn't noticed before.

"This is Charlie Lever."

Charlie shook hands. Donny stood staring down at her. Then Charlie said "Will you not sit down?" he took his coat off the chair and pulled it out for her.

"Would you like a drink?"

"No thanks, not now."

"And what brings you to the fair?" inquired Charlie

"I'm with my uncle and aunt and my cousin. I'm spending a few weeks with them. My cousin is visiting from Clones. They live here, but I'm from near Dublin."

So the man was her cousin. Of course, that didn't mean he wasn't her boyfriend. Quite the opposite.

"And how is the car running?" she turned her eyes full on Donny. They were blue as a June sky.

"Oh, fine. I never thanked you for your help last Monday."

"Oh, that was nothing."

"It's a good job you were there."

"Well, I was on my way up to the county council offices to hand in an application for a job."

"Are you looking for a job here with the council?" asked Charlie.

"Yes, I am."

"My uncle could help with that," Donny offered recklessly. "He's on the county council."

"Do you really think he could?"

"Oh, sure. I'll ask him."

"That would be simply wonderful," Victoria said, turning her dazzling smile full at him. "What great luck I met you!"

What great luck indeed. Imagine meeting her like that. He could forget all about his uncouth behaviour last Monday. She obviously hadn't given it a second thought.

She worked in a library in Dublin and had applied for the post of county librarian. The interview was in a week. As she told them about herself Donny imagined her among the books. He decided she had to love poetry.

"My aunt told me about the opening here and I decided to apply. It's a much better job than the one I have in Dublin."

"Do you think you'd like to live here?" Charlie wanted to know.

"Oh yes! I'm close to my aunt and ever since I was a child I've spent my holidays here with her."

"I'd say you're a sure bet for that job," Donny told her.

"Do you really?"

"Why wouldn't you be?"

"Well, I know I can do the work but I'm a bit worried about the interview and the oral Irish test. I've just begun to learn the language."

"I'll talk to my uncle," Donny offered again.

"Oh, thanks. That's just great. It gives me much more confidence."

Charlie, who had been watching Donny and Victoria gaze at each other, as though unaware of his presence, once again offered her a drink and she refused. The dining room was almost empty, everyone moving toward the bar. Victoria looked at her watch. "It's almost four. I must go, my aunt will be wondering where I am."

"Can I give you a lift?"

"That'd be grand."

"What about you, Charlie?" asked Donny, remembering his promise and hoping Charlie wouldn't want to go.

"Go ahead. I saw Dan Brennan go in the bar a minute ago. I want to ask him when they're going to do something about the bog road. I nearly sank to the axel on it last week."

"I'll be back," Donny promised, grateful Charlie was playing along.

"Even if you're not itself, I'll get a lift with someone."

"Goodbye, Charlie." Victoria held out her hand.

"So long now, Victoria."

They left the hotel and went down the street toward the fair grounds where he'd left the car. Donny felt people looking at them. Whispering when they had passed. He wanted to walk with a swagger, but found himself a little shy. Nevertheless, he had to find out more about her. "How long have you been visiting your relations?"

"A week. I just arrived last Friday."

"It must seem quiet here."

"Oh, I like it here. As I said, I've visited often. My aunt really wants me to get this post."

"Oh, I'm sure you'll get it."

Donny remembered thankfully that he had tidied and swept the interior of his car the day before. He usually left it cluttered with papers, bottles and jars, the floor and back seat covered with straw and old newspapers, put there to protect the surface in the event he had to transport a sick animal. Sometimes he'd take a calf over to Curtis for his opinion, although he detested doing so.

He held the car door for her and when he climbed in he prayed the car would start. When they drove away, he hoped for a long drive.

"Back up the way we came, Donny."

They drove back up through the town past the hotel and the railway station and out the Dublin Road. They were at her uncle's place in less than ten minutes.

"There, on the right."

A greystone house, a big slated two-storey. A high stone wall surrounded the property, where a laurel hedge showed above the wall. Laburnum viewed through the gate. A fine place.

As he drew up to the gate, Donny was plotting to see her again. He stopped the car and turned off the engine. They sat for a few minutes smiling at each other. He couldn't let her walk away without some plan to see her again. At last he said "Sunday night there's a dance in Ballynamon. That's where I live. Would you like to come?"

"I'd love to go," again she gave him her frank bright smile, "but I'm afraid I can't."

"Oh!" Donny's face fell.

"I'll tell you what I can do. We could go for a walk on Sunday evening."

"Great. What time will I pick you up?"

"Why don't I meet you at the Doolin Bridge. Do you know it?

"I'll find it."

"Say, half-past seven?"

"I'll be there."

A heavy, fleshy-faced man walked past as Victoria stepped out of the car. He looked hard at the car and the registration plate. He barely glanced at Victoria. Look at her you amadan, Donny wanted to say. Isn't she perfect? Have you ever, in your life, seen the like of her? But he just sat in the car and watched as she walked away and disappeared through the tall iron gate in the high wall.

So, she wouldn't come to the dance. What odds about it? They had a date. If she showed up. Bloody marvelous. All he had to do was ask. As easy as that. Just wait till he told Charlie.

He found Charlie still in the hotel, on a high stool at the bar, nursing a pint. The place was crowded, and from the snug came high-pitched voices, women talking and laughing. Over against the wall, three farmers were arguing about politics, their voices loud and rough. At the far end of the bar another huddle of country men. The Fair Day crowd just starting the usual end of Fair Day, drinking and talk.

"So, you're back."

"I am, and guess who's taking Miss Victoria Mulholand out walking on Sunday evening?"

"I thought you were going to the dance."

"I'm not. I asked her to the dance and she wouldn't come."

"You asked her to the dance on Sunday? Donny, she's a Protestant. Have you ever seen a Protestant at a concert, or a dance or a Feis or festival on a Sunday?"

"No. Come to think of it I haven't. How do you know she's a Protestant?"

"Donny, sometimes I wonder what they taught you at that university."

"Well, I don't care what she is. That old stuff is over and done with. It's different now. It's all arranged. I'm taking her out walking."

"Just don't lose the run of yourself."

"You're just jealous."

"I am! Are you having a pint?"

"No, thanks."

"Then, if it's all the same to you we'll go. I should be home to help with the evening's work."

"Oh, the life of a farmer."

When they were in the car Charlie said, "Donny, do you think you should have offered Joseph's help with that job she's after?"

"Why wouldn't I?"

"You know those appointments are all decided by the local appointments commission now."

"Sure, Joseph knows everyone on it."

"Well, Donny, it's none of my business, but that appointments commission was set up just to put a stop to that. To stop people getting jobs on a nudge and a wink and a how's your father."

"Well, there'll be a competition. There's nothing wrong with Joseph putting in a word for her."

Mrs. Lever invited him to stay for tea with the family. Charlie was twenty-five, the oldest. His brother George was twenty-two. He had three sisters, one now training to be a nurse in Dublin, and the others, Rosanne and Delia, eighteen and fifteen, still at home. George was a big man, six feet. His legs were short for his height and his tall trunk gave the impression of huge strength. He had some crazy notion about another war coming and talked about joining an outfit called the International Brigade. Charlie said it worried his mother. They'd had plenty of worry with George. First it was the IRA. Now it was Spain. Mr. Lever maintained he would eventually get sense. Of course, the farm couldn't support them all. The girls would marry and George would have to find work in the town, or a match would be found for him with some girl who had a farm. Although they had relations in America, emigration had been out of the question since '30. Many young men still left for the States but the Levers had heard stories of unemployment in New York. Even breadlines. Times might be very hard but they had enough to eat. And things had to get better.

There were seven of them around the tea table. Mrs. Lever served Friday fare. Mugs of fresh buttermilk, fried eggs and potatoes. Soda bread lathered in her own fresh butter and blackberry jam. Donny relished the food. His landlady was a poor cook and a stingy one.

"Not a bad fair," pronounced Charlie's father. "Great turnout for an early May fair."

"Prices not so bad either," Charlie said. "Pigs are paying a bit better."

"Well, four years ago that wouldn't have even been called a fair," said George.

"More business done than at the April fair."

"That's not saying much. The high tariffs have the country

ruined. Dev should pay heed to the IRA and not be threatening them."

"George, I don't want to hear another word about that crowd," his father warned sternly. "Can I get you more tea, George?" his mother asked anxiously, attempting to change the subject.

"I'm finished, Mother," George said, standing up. The black and white sheep dog got up from the hearth and followed him out.

"I think you've upset him Jim," said Mrs. Lever.

"Oh he's all right, he's gone up to finish the work on them fences in the oat field."

After tea, Donny stuffed his trouser cuffs into his socks, helped Charlie clean out the byre and spread straw beds for the cows.

"I should have done this in the morning, but I left early for the fair."

They walked down the lane to drive the cattle home for milking. The cows were standing at the pasture gate waiting for them. When the gate was opened they ambled out on creaking hooves and turned up for home.

"I like to get them in for milking before the daylight is gone," Charlie said as they went slowly back behind the herd.

"You've fine animals there," Donny complimented him, and went ahead to open the farmyard gate.

"I've good grazing, but we need rain. We haven't had a real good rainfall for a fortnight."

"So seldom we get a dry spell like this. I don't like to wish for rain, but you're right, we need it."

They secured the cows' neck chains, left them for the women to milk, and walked together to the car.

"So, George thinks there'll be another war?"

"It's just talk. He's all exercised about some commotion in Abyssinia, some fight with the Italians. He thinks it might spread."

"Declan, Nan's husband, talks the same way."

"Well, it's nothing to do with us. Let the foreign crowd fight their own battles."

They reached the car. Charlie's broad plain face looked serious. "Donny, don't be making an ejit of yourself over that lassie."

"I'm not. Why do you say that?"

"Well, you've such a notion of her."

"So, I'm interested in her. That doesn't mean I'll make a fool of myself. All I'm doing is going for a walk."

"I suppose you're right."

"Of course I'm right. Are you going to the dance?"

"Wouldn't miss it. Someone has to be there to dance with that Jessie O'Toole. She's going to miss you."

Donny opened the car door and sat in. "You'll be there in my place."

"Now, no one takes your place, Donny.

"So long, now."

Donny let out the clutch and the car slid ahead. His friend stood looking after him. Charlie was acting like an old codger. Preaching and advising. Anyone would think he was fifty years old. No wonder George was threatening to go to Spain to join some army or other. Donny felt he was above all that foolishness. He had an appointment with the prettiest girl he'd ever seen. And he was going to keep it, to hell with Charlie's warnings and sermons. No one paid any attention to that sort of nonsense any more. The whole summer was ahead of him, he'd met the right one at last. He knew he was falling in love. He accelerated a little, then geared down where the narrow winding lane was rutted. Then it became smooth and he sped between thick green hedges, past hillside pastures where cattle rested in the clover, chewing. He slowed as he approached the road, turned south, then sped up again. The car seemed to move of its own volition, floating over the light and shade-striped road, the sinking sun flashing through the trees, the wheels raising a cloud of dust golden in the slanting rays. The road curved west into the sunset. He had a sense of bright moments fleeting then vanishing.

It was dusk when he reached Ballynamon. Annabelle was waiting. She began jumping about when he turned in the laneway. He opened the car door and she put her paws on his lap and licked his face. He rubbed her back. "Good dog! Did you miss me all day? Did Masie feed you?"

Masie's place was on the very outskirts of the little town of Ballynamon. A hundred yards further was the guarda station, then fields and farms and hedges until it turned south to join the road to Obanbeg. In the other direction, Main Street ran past Sheehan's Garage and Petrol Station, past public houses on either side, a hardware shop, a butcher's shop, the Green, and on west to Slanabaille. Church Street led north from Main street broadening out to accommodate the wide gates of the creamery. Then for a short stretch there were a few houses and neat front gardens. A little further on was the Catholic church and the dance hall, and across the road the priests' house. Two swampy fields intervened before the road sloped upward past the shoemaker's house and the National School. Donny's sister Nan and her husband, Declan, lived in a cottage across from the school.

He sat for a few minutes looking at the door of his dispensary. It was small, but it was a start. He thought again about the girl. Just the thought of her filled him with excitement. He wished he had a better car to take her to Punchestown races or Bundoran. But it was so difficult to get the farmers to pay him.

There wasn't enough business in the county for two vets. How had Curtis managed? Of course, he was well set up, made his money in the war when cattle and pork exports to England brought prosperity, unseen before that time, to the farmers. In a year or so he would offer to buy Curtis out. It wouldn't take much to tempt him to give up, but first he had to do better, much better, at collecting his accounts. The thought occurred to him that maybe the farmers were taking advantage of his youth. That damn Nugent hadn't paid yet.

He could see the patch of light thrown from Masie's kitchen window on the back yard. He walked round to the back, knocked and opened the kitchen door.

Masie was sitting in a wooden armchair at the range reading *The Messenger of the Sacred Heart*.

"Anyone looking for me, Masie?"

She put down the red booklet and looked at him over her reading glasses. "Not a one."

"I had my supper."

"I knew you would. Fair Day and all."

"Did Annabelle get anything to eat?"

"I fed her."

"Thanks, Masie."

He went back around and opened his office and dispensary. The dog lay down inside the door. Donny lit a match and held it to light his way up the stairs to his bedroom above the office. In his room, he lighted the oil lamp on the table at the side of the window. The bedroom was furnished with his bed and wardrobe from the farmhouse in Slanabaille. He could, of course, have lived at home, but it was an out of the way place if his customers wanted him after dispensary hours. And he wanted his independence.

He sat for a few minutes in his chair at the cold fireplace, thinking about the girl. What luck that he happened to go to the hotel just at the time she was there. Surely it was meant to be. She was so lovely, her sun-washed curly hair that he longed to touch, her expressive blue eyes. He'd always thought his sisters attractive, Nan with her black unruly curls and big green eyes, Una, so fair she seemed like a changeling among the dark-haired Maguires. Only in her height was she like them. But neither of them, he decided, could hold a candle to Victoria. Donny stretched out his legs. Probably named for the old Queen. How old was Victoria? The old Queen's day ended in '01, eleven years before he himself saw the light of day. There'd been a *sluagh* of Protestant girls named for her. Of course, Victoria might have been named after her mother or another relative. There was so much to learn about her. And in another way he felt he knew all about her, about what she was really like, that he had always known her.

He rose and stood before the looking-glass in the wardrobe door. Darkly, it reflected back his pale skin and black hair. The high white shirt collar, the green tie, brown waistcoat and green tweed jacket, the elbows reinforced with leather patches. Behind him the jug of water and two glasses on the table and the old brass-footed oil lamp, the window with the muslin curtains, his bed. He straightened his tie. He wondered what Victoria was doing. He remembered, jealously, her leaning forward in the hotel to speak to her cousin. If he kept thinking like this he'd drive himself crazy. Anyway, what odds. It was with him she was going walking. The night was still young. He wasn't ready to settle.

Leaving the lamp burning he went back downstairs. The dog stood up from the threshold. "No luck, Annabelle! I'm going for a pint." He pulled the door shut and turned down towards the lights of the town and Flanagan's pub.

Flanagan's was small and dark, lit by just one hanging lamp over the bar. It was so gloomy it always seemed more crowded than it actually was. He drank a Guinness at the bar and talked to an auctioneer from Obanbeg named Mulcahy. He told Donny he had spent the day looking over and taking a valuation of a farmhouse and its furniture that was coming up for auction soon.

"They're Protestants, selling up and going to England."

"Sure, things are almost as bad in England as here."

"They have relations in England. You're not in the market for a place yourself?" asked the auctioneer, eyeing Donny's clothes.

"Some day I'll farm. But I haven't the money yet to buy."

"House going for half nothing," the auctioneer assured him and nodded at the barman for a refill. "Of course, the Land Commission has the land."

A grey-haired stocky man of about sixty sitting over at the wall got up and carried his glass to the bar for a refill. He nodded at Donny. "Great weather."

"Tis. But the country needs rain."

"It does."

Donny wondered if he had seen him somewhere before. He liked to know his customers. "Do I know you?"

The man paid for his porter then said, "John Farrell, from Knockmore. You're young Maguire from Slanabaille. I knew your mother, God rest her."

Mulcahy held out his hand. "Mel Mulcahy."

"Ah, the auctioneer."

"The very man."

The two men began to discuss the low price of livestock. Donny watched Farrell raise his pint, blow gently on the froth, then take a sip. The two men continued talking. Donny wanted the man to talk about his mother. He would have liked to ask him about her. He sat looking at his glass, his whole attention riveted on the stranger, listening to the talk. Tense, longing for a chance to speak, he couldn't see how he could interrupt the conversation. If he'd been alone when the man spoke to him maybe he could have got him talking. There wasn't even a picture of his mother in existence. Another drinker came over to talk to Farrell and the moment passed. The pub began to fill up.

At eleven, Donny he went home thinking, as he walked up the street, that all his life he had heard the same thing about his mother, that she had been beautiful and had died too young. But he could never imagine what she had really been like. She was in that misty part of his mind which, he often thought, if he tried hard enough he'd be able to penetrate.

Saturday, he remembered Victoria as soon as he woke, her blue eyes, the quaint correctness of her manner He wondered if she was thinking about him.

He was sitting in Masie's kitchen, half-way through his breakfast, when a boy appeared at the door.

"Me father wants you. We have a heifer very sick."

"Let the man finish his breakfast," Masie admonished.

"It's all right Masie, I'm finished." Donny stood up. "Where's your place?"

"The third farm up the Gratchies Lane."

Donny didn't know the place or the way.

"You sit in with me. I'll tie the bicycle on the back"

He took a rope from under the seat and secured the bicycle on the back of the car threading the rope through the open windows. Then they set off together.

He had just arrived back at his dispensary after that call when Masie appeared at the door. "Another lad was here lookin' for you. You're wanted over at Power's in Mullaghcastle."

"Did they say what was wrong?"

"A horse with a stoppage."

"Bloody hell!"

She turned away, muttering about bothering people on a Saturday, and never giving the vet a minute's peace. Masie was a little hen of a widow. Her son had been killed in the war. Her three daughters were married and living in America. Her husband had been a cooper. Seventy now, she lived on her pension and Donny's rent.

Power paid him for the call, unwinding the string from a greasy yellow purse and peeling the ten shilling note off a wad of bills. Donny thought he must have five or six notes in the bundle. Damn farmers! Always making the poor mouth. Anyone would think they hadn't a ha'penny.

Getting on towards evening he decided to look for the Doolin Bridge. He drove the seven miles to Obanbeg and, at the top of Wexford Street, stopped to buy petrol.

"Can you tell me where the Doolin Bridge is?" he asked the pump attendant.

"Turn right the second street down, that's Bridge Street, keep going past the Protestant church and it's just below you."

"Thanks."

He turned down Bridge Street and drove past the church; the road narrowed, and there it was. A stone curved bridge, half a dozen young lads sitting on the wall watching the street. He had driven that way before but was not aware it was known as Doolin bridge. Tomorrow he'd be here in good time and they'd walk along the river.

For a minute he considered going over to see Joseph, then he remembered he and Emer would be playing whist at Tom Plunkett's. He'd wait till Monday to talk to Joseph about Victoria's job application. He turned the car round and headed back the way he had come. Saturday nights Flanagan's served a light supper. He'd stop there for a pint and a bite.

SUNDAY EVENING he decided to take the dog. The girl might not show up; if she didn't, he would at least give Annabelle a run. But Victoria was waiting for him beside the bridge. He saw her a hundred yards away. The fair, curling hair! He left the car on the street just up from the bridge. The dog jumped out and ran ahead.

"Lovely to see you, Donny."

"Nice evening for a walk."

She took his hand and they descended the rough uneven slope

at the side of the bridge. The young fellows sitting on the parapet looked after them. They walked along the river bank. The leaves of the trees filtered the evening light and by the far bank the water reflected the trees. The grass summer fresh, here and there were still drifts of primroses.

Donny threw a stick and Annabelle brought it back. Then he threw it in the water. She retrieved it that time too, but when she laid it at his feet, she shook herself, sprinkling Victoria's legs and dress with water.

"Annabelle, you stupid dog."

"It's fine."

"I suppose I'm stupid for throwing the stick in the water."

"She's a wonderful dog."

He loved that she admired his dog.

"Donny, did you have a chance to talk to your uncle?"

"Tomorrow. I'll go out there for tea. Would you like to come?"

"No, I think not. We can see each other Tuesday."

Tuesday. So there was to be a future date. Bloody marvelous.

"Then I'll have talked to him."

"Is it not strange how we met?"

"It is indeed. I'm grateful to my old car for stalling."

"I thought you stalled it on purpose."

"Are you serious?"

"Well," teased Victoria, "I wondered! You don't look like you don't know how to drive."

He wanted to say it was looking at her caused him to stall the car but instead asked her about herself. There were no boys in her family. She was the youngest of three sisters. The others were married. She said she had grown up in the village of Blackrock. He could hardly believe it. He'd been more than four years there under the tutelage of the Holy Ghost Fathers and she had been but a stroll away. They wondered together at the coincidence. He could have passed her when the school was out for a walk or down for a swim in the sea.

"I could have walked in past those high gates and watched you playing football."

"I played a lot of football."

"When I'm here, I sometimes miss the sea."

"I can understand that. I miss our river. A river flows at the back of our house at home in Slanabaille. I'll take you there to see it."

"Maybe, some day."

Her head just came to his shoulder. Her blue dress had tiny white dots scattered over it. Her hair was tied back with a blue ribbon. So neat.

They strolled on companionably, the dog running ahead, his nose to the ground, scenting a hedgehog. The river ran at the back of warehouses on one bank and, on the other, the grounds of a boys' school.

"My uncle said today the river is the lowest he's seen it in years."

"A few good days rain will fix that. A lovely evening for a walk."

"Isn't it?"

The excitement of being with her spread through Donny. Wildly, he thought, we'll always walk on this river bank. It will be our special place, our particular walk. Further on, they passed high hedges that hid gardens and houses. Around them nesting birds drowsily twittered. To the east, above the trees, the moonrise.

"Look Donny, a half moon."

"A May moon. You know that song, Victoria, the young May moon is beaming, love."

Victoria sang in a high lilt, *"The glow worm's lamp is gleaming, love…"*

"Lovely."

"Come on Donny, you sing with me."

"You were doing so well."

"Come on."

"O.K."

"How sweet to rove…
Through Morna's grove…
While the drowsy world is dreaming, love."

"Where's Morna's grove?"

"I haven't the foggiest notion."

"Tom Moore probably didn't either.'

"He knew about love, though."

"Do you, Victoria?"

"Maybe."

"I do. I think I might be in love with you."

"Really, Donny?"

"Yes."

"We hardly know each other."

"I know."

She removed her hand from his but continued walking beside him. He saw he had startled her. What a stupid thing to say, rushing his fences like a fool. "Victoria, I didn't mean to be so forward."

"It's alright. But we should be getting back. I'm getting a little cold. It's only early May, after all."

Donny removed his jacket and put it round her shoulders. "Is that better?"

"It's grand."

They turned and in the dusk saw the distant dark arch of the bridge, the old stone buildings. The lights of the town coming on. He reached for her hand again and she did not resist him. Under the rising moon they retraced their steps toward the car. It was getting colder. When they got to the bridge, a flock of brown, shiny ducks were sheltering under it for the night, their wings spread over their young.

MONDAY EVENING, Donny drove over to Slanabaille. He walked in just as Emer was preparing tea.

"What a nice surprise, Donny. When I heard the car I thought it was Joseph. You're just in time for tea."

"I always time it for meals," he told her as he kissed her. "I know where the best cook lives."

He sat watching her move between the squat black stove and the white porcelain sink and thought how he'd like his own farmhouse.

"Great to see you lad," Joseph said, coming in.

After tea they sat in the sitting room and Joseph put a match to the fire. It wasn't cold, but it was damp and Emer liked a fire.

"Joseph," began Donny, "I have a favour to ask."

"Well," said Joseph, crouched down coaxing the fire, "you know you have only to ask."

"It's really for a friend of mine, a girl."

Emer put down her the little dress she was smocking. "A girl, Donny? Someone we know?"

"Her name is Victoria Mulholland."

Emer was immediately curious. "I don't think I've heard you mention her, Donny."

"She's from Blackrock. She has applied for the job of county librarian."

Joseph stood up from the fire. "Oh. And what's the favour?"

"Well, Joseph, would you to speak to the men you know on the commission? She's a bit worried about the oral Irish test."

"Oh Donny, anything but that. I just can't. You know we're trying to get away from that sort of thing."

"Just this once, Joseph. I'm sure she's an excellent candidate."

"I'm sure she is, but the last thing I want to do is interfere or start up that old way of everything been awarded on, as they say, 'a how's your father'."

"Joseph, I promised her I would ask you."

"And you have. It's not your fault that I won't do it."

Joseph was refusing him. It was such a little thing. Everyone did it all the time. It was the only way to get ahead.

"Who is this girl, Donny?" Emer asked. "Is she someone you're interested in?"

"She is."

"It's not a name I know."

"Like I said, she's from Dublin, from Blackrock."

"Oh. Is there anything you can do, Joseph?"

"Emer, it's impossible. It's just not right to interfere and even if I did it mightn't do any good."

"Joseph, will you at least try?"

"I can't Donny. You know I hate to refuse you, but I can't."

"Tell us more about the girl, Donny," said Emer. "How did you meet her?"

"I stalled the car on the street in Obanbeg last Monday and she helped me start it. She's really a lovely girl, Emer."

"And if she's from Dublin, what's she doing in Obanbeg?"

"She's visiting her relations."

"And who are they?"

"Her uncle's name is William Brown."

"That's the family," said Joseph, "that own the saw mill outside Obanbeg."

"Well, that's no crime is it, to own the sawmill?" Donny was resentful of the questions.

"Oh no, no," Emer smoothed over the awkwardness. "It's just that we're interested, that's all."

Donny stood up quickly. "Well, I have to go." It was clear he was wasting his time. So Joseph wouldn't even do that little favour for him. He wished he'd never asked. He'd have to tell Victoria tomorrow evening.

Joseph and Emer came to the door with him, Emer holding the dog by the scruff of his neck. Donny couldn't hide his disappointment. Emer kissed him. "I'm sorry, Donny. It'll be all for the best, you'll see."

Joseph shook hands. "I'm sorry lad, I can't do what you asked."

They watched him drive away and then went back into the house. "We won't be seeing Donny for a while. He's very disappointed Joseph. I can tell."

"Well, there isn't a thing I can do."

"I know, but he's upset all the same. I don't like to see him like that."

They went back into the sitting room. Emer took the poker and prodded the fire furiously. Sparks flew up the chimney. She sat and picked up her needlework, and then put it down, remembering Donny's hurt face.

Angry and bitterly disappointed, Donny raced the car back down the lane. He could hardly believe it. "On a how's your father!" What was all that sanctimonious blather about? As long as he could remember, Joseph was putting in a good word for job seekers, giving references, pulling strings, walking the two sides of the road, any road that suited. For anyone! Anyone at all. And now, the first time he asked for a favour, the rules changed. Everyone was suddenly above all that sort of thing. Joseph could put his lofty principles, if that's what they were, aside for anyone but his only nephew. The only time he'd ever asked anything of him.

EMER LAY STARING up at the ceiling. The moon high above the house threw its light into the room. "Joseph, I don't like this notion Donny has of that girl."

"It'll probably come to nothing."

"I thought he fancied the little schoolteacher, Jessie."

"He'll fancy many a one before he settles down, Emer. Stop worrying!"

Joseph turned his head and touched the side of her face, just in front of her ear, with his lips. Then he eased his arm from under her neck and turned over on his side away from her. In less than five minutes, he was asleep.

Long afterwards, Emer lay awake. She was remembering Donny walking away from her across the grounds of Blackrock College on a September Sunday eleven years ago, his first day in secondary school. In his school blazer and cap, she could distinguish him from the crowd only by his height. He was gone, in a flock of excited chattering boys. The uniform had made him look suddenly older, no longer a child.

Returning home in the train, she was dejected. So soon all the children had left. She knew he had to go sometime, to start his life, a life very different from hers or Joseph's. And she'd wanted him to have an education, to better himself, but everything was changing so fast. "Joseph, I hope he won't be lonely!"

"Not Donny. He'll be fine. He'll make friends. It's good for young lads to get away from home. He'll do well there." And he had done well in school, she thought, as she drifted into sleep.

As always in summer, she woke at dawn. Right away, she thought of Donny. Was he still angry? Joseph, turned away from her, was sleeping soundly and she thought again of the train journey back from Blackrock. Stephen Plunkett had left them to the train the day before and met them on their return. When they got home, Joseph lit the kitchen lamp and poked and prodded the fire into life. He added paper, kindling, and a few lumps of coal. Emer sat down in her traveling clothes in the chair by the stove. The house seemed so quiet and empty. Joseph knelt by the chair and put his arms around her.

"Let me make you some tea, Emer. I think you're a little lonesome."

"I am."

"The lad'll be alright."

She stood and took off her coat. Joseph filled the kettle and put it on the stove. When the tea was ready, Joseph poured out a cup and handed it to her.

"Emer, dear, you look so woeful. Don't be like that. You know this is the first time we've been on our own since we were married. It's going to be fine. You'll see."

He'd said that last night, too. But Emer wasn't so sure. He had been right in the earlier instance. Although the house had been empty and quiet without Donny, she had not been lonely as she had feared. In some way, they were each more themselves without the children. Every morning they woke seemed a fresh new day, almost as if they were a young married couple again. Emer joined the Irish Country Woman's Association. Craft exhibitions and cookery demonstrations. Joseph was busy with the teachers' union and the county council. In the holiday time, Donny and Nan were home. And twice a year they visited Una and Connor in Rathmines. Their lives changed again when Peadar came home and became their neighbour. Then Nan married Declan and settled in Ballynamon.

But where the children were concerned there were no small upsets. Anything that made one of them unhappy was a heartache for Emer. Donny was offended and disillusioned. He'd gone off in a huff. What he imagined was a simple request had been refused. Emer had seen that. In her heart she resented the girl, even though she knew she was being unfair. As they ate their breakfast she said, "Joseph, I don't think this girl is for his happiness."

"They'll sort it out Emer."

"But the girl's a Protestant, Joseph."

"You make it sound like they're engaged."

"No Joseph, but if he decides to marry her it wouldn't make for a good life for him, nor her either. And what clergyman would marry them? Think of what they would have to put up with. Think of what the priests would say. And you're a teacher. And Nan and Declan!"

"You're getting way ahead of things. It may come to nothing Emer."

"Joseph! Father Doyle would be against it. He might even call it out on the altar. Unless of course the girl turned Catholic. It would be very bad for Donny's practise, too. The Catholic farmers wouldn't like it and the Protestants wouldn't associate with them. They'd have to move away."

"Stop worrying. It's only a flash in the pan, Emer. It'll be over in a month," Joseph predicted.

"I don't know about that. He's the very cut of his father, head-strong when he wants something."

Joseph finished his breakfast and gathered up his books for school. "Don't be upset Emer. It'll come to nothing," he said, kissed her cheek and left.

As she went about her work she brooded about Donny and the girl. Joseph was taking it too lightly. She could see nothing but misery for Donny with this girl.

In the early afternoon, Emer went down the lane to talk to Cassie. Passing Peadar's place she saw him walking up the fields with his dog behind. For a minute, she thought she would follow him and talk to him about Donny and then changed her mind. It would feel like betraying Donny. There was such an indifference, a coldness in Donny toward his father. She continued down to Plunketts.

"Cassie, the girl is after a job here. If she moves to Obanbeg, Donny's a lost man."

"What about her people? You know they'll object. They won't want it. They'll put a stop to it, Emer. You'll see."

"Not if she's as headstrong as Donny. He's just as stubborn as Peadar."

"And Peadar was always obstinate," Cassie agreed, getting up stiffly to put the kettle on for tea.

Tuesday evening, Victoria was waiting on the bridge. Donny kissed her and they walked down to the river bank.

"What did your Uncle say?"

"Victoria, he turned me down."

"What? I was counting on him."

"But my dear, you will probably get the appointment anyway."

"Why wouldn't he do it?"

"He said that isn't done any more."

Victoria flushed with anger. "Nonsense. That is exactly how things are done."

Donny tried to convince her that it wouldn't matter, that she would do so well in the interview the job would be hers. "I just know you'll get it. You'll be the top applicant, the best."

"I'm not so sure of that."

As they walked on, he could sense how stiff and tense her body was in the curve of his arm.

"Victoria, you won't let my uncle's attitude spoil things between us?"

"No, Donny. Nothing can do that."

Donny squeezed her waist in response and they went on more slowly.

She asked him about his work and he told her about every animal he'd seen since Sunday.

"I'll never make a fortune at it Victoria, but I like it."

"Did you ever think you might have liked to be a medical doctor?"

"No. I've always loved animals, I grew up with them and I like the land. Someday, I'll farm."

Victoria's mind was again on the interview. "Does your uncle know anything about the job?"

"Well, he knew about the vacancy. The local appointments commission makes the choice, and recommends the top candidate to the library committee of the county council. That committee more or less runs the library."

"Well, I sort of knew that. But the librarian is a council employee."

"It'll be alright, Victoria. I just feel it will."

"I wish I was as sure. The interview is on Thursday. After it's over, I'll feel better."

"Victoria, why don't we go to the Punchestown on Saturday and celebrate?"

"No. As soon as I've done the interview I'm leaving, I'm taking the afternoon train to Dublin. I'll come back next Friday. Then, if you like, we could go the Punchestown on the Saturday."

"Will I call round for you?"

"No Donny, I'll wait for you here at the bridge."

"We need to leave by eleven."

"I'll be here at half-past ten."

It was dark when he drove her home. At her uncle's gate she reached over and kissed him, then touched his cheek gently with her hand. "See you a week Saturday, Donny."

"Good luck on Thursday."

He drove home filled with a wild and confident joy.

THAT DONNY MAGUIRE was walking out with a niece of the owner of the Obanbeg sawmill was not long a secret either in Ballynamon or in Slanabaille.

"That mill's losing money," declared Margaret Smith Wednesday evening, hoisting her pint.

"Are you sure of that?" challenged Oliver Higgins, who delivered bread for Mercers and knew everything that was going on in the county.

"I heard they were lettin' men go."

"That doesn't mean they're losing money."

"Maybe they're like Nugent, never wantin' to pay," Jimmy Kehoe suggested.

"You couldn't be up to Nugent," Oliver agreed. "I hear he owes Donny money."

"Well," Margaret persisted, "I know for a fact he hasn't paid Donny yet, and if he's taking out that niece of Brown's, he'll need a few quid."

"Ah, I hear she's a picture to look at, that she'd knock the eye out of your head for looks," Jimmy said longingly.

"Lads can get into lots of trouble over women. Look at the King of England and that American lassie. Poor man had to move out."

"And she's no beauty either," said Jimmy.

"Well, Donny'd need to watch himself," warned Oliver. "Them Protestants over in Obanbeg is a rough crowd."

EMER HAD NOT seen Donny since Joseph's refusal to help Victoria get the job, and did not expect to see him. But she heard gossip about the romance. Judy McDermott, when she came on Monday to help with the wash said, "There's talk your nephew is walking out with a Protestant one from Dublin."

Emer ignored her and turned her attention to the laundering. "Judy, I want you to give the sheets a blue rinse today. They should dry well in this weather. There's a good breeze."

"Yes, Mam. It's great drying weather."

Emer was surprised Judy had mentioned Donny and the girl. She took it to mean there was a lot of talk.

"Joseph, the whole country is talking about Donny and that girl. I see nothing but trouble for him there. And what about Father Doyle, he won't approve of your nephew walking out with a Protestant. It will change his opinion of you as a school principal. Maybe Donny shouldn't be seeing so much of her."

"Emer, that's the way it is these days. Most of the youngsters have bicycles. They can get them on the hire purchase. And Donny has a motor car. It's easy for him to drive over to Obanbeg."

"Maybe you should talk to him, Joseph."

"It would do no good. The heart takes no counsel Emer, and wants none. Don't worry so much."

SEVERAL TIMES during the day on Thursday, Donny wondered to himself how she had done in the competition. He didn't like it that she was going back home, that he wouldn't see her for a week.

In the evening, he went up to visit Nan. She came to the door with her baby in her arms and two-year-old Bridget hanging on to her skirts.

"Hello, Bridget."

The little girl looked up with solemn eyes then hid her face in her mother's apron.

"Come on in, stranger."

Nan went before him and sat in a big chair at the kitchen stove, the infant on her knee. Donny sat opposite her.

"Look at your Uncle Donny! Look at your big handsome uncle," she cooed at the fat baby. The child had just a few wisps of hair and big grey eyes. He sucked his thumb and stared at Donny.

"Hold him Donny and I'll make some tea."

He took the baby from her. The little boy's body felt firm, solid, warm. He kept turning his head, his eyes following his mother.

"How old is he now, Nan?"

"Almost nine months."

Bridget ran to a corner of the room where her dollhouse was set up, plopped down and began to play.

Donny told Nan about Joseph's refusal to speak to the commission.

"It's hard to blame him, Donny. You know there was a decision some time ago to stop all that favouritism. Those things are to be strictly by competition."

"It wouldn't have killed him to mention it to the commissioners."

"Donny, are you real keen on this girl?"

"I'm crazy about her. She's gorgeous!"

"You don't know her that well. Gorgeous doesn't last. Crazy doesn't last Donny. And you're too young to be so serious."

"Young? What about yourself. What about you and Declan? You were young."

"He wasn't a Protestant. And we knew the family. Una and Eilish are friends for years."

"Don't be playing the big sister, Nan. You must have been talking to Emer."

She began to spoon tea grains into the pot. "We're a bit worried about you, that's all."

Donny ignored that. "Nan, anything for a sandwich? I'm starving."

"Of course. I'll get you some ham."

His pretty sister had her wild curls pinned back with a prim black band and wore a loose green cotton dress that fell straight from her shoulders. She mixed some mustard and brought it with the ham and some bread to the table. She took the baby from Donny and put him on the floor. The child couldn't quite crawl yet but he rolled over and over till he was almost at the range. Donny wondered at the determination of humans. Nan picked the child up again, then sat opposite Donny and watched him eat.

"You have your hands full Nan, with the children."

"We don't have enough room. We're going to put an addition on and then I'll get a live-in girl to help me."

"You're doing your bit anyway, Nan. I'm always surprised Una and Connor have no children."

"Connor is disappointed. I know he'd like a son. But Una never really wanted children. She says the children she teaches are enough. And of course she's not late yet, she's only thirty-five. Lots of women don't get married till they're that age. The doctor told her there was no reason why she wouldn't have a child. It would be nice if she had a baby. She has Eilish and Peter's three nippers spoiled."

"Well, if Declan needs an extra pair of hands when you start renovating, I'm here."

"Thanks, Donny. But you have your own work. It's easy enough to get help. So many out of work."

"If things keep picking up in America, there'll be a rush to emigrate again."

"There's a rush already, more leaving than for the past five years."

Donny stayed an hour, talking to Nan and playing with the baby. As he walked home he thought enviously of his sister and her little family. He resented going back to his bare room at Masie's. Then he remembered ruefully that two years ago establishing himself at Masie's had been a huge step into the unknown, the very height of his ambition.

"Emer, that girl came first in the competition today. The appointments commission have recommended her for the job."

"Does Donny know?"

"No. The chairman, Joe Hannafin, told me in confidence. Do you think I should go over and tell Donny?"

"It might ease the bad feeling between you."

"Of course, Donny can't tell Miss Mulholland. It can't get out till the library committee has its meeting tomorrow and the council meets and sends her a letter. Still and all I think I'll run over and tell him."

"Maybe you shouldn't Joseph. From what I hear those two are so thick together he'll tell her in spite of himself. And he mightn't even be there, and you would have your journey for nothing."

"It's just that I know he was disappointed with me."

"I know that. And I'm very worried about that. But just wait, Joseph. He'll know soon enough. Then everything will be made up between you."

The library committee of the county council met on Friday at four and debated the recommendation of the local appointments' commission on the appointment of the county librarian for almost two hours.

"Are ye all agreed on that now?" Liam Boylan asked, attempting to pull the threads of the argument together. Liam wanted to get the meeting over. It was half-past seven already and he had to get home. He had a sick cow he needed to dose. Donny Maguire had told him, every four hours for three days, and he wasn't risking the loss of a milk cow listening to arguments about something that was a foregone conclusion.

"Yes we're agreed, we're all with you," said Paul Kileen reassuringly. Paul owned a pub in Ballineagh and didn't like arguments.

"What about the local appointments crowd?" asked Mel Mulcahy anxiously. As an auctioneer he believed in keeping things straight.

"To hell with them," retorted Rich Russell, another farmer who also wanted to get home.

Barry Toolin went one better. "They can just go to blazes. They're all Dublin sleevens anyhow."

"But, on what grounds are we turning her down?" persisted Mell.

"She doesn't know Irish!"

"Do you?"

"That's a different matter entirely. I'm not a librarian. She only got 250 out of 500 in Irish and I'm bloody well not standing for anyone that can't speak the language perfectly getting a job like that. I'll damn well resign."

Peter O'Keefe, the county council clerk, suppressed a bureaucrat's smile at the turn things were taking. Leave it to unelected appointees. Mary Cronin, who was there to represent both the parish and the schools looked shocked at the violence of Barry's statement.

"Father Doyle couldn't be here himself, but his worry is to get someone that will choose good moral reading material, the right sort of book," she parroted.

"See, there you are," Rich was triumphant.

Dan Brennan said nothing, risked nothing He was the county councillor on the library committee and would be taking back the decision to the county council.

"All right then, the decision is that we won't recommend Miss Mulholland. Is that the way you want it? Is there anyone who wants anything different? Is there anyone objecting?"

No one answered, but Rich asked, "And who'll get the job?"

"There'll be no appointment. The council will tell the commission to look at the list and find another candidate and send the name to us."

"It better be one of our own," vowed Rich.

"Alright now," said the chair, "do I have a mover and a seconder?'

Paul Kileen moved that the library committee refuse to accept the advice of the local appointments commission to recommend Miss Victoria Mulholland for the post of county librarian. It was seconded by Rich Russell and the motion passed easily, Dan Brennan abstaining.

"Alright now," said the chair, "we're done, and Dan you'll let the county council know tomorrow."

Brennan nodded, none too pleased with the assignment. "The clerk will bring over the minutes."

The meeting began to break up. There was a loud scraping as chairs were pushed back.

"How's the family, Rich?" Paul inquired as they left the meeting hall.

"All game ball. Thank God. What did you think of the decision?"

"Oh, proper order!"

"I'm going for a pint."

'I'll go with you."

ON THURSDAY EVENING, Emer sat in the kitchen waiting for Joseph. The table was laid for their supper. The days were lengthening. It was still light outside. It was half past eight when she heard him arrive.

"You're late home. Is there anything wrong Joseph?"

"Well Emer, there is. The library committee met last night. They didn't recommend Miss Mulholland for the job.'

"What? How can that be if she won the competition. Can they do that?"

"I'm afraid they can. I could hardly believe it myself."

"Have they that authority?"

"For that appointment they more or less do. It's a great scandal and embarrassment, but there it is."

"Did you speak up at the county council meeting?"

"Not in the terms you mean. I did try to tell them that it was wrong to turn down the commission's choice, but it was no good. You know how it is Emer. The council wasn't going to go against one of its committees. If it started doing that, no one would serve on those committees. It's a thankless job that library committee. There are always fights about what books are bought and what's suitable for people to read."

"Joseph, it's all for the best. I can't say I'm sorry. I've been worried."

"I know. It's a good thing I didn't tell Donny the commissioners had picked her."

"Did the committee give a reason why they turned her down?"

"The usual stuff. They want a local person. And they didn't like it that she was a graduate of Trinity."

"You mean they didn't like that she was a Protestant."

"We're a long way from fair play in these things, Emer."

"It has always been like this, Joseph. First the Catholics, and now the Protestants have their religion held against them. And myself, in my heart I didn't want her to get that job. I didn't want Donny to be involved with her. But of course, he may follow her to Dublin."

"He won't. Don't fret about it, Emer."

It rained a light misty rain on and off most of the week while Victoria was at home in Blackrock. The farmers said it wasn't enough, that they needed a good hard day's downpour. Friday evening as Emer looked out at her garden, the rain began to pelt down from an overcast sky. "The sweet pea has grown two inches in the past week. I'm going to have a great show of blooms."

"Good for growth, this rain," Joseph said. "It's badly needed."

It continued to pour and was getting dark.

Over in Ballynamon, Donny hoped it would ease up by morning. He could hardly see the road in front of him, the rain flogging in the beam of his headlights. He pulled out on to Main Street and drove slowly on up to Masie's place. He had just filled his petrol tank in preparation for tomorrow's journey. He was picking up Victoria at the bridge and they were off to the races. He hadn't seen her for six days. Tomorrow they'd share a long drive together, over two hours, lots of time to talk. She would tell him all about her visit home. He anticipated having her on his arm at the race meeting. He imagined her bright curly hair lifting in the wind, the dimples that came and went in the rosy, freckled cheeks.

When he turned in beside his digs Annabelle was sheltering from the rain in the shed at the back of the house. She ran forward, dripping wet, when Donny opened the door. She followed him into the house. She shook herself violently releasing a spray of rainwater.

He struck a match, went upstairs and lit his lamp. He took a book from the shelf but did not open it. He sat in his chair listening to the rain. He thought of the little hillside pastures, dark green potato fields and young crops of wheat and oats, all the way east to the coast and west to Athlone, drinking the rain. The river in Slanabaille filling, brown with mud, swelling in its rushy banks. Badly needed the rain was. Still by morning the clouds would have passed over, and it would probably have cleared. He had missed Victoria for the past week. He thought he might ask her to get engaged soon. He felt in his heart that she liked him very much, maybe even loved him. Of course, Emer and Joseph would have a conniption. Mixed marriages were rare. But the British were gone now, the old enmities were over. Sure there was the fighting over the border, but not around Obanbeg. He was young to marry, especially in Ireland. But times were changing. Everyone said so. He'd convince her that they were meant for each other, and if she agreed he'd make a go of it, he thought, getting up and taking off his coat. Someone was knocking at his door. Annabelle gave two short barks. "Be quiet Annabelle, you'll wake Masie," he cautioned. He took the lamp and hurried down the stairs. When he opened the door Victoria was standing in the rain. "Victoria, my God you're all wet."

He drew her inside. She was shivering. He put his arm around her. "What's wrong?"

"Oh Donny, I had such a row with my aunt. We said terrible things to each other."

"What kind of a row?"

"About us. She said I was betraying her. Was disgracing myself, going out with you."

"That's bloody nonsense."

"And my uncle threatened me."

"What? He has no right to do that."

"He called me a whore," she said, turning her face into Donny's chest.

"Don't cry Victoria, it will be alright."

Donny remembered her uncle from the Railway Hotel. The magisterial walk. A tough-looking customer. He'd like to put him in his place. "He had no call to talk like that. Don't mind him, Victoria."

She was soaking wet. "How did you get here?"

"I cycled."

"Come upstairs and I'll light the fire."

She sat in his chair and waited while he went out to the shed for twigs and turf. When he returned, she watched him arrange kindling and turf around crumpled newspaper, then strike the match. When he got the fire going she sat on the floor in front of the flames and dried her hair with a towel. Donny went down and put her bicycle in the shed. When he came back, she was still sitting on the floor.

"You're cold. I'll go down to Masie's kitchen and make you some hot tea."

"No. You'll wake her."

"It doesn't matter."

"I don't want you to leave me again."

"I have whiskey."

"I'll have a little of that."

He took the bottle from the top shelf of the wardrobe and filled two small glasses. She sipped a little of hers then put it on the floor. Donny sat on the floor beside her, took the towel and rubbed her hair to dry it. He kissed the top of her wet head. She buried her face in his shoulder.

"I'm never going back there."

"Do you want to stay here?"

"Yes, for tonight I do. Tomorrow I want you to drive me back to Obanbeg to get my things and then to the train. I'm going back home."

"What about the job, Victoria?"

"I'll see if I get it."

"What about us?"

"I'll write to you."

"Why do you have to go back home?"

"Because I believe I must. I won't spend another day at my uncle's."

"You could get lodgings in town."

"No. Don't make it harder for me to leave, Donny."

"Alright, as long as you come back."

"I will. And I'll write."

The room grew warm from the fire and Donny opened the window. Then he sat and held her in his arms until the fire died and the chilled air drove them to the warmth of bed. All night long they lay in one another's arms while the hearth grew cold and the curtains on the open window rose and fell in the damp night wind.

SATURDAY NIGHT, just before closing time in Flanagan's bar, Frank Gallagher, a small, stout middle-aged farmer was finishing up an evening's drinking. Any time now, the publican would walk from behind the counter with the key in his hand, the signal for all who were not bona fide travelers to leave. Those from outside Ballynamon were considered travelers and could remain in the locked pub and drink to their hearts' content. Five minutes earlier, Donny Maguire, who had been drinking with Oliver Higgins, had left for home, and right after, three men who had been sitting in the corner also left. The pub was almost empty.

"It's the height of nonsense Ollie, that rule about travelers. Here I am on a Saturday night in me own town and I can't drink in peace for fear the guards'll raid."

"Have another quick one anyway," said Oliver. "Another Guinness here, Mick."

"Could you credit it, Ollie," Frank paused for a long drink of the fresh porter, "they say we'll soon have milk inspectors smelling around my milk churns."

"Sure, they're only trying to improve the standard of the milk, Frank. Not that your dairy needs any improvement."

"The government's interfering too much in the people's business," Frank stared morosely in front of him. "You couldn't be up to them politicians."

"Maybe the dairy inspectors won't be a bad thing. Donny seems to be in support of the idea."

Frank had a couple satisfying mouthfuls before he answered. "Well, it's far from milk inspectors he was reared, out in Slanabaille, at the back of beyond."

"He's a nice lad all the same," Oliver said. "Did you think he was in bad form, Frank? A bit quiet in himself? Something bothering him?"

"Ah sure, sometimes young lads are like that," said Frank sagely, standing and draining his glass. "I'll go so. Goodnight Ollie."

"Safe home, Frank."

Flanagan followed him and locked up. In less than two minutes they heard yelling and thumping on the door. "Open up, Flanagan. Open up. There's a man hurt here."

The remaining drinkers stood up from their tables and moved toward the door. Flanagan rushed forward with the key.

"I need a hand here," Frank shouted.

Several men rushed forward through the door to help him. They carried a man, bleeding and moaning, into the pub. They quickly pushed two tables together and laid him across them. A deep gash over the man's right eye dripped blood and his mouth seemed to be swelling even as they watched. It was Donagh Maguire.

"My God," said one man, "he's half kilt."

"Someone get the doctor."

Donny rolled over on his side and tried to sit up. He groaned harshly and lay down again. The pain in his ribs was excruciating. It hurt him to breathe.

"Someone go for the guards," Frank ordered.

"Never mind the guards, useless articles, never where they're wanted," said Jimmy Kehoe, "the doctor's what's wanted."

"My young lad is gone to get him," Flanagan said.

"Give him a drink," Oliver suggested.

Donny felt his head being lifted and the whiskey stung his lips. He swallowed a sip. "I'm alright, just very sore."

"What in God's name happened?"

"I don't know. There were three of them I think. I never saw them till they were on me," as he said this he wondered if the pain would ever stop. Anger surged up and tensed him; for a minute he forgot the pain. My God, he had thought they would kill him. They could have killed him. If only the doctor would come and give him something to ease the pain in his ribs. He remembered how, as they kicked him, he knew his ribs were breaking. He had broken a rib once before, playing football. That's what they'd done to him. Made him a football.

Frank stared down at him. "I heard him moaning, just over by the hedge."

"Did you see anyone, Frank?" asked Jimmy

"No. They were gone. Must be the bloody IRA."

"Or the Blueshirts," said Jimmy.

Then they saw that Oliver was slowly shaking his head at them and they became very quiet.

But Donny was in no doubt about who had attacked him. He closed his eyes and thought bitterly of how blind he had been. He remembered the arrogant commanding aspect of the man in the Railway Hotel. And the man who had looked so intently at the registration plate of his car. He recalled sitting in the car waiting for Victoria outside her uncle's place, her quiet determined face as he stowed her suitcase. They almost missed the train and sadly he remembered it taking her away, rounding the bend out of sight. Was she all right? The whole miserable business was no one's fault but his own.

Dr. McCarthy arrived, brisk and business-like. He palpated Donny's abdomen and gently touched his bruised sides. He gave him two tablets. It hurt to swallow them. The doctor waited a short time then said, "Now lads, help him to sit up."

They helped Donny up and he sat on the table with his legs hanging down. The doctor moved a chair under his feet. Donny felt pathetically grateful for the support to his aching thighs. He winced as the doctor wound bandages tight around his ribs. He had not known his hands were injured till the doctor straightened out his fingers and began applying a splint to the middle finger of his right hand. Then, he realized he had put up his hands to protect his face. They eased him down again on the hard table.

"Better get him home now, where someone can keep an eye on him," the doctor advised.

"I want to go home to Slanabaille, not to Masie's."

"Take it easy, Donny. We'll get you home," Frank reassured him.

Oliver took his keys and fetched his car. He and Frank drove him home to Slanabaille, propped up in the front seat. He was so sore he could hardly endure the motion of the vehicle. Dawn was breaking as they drove up the lane. Frank got out to open the gate. Emer was already awake. She heard the car, the dog barking, then Frank's urgent knock. She tore down the stairs and through the kitchen. Joseph followed, barefoot, slipping his suspenders up over his shoulders.

"My God, Donny! Joseph, quick. Quick."

Joseph helped Oliver and Frank carry him into the house. They laid him on the sofa in the sitting room.

"I'm alright, Emer. I look worse than I am," he whispered. "I'm fine. I just want to sleep."

"The doctor's seen him, bandaged him up, Mrs. O'Neill. Said he'll be out to see him again this evening."

"Just rest there, lad," said Joseph, bringing a blanket to cover him. Emer slipped a pillow under his head.

Joseph walked out to the kitchen with Oliver. "What happened?"

Oliver and Frank told him what they knew. Joseph listened quietly and gravely. "Thanks, lads. We're more than grateful. Oliver, would you go and get his father?"

Donny lay with his eyes closed. He heard the low murmur of Emer and Joseph's conversation in the kitchen. A blackbird was singing outside the window. Then the cocks began to crow. The medication the doctor had given him made him drowsy. He fell asleep.

He awoke when the dog barked, then there was Peadar's urgent step in the kitchen. Donny opened his eyes. Peadar was standing looking down at him. He hunkered down beside him, took the swollen, bandaged hands gently in his and looked at them for a minute. He laid them back on Donny's stomach.

"Does it hurt much?"

"No. It's easing now."

"Rest there."

He closed his eyes and heard Peadar stamping out to the kitchen. "Someone will answer for this, Joseph. I swear they will."

"Take it easy, Peadar. It's alright. The law will deal with it."

"If they don't Joseph, someone will answer for it. I swear to God they will."

"Hush, Peadar," Emer admonished, "you'll upset Donny."

Donny heard the door open and close. Joseph and Peadar were continuing their conversation in the yard. Emer came into the room. "Donny, you should take something to eat."

"Maybe just some water, Emer. I don't feel like eating. My mouth is sore."

"How about some soup?"

"Just water for now Emer."

In the afternoon, the doctor came to check on him. He removed the slices of raw beef Emer had placed on his eye.

"The swelling is lessening. Now, if his ribs would heal as fast. I was worried about internal bleeding. But everything seems alright. You're a strong lad."

He snapped his bag shut and went out to the kitchen with Emer. "Make sure you get him up on his feet every two hours, Mrs. O'Neill."

When the doctor left Peadar came and sat beside him. "How are you now, son?"

"Better. I'm mending fast."

Donny turned over on his side to face Peadar. It was an effort to talk, all he wanted to do was sleep, but he had to talk to his father. "There's some part of this my fault, Father. I didn't think of the consequences when I took up with Victoria."

"It was not your fault! That was between you and the girl. No one has any right to do what was done to you."

Donny closed his eyes and said no more. In a while he fell asleep.

He lay in his old bedroom on Nan's bed. He slept and woke and lay looking through the window, watching clouds and showers passing over, and slept again. In the daytime, when Joseph was at school, his father came and helped him out of bed as the doctor had ordered. At meal times Donny walked painfully to the kitchen table, his arm over his father's shoulder, Peadar's arm supporting him around his waist. He was surprised at how hard-muscled his father was.

By Wednesday, he was spending the days on the sofa in Emer's sitting room looking out on the garden. Was it all lost? All gone? Write to me Victoria, he said, looking at the afternoon shadows the sunlight made in the garden. Write to me, he wished, his eyes searching the room, noting with another part of his mind the books in the bookcase, the geraniums on the window sill.

By Friday he was walking about the yard. He sent his father to Masie in Ballynamon to fetch his post and bring Annabelle over to Slanabaille.

"I'll keep her at my place," Peadar said. "That dog of Joseph's has no manners. She's better with me."

Donny riffled through the post. No letter came from Victoria.

"You've heard nothing from the girl?"

"Not a word, Emer. She promised to write."

"She may yet."

"Do you think she's alright Emer?"

"Oh yes, I do. Her parents are city people. They'd be less strict about things than her uncle. I often wondered at the Protestants like her uncle or Nugent staying on here after the Treaty. Most of the gentry moved to England."

"They're not gentry."

"No, but they're landlord class."

"I wish she'd write."

"Donny, she may have decided to put it all behind her you know."

"That's what I'm beginning to think, Emer."

His bruises faded to yellow and his appetite returned. He felt himself recovering his strength and began to walk down to the river every day with the dog. By the middle of June he was ready to open his dispensary again. The second Monday in June he drove back to his digs at Masie's place. He was ready to work again. He pulled into the lane. Annabelle barked and he reached round, opened the back door and she jumped out. Donny looked about him at the house, the door of his dispensary, the hedge and the lane. For a second he had the impression he had never seen the place before. His vision seemed sharper. He saw flustered sparrows flying from their nest in the eves as clear as if he held them in his hand. Then he stepped out and began to unload the car.

Each day he felt stronger, but in the beginning the work quickly tired him and at night he drowned in sleep. The bleakness of his mind did not lessen. He felt himself immeasurably older. He realized he'd been blind to the realities of life in Ireland in 1937. He'd made a mess of things.

THE GUARDAI TOOK a statement from him and from the drinkers in Flanagan's pub, but there was no sign of an arrest.

"George says they know very well who they are," said Charlie. "Why don't they pick them up?"

"No proof, Donny, no one talking. But it's early days yet."

"Have you heard from the girl?"

"No."

"What are you going to do?"

"Nothing for now. I'm trying to forget about her."

"That's the best thing Donny. There's as good a fish in the sea as ever was caught."

"I know, but I'm not fishing."

He still believed he loved her, her absence a great emptiness inside him. Sometimes he felt guilty of some great blunder, as if he'd been a fool. Sometimes he plotted to drive to Blackrock. He knew she lived in Seaview Terrace, but he didn't know the house number. He could enquire which house it was, or go to the library where she worked.

When it became known she hadn't been awarded the job, he accepted that it was over, she was gone. It helped that his work kept him busy. He knew the affair was the talk of the townlands, but he forced himself to ignore that, although he suspected the talk was entirely sympathetic to himself.

WILLIAM BROWN'S lumber yard and sawmill covered four acres of enclosed ground, a quarter mile from his house on a by-road that led off the main Dublin road. Finished lumber was stacked eight feet high on the east end of the yard and on the opposite end was the sawmill and the piled raw wood. The wire fencing that ran around the perimeter was nine feet high.

On the twenty-ninth of June, St. Peter and Paul's Day, as was the rule, summer work was interrupted to mark the feast. Times in the country were still very hard and the Peter's Pence collection was small. Still, it was a holiday from work, and people celebrated. Halls and crossroads were loud with dance music till late in the night.

Charlie persuaded Donny to go to a dance in Mountnugent. "It's time you stopped moping. There's a new band from Cootehill playing. Foxtrots and quicksteps. All the latest."

Donny danced a waltz with Jessie O'Toole. It tired him out. His sides still sometimes ached. He spent the rest of the evening with a few men at the refreshment stand, watching the dancers. Charlie's sister, Delia, was dancing with the creamery manager from Ballynamon. Jessie was dancing with Charlie. She smiled at him as they whirled past. Donny was feeling a bit sorry for himself. It seemed everyone was enjoying the evening except him.

With so many people out in the country that night it was a great wonder no one saw the fire till it had consumed almost all William Brown's mill. By the time the fire brigade arrived at the locked gate, the stacks of raw and finished lumber were starting to burn. The firemen broke the lock with an axe. A small crowd gathered, country lads on bicycles and some from the town. They followed the firemen's lorry through the gate. Hordes of panic-stricken black rats that nested in the stacked raw wood ran scurrying about. The boys pounced on them, seized their long wire tails and flung them squealing back in the flames. There was a smell of roasting flesh. The heat was intense, the dry wood burned like matchsticks. When the pile of lumber crashed in on itself, they sent up a cheer as for a goal scored at a football match.

Thin streams of water from the hoses played in the sinking fire. The stacks of wood shrunk to low, steaming, sizzling heaps. Fragments of black soot and ash rose and floated on the air, drifting down to settle on the onlookers clothes. The crowd dispersed, young lads cycling down the road under the bright moon, three and four abreast, hands on one another's shoulders, their bicycles wobbling dangerously. They sang as loud as their voices could carry.

"Ireland was Ireland
When England was a pup,
And Ireland will be Ireland
When England's buggered up."

It was a four-line item in the Dublin newspapers. In the country it was talked about for weeks. In Flanagan's the gossip was that Brown had set the fire himself, to collect the insurance.

"That's a load of rubbish," Oliver Higgins maintained. "The insurance he had wouldn't pay for the lumber, let alone the mill!"

People claimed the fire brigade had been slow in responding, that they were incompetent. The Anglo Celt called for additional training for the firemen.

Suspicion naturally fell on the IRA. But that group made no claim to have pulled off such a spectacular event. Then the Blue Shirts were blamed, but the guardai ruled them out: they were considered too disorganized and preoccupied with their own squabbling to plan arson.

"Who do you think did it, Charlie?" Donny asked one Saturday evening when they were having a pint in O'Briens.

"I couldn't say. George might know, if he hadn't left for Spain last Monday."

"How do you think he'll get on over there?"

"Well, we all hope he'll get whatever is bothering him out of his system. But it's hard on my mother. We should have tried to stop him. But we didn't know he was planning it. There's nothing to be done about it now, nor about Brown's sawmill either," said Charlie, fatalistically.

Donny wondered about his father. But he thought him a sensible man. A man who didn't take risks. Of course, his father had been all those years in America. What had he been doing over there? Did anyone know? Did Joseph know?

When he asked Joseph, he merely said, "Leave well enough alone lad. Lots of people didn't like Brown. There's plenty had a grudge against him."

It occurred to Donny he had seen a lot of his father lately. Not up close, but out on the edge of his world, on the perimeter. Once, at a football match with Charlie and Jessie, he looked up and noticed him sitting above him in the stand. And there was the Saturday evening he was leaving an auction, where he'd gone with Charlie to check out the price of a farmhouse, and he saw Peadar walk ahead of him back up to the lane and step up into a trap with another man. He didn't know the man. One Sunday evening, as he drove up the Green he thought he recognized him in a group of men watching a game of handball. The man was faced away from him watching the play, still Donny was sure it was his father. Had it always been like this? Had Peadar always been around and had he just not noticed him?

As July turned to August he took to looking back on the weeks he had been ill at Emer's. It seemed to Donny it had been much longer than three weeks, that he'd had to crawl back into himself. It was as if he had been away on a difficult journey. A journey which had somehow changed him. He remembered his father bringing him newspapers and the post. He recalled waking and finding

Peadar sitting over by the window, just sitting there watching him, waiting for him to wake up.

Going about his work, driving the tilting roads and winding lanes, he had time to think, and he thought a great deal about his father. He considered Peadar's behavior when he was ill, his keen anxious scrutiny, his strong arms assisting him out of bed. He went over every detail, remembering every word Peadar had spoken, and was surprised to find himself filled with a fierce mixture of emotions which in the end he concluded was probably love.

Donny's practise was busy through July, August and early September. His difficulty with the customers' reluctance to pay their bills seemed to have disappeared. It was a matter of pride now for a hardened old farmer to volunteer the payment. "What do I owe you now, Donny?" or more often "What's the damage today, lad?"

He had begun to make regular payments on his debt to Joseph and to talk, and dream, of buying his own place. In the evenings, passing a particular field where a magnificent mare and her spindle-shanked foal ruled the summer days, he'd slow the car, searching hopefully for an auctioneer's sign that wasn't there.

He drove by another small farm, near Knockmore. Charlie said it might soon be on offer for sale because the owner, an old fellow of eighty, was said to be going to live with his daughter in Obanbeg. A small thatched house on a low hill. The thatch would have to go. Then he realized the location was too remote for his practise.

"All in good time Donny," Joseph said, when he told him about these ambitions for his own place.

He was doing so well he neglected to pursue the bill Nugent owed him till he was awakened one morning, near the end of September, by a loud hammering at the door of his dispensary. Dawn was just breaking when he opened the door to a guarda.

"You're wanted at Nugent's in Slanabaille. They rang up on the telephone. It's an emergency."

Donny stared at him for a minute. "Did they say what it was?"

"A cow in trouble."

"Thanks, sergeant."

As he drove to Slanabaille he considered the money Nugent owed him. They didn't mind getting him out of his bed at the crack of dawn.

The avenue branched just before the front entrance to the house, the left fork leading to the back of the property and a high stone wall enclosing the yard and farm buildings. Wallace, Nugent's manager, was waiting for him at the double doors set in the wall. Donny parked the car and stepped out.

"I thought you'd never get here."

"I came as soon as I could."

He went before Donny into the large square yard. At the far end were the stables, at the left the pigsties and to the right the cattle byres. He could hear the pigs grunting. Breakfast time.

"What's the difficulty?"

"A calving coming wrong," said Wallace over his shoulder; he led the way to the first byre.

The cow lay on the straw, her beseeching eyes turned back at a farm hand who was kneeling beside her. The man rose when Donny came in. Donny knelt and examined her. As she heaved and strained, the calf's feet and head protruded and disappeared again.

"The position of the calf is alright. Has she been labouring like this long?"

"Since three o'clock."

Donny walked back to the car and returned with a length of rope. He left the door in the wall open.

"When did her water break?"

"Maybe an hour and a half since. Can you save her?"

"I don't see why not. The calf's a bit big, that's all."

Donny knelt behind the cow, waited till the appropriate moment and carefully looped the rope over the calf's head, behind his ears and through his open jaws. Then leaning back slowly and firmly, he began pulling on the rope, matching the pace of the cow's contractions. It took him almost an hour of slow, painstaking manoeuvering of the taut rope to free the head, a few more contractions, and the cow gave a great heave and pushed her slick blue calf out on to the straw.

Donny rested back on his heels. The cow eased herself over on her stomach, stretched her head back and began to lick her calf. Wallace stood at the door looking at him. For a second Donny felt he would faint. Sweat poured down his back and legs. The bones behind his ears ached. Shaken, he stood up and walked out to the yard pump. He worked the handle and when there was a good flow stuck his head under the cold water. The shock of it on his neck and ears cleared his brain. He straightened up, still trembling slightly. He washed his arms, hands, and the rope. He took his time, letting the water flow freely, pumping the handle as was needed. After a few minutes he felt himself quite steady again. The farm hand stood staring at him from the door of the byre. Wallace walked over.

"Was there any reason you couldn't have done that yourself? It was more or less straightforward."

"She's a prize cow, you know. We wouldn't chance it."

Donny stood looking at him for a minute. He knew what Wallace meant. He hadn't wanted to take responsibility should anything happen to the cow.

"You people here owe me for the last two calls I made."

"Well, the master's away. I'll remind him when he gets back."

Horse Show Week was long over. Was Nugent still in Dublin? Times weren't that hard obviously.

"And when will that be?"

"In a couple of weeks."

Donny turned away and walked over to the pigsties. Wallace stared after him. He opened the door and surveyed the pigs. They would do. He stooped and took a pig under each arm and turned to walk out to his car. Wallace barred the way. "Look here, you've no call to take those."

"Just step out of my way."

Wallace stepped back, Donny walked to the car, opened the door and deposited the squealing pigs in the back. He looped the rope loosely around each of their bellies, knotted and secured it to the front seat. Wallace was standing watching him. Donny slammed the back door, got in the car, started it and drove off to a chorus of blue ribbon squealing. He knew Wallace and the workman were staring after him. To hell with them!

He sped down the avenue and out through the gates, over the bridge, through the village, on past the church, on to the highroad, and turned off at the lane that led to Lever's farm. He slowed a little in the lane. He felt invigorated, triumphant. Bloody marvelous. He wondered what McCarne's bacon factory was paying for pork this week. Charlie would know.

The black and white sheep dog ran out barking. Charlie came from the stable and hurried over to open the gate. Donny drove in and stepped out of the car. Charlie looked in at the squealing pigs.

"Fine specimens!"

"Do you have room to board them?'

"Sure. No charge either."

Charlie spread straw in a spare pen and Donny carried over the animals. Their squeals set off Charlie's pigs, and the yard was filled with the sound.

"Where did you get them?"

"It's a long story."

"Will you come in for a cup of tea?"

"I will. I'm starving. I had no breakfast."

"Come on then, my mother will cook you some eggs."

They washed their hands at the pump, soaping well. Then they walked over to the kitchen together. Donny was looking forward to breakfast and to telling the story.

Charlie sat sipping a mug of tea, watching his friend eat and listening with enormous enjoyment on his broad, sunburnt face. The account of the morning's activities was the best yarn he'd heard in a long time. When Donny had finished Charlie said, "So you played the Piper's Son, Donny?"

"Well, not exactly, that was my third time out there without being paid. I just decided I'd been patient long enough. It wasn't as if Nugent hadn't the funds."

"You were perfectly right, Donny! I tell you lad, this morning's work will do your name no harm. It's not before time that Nugent was put in his place."

"It drove me half crazy that the likes of him wouldn't pay, and even the poorer farmers so quick to pay up."

"If you keep this up Donny, you'll be able to talk to the bank about buying the farm you're looking for."

Fixing the Roof

"If I never fought for Ireland they'd fix my roof. They give grants to men who hid under the bed," Jack declared furiously, stabbing the shining, crooked awl into a black boot. He straddled the bench, boot last between his knees, boot stretched on the last. More boots spilled off the shelves behind him in dusty black tiers, some with buff tags looped through the eyes and names in big black letters, others anonymous. A few high-heels stood on the window sill at his right. The villagers said Jack kept the anonymous ones to exaggerate how much work he had. "I can't promise," he'd say, "you see the work ahead of me before Sunday."

Seven-year-old Finn Hoolihan sat on a little three-legged stool, hugging his knees and watching Jack. Finn didn't believe what people said. Jack was his hero: a short, sturdy man of forty with abundant black hair and a very brown face. That Jack always addressed him as MacCool, in honor of the legendary Irish giant Fionn MacCool, made Finn feel ten feet tall. Father Byrne, the curate, said Fionn MacCool was a pagan, and no proper person for a Catholic boy to admire. So when the curate came to talk to the First Communion class, Miss Callan introduced Finn as Finbarr, a name no one ever called him unless he was getting a scolding. Father Byrne would rest the heavy heel of his hand on Finn's head and swivel his fingers in Finn's curly hair. That was supposed to make Finn feel good, but it didn't. Finn's face would flush and his ears heat up. He wished Father Byrne wouldn't do that. Half an hour later his scalp would still be aching a little. Father Byrne always made him feel small and insignificant, at fault somehow, guilty of something and out of place. Jack wasn't like that. He made Finn feel alright. "Come in MacCool, sure the sight of you would gladden a blind man." That was the difference between Jack and other people.

"The crowd in the county council weren't long forgetting who put them there, feathering their own nests, that's what they're at, not caring if I drown with the rain leaking in this winter," Jack muttered.

Under the window, a side of heavy tan leather soaked in foul-smelling, brown water in a huge, black iron pot. The part of the leather under water was tinged grey and purple, like the fur of a dead mouse. It was for cutting into soles for boots. The skin Jack used to repair the uppers of shoes and boots was soft as knitted wool. It sat on a shelf above the pot. The water-softened leather was more pliable. Finn was waiting for Jack to finish stitching the patch on the boot; he wanted to see him cut the sole.

With a grunt of satisfaction, Jack pulled the last thread through and set the boot on the floor. He took the side of leather from the pot and shook it free of water. Then, he held the dry side to his chest and the soaking end in his left hand. Measuring only with his eye, he took a wickedly sharp knife and cut a perfect sole. He fitted the boot on the last and the sole to the boot. Almost perfect. Jack trimmed it neatly.

Finn gathered up the slivers of leather and put them in his pocket.

"Good man yourself, MacCool," said Jack. "You'll soon have the hang of my trade." He inserted a row of tacks between his lips. Finn watched in awe. One by one, Jack took the tacks from his mouth and, with just the right number of taps of his little hammer, drove each in turn into the sole, securing it with a loop as neat as if drawn by a compass. Then he took up the awl again to stitch the sole. "I'm making short work of it. I'm saving more soles than the priest, MacCool."

Finn grinned back.

Jack's workshop was half the kitchen, the half nearest the door. From the back wall, steep stairs led up to two little bedrooms.

Above the stairs the ceiling was stained brown where rain leaked through. On rainy days, a pail on the bottom step caught the drips. A long beam of sun slanted in the window and glinting on rows of plates and mugs on the dresser in the kitchen. It turned the red fire grey, except for the rosy spot where the big hanging pot cast the coals in shade. There, they glowed like a heart.

"Your Mother's looking for you, Finn," Jack's sister Katie said from the door. "It's time you were home anyway."

"Sure he's only just here," Jack responded, defending Finn.

"Well, he's wanted at home," Katie carried the stool and the paper she'd been reading into the kitchen. She was a tall, thin woman with greying hair, parted in the centre of her forehead and secured in a bun at the nape. Finn was afraid of her. She seemed to boss Jack around. Katie had been to America, working in New York as a seamstress and had brought home illustrated papers with pictures of men in pigtails and women with smooth, pale, perfect features and hair massed on top of their heads.

"Heathens, MacCool, every last one," Jack remarked.

"What's a heathen, Daddy?" Finn asked that evening, as his father listened to the news, his head on his hand, ear bent to the wireless.

"Someone who doesn't believe in Jesus," said his mother, Nan, sewing a button on a shirt, holding the work out from her body to catch the fling of light from the Aladdin on the table.

His father switched off the wireless. "It's time you children were in bed."

Finn's older sister Bridget was curled up on the green horsehair and leather sofa, looking at a book. "Tomorrow is Saturday, can we stay up a little longer?"

"Why won't the county council fix Jack's roof?" Finn asked, to turn the conversation away from bedtime.

"Yes," said his mother, "what's the delay? Declan, I thought you helped him fill out forms for a grant months ago."

"I did, but maybe the council is low on funds. Anyway, Brennan is useless."

"*Ta clusa mor ag na sionnach beag,*" his mother warned in Irish, but Finn knew what she meant. The little foxes have big ears. Nan didn't want the children to hear their father criticize the local councilor, though Finn knew his parents disliked big, red-faced Brennan who had dropped by the house every couple of weeks, for as long as Finn could remember.

"Can we get a dog?" Finn asked.

"No. Now off to bed," his father said.

"Uncle Donny said every boy should have a dog."

"I told you before, Finn. A dog is too much work, a puppy has to be trained, and Rose has enough work to do. Now, off to bed."

"I'll train him."

"No, Finn. Off to bed."

On Sunday morning, parishioners hurrying to mass saw Jack sitting astride his roof. From below, it looked as if Jack and the roof were perched in the dusty, blue fruit of the plum tree ripening in the autumn sun. The second bell for mass was ringing, so no one stopped to investigate. On their return, Katie was at the top of the ladder, her head sticking out of the plum tree branches, in earnest conversation with Jack. He sat brazenly smoking a cigarette. People were a little shy of Katie since her return from America. She was a bit uppity and didn't mix with the neighbours. She didn't seem to realize that when you came back from America you had to make an effort to fit in. Kate had come home in '39, just before the Atlantic got dangerous and even now, four years later, she was a bit of an outsider. So they ignored the unusual sight of Jack on the roof. Each passed the scene with their eyes averted and the usual, "Fine day, thank God."

"So they had a row, a little set to. Who hasn't had," people mused as they walked on, "and decent people passes no remarks at something like that." Everyone was hungry and wanted to get home for breakfast.

By early afternoon, it was known throughout the townland that Jack was determined to sit on the roof until the county council approved his grant.

"He'll come down when he gets hungry," Finn's father said at tea-time.

"That's where you are wrong. He said to me, `MacCool, I'll never give in,' and anyway, I saw Katie bring him his tea in a bottle and sandwiches in a bag," Finn answered.

"I don't like him calling you MacCool," his mother interrupted, "your name is Finbarr, and I don't want you over there again climbing on the ladder talking to him. What if you fall?"

"Katie said Father Doyle might write to the county council about it."

"I doubt that," said his father.

IN THE EARLY EVENING a small crowd gathered at the end of the short laneway and stared up at Jack. He appeared to be reading the paper.

There were shouts of encouragement. "Me life on you Jack," and "Good man yourself." Jack was demonstrating for every grant-seeker in the parish.

Everyone assumed Jack's protest would end with dusk, but as the sun went down Jack sat straight on his perch. With daylight gone the crowd dwindled, home for tea, lamplight and warm fires. There was no moon. Jack's cigarette glowed faintly in the branches of the plum tree.

FATHER SEAMUS BYRNE, the young curate, heard about it at Benediction on Sunday evening. He told Father Doyle, his parish priest, about Jack's protest that night as they stood in the hall of the priest's house. Father Doyle was on his way up to his bedroom. He raised his bushy, grey eyebrows. "We'll see how long that performance lasts," he said and went slowly and deliberately up the stairs.

Father Byrne, an athletic young man with black hair and an open, boyish face went into the sitting room and sat, downhearted, staring into the fire. He hated the parish. He thought about autumn evenings in the seminary, saw the lowering clouds over the playing fields, felt again the tremor in his arm of the loud crack as his camann struck the hurling ball. He heard the thrilled cheers of the lads when he scored. He remembered Joe, his best friend, now an armed forces chaplain in France and imagined him bringing the Host to the wounded, or bending to hear confessions of frightened young men on the eve of battle.

Father Byrne had arrived in Ballynamon full of enthusiasm. The village was setting up the local defence force. They had meetings in the parish hall and drew up procedures in case of an air raid. They had lectures on maintaining a blackout. But no air raid ever came. The papers said a few German airmen had parachuted out of doomed planes on the east coast. They were arrested and held in a camp at the Curragh. The local defence force became an excuse for men to play cards and drink on winter nights.

The farmers were comfortable smuggling sides of bacon, boxes of eggs and cart-loads of chickens to the North for shipment to England. Everyone knew they did it. The customs officers looked the other way. Some young men joined the British army and some worked in armaments factories in England. They sent money home to their families because there was nothing to buy in England. And nothing to do here, Father Byrne thought morosely. He wished he had joined the foreign missions, or the army.

Monday morning, Frank Gallagher, driving the early cart collecting milk cans for the creamery, reported everywhere he stopped that Jack was still on his perch. Tuesday, the situation was the same. There was speculation that Jack came down at night. A few of the lads persuaded the owner of the village hackney car to drive over after dark and park with the headlights trained full on Jack's house. But the cone of light from the car illuminated the trunk of the plum tree and the porch of Jack's house and threw the roof into inky darkness. The car owner complained of wasted fuel and battery, secretly terrified of a scolding if the light and noise disturbed Katie. "I have my business to think of," he muttered, "and I'm only supposed to use my car for business." The scheme was abandoned.

Wednesday, a steady drizzle kept gawkers away. Jack held to his purpose, protected by a thick rain cape and fortified by hot tea handed up by a weary Kate. He now had a chair-like contraption nailed to the roof, his feet supported by a plank fastened just above the eaves. He even had a cushion in the form of a potato sack filled with straw. Customers coming to fetch footwear left for repair were turned away.

Down at the pub, the barman was holding bets on the length of time Jack would survive on the roof. Opinion was divided. For those who bet on a short stay, Jack's stature fell in proportion to their losses. Some said he was crazy, others said he was shamefully stubborn.

"What's wrong with him is a terrible dose of laziness," said one drinker, "the man has the life of Riley, and a fine view of the rest of us at our work in the fields."

"The priest should deal with him," Jimmy Kehoe declared. "After all, Katie is first to seven o'clock mass every day."

"What difference does that make?" said Paddy Shanahan. "What does the priest care?"

"They do care," said Jimmy, "they care about the people."

"No, they don't."

"They do, Paddy."

"Only an ejit thinks that," Paddy was getting a little drunk.

"Are you tellin' me," said Jimmy, "that a good woman that goes to seven o'clock mass every day doesn't deserve the priest to speak up for her?"

"No," Paddy was shouting at him now. "I'm tellin you even if she goes to mass morning noon and night every day of the week the priest doesn't give a tinker's dam about her."

"Easy, easy," said the barman. "None of that in here."

"Ah, to hell with Jack and the priest," said Paddy, "give us a double Powers."

WHEN FINN'S father called him for breakfast Wednesday he found him already awake and determined to stay in bed in solidarity with Jack. Declan stared at the sweet, beautiful face of his son. He considered dragging him out of bed. Then, shaken by the force of his own irritation, he turned away and went to consult his wife. To his amazement, Nan laughed heartily at his predicament.

"It's just a figare Finn has. Just leave him. He'll get over it. It's a joke."

Declan became furious with her. He was the village school-master, after all. And she was a teacher herself.

"What does it look like if our only son lies in bed and refuses to go to school? And I'm taking attendance and sending notes to parents to remind them to send their kids to school, and reporting the slackers to the guards."

"Declan, it's not that serious. No one will know but Finn is sick. And by tomorrow he'll probably be tired of being home."

Declan realized he didn't know his wife at all. He remembered her opinion on the harvest days. Though a farmer's daughter, she bitterly resented the policy allowing parents to keep their children home from school to help with the harvest.

"Education is their only way out of this place," Nan said defiantly. He, on the other hand, saw the need to save the harvest. Every September they disagreed.

Now Declan walked out to the side of the house with his wife, carrying her lunch. He put the lunch in the basket of her bicycle, along with her rolled-up raincoat.

"Nan," he said, trying to be reasonable, "Nan, you have the lad spoiled."

"He's only a child," she told him, tossing her black curls. She hopped up on her bicycle and rode away to the little one-room school she ran in Slanabaille, three miles away. Watching her ride off, Declan looked miserable.

WHEN FINN HEARD the front door close, he knew his father and Bridget had left for school. He slipped out of bed and went over to the window.

A misty morning. White fog thick on the sloping fields that rose gently beyond the garden hedge. Finn saw three dragons squatting on the hill opposite, puffing smoke straight up in the sky, black eyes staring back at him under matted straw hair. He narrowed his eyes and squinted, rested his hand on the window sill, index finger pointing. "Bang! Bang! Bang! You're dead," he yelled.

"What are you doing home from school? Are you sick?" Rose, the housekeeper, stood in the doorway.

"I'm on strike. I'm not going to school till Jack's roof is fixed."

"Jack Foley is a right ejit, and if you don't go to school you will grow up to be a dunce!"

"I will not. I'm the best reader in second class."

Rose walked over and stood behind him. She looked out over the garden and the rising land. "The fog's lifting Finn, and not a breath of air either to blow it away. See, over there, the smoke rising straight up out of the cottage chimneys."

Finn turned and strode over to his bed. He sat with his arms folded and his head down. From under lowered brows he looked at Rose. She spoiled everything. But he had slain the monsters, they were dead. Of course, they'd come back tonight, their red eyes would stare at him again and he'd have to shoot them again.

"Anyway, come on downstairs. I'll make you an egg and fried bread."

Finn jumped off the bed and followed her down the stairs. He sat at the scrubbed deal table and watched her fry bread on an iron pan on the kitchen range. The edge of the egg white was lacy. He could smell the bacon fat, hear the bread sizzling in it.

A door at the side of the range led into Rose's room at the back. On the other side, another door led to the pantry and yard. The kitchen and Rose's room were the original cottage. A second storey addition gave them two rooms leading off the front hall, stairs leading to three bedrooms and a bathroom above.

Rose had a cigarette in the side of her mouth. Her sharp, very blue eyes squinted in the smoke. She was a sturdy woman of twenty-five, with her tightly curled red hair cut close to her small head and round freckled face, and a flowered overall belted tight about her strong body. She slid the food on a plate and put it in front of Finn. He was very hungry.

"You should stay away from Jack till he comes to his senses."

"He's not coming down till they give him the money to fix his roof."

"*Mor dhea*, as if anyone will pay him to sit up there. Does he think he's an acrobat in Duffy's Circus?"

"Jack says Hitler will win and then every one will have one of those cars the Germans use in the desert," Finn was changing the subject.

"That's not what your father thinks. I heard him say they were done for when the English sank their big ship a while back."

"They didn't sink it. Jack says the Germans sank it themselves so the English wouldn't know their secrets."

"*Mor dhea*. Don't mind that fellow, he doesn't know what he is talking about."

"He does so. He remembers when we had a war with the English when he was small. He carried messages for the IRA. Half the time he didn't have to go to school."

"That's the reason he can hardly write his name and that's what you'll be like if you don't go to school."

"I hate school, the big boys say I'm like a girl because my hair is curly."

Rose lifted the black locks from Finn's forehead. "On Friday, when I get a chance, I'll cut your hair and then you won't look like a girl."

"That's worse, then it curls more and they say my hair is like the hair on a cock and they pull down my trousers."

"God damn them to hell," spluttered Rose, "the bloody begrudgers! It's because you're the best scholar." She lifted the top off the range, flung her cigarette in and slammed the top down again.

Finn was delighted; there was nothing in the world so satisfying as Rose cursing.

"Never mind, I have a surprise for you when you're finished your breakfast."

"I'm finished now. What is it?"

"You guess."

"Urney's chocolate?"

"No, guess again."

"A *Dandy* comic?"

"Good man, sure you're a great guesser." She went to fetch the comic from the dresser drawer.

"That Hitler's a bad article," said Rose as she handed Finn the *Dandy*, "that crowd is bombing Birmingham every night and my mother's fingers are worn to the bone praying for my brother over there in case he'd be killed." But Finn was already absorbed in the comic.

"You better go back upstairs now, Finn."

"Why can't I stay here?"

"Ned the postman will be here soon and you don't want him to see you, you're supposed to be sick."

"Will I be let go to pick apples on Saturday?"

"And you mitching from school? Have a bit of sense."

"I'm not mitching, mitching is if you pretend to go to school and then mitch off."

"Up to bed with you, quick."

Finn climbed the stairs slowly. He sat on the edge of his bed. Soon it would be morning recess at the school. Downstairs Rose was singing.

"Bless them all, bless them all, bless them all
The long and the short and the tall.
Bless De Valera and Sean MacEntee
They brought us black bread and a ration of tea,
They're not rationing Fianna Fail..."

That was a great song, Jack's favorite song. Finn punched his pillow up to a satisfactory height and opened the comic.

AT THE GUARDA station, the sergeant was pulling rank on the guarda, ordering him to get on his bicycle, ride to the shoemaker's house and order him down off the roof.

"And what will I do if he won't listen to me?" the hapless guarda pleaded.

"Go up and pull him down," roared the sergeant. He was enraged at being put in the position of ordering his subordinate on such a ridiculous mission. But he had received a telephone call from the superintendent in Obanbeg who had received a call from the local county councillor. Not orders, just a hint that the demonstration by the shoemaker was becoming an embarrassment and the council would be much obliged if the sergeant could, "put a stop to the codology."

Katie invited the guarda in for tea. She served scones and black-berry jam. When she pointed out the brown stain from the leaking roof, he forgot his mission in his indignation over the negligence of the county council and their treatment of a decent man like Jack, who worked hard and faithfully paid his rates. "Show the buggers what you're made of, man," he encouraged Jack as he departed.

FATHER DOYLE was informed of these new developments by his housekeeper as he and Father Byrne read the previous day's *Irish Independent*. She placed the tea tray on a table a little back from the fire, began pouring the tea and complaining of the council's neglect of its duties, the cold, wet winter fast approaching, poor Katie worried that Jack's health might be ruined from sitting out on the roof. Father Doyle's eyes never left the newspaper. "Thank you, Mrs. McIvers."

She withdrew.

"I wonder," said Father Byrne, "is there anything we can do?"

"These things are matters for Caesar, Father Byrne," Father Doyle said coldly, folding the paper lengthwise so he could hold it in one hand and his teacup in the other. The curate looked back resentfully. Father Doyle ignored him.

On Thursday, the *Anglo Celt* sent a reporter to interview Katie. A steady stream of gawkers walked and cycled past the house.

On Friday afternoon, word reached Katie that the hackney driver had taken a consignment of shoes to Obanbeg for repairs. Katie put on her Sunday coat and hat and went to see the parish priest.

The priest's housekeeper saw her coming and relayed the news to Father Doyle, who was walking in the back garden.

"I'm saying my Daily Office," said the cleric, "let the curate deal with her."

The housekeeper took Katie's coat and ushered her into the sitting room, where Father Byrne sat smoking a cigarette, resentfully considering his future. How could he continue to endure this dull, lifeless parish with its ignorant, stodgy, backward people? The smell of blue peat smoke always in the air, the damp church, the endless, boring nights of the coming winter stretching into grey years ahead until the day his bishop would transfer him. Somewhere, there must be a way to distinguish himself, some great work, some noble undertaking to lift him above the raw recruits of the diocese.

"Katie wants to have a word with you, Father." The housekeeper and Katie were standing in the doorway looking at him.

"Oh come in, come in, Katie."

"She wants to get your advice about the trouble with Jack, Father."

"Oh the very thing, the very thing," and Father Byrne stood up and waved Katie into a chair.

"Now, tell me about it," he encouraged sitting opposite her. The housekeeper left and closed the door.

Father Byrne dragged furiously on his cigarette as Katie told her story. It was clear to him Jack was acting like a spoilt child.

"He pays more heed to that young lad Finbarr Hoolihan than he does to his own sister," she told the priest. "Although since he took to sitting on the roof, I haven't seen hide nor hair of that child."

"He's sick in bed," said the priest, "chicken pox or something."

"Chicken pox, how are you! He had chicken pox last year Father. I'd say it's a dose of the sulks he has."

Father Byrne did not reply. Katie continued her list of complaints: anxiety for Jack's health; exhaustion from the labour of carrying up his food; apprehension at the loss of his earnings; remorse for her initial decision to support his protest. Father Byrne reflected on what a different light hindsight throws on events. Who could have believed the protest would have lasted this long."

"And how does he manage to go to the lavatory?" he asked with sudden curiosity.

"Sure, how would I know that?" responded Katie, appalled by such an indelicate question. "All I know, Father, is he is up there when I go to bed at night and he's still there when I get up in the morning."

The curate stared in wonder at such self-command.

"Would you talk to him Father?" Katie pleaded. "He'd listen to you."

In one quick motion the priest slammed his feet against the floor and stood. "I'll go back with you Katie, and give it a shot."

FINN WAS SITTING at the top of the stairs, waiting for the postman to pass the house. Then Rose would let him come down to the kitchen for a cup of tea. The postman was very late. Even if he had no letters for the family, he would still stop by to talk to Rose. Time seemed to pass very slowly. Finn was very tired of his room. He wished he could go back to school. He wished Jack would come down off the roof. He wished Jack would get his roof fixed. Tomorrow was Saturday. He'd still be in his room and he'd have to sneak out to the top of the stairs to listen to what was going on downstairs.

His mother and father weren't talking to each other much. His father just answered any question his mother asked in as few words as possible. Then he'd go outside and pump water from the well up to the tank on top of the house. Squeak, squeak of the pump, then water splashed into the tank. Finn knew the bad feeling in the house was his fault. Tomorrow afternoon his father, Bridget, and Rose were going to Great Uncle Joseph's orchard over past Slanabaille to pick apples. His mother never went to pick apples. She didn't like anything to do with farming. She said she went to Slanabaille every day anyway to teach in the school. And if his mother went, Rose couldn't go, his father always wanted to spare the pony.

Apple picking was the best day of the year. Great Aunt Emer would have dinner ready, including a fresh baked apple tart. After the apples were picked and dinner was over they would go down the lane to his grandfather's. Bridget and Rose would stay with Great Aunt Emer. The men would walk down the hill to O'Brien's Bar in Slanabaille, talking about the war, Dev and Lemass, Great Uncle Joseph holding his hand, the dogs following them nosing and snuffling about in the hedges, Grandfather swinging his stick, knocking the heads of thistles.

Finn thought his heart would break if he couldn't go. He remembered last year. Great Uncle Joseph set him up on a high stool at the bar and said to the barman, "Frank, a bottle of minerals for this man!" The barman had poured him a big glass of fizzy orange drink and he sat on the stool, watching the heads of Joseph and his grandfather towering over his daddy's head in the looking-glass behind the bar, even though his father was a tall man. He could not stay home. He wanted so much to go, especially to the bar with the men.

Afterwards, they might walk down to the river past the blacksmith's shop. Last summer he had gone there with his grandfather to get a horse shod. His grandfather told him the blacksmith's shop had been a forge years and years ago, then a lone woman had lived there in the little house and kept hens in the forge and goats on the land, but now it was a forge again, because of the war and everyone having horses now.

His grandfather was very wise, he knew a great many things, he had lived in America for a long time. Billie Kehoe, who was in Finn's class in school, said his grandmother was from Slanabaille and she told him that the woman who used to live in the little house beside the forge was a witch.

"She could put a spell on you. With one swipe of her shawl she could knock a strong man out of where he's standing."

Finn liked to imagine that old witch at the forge flinging her shawl about. He asked his mother about it. She said that was nonsense. Lizzie Scanlon was a fine woman. She had known her well.

Finn told his Great Uncle Joseph the story when he had gone to stay with him and Emer in the holidays. "Finn, all the women from Slanabaille had a bit of witchery in them," his great uncle said.

Finn would miss it all, the whole great day, if he had to stay in his room. But he knew what his father would say, "If you are not going to school, Finn, you must stay in your room."

And his mother's answer, "Declan, you're too hard on that child."

As Katie and the curate neared the house, Father Byrne was full of confidence. He rehearsed his approach in his mind. He would take charge of the situation, sort this fellow out. Talk to Jack man to man. He saw himself talked about, written about, and maybe even immortalized in song, as the man who negotiated with the roof sitter.

Father Byrne hesitated only once, when he saw people gathered at the end of Jack's short drive. The small group had seen Katie and the priest approaching.

"This'll be good craic," said Frank Gallagher, who had stopped his cart on his way home from the creamery.

"Should be great value altogether," promised Paddy Shanahan.

The crowd parted respectfully. Father Byrne walked to the house and deliberately climbed the ladder. Katie stood at the foot of the ladder, a serious but encouraging expression on her long, thin face.

Father Byrne stood on the second step from the top and addressed Jack in tones of admonishment. "You should be ashamed, making a show of yourself like this and worrying your poor sister."

Jack continued to smoke nonchalantly and the crowd, sensing drama in Jack's apparent defiance, moved forward to hear. The priest began to get angry. This was more difficult than he had anticipated. "Have a titter of wit in your head man, get down off there."

"Where's the fellow that's going to make me?" Jack shouted back insolently, crossing his legs and leaning forward.

Father Byrne was taken aback and a little embarrassed at snickers from the crowd below. Maybe he had been too hasty. Now Jack began to blow smoke rings and leaned back to watch them admiringly, resting his feet on the plank he had nailed to the roof. The priest reconsidered his tactics. The aroma of Jack's cigarette reached him. He'd ask Jack for a cigarette. That would soften Jack's indifference. He climbed up on the top step and leaned on the roof.

"Could I ask you for a smoke, Jack? I forgot my own."

"Sure," said Jack. He reached into his shirt pocket and tossed a packet of Woodbines in Father Byrne's direction.

The cigarette pack slid along the slope of the roof, a little to the right of the priest. He reached for it. His fingertips brushed it out of reach. He leaned further over. The ladder slid. Father Byrne grasped desperately at the gutter, heart racing in terror. The gutter began to crack. He clawed furiously, but the eaves trough broke off and came away in his hands. He screamed. "Oh my God Almighty," and crashed to the ground. He lay crumpled at Katie's feet, his legs bent at an unnatural angle. Some of the watchers, not wanting to be involved with any mishap to the priest, left quietly. A few crowded closer. Jack stood on the roof looking down, dumbfounded.

"One of you gawkers go quick for Doctor McCarthy. Quick, run," cried Katie, taking charge. She crouched over the priest.

"Good God Father, what happened to you at all?" she asked. The priest groaned.

"What about a little whiskey till the doctor comes?" Katie took off her cardigan and put it under his head. "Jack, you ignorant *amadan*, will you get Father a drop and be quick about it," she called to her brother, who was lowering himself down by the drain pipe. "And don't fall in the rain barrel and pollute the only drop of water I have."

Father Byrne lay on the hard ground, looking up at a ring of faces. His whole existence centered on the excruciating pain in his hip. He had never imagined such pain.

Jack came back with the whiskey. Katie lifted his head and he sipped. The whiskey deadened the pain a bit and Father Byrne felt a great sense of vindication. He had known all along it would end like this, he a martyr and the ignorant bogtrotters shown in their true colours. Katie held the cup to his lips again and he drank. Then he laid his head back on Katie's cardigan. He tried to speak but no words came. A blackness smothered his sight. It's over, he thought, so soon, so very soon.

FINN WAS TIRED of sitting at the top of the stairs. He heard Rose talking to Ned the postman. He moved down two steps. He still couldn't make out what they were saying, but Ned sounded excited. Finn crept halfway down the stairs.

The front door was open and Rose was standing on the front

step with her back to Finn. Just below her, in the drive, Ned was leaning on his bicycle looking up.

"Well, if that doesn't beat Banaher," Rose exclaimed, "that ejit could hang for that."

"The devil a hang," said Ned, "that fellow's neck's too thick, they couldn't hang him."

"Hanging's too good for him if you ask me," Rose turned back into the house and started up the stairs.

"So, you're out of bed," she said when she saw Finn. "Well, there's a halt to Jack Foley's gallop now, he's after killing the priest."

Killing the priest? Jack killed the priest? He must have got down off the roof to kill him. Was Jack gone mad? Maybe he was always mad. A cold terror descended on Finn, he felt it overpower him, his blood race in fear. Then he thought, it's over, I can go back to school. Maybe he would be blamed. Maybe it was his fault too. Still, everyone would be so upset about the murder they'd forget about him. He wished he could make himself invisible, like the man in that book he'd read. What if they hanged Jack? The English hanged Kevin Barry. Finn felt his whole world close, dark and smudged, himself very small and alone.

Rose's face was set in a hard, satisfied look. Finn turned away and trudged up to bed. Rose followed and sat on the side of his bed. Finn buried his face in his pillow.

"Ah sure, maybe it'll be alright, maybe there's two sides to the story, maybe the priest was asking for it."

Finn sat up quickly. "Do you think maybe they won't hang Jack?"

"Well, maybe he didn't mean to kill him. Ned's after telling me Father Byrne went up on the roof to talk sense into Jack and Jack hit him a blow and knocked him off the roof and killed him. It might be only manslaughter, that's not as bad as murder."

"What's manslaughter?"

"It's when you don't mean to kill someone."

"Jack didn't mean it!"

"We'll see what your father says."

His father would be home soon with his tight, worried face

that made Finn feel sad and guilty. Finn knew he'd have to go back to his room and stay there all evening. After tea, it would begin to get dark and he'd have to try not to think of the infinite stairwell hole just outside the door and what might be in it; a dragon like the ones that sat on the hill and puffed sooty smoke, waiting to pounce; every morning, standing at the window, he shot them.

Just then they heard the front door open and his father come in. Someone was with him.

"There's your father home! He's early! He has someone with him," Rose stood up. "It's late," she fussed, "your mother will be home soon. I have to get the tea. I'll go down, so."

When Rose left, Finn stole back to the top step of the stairs. His father was in the sitting room. The door was open. His father was talking to Brennan, the county councilor. Brennan's voice came up the stairs.

"I tell you Declan, if you give us a hand here you won't be sorry. The thing has to be done quietly. That's what the council wants. If it gets out that we paid for that ejit's roof just because the priest was nearly killed we'll be the laughing stock of the country."

So the priest wasn't dead! Finn eased himself down a step on the stairs. He heard his father's voice, "I'm willing to try, but Jack Foley is a stubborn man."

"It has to be done, and you're the man to do it, just quietly get the roof fixed, the council will pay, a cash transaction, and make sure Foley says nothing about it."

Brennan sounded as if everything was settled. They were going to fix Jack's roof. It seemed odd to Finn that if Jack nearly killed the priest they would still fix his roof. Maybe they were sorry for him because they were going to hang him, or send him to jail. Finn crept down a few more steps. He was almost to the bottom of the stairs.

"I'll work through Katie," he heard his father say, "she's a rock of sense. I'll go down and talk to her and try to get the thing done."

"I wish the priests would stay out of where they're not wanted." Brennan sounded cross.

"Ah, he meant well."

"Tell me, Declan," said Brennan, "how's your young fellow? I hear he's not well."

"Oh Finn, he's not himself, my little Finn, not himself at all. I don't know what's come over him. I'm worried, very, very worried about him."

His father sounded sad and upset, almost like a little boy. His father, who was always so sure of everything. A great pity for his father enveloped Finn, he hugged his knees to his chest and bit his lip to stop the tears welling in his eyes.

"Do your best Declan!" Brennan was leaving.

Finn's father followed him to the front door. He turned and saw Finn on the stairs.

"This is my boy now, Frank," His father lifted him in his arms. Finn's feet hung down awkwardly. His pajama legs were too short. It was a very long time since his father held him.

Brennan ruffled Finn's hair with his big hand.

"Sure, that's a great man you have there. Not a bother on him."

Finn turned his head away, his eyes full of tears. But he was not going to cry.

"I'm off so," Brennan waved his hand as he descended the steps.

At last a great sob escaped Finn's tight throat. "Rose said Jack killed Father Byrne, and he's going to be hung, so he is."

"Nonsense," said his father. "Where'd she get that idea?"

"Ned the Post said it," Finn sobbed.

"It's too bad Ned wouldn't just deliver the post and never mind carrying stories. Father Byrne fell and broke his leg. He's gone to the hospital."

"Did Jack hit him?"

His father put Finn down and sat beside him on the stairs.

"Not at all, Father Byrne leaned over on the ladder when he was talking to Jack and he fell. Haven't I always told you Finn, never lean over on a ladder?"

"I never do," sobbed Finn, tears flowing now, but still he was thinking about picking apples.

Rose came out from the kitchen. "So Father Byrne fell off the ladder?"

"Yes," said Declan, "he leaned over and fell and broke his leg."

"Is that all?" said Rose. "He'll mend so! Don't cry, Finn, I tell you the whole thing is of absolutely no importance whatsoever."

"That's right," said his father, "as far as we're concerned it's of absolutely no importance! What's important Finn, is that you promise me you'll be back in school on Monday."

"I want to go back. I hate missing school. Am I far behind in the lessons?"

"Nothing to worry a smart lad like you," his father told him, "anyhow, I brought home the books."

He handed Finn his handkerchief. "After tea," said his father companionably, "we'll go down to see Jack and Katie. I'll talk to Katie out in the yard. You can talk to Jack. But we can't stay long, you know."

SATURDAY MORNING, Finn held the yard gate open; his father drove the pony and trap out on the road around to the front of the house and waited for him. Finn shut the gate, ran and climbed up beside his father. His mother and Rose came down the steps from the house. For a minute Finn thought he might have his father and Rose and Great Aunt Emer and Joseph and his grandfather all to himself but no, there was Bridget running down the path and stepping up into the trap as if she was Princess Margaret Rose. She settled herself with her book on the seat and tossed her black ringlets. She had a big, floppy, white bow on top of her head.

"Good girl," said his father, "you decided to come. What are you reading now?"

"*What Katy Did.*"

"Are you liking it?"

"It's the best Katy book yet."

Miss prim. If his father hadn't been watching, Finn would have kicked her, above her crossed ankles, just a little kick. Then she'd take her head out of the book.

Rose put two tea chests under the seat and sat up beside Bridget.

"It's a grand day for an outing Nan. Are you sure you won't come? Rose could cycle or I could."

"No, Declan. Saturday is the only day I have to myself. I have sewing to do and letters to answer and remember, next Saturday we're going to Dublin to see Una and Connor. Tell Emer I'll drop up for tea after school on Monday."

She waved them on and turned back into the house. Finn felt sorry for her, alone in the house all day. He thought she'd enjoy picking apples if she came. His father flicked the reins and they trotted down the hill past Jack's house. Katie was sitting outside reading the paper. His father raised his hat. "A grand day, Katie."

Jack, thought Finn, is inside catching up on the shoemaking he neglected when he sat on the roof.

The village was quiet, too early for the farmers to be in. They passed the Ulster Bank and Flanagan's Public House and then up by the Green and on to the dusty, white road to Slanabaille.

Uncle Joseph and Stephen Plunkett were waiting in the orchard, sitting on the stone wall. Stephen was smoking. Uncle Joseph's black collie, Hogan, danced about, tail wagging, excited to see Finn. Finn jumped down and raced the dog to the old house and back. Stephen's pigs were loose in the orchard. They ran squealing out of the dog's way. Stephen was farming Uncle Joseph's land because of the war, and the compulsory tillage orders requiring anyone having land to farm it or let it to a farmer.

"Settle down, Finn," said his father. "Pigs don't need exercise."

Finn called the dog and walked back. The dog wandered off to snuffle in the hedge for the scent of rabbits.

It was an abundant crop of apples: as many on the ground as in the trees. Cadres of wasps burrowed in the windfalls, gorging themselves. They buzzed angrily in the pigs' faces and hovered menacingly about their eyes. Sometimes the insects settled around their snouts. Heedless of the wasps, the pigs grunted, squealed and gulped the fruit.

"Won't they choke?" asked Bridget helping Rose gather windfalls for jelly.

"Well, if they do itself 'tis no bother," laughed Stephen. "We can always do with more pork steak."

Bridget shuddered and looked disgusted. Finn thought she was a sissy. Where did she think their bacon came from? Even if she was nearly nine, she was still like an infant in a pram. A few months ago they had a party for Great Aunt Emer when she was sixty-five and his grandfather had one over the limit. He sang *The Old Bog Road*, a sad song about America and the poor Irish labourer longing for home. Bridget acted like a big baby.

"My feet are here on Broadview
This blessed harvest morn…"

And when he got to the part about the emigrant's mother dying:

"But here was I on Broadway,
Building bricks for my load,
When they carried out her coffin,
Down the old bog road," Bridget started to cry. Great Aunt Emer said, "that's enough of that Peadar. The child is overwrought! That's not a song for what's happening here!" Only Great Aunt Emer would tell his grandfather to shut up.

Stephen positioned the ladder against the trunk of the tree and held it while Finn climbed up.

"Pick away there, lad."

Finn pulled at the apples. It was hard, until he got the hang of it and gave the apple a little twist. He handed the apples down to Stephen to put in the tea chest. Uncle Joseph was picking behind him, standing under the tree and reaching. His father was working on the next tree. "Don't lean over, Finn."

"How's the priest anyway?" Stephen asked.

"Oh, he'll be out of commission for a while, maybe three months, Dr. McCarthy said."

"That's no loss! He's lucky, leaning over on a ladder like that."

"It's good to see the land under crops, Stephen."

"It's the best of land, Joseph, and I'm getting a good yield. I have to thank the compulsory tillage for that."

"Well," said Joseph, "there's men couldn't farm a window box farming now."

The apples were firm and slippery. The bags and tea chests filled up. Silver paper lining the tea chests reflected the apples.

"Look," said Bridget, "the paper is like a mirror."

"Silver apples," said Joseph.

"*Silver apples of the moon*," said Bridget.

"Good girl."

Their voices rose through the leafy branches and floated up to the blue sky. Finn looked down. Dappled shadows trembled on the apple-dotted ground. So many fallen and still plenty left on the trees.

"Tomorrow, I'll get the rest and store them for Emer."

"A great crop, Joseph!"

"Ah, the younger trees are producing, those six I planted in '13 for my mother, God be good to her."

Going back, Finn sat in Joseph's trap with Stephen. The dog loped behind the trap.

"He needs the exercise," Uncle Joseph said. He gave Finn the reins. Rose, Bridget and his father followed. The men were talking about the election held the previous June. Finn tried to commit it all to memory.

"Dev, with his blather about comely maidens at the crossroads, nearly missed the boat," said Stephen

"He might have waited too long to call the election. He's still driving the train though, mainly because Labour is split and Fine Gael needs a new leader. Cosgrave is fed up of politics. I'll bet we have a re-run soon."

"Well, I'm not for Dev, though he kept us out of the war. We're not profiting like we did in the last war. I remember how well my father, God be good to him, did from '16 to '18."

"The Brits have fixed the prices. Just be glad you're not a wage slave, Stephen. Pay frozen for the last two years at least."

Finn could have listened for hours. Later, he would repeat every word to Jack. And Jack would have opinions. He didn't like Dev. "An auld bollocks, MacCool," he'd say.

They reached Stephen's house. "Will you come up for dinner? Emer would be glad to see you."

"I'll not Joseph, not today, maybe tomorrow I'll drop by," Stephen stepped down.

"Let the pony take his own time, Finn. He knows the way."

Finn drove on up the lane into Uncle Joseph's yard. His grandfather was sitting on the front step, reading the paper.

"Ah Finn, good man yourself."

Emer came out when she heard the pony's hooves. "Didn't Stephen come back with you?" she asked, after she had kissed Finn and told him he was getting as big as a house.

"No, he's busy I suppose. He'll come up tomorrow."

The dog trotted up and Finn jumped down to play with him.

"Come on Finn lad, give me a hand here."

Joseph backed the trap over by the haggard and loosed the pony. He gave the reins to Finn. Finn led the pony over to the paddock, opened the gate, unfastened the bridle and the pony trotted away. Declan drove into the yard and Emer went over to shake his hand. She kissed Bridget. "Such a great girl you are, more like your mother every day. Come on in. Dinner's ready."

There were three apple tarts on the leaf of the dresser. Finn calculated there was one to take home. He smelled roast chicken and gravy. He was ravenous.

"I'm not very hungry," said Bridget. She'd eaten two apples.

"I hope you weren't eating windfalls, Bridget."

"Oh, I wouldn't let her do that," said Rose.

Rose heaped Finn's plate with chicken and vegetables. The carrots were perfect orange disks. He couldn't wait to taste the chicken.

"So, you think there'll be another election in the spring, Joseph?"

"There has to be, Declan. They can't keep going without a majority. Next time Fianna Fail will propose rural electrification. That'll bring the farmers back."

"What's rural electrification, Uncle Joseph?"

"It's when you have your farm wired up for electricity and you just have to switch on the light, even in the barn."

"Yes," said Emer, "and you wouldn't have to bother with smoky oil lamps and candles. I'd love to get rid of the cans of paraffin oil, the smell of it can't be healthy."

"Well, I'll go out and campaign for that myself," vowed Rose. "Who wouldn't?"

"The country is going no place till we get it."

Rural electrification, the very words were pure light, brightness, a glowing bulb in an inverted white saucer over Jack's work bench. Finn could just imagine it. To flip a switch and everything was lighted, the yard, the kitchen, the byre. Just like when his father took him to Athlone, to visit his aunts who had a pub.

"Excellent potatoes, Emer," said Declan, helping himself. "Are they your crop?"

"Those are Stephen's kerr pinks. They are very good."

"It's a wonder," Rose said, "that Stephen never got married."

"Well, he's not late yet, sure he's only about forty-three."

"He's a bit older than that, Peadar."

"Well," Joseph reasoned, "he still has lots of time, everyone doesn't have to get married just as soon as they are out of short trousers."

"Stephen only wanted one girl and she never even looked at him, so he'll just be another Irish bachelor," Emer declared, "and that's a shame. Cassie, God rest her soul, would have wanted children running about."

"There's lots of fine girls about the country," Rose said.

"That's true," Emer answered, "I tried to get himself and Greta Smith together years ago, before Greta went to work in England, but it was no use."

"Sometimes," Joseph said, "love is no short sentence."

"Still and all, he would have made a good husband and that's a fine place he has now," Declan said.

"She's much better off where she is, with the man she's got," Peadar said firmly, ending the discussion.

Rose got up to clear the plates and make tea. Emer began to slice apple tart. Bridget took up her book to read.

"Don't read at the table, Bridget," said her father.

"Oh, it's all right, Declan."

"Aunt Emer, I just have one page left to finish the book."

"Read away, dear."

Finn was resentful. Aunt Emer let Bridget do anything she wanted just because she was a girl. He never got off with anything. He ate two pieces of tart to console himself. There was lots of cloves and cinnamon in it. The waistband of his trousers felt tight.

"The tart is perfect," said Rose.

"Neither Joseph nor I take sugar in tea. We save our ration for sweets and jam."

"What she means," joked Joseph, "is that I'm not allowed to have sugar in my tea."

"It's not good for you, Joseph."

"How about a pint now?" Peadar said, when they had finished.

"Yes," Emer agreed, "go ahead. Rose and myself and Bridget will have another cup."

"Come on Finn," his grandfather called. Finn hesitated a minute. He felt sure Rose and Emer were going to talk about Stephen and the mysterious girl he'd been in love with. He wanted to stay and hear about it. There was a secret hidden in Great Aunt Emer's saying, "But she never even looked at him." He also wanted to go with the men, listen to their talk, especially about rural electrification. He would have a great report for Jack about getting all the farms and houses wired up for electricity. And he didn't want to miss going to the pub.

"Come on lad," said Uncle Joseph from the doorway.

Jack wouldn't care about some silly love story. "I'm coming, Uncle Joseph, I'm coming."

Uncle Joseph's collie bounded after them.

"Your mother told me you weren't yourself for a few days, that you missed school."

"I'm going back on Monday, Uncle Joseph."

"Good man. School's important."

His grandfather took his hand and they walked just behind the others. When they passed his grandfather's house Cu, his old hound, ambled out too and followed them. The two dogs ran ahead.

"That's a high mackerel sky, tomorrow will be fine."

"Great weather," Declan agreed.

"Declan," his grandfather called, "it's time this lad had a dog."

Finn held his breath. His father never disagreed with his grandfather. His father turned his head to answer.

"Well, Nan and myself have been talking about it. We're thinking about it. Maybe next spring."

Finn breathed again. Spring. First, it would be Hallowe'en, then winter and Christmas, and then spring.

"Donny told me he's intending to breed that new kerry blue he has. You could ask for one of the litter."

"I think I will. I like a kerry blue myself, they're smart dogs, and a good size too, not too big."

They walked on past Stephen's house, toward the village. Grandfather swung his stick at the thistles on the side of the road. A line of swallows sat in a row of black commas along the rusty top bar of the open gate. Any day now, Finn knew, they would be flying south. And when they came back, it would be spring.

ACKNOWLEDGEMENTS

I received much support while writing *The Music of What Happens*. I would like to express my gratitude to the following: my family, who were encouraging from the beginning; Dympna Power and Dr. Barry Martin, Jill Arthur and Virginia Johnson and the late Cecelia Ruddy read early versions and provided useful comments. Dr. James McCarthy and his wife Carmel provided hospitality in Dublin and help with the spelling of many Gaelic words. Thanks to Bobby Crichton for the loan of his mother's Mass Prayer Book.

Mehri Yalfani, writer, poet and workshop partner was an inspiration. Ann Decter, writer, editor and teacher had faith in the project and kept it going when it seemed it would never be finished. Noreen Shanahan did the final edit and provided much good advice.

For historical detail two books were invaluable: Liz Curtis' *The Cause of Ireland* and J.J Lee's *Ireland 1912-1985*.

To all many thanks.